THE COVENANT OF SHIHALA

The Fires of Qaf: Book One

KYRO DEAN & LAYA V SMITH

EIGHT MOONS PUBLISHING

The Covenant of Shihala is a work of fiction. Names, places, and incidents are either a product of the authors' imaginations, or are used fictitiously.

Copyright © 2022 by Kyro Dean & Laya V Smith. All rights reserved.

No portion of this book may be reproduced in any form without written permission from the publisher and authors, except as permitted by U.S. copyright law.

Cover illustration copyright 2022 by Eight Moons Publishing.

Published in the United States by Eight Moons Publishing, LLC.

Paperback ISBN: 978-1-957475-01-1

Hardback ISBN: 978-1-957475-02-8

EBook ISBN: 978-1-957475-00-4

Printed in the United States of America.

www.eightmoonspublishing.com

I'd be remiss if I didn't give the biggest thanks and all the love to my children who mean more to me than anything in both worlds. All the appreciation to my Heavenly Father who blesses me daily. And of course, all the feels to Laya whose fire sustains me through life's storms. When others have chosen to walk away, they are always left, helping me stand.

—Kyro

For my brother, Aaron. I miss you every day. And for Carolyn, the friend I didn't know I so desperately needed.

—Laya

QAF, THE UPPER CONTINENT

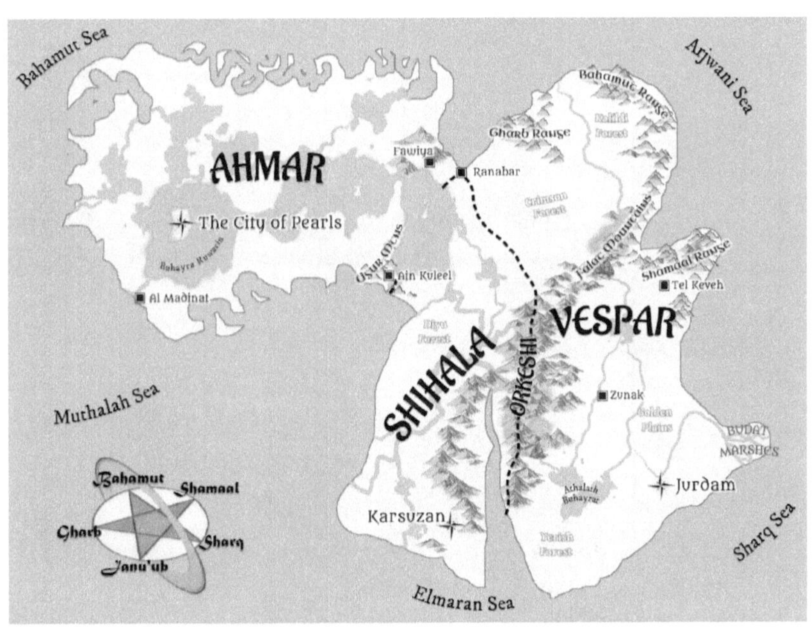

The Royal House of Shihala

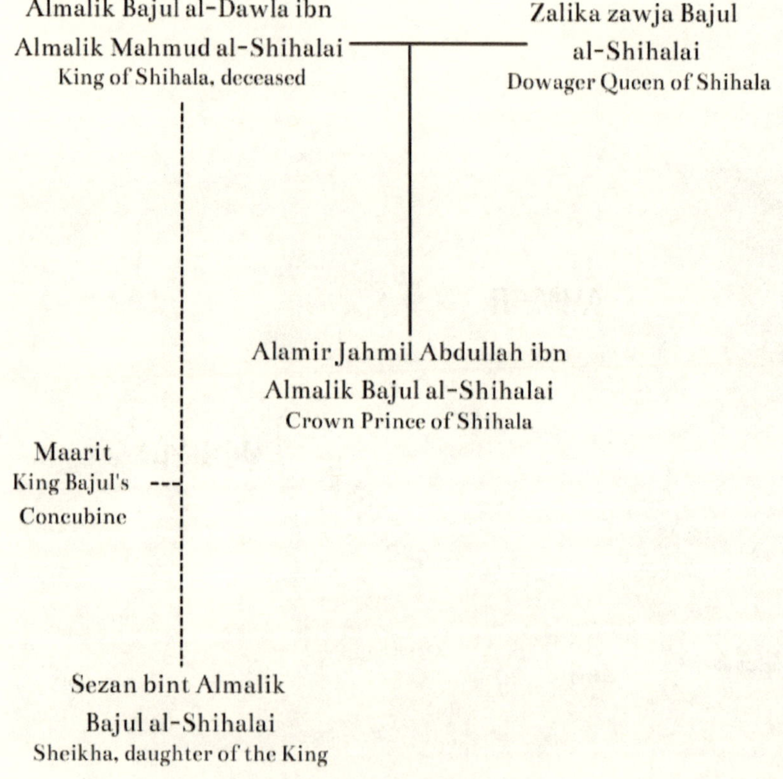

The Royal House of Vespar

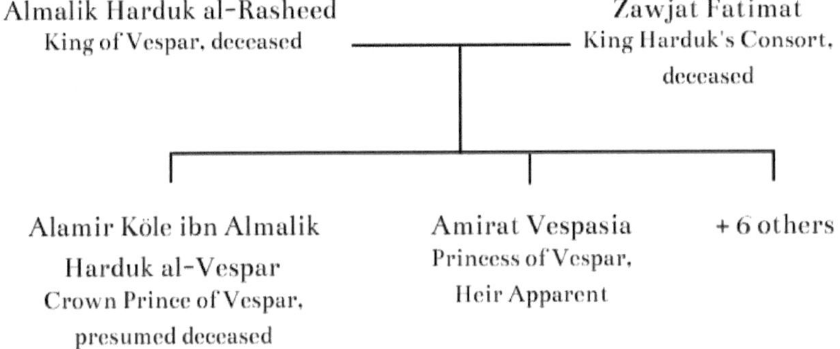

CHAPTER ONE

JAHMIL

ONCE AGAIN, JAHMIL HAD been summoned to stand before the Queen of Ahmar. The lives of six thousand people hung in the balance, and he had no offering. Again.

"*Al'ama*," Jahmil cursed and snapped the doors of his jewelry cabinet shut.

Nothing but empty pouches and his grandmother's opal necklace. He would die before he gave that up, even for the sake of saving lives. Not to Queen Qadira. It would be worth nothing to someone like her. A trinket against her obscene collection of diamonds, pearls, and wonders mined from the Five Corners of Qaf. But Jahmil had already given his querulous fiancée as much of himself as he was willing to part with. That necklace was meant for someone special. Someone he would never meet now.

He had to come up with something. The one time he had gone to see Queen Qadira without bringing a gift, she had him publicly censured before her muster of vapid, peacocking courtiers and threatened to tattoo her name on his cheek should he ever make such a miscalculation of conduct again.

Jahmil rolled his neck from side to side until it cracked. His bones felt like clay left to blister in the sun. A bit of public humiliation and scarification was the least of his worries. Keeping Qadira happy was a matter of life and death. The Queen of Ahmar had not simply inherited her position. Like every previous ruler of her kingdom, she'd had to beat out and murder every one of her siblings in order to rise to prominence, which in Qadira's case left two princes and four princesses in marble sarcophagi. If she had gleefully done that to her own siblings, what was to stop her from doing the same to a fiancé who could not even bring her an acceptable present? Never mind that Jahmil was a penniless refugee. Never mind that he had ten thousand other matters weighing on his mind. None of that made any difference to Qadira.

She would have her present or she would have his head.

Snatching up his purse, Jahmil dug his fingers inside. Two opals. Barely enough for a plate of kofta. He walked to the window and gazed up at the sky. The rusty circle of the First Moon was nearing its zenith, its coppery glow spilling warmly upon his face. The Shadow Moon peeked over the glimmering parapets of the City of Pearls, blocking out a perfect circle of stars for a year at a time. Finally, his eyes found the tiny, pale pink Third Moon, tucked neatly in the crook of the Horseshoe Nebula.

Jahmil lifted a hand and gazed through his fingers. He aligned his thumb to match the angle where the paths of the two moons would cross. Some fifteen degrees to spare. Enough time to slip to Ard and buy a fat slab of sticky baklava to satisfy the queen's insatiably greedy mouth. The confection might yet have the added benefit of gluing it shut.

A *whoosh* sounded behind his back, and a quick rush of heat that smelled of lily of the valley licked his shoulders. It was rude to apparate directly into any djinn's home, let alone a prince's private chambers. Only one person in both worlds ever did, and even she wasn't supposed to.

"*Marhabān*, Mother," Jahmil said, turning slowly.

The dowager Queen of Shihala had royal blue skin that glowed like lapis lazuli in the warm light of the First Moon. Thick black ringlets shimmered under her transparent veil like the ocean under the night sky. Teardrops of obsidian hung from her ears, her dress a checkered wonder of gold and black. Her upper lip curled like a desiccated leaf, a practiced sneer of superiority and contempt. A queenly expression if ever there were, though she was forbidden from wielding any power. When Jahmil became engaged to Queen Qadira a year before, his mother had relinquished her title and accepted house arrest in Ahmar's royal harem. But Qadira had greatly underestimated the ingenuity of the dowager Queen of Shihala. Everybody always did. Jahmil himself had often been guilty of the same offense, though he quietly prayed his mother had one more trick up her sleeve.

"*Salamo 'alayka, al'asad,*" she said, lacing her fingers together at her waist with bent elbows. Her full skirts swished loudly as she stepped closer. "Qadira came to speak with me again this morning."

"Commiserations." Jahmil slipped past her shoulder, pushing a breath out through his nostrils to avoid inhaling her overpoweringly floral scent. His bare feet were silent on the white marble as he crossed to a divan near the center of the cavernous bed chamber.

"Why won't you just sleep with the shrew?"

Jahmil scoffed and snatched up his soft leather boots. "Please, don't hold back, Mother. Tell me how you really feel."

"I don't understand your hesitance, Jahmil."

"Surely you're not suggesting I sleep with her before we are married." He looked into her clear diamond eyes, anticipating her answer and wary of it all the same.

"Qadira is no virgin. She's never once had a patriarchal protector standing guard over her womb…"

"Then she's well overdue."

His mother gave a queenly roll of the eyes. "When a woman sleeps with a man, she draws him into her confidence."

"Thank you for educating me on the ways of women, Mother. Allah knows, I have no experience."

She scowled, the skin under one eye twitching. "Back when you were running around with General Bakr and those Orkeshi hoodlums, I questioned if a single woman remained in the court of Shihala whom you had not taken into your bed."

"That is nonsense." Jahmil blanched at the mention of the old, yet incredibly persistent, rumor. "I know a man is judged by the company he keeps, but I was never a party to my friends' indiscretions."

She eyed him suspiciously, as she always had. The damage his association with Bakr had done to his reputation had proven insurmountable. Still, Jahmil would not have given up any part of their friendship. Not a single minute.

"I keep a list of the women just in case any bastards pop up, *nauzubillah*." She scowled and her eyebrow twitched. "If you care to see the list, you'll have to come to my chambers. The roll is far too long and heavy to carry across the palace grounds."

Jahmil's muscles tightened. He rolled his wrist until it cracked and stroked his trim beard. "Whether I was unerringly chaste in my youth is of no consequence. Allah eagerly forgives sins for which we cannot forgive ourselves."

"*Inshallah*," she sighed, then took a quick step closer. "You are only twenty-six, Jahmil. Your youth is not over."

"I beg to differ." He dropped his shoed foot to the floor with a hard *thud*.

Her upper lip curled so hard that vertical wrinkles formed around the edges. "My charming, handsome son, if only you would lie in her bed, I'm certain Qadira would finish falling in love with you."

"Qadira loves no one and nothing but herself, and even on that she has but a tenuous grasp."

"It would cement our position and, I dare say, give us some degree of security."

"I thought the whole point of abandoning Karzusan and coming to this ostentatious nightmare of a city was that you thought we would be safe." Jahmil shot her a hard look. "If you feel threatened, maybe you'd rather go back to Shihala."

Her face hardened to stone, tiny wrinkles crackling in her lips. "That is *not* funny, you ungrateful, self-absorbed man-child."

"I would rather be eaten alive by Vespars than by Qadira."

"We must employ every resource at our disposal."

Jahmil smirked. "If you're so keen, why don't *you* sleep with her?"

Another wrinkle formed in her lower lip. "The deal has already been struck and there is no changing it."

"Thanks to you and your deal, Qadira has taken our fortune, our titles, and our dignity."

He pressed his thumb and forefinger into his eyes, trying to keep his blood from boiling over. He still held out a vague hope of avoiding the entire affair, but informing his mother of his plans could only serve to exacerbate her. He didn't want to give her the opportunity to meddle any more than she already did.

"You've lashed me to her golden string to make me a puppet. She sees me as nothing more than a dispossessed refugee with no inherent value but the nobility of my blood."

"Then allow her to see you for the beauty of your body."

"I am not a bed slave!" White plumes of fire ignited around his fists. Jahmil burst from his seat and flipped the coffee table. It smashed against the near wall, shattering into a cascade of splinters. "Qadira's embrace is that of a constrictor. Her kisses are iron spears impaling my flesh. And for this, you expect me to fall down and be grateful?"

"Jahmil, we have all sacrificed." His mother lowered her gaze and shook her head. "You have already agreed to marry her. You would not back out."

He couldn't tell if the last statement was a question or a threat.

Chuckling coldly, he rolled his head back until his eyes came to rest on pearl-encrusted chandeliers lit by the smokeless yellow and white fires of his servants. How ridiculous to be constantly couched in luxury, yet still lack the funds to buy even a new set of clothes.

"Even now, Qadira takes Vespar lightly," he said. "Shihala fell, and still she is confident Buhayra's waters would repel the tides of Iblis himself. But she is wrong. When her beloved citadel is breached and overrun by magic-wielding Spiders, which it will be, Qadira will remember the ally she has made in me. And she will fall on her knees to beg for my help. Perhaps, I will even grant it."

His mother cleared her throat and swallowed hard. "If making yourself indispensable is the goal, what better way than to impregnate the queen?"

"Impregnate her?" His breath was harsh, shaking in his chest, and his words came out caked in blood and venom.

It was the first time his mother had ever made the suggestion outright, though the implication had been there since he signed the document of trothplight. Never mind his abject disgust and hatred for Qadira; he would sooner die than see his own children as princes of Ahmar, forced by barbaric practices to fight and murder each other to decide who would inherit their mother's throne. He wanted to be incredulous that his mother would suggest such a fate for her own grandchildren, but given the depths to which she'd sunk since fleeing their homeland, he put nothing past her.

"I will do anything for my kingdom," he said, trying a hand at diplomacy, "but I will not sire a child until I retake Shihala and smokey fire no longer burns in Orkeshi. Until our people are no longer refugees scattered throughout the Nine Kingdoms. And every Vespar lies dead in a puddle of his own filth."

She met his gaze, flashes of white and yellow shimmering in her irises. "You sound like your father."

The skin tightened around his eyes. She meant it as an insult, but the words pleased him nonetheless. "If I can never call myself a king of anything more than smoldering rubble, there will be no heir. I would sooner our family line die out completely than leave such a legacy."

"Only Allah can know what the future holds," his mother said, her voice colder than the kiss of Janu'ub. "If you refuse to lay with Qadira on your wedding night, there will be severe consequences."

"I am a prince and a general, not a stud horse to be bred at will." The fire wreathing his knuckles burst brighter, and he punched the wall. The thick brocade covering the wall ripped, and wood shattered beneath, flares of smoky orange fire igniting the splinters.

His mother's eyes flashed white before she shook her head coolly. She snatched a goblet of water from the central table and tossed it on the smoldering wall without looking. "You are a proud fool."

"I am contractually obligated to lie with Qadira on our wedding night, and I always honor my obligations. I will do it once, and I will make her scream my name so loudly every ear in this gilded prison hears it, so that they may bear witness that our contract can never be annulled, no matter how she grows to hate me. But on that night, I will drink poison to ensure that my seed is rotten and will not sprout in her rancid womb."

His mother cast her gaze aside. Her eyes were silver mirrors, shimmering in tones of starlight like backlit diamonds. His own eyes.

"We must all endure scourges," she said.

He stood silently for a moment, gazing at the hole he'd punched in the wall and tempted to make it larger. Instead, he turned to his mother with a sneer. "Queen Qadira would be upset to learn you've wandered outside the harem."

She cocked her head to one side, registering his threat, and somehow stood even straighter. "Fine, I'll go. But I warn you, your continual refusals of her advances only make the queen's fire for you burn brighter."

"Your concerns have been duly noted, Dowager Zalika." A growl simmered in his throat. "Now, go from me."

For a long moment, she did not move. Even the colorful fractals in her eyes held still. Then, with a heavy sigh, she disappeared in a puff of white fire.

Relieved of her oppressive presence, Jahmil's nerves began to relax. He walked to his bed and picked up his jacket, pulling the blue leather tight over his shoulders and fastening the buttons. There was no point in being angry with his mother, as much as he despised every word she said. He had to keep Qadira happy. If his other plans fell through, the capricious queen was his last hope. Though he couldn't help worrying that the amount of time he was forced to expend on his backup plan hurt the chances of his first being successful.

Jahmil glanced at his sword resting against the wall in one corner. The double-edged obsidian blade had sat untouched for months, and gray dust had formed on the scabbard. As always, it occurred to him to strap it over his shoulder, to proudly wear the symbol of his people as he used to before his mother and Vespar stole his dignity. But, as always, he let it be.

Closing his eyes, Jahmil pulled on his fire and opened a small tear in the fabric between worlds to slip through the veil into Ard—the world of sunlight and the birthplace of Muhammad, *sall Allahu 'alayhi wa sallam*. He aimed for his favorite city, the capital of the so-called Ottoman Empire, which stood at the center of the world. A crossroads of trade that showcased all the best human beings had to offer. Qadira could not resist the pretty trinkets humans produced, which was lucky since they were freely obtained by any djinn brave enough to venture into their world. Besides, Jahmil needed a moment to compose himself, to bask in the illusion of freedom Ard's sunshine always provided. If he was going to convince Qadira to give him what he needed, his smile had to be at least partially genuine.

He had always been a terrible liar.

CHAPTER TWO

Ayelet

Ayelet worked her way through the busy streets of Edirne, her slippers caking with mud from last night's rain. She gave her bare ribs a good rub as a woman with a dark hijab pushed past her. Ayelet spun in an easy circle with the bump, walking backward a few paces as she tried to separate the smells in the market.

Bread.

That's what she was on the prowl for. But the Empire was known for more than just its fragrant markets, and the smell of animal dung and spruce incense was just as strong as the tantalizing whiffs of baked goods.

Luckily, she hadn't traversed all of Anatolia and Thrace with only her lyre without having learned how to sniff out a good loaf. At last, her eyes settled on a *fırıncılık* near the end of the street, its dull blue awning the same shade as the sky. Plaster walls on each side of the doors were painted with golden murals of her prey. Flat pita. White, fluffy *ekmek*. The deep brown ovals of rye. Her stomach gurgled. Empty, empty, like her pockets.

She sighed and popped her lips together a few times. She didn't usually steal. Not anymore, anyway. It wasn't worth the attention it drew if she were caught. But she also hadn't eaten in two days and maintaining anonymity to ensure her survival did nothing if she perished from want of bread.

As her eyes swept the local wares, a dirty lavender scarf disappeared behind a stall. Ayelet smirked. She eased between two skinny men with crooked beards who grunted at her and around the other side of the wooden stall, then counted down. *Üç. Iki. Bir.*

Right on cue, a child's hand reached around the side of the planks, patting gently atop the counter for something to snatch. Ayelet slipped the empty locket from around her neck and dangled it within reach. When the little fingers grasped it and pulled, she yanked back and dropped to a crouch. Serap tumbled out from under the stall, eyes wide and cheeks flushed.

"Caught you." Ayelet grinned.

Serap gasped and let go of the necklace, her brown eyes wide over hollow cheeks. "You scared me! I thought Old Emre had found me out."

"You're lucky he didn't."

"Boo. I could outrun him any day." Serap scowled and folded her arms. "He's so well-fed you can see the fish still wriggling in his belly. Lucky dog."

Ayelet smiled and shook her head. "Up, you. If you insist on having sticky fingers, use them for bread, not trinkets."

Serap sighed, the effort outlining hungry ribs through her ragged dress. Ayelet bit the inside of her cheek and helped the girl up. There were a wealth of reasons she preferred to work alone, but something about Serap's innocence had always pulled at a part of her she thought long dead. A part of her she sometimes wished was. But there wasn't anything for it. She wasn't about to let the little thing starve.

She brushed off Serap's tattered hem and straightened her shoulders. "Besides, after the years you spent studying under that crazy Frankish acrobat, you shouldn't be wasting your time on the ground."

"Because acrobats are nimble little things with no fear?" Serap looked up at her with a big smile.

"No. Because acrobats are highly capable and extremely driven. Now, come with me. I've spied a bit of pide."

Ayelet rubbed her slippers one over the other, then pushed forward with Serap in tow, determined they would live to play another day. Closer and closer, she scuffed through the soggy dirt. Hands itching, heart pulsing. The smell of crispy crust and spongy insides made her stomach rumble impatiently. Then, Serap gave her a wink and disappeared around the far side.

A small outburst broke out on the other side of the crowd as the little girl caused a distraction. Ayelet smiled guiltily, then snuck behind a man with white puffy pants and curly boots. There, she found the woven basket full of round pide baked with soft cheese. So close. Just a hand's grab away. She bit her lip, wiggled her fingers, began the painfully slow stretch of limbs toward the basket, then froze.

She could have sworn she saw a flash of dark blue skin in the corner of her eye. Her stomach knotted like a rug. She snatched her hand back to sign against the Evil Eye and spun on the ball of her foot so she could hurry along the other way. She let out a sharp whistle to let Serap know she should run in the opposite direction and offered a small prayer that the little one would escape safely. No amount of bread was ever worth encountering a djinn.

And a djinn it was, heading in the same direction that she had taken to escape. At least that meant he was headed away from Serap. The night keeper was a male, as so often they were. Lean and stately. Dressed far too nicely for the south side of town. It was the brightly colored skin that gave away what he was. And she was sure if she could see his eyes, they would flash like colored gems. He strolled lazily through the market with a small pastry box in his hands, occasionally bending one way or another to avoid colliding with the lucky humans who had no idea he was even there.

She picked up her pace, trying to avoid the djinn's path without him noticing that she noticed him at all. She had learned long ago that if she didn't let them know she could see them, they assumed she was like the rest of humanity and gave her no more notice than a gnat. But if they realized she *could* see them...

The shadow of beetle legs rippled down her spine. She had been cursed at in strangely accented Arabic, had been the target of smokeless, rainbow-colored fire shot from their fingertips, and once had been chased down the streets by one that had transformed itself into a snarling dog.

Ignorance.

Feigning ignorance was the best policy when dealing with djinn. All she really knew about them was that they, like any human she'd ever met, could not be trusted. Not one living creature on earth could be, except for herself.

She glanced at him from the corner of her eye, praying to Allah and His goodness that there was only one of them and that no other dark magic followed their trail. For where there was a djinn, there often was a wisp. And with the wisps came evil. Another chill squiggled down her spine despite the summer sun.

At last, the blue-skinned djinn took a different turn and ambled out of sight. Ayelet ducked to the side of the dusty street and slouched against the wall of a building beneath a sliver of shade. The warm waft of bread had dissipated, leaving her with the smell of sweat and the sound of her thrumming heart.

She pulled at the glass beads that hung over her forehead from her silk headband. Her stomach complained at her once more, and she shushed it. It was her own fault she was hungry. Even the best music grows dull to people who hear it every day, and the crowds of Edirne were no different. The smart choice would be to move on like she had hundreds of times before. To pick a new city to ply for monetary appreciation until their pockets—or generosity—ran dry, too.

An ant tickled the skin of Ayelet's foot, and she kicked it off, then bent down to rub away the sensation. "Little pests," she muttered.

Her hand brushed the cool scar on her ankle. She shivered and yanked the hem of her dress down over the gnarled "K". She hugged her knees tight.

"What's wrong, child?" A crooked old woman looked up from where she sat under a dirty cloth tent that tilted precariously to one side.

Ayelet should have noticed her sooner. She did not want to become cruel like the rest of the human race and ignore suffering because it was easier. Though neither did she want to become a part of it. Still, life on the run could afford a little kindness. Ayelet turned, still crouching, and smiled at the woman.

One of the elderly woman's makeshift awnings had slipped off, leaving her exposed to the rainstorm of the night before, and she was busy wringing out her few possessions. Not that they'd ever dry. Not in humid Türkiye. Her legs were emaciated and her face blemished by the sun.

"You shiver. Are you cold?" the woman asked, her voice dry and brittle like the husk of an onion.

"I am, *Nene*. And I am not." She glanced at the dirty, toothless grandmother once more and sighed. She should offer more than a smile. "Is there something I can do to help you? Perhaps a song?"

She reached over to adjust the fallen piece of the woman's tent when a knobbly hand smacked her away.

"Not from you." The old woman's formerly open face scrunched tight with narrowed eyes and angry lips. "Those who shiver in the sun are marked by the devil and will make their home in Jahannam someday."

Ayelet's heart darkened. "Then I will not help you, *Nene*, and all the better for it."

"See?" the woman rasped and held up a shaking, bony finger. "See how easily your tricks are revealed? You weren't going to help me, you were going to eat me."

"I should not like to eat someone like you—there is no meat on your bones." Ayelet stood and crossed her arms. She had been cursed at before, but never because she had felt a chill. And not once by such a terribly unpleasant grandmother.

"Gach!" The woman spat through the holes of missing teeth in her mouth. "Devil worshipper. Djinn lover. I bet you dance under the moon with ghouls."

Ayelet stared at the woman and rubbed her thumb over the smooth wood of the lyre she kept tied to her waist. *Her* lyre. And the reason encounters like this started happening. She narrowed her eyes and leaned forward. Then, she snatched the bit of fallen tent and pulled it up to its proper place before the spotty old hand could bat her away again. She smiled as the old woman's face contorted.

"You witch. Sorceress. Lilith. Harpy. May whatever makes you shiver find your soul and drag you back to Jahannam."

"Thank you, *Nene*," Ayelet said solemnly. "I had resigned myself happily to just such a raucous fate, but now I will do my best to avoid it so that we may revel in each other's company once again."

The old woman scowled and tossed a handful of soiled hay in her direction. Ayelet narrowed her eyes and shrugged off the mess, then slipped back into the main street, her starving stomach now unsettled by a stew of the woman's curses. As soon as she was out of sight, she signed against the Evil Eye and prayed the woman's curse would not come true. Hunger was nothing compared to the fate that awaited her if she were ever caught.

Nevertheless, her bone-dry stomach complained its needs were more urgent. And if she was too haunted by djinn to swipe a bit of bread, she was back to swiping the old strings for a bit of coin instead. Maybe there was a pocket left in the city that hadn't yet been turned. Serap was probably looking for her, anyway.

Ayelet sighed and twisted her feet toward the west gate, where she was supposed to meet Balian, a mess of a man who was Serap's cousin, her drummer, and the only person who had known her from before her life on the run. He would tease her for coming back empty-handed after she had scoffed at him that morning, but there was nothing for it.

Ayelet slipped through market stalls filled with apricots and herring, silks and rugs, heading for the square. She ran her fingers over each one, enjoying the change in textures until her heart caught in her throat.

The chilly white mist of a wisp whipped through the market, teasing the ends of scarves and skirting around hurried feet.

Ayelet's stomach sank. She had not seen one in the five weeks she had been in Edirne, and she had grown complacent, foolish. She should have known better than to tempt fate and put herself or Serap at risk. A burning sting filled her throat as she imagined Serap suffering a similar fate to what she had at that age. The djinn in the marketplace had just been the start. Any sign of glittering white in the wind was a swift call to evil. She had stayed too long.

Shaking the goosebumps from her arms, she couldn't help but keep an eye on the sparkling tendril. It floated lazily now, catching updrafts as merchants aired out silk and flinching at the bang of pots and pans. It snaked through a smaller crowd of people near the far end and disappeared behind tense shoulders. Ayelet blinked and followed the uncomfortably straight line of the back up to a familiar azure face that turned and scanned the crowd in her direction. She inhaled quickly and coughed to cover it up.

Gem-blue skin. Faintly glowing eyes. And that ever-present look of disdain.

The djinn she had evaded in the market. Allah, save her. If wisps were the call to evil, surely the magical beings were the manifestation of it. But this time, his presence held her gaze. He was still in his natural form of a man, not pretending as an animal or beast. From this angle, she could see his dark, neatly trimmed beard and diamond eyes. Through the wavy haze of magic surrounding him, she could see he was polished, fit, and neck-craning tall. As far as djinn and their brightly-colored skin went, he was painfully handsome, though his scowl suggested he either did not know it or took it for granted.

Indeed, she was certain mirth had never once crinkled his face or played mischievously in his eye.

His back was as taut as the strings on her lyre, his flashing, crystal-like eyes far too serious, his clothes pressed stiff, and his frown curled into something permanent and forlorn. She hadn't seen a face so miserable since the night her father drank himself to death. And even then, her father had the decency to hiccup a lullaby before sending himself off. She doubted the djinn sang at all, much less laughed. The sticky baklava he carried almost seemed a farce in comparison and made her stomach rumble all the same.

Good thing only she could see his pall of gloom and dusky skin. One sour face could turn an otherwise giddy crowd and end her day's performance with too little to buy even a bite of burnt bread. Not that he would know what that was like, whoever the djinn was. His crisp kaftan and shiny buttons alone could buy her food for a month and told her all she needed to know about what his life must be like. Lamb shanks for dinner. Cinnamon peaches. Naan piled high. Easy and untroubled as he strolled the human markets for a bit of luxury. Not that he'd have any coin, of course—the stories of genie-trapping chains made of burning iron were well known. But there were whispers of cities made of sun-streaked marble and streets cobbled with gems.

Hiding behind a passing camel, she eyed the djinn and decided the rumors must be true. The crystal ring on his finger caught the sun greedily and mocked her with its light.

The hairy, humped beast she hid behind bleated and flapped its wide lips, drawing eyes. Ayelet left its side and picked her way through the crowd, her gaze fixated not on the gem the djinn wore on his finger but the ones in his eyes, misted with worry. Maybe she had been going about this all wrong.

She had never intentionally engaged with a night keeper—only tales of woe came from people who dealt with the other-worldly beings—but fate left her little choice. She had maybe a week after seeing a wisp before the faceless man would come to find her, and she had to be gone before then. Her music had caught the attention of djinn before. Too often would they turn an ear as they passed or peek curiously around a corner to watch her. If djinn minds could be touched by melodic sounds, could their hearts? Did they have hearts?

She caught herself staring at the crystalline gaze of the stately djinn and bit her lip. With misery clear in his sparkling eyes, he must have one. Something in a minor key that pulled at the soul would be the perfect bait. He wouldn't have to know she saw him, just be compelled enough to discreetly toss a favor in her bowl.

Besides, those who did not deign to make time for music were usually swayed by it the most.

Taking a risk on his sad face was better than the risk of encountering a man—or djinn—without one. She untied her lyre and stepped through the crowd to the center of the square. All she had to do was play.

CHAPTER THREE

Jahmil

Of all the beautiful things he didn't have time for anymore, Jahmil missed music most of all. As much as he resented Qadira constantly wasting his time with her greed, ego, and caprice, browsing for her presents was some of the only time alone he could justify anymore. If he married the queen, even that would evaporate with the cadre of expertly trained servants he'd have to handle all the mundane and pleasurable aspects of life.

Once he had secured a large slab of baklava, he had ten degrees to spare, so Jahmil made his way into the town square, hoping to find a street musician plying their trade. The clumsy strum of a *guitarra morisca* or the sliding lilt of a *kaval* were common sounds in the crowded markets of Edirne—wild and artless and diametrically opposed to the carefully polished sounds that shivered through Ahmar's Palace of Pearls.

The twang of a lyre touched his ears as he entered the square. Jahmil found a spot far at the back of the crowd, standing close to the white-washed wall of a small mosque. The humans could not see him if he did not want them to, and it was much safer to remain invisible. His body stayed tangible, but it was easy enough to move amongst them without being noticed. Most humans were so self-absorbed they would not have noticed a drakonte in their midst, let alone a single djinn minding his own business.

One song ended and another began. Jahmil turned to be on his way when the crowd parted, and he caught a brief glimpse of the lyrist. The edges of the world blurred around her so all he could see was the shine of glass beads sparkling on the band of her transparent veil and the dance of her long, dark hair.

The bellow of shopkeepers, the stench of fish, and the scrape of wind through dry leaves faded into nothing. There was only her and her lips of a budding rose. The corners of Jahmil's mouth turned unexpectedly, the suggestion of a smile. *Ya Allah*, she was beautiful.

The wind wrapped around her, her fingers expertly stroking the lyre as she danced, her eyes closed, and Jahmil was suddenly and irrationally tempted to show himself. He longed to feel her eyes brush over him. Would her gaze linger, or would it sweep past even as her music swept through the wind?

There was a man with her, sitting in the dirt and patting on a drum. Who was he, Jahmil wondered. Her husband, perhaps. Or a lover. Certainly a woman with such storms in her eyes and flourish in her wrists did only as she pleased, allowing herself to be a subject of adoration so long as there were no demands made on her, no price to be paid. The stars care not for the admiration of mortals. They shine and sparkle whether anyone watches.

When the song ended, she leaned close to the man and whispered in his ear, perhaps directing the next measure of music. He was barefooted and poor, his hair hanging from his head in ragged tendrils and his face smeared in dirt. Jahmil envied him so much that it stung. He was blessed, and he didn't even know it.

"Jahmil Amir?" a sniveling voice cut into his thoughts like shards of glass.

He looked up at the twitching, tight face of his advisor, Zamir. A mop of tight curls curved down to meet his chin in a thick, wooly beard and watery black eyes that always seemed on the verge of panic. Shadows and lines marred his dark blue skin, as if forty hard years had fallen on his back instead of two.

How had Zamir found him? Had his mother put him on his tail? Even the human world that had always been his escape had been invaded. So much had changed since the Vespars began their march across Shihala. There was no more music, no laughter. Only the looming threat of annihilation, and hope but the fleeting whisper of a treacherous sylph. Memories were of no use. Neither was pain other than as a bellows set to fire the hatred in his guts. Even in his imagination, he could not be free.

Jahmil sighed, trying to cast off the spell the woman and her lyre had cast over him. She was a dream, and he had no time for such distractions.

The call to prayer broke through the thick air of the market, the haunting lilt of an iman's voice like hooks in his skin, dragging him back to the world he could never leave.

"What do you want, Zamir?"

Zamir nibbled his bottom lip, his shoulders held in close to avoid being brushed by passing humans. "Forgive the interruption, *Amiri*. You asked to be informed the moment word came from the Seventh Legion. They have fallen back to the keep and are requesting reinforcements."

Jahmil pinched the bridge of his nose and turned his face down. "And?"

"The drakonte cavalry still have not been spotted, *Amiri*," said Zamir, an uncertain shake in his voice. "Our forces have combed the Ugur Mountains and surrounding lands. It's as if they..." He took a deep breath and shivered it out. "As if they have simply vanished."

"Vanished?"

A harmonic trill rushed through his blood, scattering his anger before it blinded him. He turned his gaze back to the lyrist. The man in the dirt was speaking to her, and she was laughing so that her entire body quivered. The sting of envy that bit into Jahmil's heart threatened to steal his breath. To make such a woman laugh would bring warmth to even the Moonless Night. And here he stood, a cold nothing to her and everything to his scattered people who looked to him, their prince, to come to their rescue. The needs and desires of his own heart—his life itself—were inconsequential.

Jahmil chewed the inside of his cheek, already ragged from the ravages of his sharp teeth, and turned back to Zamir. "How exactly does one lose an army of gigantic flying snakes?"

"There is word that the Spider of Karzusan was at the battle of Ain Khuleel," said Zamir, lowering his gaze. "We must accept the possibility that the cavalry met defeat."

Mention of Vespar's most powerful magic user—who had breached the walls at Karzusan, murdered his father, and forced him and his mother into exile—sent a shiver up Jahmil's spine that transformed into fire where it touched his brain. "Don't be absurd. I would know if Takisha Alqayid were dead. She is family. Her blood is my blood. Her fire burns inside my own."

"Of course, *Amiri*." Zamir looked down at his knees and wrung his hands together.

Jahmil felt sick looking at him. Of all the members of his old clique, Zamir was the only one who had made it out of Shihala alive. He'd lost Bakr, his right hand and best friend, at Karzusan. And Dhikrullah, head of his secret bodyguard and unhinged daredevil, had been captured by the Vespars, drawn and quartered after leading an unsanctioned charge into their territory. Chadli, Ajda, Fahti, Yusuf—all of his friends were gone. All he had left was his cousin Zamir, a wet blanket on the best of days, who had only gotten worse since they'd gone into exile. More cautious, more suspicious. More duplicitous.

"Is all well between you and Queen Qadira?" asked Zamir.

Jahmil forced back the bile that rose in his throat whenever he heard his fiancée's name. His body tightened, and his face twitched with dull spasms. "As well as it can be."

"Forgive me, *Amiri*, but she requested your presence at the dawn of the Seventh Moon. It would be wise not to upset her."

He flinched at the veiled admonition and turned his gaze back to the lyrist. She had begun a new song, this one smooth, slow, and intense—lines of heat rising from white sand on a hot day. The secret promise of a veil of black lace drawn across dark, kohl-lined eyes. It snaked down his throat and filled his chest to bursting with the heat of the desert, dry and shimmering, but with an illusion of water beyond every horizon.

Unfulfilled. Impossible.

He closed his eyes and tilted his face to the blistering, cloudless heavens. The light seared his moonlight eyes, his dusky skin, but he relished the feeling. Warmth, light, beauty; these things went hand-in-hand. And he was a creature of sunset.

"Your fiancée is not a patient woman," said Zamir quietly.

It flashed through Jahmil to break Zamir's sniveling nose. Instead, he blinked and let out a heavy, sandy breath. He didn't need anybody to remind him what Qadira was. More than that, there was no point in talking about her. That situation was as impossible as the first. He needed to focus on matters he could control.

Every day, the threat of Vespar grew and his options dwindled. He could not afford to trust in fate, for she was a duplicitous mistress. He had to make his own luck, fight his own battles. And if the drakontes were gone, that was impossible.

"We could send an emissary to Fyre," Zamir suggested. "The king would at least be able to say whether the drakontes still live."

Jahmil turned hot eyes on him. "And what do you think the chances are the Ah-nis will be willing to provide more when he learns we've lost track of the four hundred drakontes already in our arsenal?"

"Forgive me, *Amiri*. I just thought…"

"You're out of your element, *'ibn 'ami*," Jahmil snapped, then he leaned back and stroked his beard. "Faris Khayin would know where they are."

Zamir's face paled. "The traitor?"

"Go now to Ashkult prison."

"With respect, *Amiri*…"

"Feed him, clothe him, and bring him to me by the height of the Fourth Moon."

Zamir shook his head and hissed through his teeth, "That traitor is not to be trusted."

"Did I tell you to trust him?" Jahmil turned flashing eyes to Zamir's frightened, pale face. "The Vespars will reach Ahmar within the month, and without the drakontes, our fate is already sealed. Khayin was once their commander. *Inshallah*, he is the only one who might be able to find them in time."

Zamir's face morphed like he had just drunk poison. "Yes, *Amiri*."

"Bring him to my apartments in the City of Pearls."

Zamir bowed, then hastened through the gathered crowd, disappearing as he passed under a ladder. There were a thousand ways for a djinn to return to the Qaf from the human world—wherever three lines met to form three corners. Ladders leaned against buildings, the doorway of a tent, below a certain bridge, between the crags of rocks, under a fallen tree branch. If nothing else was available, a djinn could turn himself into a cat or a lizard and scurry through the triangle formed by a human's legs and the earth.

He could not afford to linger, yet Jahmil's gaze drifted once more across the plaza to the lyrist. Her filthy drummer had gone, as had the crowd as most of them hastened to the Dhuhr. She rested now, her back leaning against the stones of a nearby building to take advantage of a small line of shade. When he left this place, he would never see her again. He didn't know her, had never spoken to her, yet the pain of leaving her was as real as any he had ever known.

He opened his purse and found a single opal the size of his thumbnail. It shimmered in the sunlight in shades of red, orange, green, and purple. It was but a small change in his own world, and he couldn't remember if it had much value to humans. They made their money as pounded metal circles called coins, but Jahmil had none of those. Metal was as acid on a djinn's flesh. Some, like gold and silver, were merely irritating, though they sapped all magic. Others, like iron and quicksilver, burned with the fury of a thousand suns.

He hoped an opal would be worth something to her and wished he had more to give to thank her for the brief moment of respite he'd found in her music and her laughter.

The crowd thinned, allowing his approach. He tossed the stone into the bowl she had left out for collection, and once more his eyes swept over her. He was now so close he could see red highlights in her dark hair and rolling thunderclouds in her eyes. It set his heart on fire and smothered it all at once.

Her eyes shifted to focus on his face. The intensity of her gaze stole his breath, and his feet sank into the hard earth as if into sand. Her lips parted, and the corners lifted in a smile. But it was a coincidence, nothing more. She could not see him. She gazed through him at whatever was behind his back.

"You are beautiful," Jahmil said. Then he turned and walked away.

CHAPTER FOUR

Ayelet

Ayelet barely caught the end of Balian's quip about the baker's wife and the winemaker disappearing down an alley with her skirts already halfway up.

She cracked a smile and barked out a laugh. Not that his wit was any sharper that day than usual. Time in that miserable city just moved faster when she laughed, so she did her best to do so whenever occasion afforded. And often when it did not. And with the wisp still ruffling in the breeze and a djinn nearby, this was definitely the latter.

He sighed. "You're not even listening, are you?"

"I should not want to listen to you too much or you might become accustomed." She pulled her gaze away from the serious eyes across the market and turned to her bedraggled companion. His square jaw sported the shadow of a molasses-colored beard, and she could walk two fingers along his sharp cheekbones.

"You're as generous as the people. A lot of *eli sıkıs*, this crowd," Balian murmured.

"Then we shall have to play better. No more skipping beats just to see if I can keep up." She shot him a look with pursed lips.

"Ah, but where's the fun in that?" Balian slapped his drum once and pushed back his tangled hair. "You don't complain when I tease you in the warmth of your sheets." He wrinkled his nose and jutted his chin up with a smirk.

"What have you to boast of?" She smirked, then held her lyre up and shoved her foot square into his chest. He tipped back, almost knocking over his drum with a deep *thwump*. "Don't make me rub your face in the dirt," she added, crossing her arms. "If you collect any more filth, you'll blend right in with the streets."

He reached for her hand with a good-natured chuckle. "I wouldn't be talking if you were playing."

"And I would be playing if you had kept your eyes on your drum and not on the baker's wife." She pulled him to a seat and wiped the dirt off his back. "*Boş ver*! I've just the thing to catch us some dinner. Play me something slow and steady with a three-four lilt."

Balian frowned. "The people 'round these parts tend to prefer something a little more lively."

"And what has that gotten us recently? I'm netting for bigger fish."

Ayelet snuck a glance once more at the finely dressed djinn. His solid blue skin caught the sun like the waves of the ocean. *Lovely*, she thought, wanting for the briefest moment to be seen. She gave her arm a hard pinch.

She loosened her shoulders and curved her fingers. "Give me the beat."

Balian shrugged and began to drum, a solemn thrum with just enough skip to awaken the heart and hint at baleful secrets. She offered him a smile, then cast her sight once more to the back of the crowd. The gloomy djinn was still there, speaking to his slouching companion, the second a crumpled, washed-out version of the first. Of course, he came in a pair. She bit her lip and pressed a thumb to her forehead to ward off the Evil Eye, then took up her lyre. If evil was about, she might as well make it work for her.

She dropped her eyes to her slippered feet and strummed her first chord. The music spread through her chest and up her neck, the gentle tingle of a kiss far finer than any lover's she had ever known. Her worries melted as she swiped her fingers across the strings once more. She lifted her foot and held her breath in anticipation. Then, when the beat of the drum had filled her to bursting, she flashed her eyes up to the djinn and landed her heel in the dirt with a strum of the third chord.

Her body swayed and curved as music she didn't know she knew poured from her lyre and her fingers navigated a foreign scale. The marketplace shimmered to a blur of colors. The chant of sellers and murmur of crowds dwindled to silence until she heard only the pluck of strings. Only once had she played like this before, and the rush of magic pulled the memory. Twelve and on her own, she had picked up a lyre from the trinket-strewn wagon of a traveling peddler with bottomless eyes and a terrifying sneer. She had held it awkwardly, all elbows and uncomfortable angles, until the peddler showed her where to place her hands and muttered strange warnings under his breath.

Music, the folly. Magic, the call. When one kingdom rises, another must fall.

One pluck of those fated strings had been all it took to send her young heart racing and her fingers dancing. Faster and faster in a flurry of feet and heart and chords and color. Never had she felt so free. And only when her feet had ached with blisters and her lungs had burned for air had she collapsed in an exhausted heap on the ground.

The seller would not take the lyre back. "A strange and beautiful gift for a strange and beautiful girl," he had said. But the crowds whispered differently. She had been marked by the Evil Eye. She had been blessed by Allah. She had sold her soul for a favor from the djinn, or been possessed by one. All she knew was from that time forward, she could play songs she'd only heard once and whispers of songs she hadn't. Songs deep and sorrowful and ethereal. And that since then, she would catch glimmers of magic on the wind and see the soft, gem-hued skin of the night keepers.

Ayelet's feet slowed as her mind returned to the present, matching Balian's beat even as her heart raced to a finish. The crowd came back into focus and with it those serious eyes, watching her. Their sorrow pulled at a spring deep inside. She fought to keep it away, but it welled up, threatening to spill out onto her cheeks. She fingered the last scale, ending with a single note that felt as lonely as she did when she looked at him.

"*Deh.*" Balian snapped his finger in front of her nose, startling her to attention. "Who are you staring at with cheeks as red as that? I told you to only look at me that way."

She had to blink twice to chase away the blurry edges around Balian's face and the suspicion in his boat-brown eyes. It was like she had entered the magic and stared at the real world from within.

"Sorry," she said, the word half-formed. "I got lost a little on the way back in."

"I didn't hear anything off. You played perfectly, as always."

Her knuckles showed white where she gripped the lyre. She loosened her hold and shook the heaviness from her fingers. "Right. So, what was our haul today? Enough to eat?"

He sifted through the bowl, counting the few measly coins. "Better than usual. A small loaf of bread for both of us, if it's a little burnt, and a swallow or two of grapes."

Ayelet tried to catch sight of the djinn, but the crowd had shifted, blocking her view. Had she failed to sway him? Her stomach growled, and she pressed her hand against it in chastisement. "What about Serap?"

"That's not your concern," Balian said stiffly.

Ayelet sighed, that morning's failure fresh on her mind. "Does she need the food or not?"

He turned and glared at the sandy wall beside them.

"That's what I thought." She eyed the money as her stomach begged for food. "Take my share for her. No little girl should have to go hungry or work herself dead to eat."

Balian squeezed the coins in his hand before opening them back up to the sky. "And what will you do? If you stumble and break those fingers of yours, I won't have enough money to buy any food. No one wants to hear me pounding away if something beautiful isn't there to cover me up."

"Flattery won't feed me," she said with a chuckle. "And neither will your worry. You don't even know if I'll be here tomorrow."

"You've been saying that for a month now." He pinched her hip hard through her dress. She yelped. "Yep, still here. Maybe this time I've charmed you enough to stay."

She swatted his hand away, then forced a smile to keep the bitter taste on her tongue from spilling onto her lips. "I found a loaf earlier in the market."

Visible relief filtered over his face even as he narrowed his eyes. "Really?"

"Really," the lie rolled off her tongue as easily as notes from her lyre. "Let your worry be in the past. Now, off with you."

He kissed her cheek, then weaved his way down the street and out of sight.

She leaned against the rough stone wall, squeezing herself into a small slant of shade, and hugged her lyre to her chest. Balian was right. She should have left weeks ago. She had gotten too comfortable, stayed too long, and now the mark of her fate was coming for her. No one could be trusted. Not strangers, not acquaintances, and certainly not friends. Why hadn't she learned her lesson, yet? She kept finding excuses, telling herself that she just needed to play one more song, to pull in one more haul.

A hundred songs and half as many hauls later...

And for what? There was no bread. And it wasn't Balian, though he was rugged and handsome under the filth of poverty, and though she had let him slip into her bed a time too many. She had been with others like him before, and she would be again.

No. It was Serap and her sunken cheeks. Her too-big eyes and industrious little fingers. She was too easy a target. Hunger and the spice-trade slavers both vied for her life, while death waited lazily for what would be left of her soul. Ayelet saw too much of herself in those cracked lips that split when she smiled. It had made her foolish enough to think she could stay in Edirne and make a home. But she should have known better. She had grown too attached and now it would hurt ten times more when she left.

A soft, white shimmer blurred her sight from the left. She slid her eyes over to look through the haze. Aside from when she played music, she had never felt magic this close before. She waited for dread to consume her, but curiosity proved stronger. She almost reached out to touch it when sparkling eyes, bright blue skin, and lips curved with despondency emerged from the cloud.

She did not scream. Did not back away. She had been waiting to net him, the heart-aching song her lure. And whatever force had imbued her with her gifts must have favored her that day, because here he was, called by music, or magic, or a little of both.

He stepped closer, and she caught a whiff of moon-kissed breeze still warm from the sun's journey across the sky. He tossed something into the empty bowl at her feet, but she was drawn to him. To his oh-so-serious eyes of diamond that shifted with shades of deep purple, soft blue, the tiniest ember of red at the centers. She couldn't help it. She broke her rule and looked at him. *Into* him and the never-ending night he carried both in his heart and on his skin. She did not feel the chill she was expecting. Maybe it was the magic she now breathed in her lungs, or maybe it was the crisp, princely uniform that hugged his chest, bright white against stormy blue, but something in her caught like wool beneath flint.

With the tiniest flutter in her breast, she smiled.

"You are beautiful," he said, his voice gruffer than his smooth face led her to assume. His brows creased in a look of resigned dejection. Then he turned, and he left.

Ayelet stood frozen in place. Not once had a djinn ever come so close, much less spoken to her. Again, she waited for the chill of evil but felt only warmth. She watched him go for far longer than she should have, hoping to catch the scent of a summer's night on the breeze. With his broad shoulders out of sight and only the stink of fish under her nose, she bent down. Her eyes widened. From the bowl, she pinched a shining opal the color of fish scales and stars and held it up to the light.

Her eyes flashed past it to where the djinn had disappeared into the crowd. She hadn't netted a fish at all; she had netted a whale. A whale who just handed her and Serap a lifetime of full bellies and freedom. A way to escape the faceless man for good if she moved quickly enough. She laughed, a soft bubbling inside her chest, both genuine and fresh.

"*You* are beautiful!" she yelled across the market, knowing he could not hear. She popped the opal into the metal locket she wore low between her breasts and skipped home like a child to a full plate of dinner.

CHAPTER FIVE

Jahmil

He was cutting the time very close when he arrived at the edge of Buhayra Ruwarin, a silver lake of unparalleled clarity. Situated at the center was the City of Pearls, home to the Seat of Ahmar, the greatest of Queen Qadira's palaces. He could have simply blinked into his apartments, but Qadira frowned upon such antisocial behavior. He was her future husband, and he was supposed to be seen.

Within moments, an escort rode out to meet him—a carriage drawn by four winged, white horses accompanied by no less than a dozen armed soldiers. He wished he had the time or freedom to walk the long, tortuous bridge on his own, but that too was unacceptable to the queen. He needed to maintain the dignity of his station and could not simply walk through the gate into a swarm of commoners, as he had often done in his own kingdom, where royalty had more to do with leadership than pageantry.

As they moved along the floating bridge that snaked towards the palace, he watched rainbow fish, fifty-foot-long whales, and the bejeweled backs of sea turtles the size of small houses move in the depths of the water. The mirror of the lakebed reflected the sky above—three crescent moons nestled in twists of pink, black, and purple. And the palace itself, ten stories of towers capped with domes of blue glass and white marble.

Jahmil twitched anxiously, wishing the winged horses would move faster. He should not have lingered in the market. The lyrist's song still echoed in his ears, an image of her flickering in his mind's eye. A shadow dancing before a fire. Gray eyes sparkling in the light of a desert sun. And a smile that felt like it belonged to him.

He closed his eyes and shook his head. There was no time for fantasies. His drakontes were missing, and every moment they were gone brought him closer to the inevitability of marriage.

The coach took him through the City of Pearls to the great palace. When he arrived, they allowed him to freshen up, and then four guards ushered him to Qadira's apartments. Prince and future king he may have been, but he did not have free access to Ahmar's palace. Not yet. Perhaps not ever.

Nauzubillah, let it not come to that.

A raisin-skinned eunuch greeted him at the door, Qadira's own blood servant and master of slaves. His body was so padded with fat that he could hardly walk. Every heavy step elicited a low grunt. Qadira kept him that way on purpose. Him, and all of her other personal servants. She fed them six meals a day so that their very bodies would be a reflection of her tremendous wealth: the fattest servants in all of Qaf to serve the whims of the most powerful queen.

The eunuch announced him, and Jahmil was allowed into the drawing room of Qadira's private apartments.

Opulence didn't begin to explain it. The pearl and sapphire encrusted chamber was more garish than the Ardish sun. Every surface was coated in dust from crushed diamonds so it glittered and shifted in the rainbow-colored fires burning in the chandeliers. Before he acclimated himself to his luxurious and sparkly new surroundings, she rushed into his arms.

"*Taw'am ruwhi!*" she cried. *My soulmate.*

Jahmil took a step back and bowed politely. "*Malikati.*"

"You are cutting the time very closely, *habibi*," she said, her smile tightening as the brown fires of malice sparkled in her eyes. "I thought you had learned your lesson the last time."

Jahmil flinched, biting back the anger that flared in his gut to keep it from reaching his eyes. The last time he had dared to be tardy, she had recalled three regiments from the front to punish him. Six hundred civilians had died in the resulting massacre—Qadira's own people. She cared no more for them than she did for anyone else. Their lives were merely a device she used to keep him in line so she could laugh at him. The weight of those souls pressed down on Jahmil, forcing him into submission.

"Nothing," he said, his voice calm, even affectionate, "not even the King of the Eastern Elm, could keep me from you."

She folded her arms and pouted like a child. "Well, that is as it should be."

"May I ask why you requested my presence?"

"Does a fiancée need a reason?"

He bit his tongue to keep from saying what was on his mind and forced a smile. "Of course not." Jahmil reached into his pocket and took out a small wooden box. "A gift, *malikati*."

"You shouldn't have." Qadira squealed when she opened the box and discovered the baklava inside.

She had a sweet tooth and a passion for the novelty of all things human. The creatures of Ard had a reputation for danger, evil, and caprice throughout Qaf, and most djinn never dared visit their realm of metal and sunlight. It was true enough that human cities were filled with iron, disease, slaves, and poverty. Qadira enjoyed knowing Jahmil had taken some personal risk to procure her gifts. She didn't know he enjoyed it. He planned to keep it that way.

Qadira broke off a small chunk of the syrup-soaked pastry and placed it delicately between her large, birdlike lips. Her golden eyes met his as she moaned with pleasure. She was not unattractive. Sharp bones, a thin nose, a mop of black braids so long they brushed the floor, laced with diamonds and rubies. Her pasty purple skin was always dusted with shimmery powder so that it glimmered in the soft candlelight, and it got all over him whenever he was forced to touch her. She was tall and sharply angled; her hips did not curve so much as they jutted past her flat stomach. She always wore long, loose pants that swirled about her legs like smoke with a bejeweled lace bandeau covering her tiny, triangular breasts.

She broke off another piece of the pastry and lifted it towards his lips. He reached up to take it, but she held it back and shook her head. Stifling a sigh, Jahmil closed his eyes and opened his mouth so she could place the sweet morsel on his tongue. When her fingertips brushed his bottom lip, he knew it wasn't by accident.

Qadira grabbed his shoulders and pulled herself close to his chest. The touch of her body was as ice on his skin. He met her eyes.

"Sleep in my chambers tonight," she said, tracing a long fingernail over his chest.

He forced himself to smile. "*Malikati...*"

"Our wedding is but ten days away. What would be the harm?" She combed her fingers through his hair, the tips of her long nails against his scalp as tantalizing as the scrape of a razor. Pressing her lips into a pout, she gazed up from under plush black eyelashes. "We are the rulers of this land, Jahmil Amir. There's no reason to stand on ceremony."

"On the contrary, we *are* ceremony."

She pressed her hand against his chest, her fingers snaking between the buttons of his jacket to rumple his kaftan undershirt. "Did you come here to ask me to send a fresh regiment to Fawiya?"

I came because you summoned me, he almost said.

"I could not bear another moment away, *malikati*." He ran his fingertips over her cheek and she quivered under the light touch, her eyes aching to fall closed as if anticipating a kiss. He dropped his hand. "Unfortunately, the war rages around us and we must address it."

Her lips curled, eyes still closed, face still tilted towards his. "I'm afraid I cannot afford to spare it."

"With all due respect, *malikati*, you cannot afford not to. If Fawiya should fall, it will open the Vespars' path through the pass at Barina, and then..."

"Shh." She set her sickly sweet finger on his lips and opened her eyes. "I despise when you talk strategy. It makes you sound like a common general."

"I am a general." Jahmil bristled, fighting to keep his muscles from tensing and to stop the colors from rising in his eyes.

She leaned in closer, catching her own wrist behind his neck and dangling her meager weight from his solid frame. "Perhaps there is a way you could convince me."

Without warning, she went up on her toes and kissed his lips. Fighting the instinct to recoil, he laced his hand around the small of her back to draw her closer, but only for a moment before breaking off the kiss.

"*Jamilati*," he said, his voice husky though the words were chewy as old milk, "you know I long for our union as much as you, but ten days is not so very long when we have but one opportunity to do things properly." He lifted her hand to his lips and kissed her bony knuckles. "And what if the inevitable should occur? The birth of an heir is far too important to leave any room for claims of bastardy, even a scant few days."

"I suppose you're right, though I hate you for it." She ran her sharp, sparkly fingernails down the length of his cheek, then gripped his chin and drew his lips so close to hers that he tasted her minty breath. "I dream of you each night, *habibi*. Do you dream of me?"

He enfolded her fingers in his and looked into her eyes, thinking of the human lyrist so that the colors that flashed through his irises would reflect desire rather than disdain. "When the First Moon rises in my window and I wake, your face is all I see, and I long to sleep but to dream again."

Jahmil swallowed hard. There was only one way he would convince her to give him the troops he needed. If he didn't send reinforcements, Fawiya would be lost, and the Vespars would slaughter every soldier and civilian. He had no choice.

For Shihala, he thought. Then he cupped Qadira's jaw in one hand and kissed her. Her tongue came to alight on his bottom lip, hard and pokey, a battering ram demanding entry. He parted his lips, and she plunged inside. He fluttered his tongue over hers like the beat of a butterfly's wings, and a soft *mmm* rose in her throat, the same sound she had made when the baklava hit her tongue. When he pulled back, she nibbled on his bottom lip, holding it lightly so it stretched as he pulled away.

Her breath was heavy, eyes still closed. "The way you kiss me, Jahmil..." She sighed and bit her lip. "You may leave me no choice but to order you to stay."

"Have patience, *malikati*," he whispered. "And on our wedding night, I shall write poetry on your skin with my fingers and come away with your scream tingling on my lips."

She shivered and looked up at him, her eyes pulsing with hunger like a lioness about to leap on her prey. Then she moaned and pressed two clenched fists to her forehead. "Oh, go on and have your regiments."

"Thank you," he said, a wave of relief rushing through his blood and scrubbing away some of the shame. "*Ahlam jamila.*"

"Sweet dreams, *habibi*," she purred and her lips twitched, longing to be kissed again. But he turned and strode away.

When Jahmil was out of her sight, he wiped his lips and spat on the floor.

Being around Qadira always made his anxiety flare and his stomach curdle, but today was far worse than usual. The news Zamir had brought him about the drakontes was swirling around his brain, coloring every thought with blackness. The last year of living in the Palace of Pearls and playing at being Qadira's plaything had always been colored by the vague hope that he could find a way to retake his kingdom without having to fully prostitute himself. But with only ten days until the wedding and with his drakontes missing, his dreams of remaining a bachelor were fading into the din of encroaching battle.

Jahmil put his head down and hurried across the palace complex toward his apartments. The traitor Khayin was his last hope, and no thought could be darker than that.

CHAPTER SIX

AYELET

AYELET HURRIED ACROSS THE city, the opal—the djinn's gift of freedom—adding a spring in her step and softening the pang of hunger that growled within her. Even so, the ringing call to evening prayers stopped her progress, and it was dusk by the time she drew near the tents that made up a hodgepodge camp of local performers and passing vagrants. The tattered array of colorful fabric and the hazy smoke of fires rested on the edge between city lights and the dark abyss of wilderness.

Except, tonight there were several fires too many. Unexpected guests. She slowed her skip and dropped behind the scrub of bushes to the side of the road. The only reason caravans dropped in unannounced was because they knew they'd be unwelcome if the locals heard they were coming. Caravans full of Klephts and Armenians, of mercenaries or—Ayelet shivered despite the warm night—slavers. One foot in front of the other, she hedged forward.

"*Yuh!*" A voice scraped at her ear.

She turned around and shoved her forearm into the interloper's throat, then sighed with exasperation. "Balian, you hog tusk! You know I hate it when you do that."

He smirked. "I like getting you all riled up. You should know that by now."

"I would if you were better at it." She leaned in so their noses almost touched and fluttered her eyelashes.

He blushed in the moonlight, and his easy demeanor loosened the tension that had been building in her muscles.

"Why are there so many fires at camp?"

"That's just what I was heading out here to tell you. Kadri's in town."

"The traders aren't supposed to be in town until after harvest. That's a month away." Unease settled on her shoulders, and her smile faltered. "They're never early."

"Traders may not be early. But smugglers arrive exactly when they know there's a profit to be made."

"And Serap?" she asked, unable to fully shake off her worry.

"Safe, fed, asleep, and *away*," he said, reading her face. "She will be fine."

Ayelet cast a wary gaze on the orangey glow in the distance.

"Come," Balian said, holding out his hand. "Let's go make merry at camp. The cider's on Kadri for our gracious hospitality."

Ayelet slipped her fingers willingly into his rough palm and followed him to camp. A raucous party was underway, the tambourines and drums in a galloping beat that made it easy to dance with a drunken swagger. Kadri reposed on the far side of the fire, gold bracelets spilling down her arms and her hand clutching a stick, scribbling notes and calculations in the dry dirt. Her dark hair frizzed around her face, braids wound tight with ribbons and strings, their ends tufty and dry. Her bright blue eyes could be seen from anywhere, sparkling pools that saw everything and forgot nothing.

Ayelet fingered the charm through the muslin of her dress. Kadri would pay a pretty penny for it and only stiff her half as much as a normal customer. A camp full of boozy paupers, however, was no place to go flashing gems.

She separated from Balian, grabbing a tuft of the soft brown bread in his hands before he gambled it away, minus Serap's share. She shoved it in her mouth and wove her way through jostling elbows. The morsel was just enough to remind her stomach how empty the rest of it was.

In a lump of furs and strange smells, rested Nadir, a wolf of a man whose bite was far worse than his bark. He rarely traveled with Kadri's caravan and was a procurer of travel accommodations for those looking to start a new life. A trafficker who, for the right price, would just as easily help a slave escape as he would return one to their master. Rumor had it he also trafficked djinn and other magical beings when he wasn't at his abandoned castle working magic with his ghost of a stolen bride and reclusive son. His wagon always jostled with iron chains and bottles of frost that never warmed. And at camp, he could often be found alone, eyes staring keenly at nothing, as he whispered from his religious scrolls in tones that made the prayers sound like curses.

Ayelet had once used his skills to flee, and for that, she kept her mouth shut, but his presence at camp sent her skin crawling. Bad things happened to innocent people when Nadir was about. She offered him a curt nod that he returned before nursing his giant mug of cider.

At last, Ayelet pushed her way to the circle of dancers by the fire. The wind blew her way, coating the air in stinging smoke. She coughed once, grinned, and jumped into the fray. If she never danced when she was hungry, she'd hardly dance at all. She hooked her elbow into the nearest partner's and swung around with a giggle. Keeping in time with the plucky beat, she kicked, dipped, spun, and laughed until her breath was short. Then she pulled free on the other side of the fire and rubbed the corkscrew stitch in her ribs. With the levity of music pumping in her veins, she was able to put up a charming smile. Kadri hated solemnity even more than Ayelet, only she'd been known to kill over it.

Not that Ayelet blamed her for it.

Kadri was the queen of the black market because of her willingness to do whatever it took to stay that way. A woman working *like* a man but not *as* one in a world that cared very much about precisely that. She had cut the feminine ending from her name young and built an empire by batting her eyelashes just long enough to slit the purse strings of any man stupid enough to underestimate her. Now she wore her skirts simply to mock all the men who couldn't keep up with her shrewd decision-making, ruthlessness, and infuriatingly intact womanly charms. Ayelet had always admired her for her ability to survive in a world stacked against her. But she also knew Kadri could be far more dangerous than even the likes of Nadir, so she kept her at arm's length and worked hard to keep up a friendly acquaintance in case a need for just that kind of cruelty ever arose.

Ayelet clenched her stomach muscles, checked her smile once more, and stepped forward into the firelight with a slight bow. "Kadri, Kadri! Your visit is a blessing."

"Ayeleta, I was wondering when you'd show up." Kadri waved her over with a smile, but her eyes were as sharp as ever. "My ears tell me that you are easier and easier to find these days. Planting a garden of roots here, are we?"

Ayelet slipped onto the green, silk pillow next to her. "A woman must eat. If I'm planting roots, it is so I can harvest later."

Kadri's eyes narrowed. "What a charming way to not answer my question."

She was fishing, trying to see if Ayelet would become a simple housewife to some poor performer, with seven babies and nothing to offer the Queen of Black Trade.

"I plan to leave before the week's through," Ayelet said, refusing to bite. "Perhaps with you? How long do you stay in Edirne?"

"Three days." Kadri lifted her brows. "It has been too long since you traveled in my camp. I miss the thrill of your music. And word of your talent travels in important circles. I might gain some valuable customers with you at my side."

"I don't play for highbrows." The thought soured in Ayelet's stomach.

She *had* stayed too long. So long, the same people had begun to recognize her, to talk with their friends, who talked with acquaintances, who talked with scum, who talked with *him*. And just like every other time, he would find her. The wisp in the market attested to that. There was a reason she had turned down countless offers to live comfortably in the palace playing for the sultan himself. Nowhere was safe, and she was better hungry than caught.

"As long as you play for me, you are welcome." Kadri waved casually.

Ayelet put up a serene smile. "It is settled then. We leave in three days. So, what brings you to Edirne ahead of harvest, anyway?" she asked, keeping her tone a pleasant shade of neutral.

"Trade."

"Before the money counters come to town?"

Kadri raised her stick to poke at a passing servant. The scrappy man nodded and hurried out of sight. Then she turned back to Ayelet. "Is there a rule that says I should not?"

Ayelet grinned. "What a charming way for you to not answer my question."

Kadri furrowed her brows, then released them with a bark of laughter. "See, this is what I've missed! It is settled, then. In three days, we leave this place and head past the mountains."

The servant returned, carrying goblets filled with honey-colored liquid as thick as tree sap.

"Apricots." Kadri held her goblet up so the green glass twinkled in the fire. "Some honey and spices, too. You've never tasted anything so good as this."

"And what do I owe you for such libations?"

"What do you think?" Kadri asked. "A song."

Ayelet chuckled. "Such a low price. I'm flattered you think my tunes are worth as much." She made to stand, pulling her lyre from the satchel she kept tucked around her waist, but Kadri stilled her.

"Not yet," she said, her voice quiet and her eyes glittering as she looked into the crowd.

Ayelet hesitated, then sat back down. She scanned the revelers for trouble. A nefarious sneer, perhaps. A drawn blade. Or the shadowy doings of a mystic and their city-burning fireworks.

She saw nothing. Nothing but lingering smoke that pooled in a pocket of air on the far edge of camp. It swirled between the tents and Kadri's wagons. A breeze blew against her face, but the hazy tendrils continued to lace themselves among people and crates, a tapestry of silken threads made of silvery gray air. It was beautiful. Like a spring of magic mixed with smoke if ever that much gathered in one place at a time. Lowering her guard, she took a sip of the apricot cider: tart and spicy and teeth-hurting sweet.

Ayelet leaned back against the cool pillows with Kadri, their arms touching, and watched the haze tease with shapes that hinted of animals and flowers, of stars and longing. Twice she swore she saw the handsome azure djinn from the market and felt the sorrow he carried. Twice she took a large gulp of apricots to chase it away. Halfway through her mug, her thoughts were buzzing. She had always been a lightweight. Then again, this was the first she'd had of anything to eat in over a day.

Giggling, she leaned closer to Kadri. "This isn't juice."

Kadri cracked a wry smile. "Indeed. No more for you, though." She took the goblet from Ayelet's hands and handed her a warm piece of bread. "Eat up and get up. Your payment is about to come due."

Ayelet blinked through the heaviness that coated her mind like muslin. If the magical trance that happened when she played earlier that day overtook her once more, she may well fall flat on her face. Kadri would never let her live it down, and her reputation as a lyrist who could summon the djinn and control the currents of the four winds would be mud. And now that her name was on the breeze and talked of in *important circles*, a blunder like that would only draw more attention.

Kadri stood, and the thumping music died down. A few drunken voices muttered on until the crowd *shushed* them quiet.

"Revelers," Kadri spoke with an easy, commanding air. "Our gracious hosts have offered us a taste of their talents." Her men whistled and stomped their feet. Kadri reached her hand back, and Ayelet took it, stumbling slightly as she found her feet. "The famed Ayelet, named and marked an instrument of the gods themselves, will play her lyre for us tonight."

Hoots and howls hit Ayelet with a force that smelled of bitter, illegal wine. Her mind still hummed as she ran through her list of songs. She would play it safe. A lullaby. There was a charm to pieces that touched the hearts of both children and men. They were also easy to remember. Kadri lay once more behind her, and Ayelet took out her lyre. The flicker of fire reflected off the worn, smooth sycamore wood and shifted between opalescent hues on the ensconced turtle shell inside the rounded sound chest. Ten rough strings ran from the top of the two curved arms and to the bottom of the rounded base.

She ran her fingers across the strings, back and forth in a scale of skipping thirds. Magic did not take her this time, but the smoke in the back swirled and swayed with her tune, drawing her in as she seemed to draw it.

She sang:

Dandini dandini danadan

Bir ay doğmuş anadan

Kaçınmamış yaradan

Mevlam korusun nazardan.

Dandini dandini danadan

A moon was born from a mother's womb

spared from all harm

and protected from the Evil Eye.

As she neared her final chord, the smoke withdrew. By the time she plucked the last note, all the haze had disappeared, and the stars showed crisp and clear. An eerie quiet hung in that pause of breath that always succeeds a bout of well-played music. Then a woman on the left smacked her tambourine with a cheer. The crowd broke out in a mixture of praise, laughter, and their own gurgling renditions of what she had just sung.

"How was that?" she said, turning too fast to look at Kadri. She had to catch herself on the arm of a passing servant.

The green pillow sat empty, the thin fabric creased from where Kadri had lain.

Ayelet frowned. She grabbed her goblet and downed another deep swallow. "I'm taking my spoils whether you listened or not, Kadri," she called to the empty wagon nearby.

The same servant who helped hold her steady approached with head bent. "*Efendi* begs your apology at her departure and asks that you relax and enjoy yourself until she returns. You may have more cider as you will." He bowed low, the golden liquid he carried spilling lazily over the edge of the pitcher.

Ayelet looked down into her cup. A red-eyed reflection of herself stared back. Kadri would not treat an important customer like this. And with the opal in her locket, she was an important customer now, whether Kadri knew it or not.

"Kadri is not *my efendi*." She snorted. "I am no one's servant. And I will not wait."

Ayelet stepped over the pillows and nearly tripped. She regained her composure and marched through the row of wagons despite the servant's protests.

"Kadri! Kadri Muhtasib!" She ripped back the curtains of a wagon only to startle a pair of lovers in the throes of passion. "Allah's blessings," she said and ducked back out. "Love the tattoo."

She scurried off, hoping the man inside would be too busy consoling his woman to chase after her. The black egret on his ankle *was* lovely, but it also meant he was military. She did not need any government trouble on her hands. The sultan and his Ottoman rulers were just like every other dictator that ruled the world: spoiled, entitled brats who caused more trouble than they solved.

At last, she neared the final wagon at the back of camp and heard whispers on the other side and the deep, husky voice of Nadir chanting what sounded like a garbled prayer.

"Cork it tight," Kadri said in a hushed tone. "All the way down. Make sure it's smooth. No gaps."

Ayelet paused, swaying a little from the motion. She wrapped herself around the back of the canvas covering and to the other side. Then she peeked around the corner. Kadri stood with Nadir and two men, seven large glass jars between them, all full of hazy white. As soon as they had properly sealed the bottle, Nadir's chanting stopped and they all leaned in to inspect the jar.

"What is this?" she asked, forgetting to keep her mouth shut.

The four jerked their heads in her direction.

Ah, well. She stepped into the light.

"What are you doing here?" Kadri's tone rang far from the hospitable one she had welcomed Ayelet with earlier.

"Looking for you."

Kadri offered a tight smile. "I guess you would've found out soon enough."

"Found out what?" Ayelet asked. She tried desperately to pull all the strings of her mind and knot them together, but her thoughts were honey.

"I came to Edirne looking for you."

Ayelet blinked at the swirling mist inside the jars. She fought the urge to kneel and press her face against the glass. "Why?"

"To make you a proposition." Kadri grabbed her hand and placed it on the nearest container. The glass warmed her fingers, and the silver tendrils inside swirled rapidly to meet her touch.

"I'm not smoking whatever's in there," she said flatly. Even drunk, she knew that much.

"No." Kadri laughed. "It's not for smoking. It's for drinking."

Ayelet frowned. The glint of the bottled wisp thinned the honey in her mind. "The apricot cider?" she asked and glanced up at Kadri.

"Precisely," she crooned. "Have you ever tasted anything so sweet? So energizing? It seemed to hit you pretty hard, though. I've not seen that happen before."

"Seen what exactly?"

"Seen someone get drunk on magic."

Ayelet crouched lower and peered into the jar. Of course. She already couldn't handle her human spirits, so it only made sense that the supernatural equivalent would leave her wrecked. She poked at the wisp, and it rose to meet her. Wherever her finger trailed, the magic followed. "You caught a spirit?"

"No," Nadir spoke for the first time. "It is not a creature."

Ah. That's why he's here. "So, you traffic air now? Times must be good in the Empire if your business is that slow."

Nadir crossed his arms. "It's not air either. Call it an essence if you must. But it's the pure form of magic."

"And you can see it?" Ayelet asked. She thought she had been the only one.

Kadri leaned down, looking through the other side of the jar, so her irises were as wide and blue as a *nazar boncuğu*. "Can you?"

She bit her tongue in time to keep back the truth. "I see only the glittery stirring of dust in a jar full of air."

"Me too." She sighed. "Though if the magic is condensed enough, and you shine light on it just right, you can see more of a hint of shimmer, like a mirage on desert sand distorting anything on the other side."

Ayelet leaned back on her heels, and the magic retreated once more to the center of the jar. She definitely saw more than a mirage. "How do you find something you cannot see?"

"My Ayeleta, that's where you come in."

Ayelet sat back and turned her eyes to the starlit sky. She didn't know what Kadri meant, and she didn't care. Kadri's highest-valued commodity was her willingness to embrace trouble. Ayelet wanted none of that. Besides, "old friend" or not, Kadri was human. And no human could be trusted. That was a truth carved into her bone.

Playing with magic was fire in hay that called to her nightmares. How many wisps were about in Edirne? And—air caught in her chest and left with a painful hiccup—what if they truly were the reason she could never stay hidden? If they revealed her once more and *he* found her when she was with little Serap... it was too painful to think about, even dulled with spiked cider. That Kadri suspected she had anything to do with the wisps made them all the more dangerous.

She closed her eyes and breathed in the dry evening air, missing that hint of moon-kissed breeze she had felt in the market earlier. The darkness of her mind glimmered as brightly as the night sky as she thought of crystal eyes that were oh-so-serious. If only she could disappear as the djinn did so easily. What freedom it must afford.

Not so, for her.

Three days was far too long to wait. She would have to run tonight.

CHAPTER SEVEN

Jahmil

HE FLUNG HIMSELF ONTO the divan and summoned a puff of white fire to his fingertip. He lit his hookah, the cool smolder lending a gentle blur to the fray of his nerves. With a heavy draw, he read reports from his commanders.

Of Queen Qadira's twenty-seven active generals, fifteen had privately sworn their allegiance to him as their future king. In the remaining forces, Jahmil at least had a captain or major who was loyal to him, secretly relaying information and guiding their commanders with gentle hands away from the singular will of the queen.

Jahmil did not see these men as traitors; their decision to back him was based on their personal experiences with the merciless and unfortunately clever Vespar army. When Jahmil showed them how Queen Qadira still took the threat lightly, some fell on their knees to beseech his help. Her grandiosity may have intimidated the peasants, but it did not have the same effect on the military. As commander of all of Shihala's forces since the death of his father, and a secondary general for years before that, Jahmil had more experience fighting Vespar than anyone alive. And even though he had been forced into retreat after the travesty of Karzusan, he had won often enough and caused the Vespars enough pyrrhic victories to slow their virulent spread. Most importantly, he had bought his people, and the peasants of Ahmar living on the border, the time they needed to get out safely.

He broke the wax seal on a scroll with his pinky and glanced over the report, but his gaze was drawn across the room. In a corner resting on a bed of crushed black velvet lay his ney. The flute was one of only three personal effects he had salvaged from Karzusan, the others being his sword and his grandmother's opal necklace. He hadn't touched the instrument in over a year, dust accumulating on the long tubular body of the reed. Whenever he looked at it, a soft whisper tugged at his heart.

Usually, it was easy to ignore, but today it was amplified by his experience of the lyrist in the market. Memories flashed through him of sitting on the roof of Karzusan palace with his friends—with Bakr—playing to a pulsating, responsive sky and imagining what journeys may lie ahead. Even back then, he had known it was nothing more than a fantasy, but he used to imagine what it would be like wandering Allah's worlds with his ney. Making a home wherever he made his fire, allowing destiny to blow him about like a feather in the wind.

The gray-eyed woman played on his thoughts as deftly as she strummed her lyre. Jahmil allowed himself a moment to wonder where she would be now. Seated around a campfire conversing with friends, laughing that laugh that was more beautiful than her music. Or would she be lying in a tent kissed with sweat as that filthy man—maybe her husband, but certainly the luckiest man alive—showered her skin with adulation? For her sake, he hoped the man was skilled. That he brought her some measure of the pleasure her body had been designed by Allah to experience.

The door banged open, and Zamir scurried inside. "*Amiri*," he said, bowing, but the expression on his face was unmistakable.

Jahmil set aside the scroll and sat up, his mouth dry and his eyes wide in anticipation. "You have him?"

Zamir nodded. He was out of breath, his fingers twitching as if searching for a weapon. "He is chained up in the stables."

"Bring him."

"With respect, *Amiri*—"

Jahmil's eyes flashed, and the room flooded with white followed by a swift crack of thunder. Standing, he straightened his back. "Bring. Him. Now."

Zamir bowed quickly then straightened his own back, perhaps trying to salvage a scrap of dignity, and hurried through the door.

Alone, Jahmil chewed on his lip and began to pace. Logically, he knew the creature he had built up in his imagination would bear little resemblance to the actual man who even now was being dragged up from the stables. Khayin was just a man. Perhaps he was no longer mortal, but that did not make him a god.

"*Lā 'ilāha 'illā-llāh,*" he whispered. *There is no God but God.*

Still, Jahmil's pulse quickened and sweat condensed on his brow. Perhaps he had made a mistake, but what other options had he?

The door smacked open and Jahmil turned. One soldier wearing thick gloves hurried inside and placed a golden chair at the center of the room. All metal was harmful to djinn, but the effects varied. While iron would melt through flesh and bone alike, gold was a slow burn like the Ardish sun on pale flesh, but it deadened magic like nothing else, trapping a djinn's fire inside their flesh. The guards of Ashkult who were Khayin's sentinels would take no chances with such a prisoner.

Six heavily armed Ghaluman soldiers stepped through the doorway. Each was at least as tall as Jahmil, and all were broader with puffy muscles and vicious eyes that sparkled with specks of yellow disgust and pink anxiety. Their red skin burned like hot embers under the light of white fire in the wall sconces. Like all Ghalumans, they had no respect for royalty—no respect for anyone outside of their own country. They each glared at Jahmil in turn as they led a cloaked and hooded figure inside.

Jahmil resumed his seat on the divan and leaned back against a cushion, careful to throw his arm over the back and relax his shoulders. "Leave us."

The Ghalumans shared wary glances, as black tendrils of fear raced through Zamir's eyes. The guards secured the traitor's feet to the legs of the hideous golden chair and forced him to sit before allowing Zamir to herd them out of the room.

Jahmil took a slow breath, his gaze poring over the anonymous figure. "Remove your hood."

The head lifted and cocked to one side. Under the hem of a cloak of brown sackcloth was the sharp outline of a chin—rubbery, greenish-gray skin caked in dirt. The teeth inside the mouth were brown and pointed, the front two hanging over the top of the bottom lip. They were textured and craggy like chunks of rotted wood.

"*Marhabān mujadadān, al'amir alsaghir.*" Khayin's voice was at once deep and breathy, tinged with the hiss of hot metal plunging into cold water. Or was that the burn of his skin on the golden chair?

Jahmil's breath caught. The traitor remembered him. He had been only nine when they met, a snot-nosed princeling gushing over the great knight's exploits. Even in those days, Faris Khayin D'Jaush was not often in court, far too busy wrangling cyclones and stealing diamonds from hunched immortal gorgons. He was the stuff of storybooks. Faris Khayin had sailed to the edge of the world, fought the sorceress of the Far Flying Mountains, and charmed a sphynx into giving away her treasure. He had descended into Jahannam and then been lifted to the edge of paradise on the wings of angels, returning with the ability to see the unseen and know the unknown. The man was a legend then, the purest possible embodiment of freedom, adventure, and romance.

Everything Jahmil had ever longed for. And now...

A cackle broke from Khayin and he bared the rest of his hideous teeth. Rotted meat and sulfur curdled in the air. Jahmil's mouth blanched and his shoulders tightened. He took another hit from his perfumed hookah just to cover the stench.

Twisted hands with huge, swollen knuckles gripped the hood and threw it back, revealing the remainder of the face. The eyes had not changed, pure black that shined with rainbow iridescence like oil slicks, now shrouded in loose skin that hung down the sides of his face, pooling at his neck in curtains. His long ears stuck up, then drooped out to the sides in points.

He had always been hateful to look at, the result of a nameless curse placed on him decades ago. There were many versions of what had happened, but that was the only of Faris Khayin's many exploits that the great knight had always refused to speak of.

"I remember you, *al'amir alsaghir*." Khayin grinned with those horrid, mossy teeth. "When last I saw you, you were little more than a suckling babe hanging from the breasts of your wetnurse."

Jahmil turned the rock crystal ring on his finger with the edge of his thumb. He could not let on how nervous he was, especially since he wasn't sure why he felt that way. Was it because Khayin had once been his hero or because he was now the stuff of nightmares?

Cold sweat stained Jahmil's hands. He took a handkerchief from his pocket and dabbed his forehead. "Much has changed."

The traitor cackled, his slight shoulders shivering under his cloak. "Almalik Bajul is dead."

Jahmil steeled his expression. "He is."

"Swarmed by a horde of *bial'dabaye* and torn to pieces." Khayin's blank eyes gazed at everything and nothing. "Even as his son and wife fled in the other direction."

Every muscle in Jahmil's body tightened. "He was already dead."

"Who says he was? Your mother the coward?" In the reflection of Khayin's black eyes, Jahmil saw his father clawing at a stone wall as he fell from the ramparts of Karzusan Palace into a swell of scrambling arms and legs. Of teeth, blood, and claws as long as daggers. His father's scream echoed through the room, closing in around him from all angles.

Tears stung at Jahmil's eyes, but he hardened his face and clenched his teeth. What magic was this that Khayin could wield even with his back pressed against gold?

"You left him to die, *Amiri...*" came the cold whisper. "You should have been fighting at his side. Instead, you fled like a rat."

"He was already dead."

Jahmil had been telling himself the same thing every day since he lost his father. He was already dead and there was nothing anyone could do. The walls were breached by a tremendous explosion of fire and raw magic—the Spider of Karzusan working his hideous magic. Vespars poured into the keep with their swift, needlelike swords and insatiable thirst for blood, slaughtering everyone in their path. Jahmil had fled to protect himself, to protect his mother. Because without them, there was no Shihala. If they had died, the war would have been over that very night.

That was what his mother always said, and Jahmil longed with all his soul to believe it, even as he reviled her and everything that led to that moment.

"General Bakr stayed and fought to the end," Khayin said, and another scream cut the air.

Bakr's voice, which had always laughed so easily, transformed into a hideous gurgle as he choked on his own blood.

"Your own best friend, who might have been your brother-in-law, cut down trying to win your battle, and you left him bleeding on the battlefield under a pile of corpses."

One of the tears stinging in Jahmil's eyes raced down his cheek like a stream of lava. He opened his mouth to protest, but his tongue was dead and desiccated, coiled at the back of his throat.

"Bakr," he rasped.

"And what have you accomplished with the gift of time they gave you?" Khayin lifted his brow and turned his head to one side. "Because of you, the Shihalan people are refugees. Parasites sucking on the underbelly of other kingdoms. Hated, reviled pariahs. Your coffers are empty, your list of allies thin. What did your father die for? What did Bakr die for? A prince that would rather preserve his own wretched life than honor their sacrifices."

Jahmil's eyes flashed, drenching the room in white. He jumped to his feet and smacked the glass hookah across the room. Khayin flinched, and with eye contact broken, the screams faded to nothing. Jahmil finally managed to take a single, desperate breath, but Khayin's laughter cut into him like poisonous smoke.

Jahmil's chest heaved. Even though the sounds and images were fading, he could still hear them echoing in his heart. His father's shriek, his best friend's helpless rattle.

Ya hasrety, what had he done? How could he have left them?

He clenched his fists and his eyelids. He couldn't let himself think such things now. He would honor their sacrifices. Every day, he worked to honor them. And no, it would never be enough. And that was why he could never stop.

Jahmil's heart tightened, but he breathed it out. He had to focus. Whatever he had once admired about Khayin was long dead. What sat before him was a monster. The traitor who sold out Shihala before the battle at Rananbar, where the Vespar army anticipated every Shihalan trick and ten thousand and five loyal soldiers had been slaughtered. If Khayin hadn't been immortal, he would have been executed for selling court secrets to Vespar. Instead, he was sent to Ashkult prison to suffer a fate worse than death.

"Have at it," Khayin said, cocking his head far to one side and not blinking once. "Let's hear your threats, *al'amir alsaghir*. Or is there no thunder behind those eyes of lightning?"

Jahmil flattened his chin. Losing his temper was not going to win Khayin's help. "After so much time in Ashkult, I can't imagine much remains in this world that frightens you."

"All men are frightened until they are dead."

Jahmil's mind burst with memories of the conversation he and Khayin D'Jaush had shared when Jahmil was so young. He had asked Khayin, begged him, to tell him how to find the Eternal One so that he too could be given her Kiss of Life.

Those black eyes had turned to him then, and a screeching laugh had torn from Khayin's throat. "*Immortality: a fate worse than death.*"

Jahmil knew there was only one card he could play with the traitor. Only one thing he could offer that would be of any interest. The only problem was the card wasn't in his hand. He would have to bluff. He had never been a good liar, never been able to master the fine art of holding his emotions back from his own heart so they did not shimmer in his eyes. To believe his own lies like an Elmaran lawyer, to the extent that they no longer reflected in the constant shift of his internal fire.

He could find the answer in time, Jahmil told himself. And he believed it. Which meant this wouldn't be a bluff. Not really.

"I can kill you," Jahmil said.

"Kill me?" The laughter redoubled so that the very room seemed to quiver. Khayin breathed out, and it sounded like the low growl of a leopard, blood bubbling in his throat. "I cannot be killed. *Yalak min 'ahmaq.*"

"I know that, you idiot." Jahmil resumed his seat on the divan and kicked his feet up on the ottoman with a passionate sigh. "Everybody knows that. It's only been twelve years since you were put away, not a thousand."

Jahmil stuffed his ring back onto his finger and stroked his trim beard. "But twelve will become a hundred. And then a thousand. And then ten thousand."

Khayin snarled and his face twitched, searching to meet Jahmil's eyes again. Jahmil kept his gaze on the ceiling.

"I've never been to Ashkult," Jahmil continued, "but I have been told stories about that place since I was a boy. Is it true they keep you in a golden box so small you cannot even move your limbs? That they never feed you, never water you? And they keep your box buried under heavy stones so that you cannot hear a sound, nor see a whisper of light?" He laughed coldly, determined that his own growl should match the vitriol in the traitor's face. "Really, we should both be grateful they remembered where they'd buried you."

Khayin's nostrils flared and the black pools of his eyes widened. "Are you offering to free me?"

"I'm offering to kill you."

"That's impossible."

"Why?" Jahmil lifted his brows. "Because you shook hands with the Bahamut?"

The look of disdain that coated his face felt strangely like a victory. "I received the kiss of the Eternal One."

"What's in a kiss?" Jahmil smirked. "Better a handshake. At least hands hold weight."

Khayin's face further contorted, brows raised and lips parted. Incredulous, and yet undeniably curious. Jahmil watched the curtains of skin twitch, searching for clues as to what ineffable thoughts might be racing through the mind of the immortal traitor.

"I cannot die," Khayin said again.

Jahmil laced his fingers behind his neck and stretched his back. "Only emptiness and Allah are immortal. The rest of us live on stolen time."

"Look into my eyes and say it." Khayin leaned forward. There was no venom in his voice. Indeed, the faintest tremor.

"I would sooner die," Jahmil spat, his gaze fixed on the ceiling. "Take the deal, or go back to your box."

Khayin's head twitched to one side like a wild animal. "What do you want?"

"I will ask you questions. And you will answer them helpfully."

"Three questions."

"As many questions as I like."

"No. You will never run dry of them and keep me alive forever." Khayin extended his long, skeletal hand. "Three questions, *Amiri*. Three answers. And then, you will end my wretched life."

Jahmil scrutinized the hand: the swollen knuckles, the skin caked in black filth. Swallowing the bile rising in his throat, he clasped the fingers and shook. "Tell me where to find my drakonte cavalry."

Blackened lips curled around sunburnt teeth. "Is that all?"

CHAPTER EIGHT

Ayelet

To say Balian was unhappy when she told him she was leaving would be like calling the sea a puddle. Perhaps she should not have told him immediately following a romp in the sheets. She had meant it as a goodbye gift. He took it as a betrayal.

"I thought you would stay this time." He pulled the sheepskin blankets around him and sat up next to her.

"I told you I would not."

"But you did."

"And now I am not."

He sighed and laid his chin on her shoulder, whispering in her ear so that chills slipped down her bare back. "Do I not make you happy?"

"On occasion," she said, fighting the goose pimples that grew on her skin wherever his lips touched.

"Ha!" he scoffed. "Is that why you leave? Because you are not elated at all times? Life can be hard, Ayelet."

She had a mind to slap Balian. To rant and rave about how she knew more than he ever could about how *hard* life could be, especially when one's best friend abandons them. But it would accomplish nothing more than prolonging her departure and expending her heat. No matter how many times they had the conversation, he would never be sorry enough for anything to change.

"It is not the only reason." She sighed, eyeing the door of the tent with a growing sense of longing.

"Oh? And what else pushes you away so urgently?"

"Your eyes."

He pulled back. "What of my eyes?"

She looked at them once more, the brown mirrors of his heart, tracing the eternal curve of his irises and the shimmer of longing that lingered there. "They tell me you care far too much."

"Is that so bad?" He kissed her shoulder, moving along to her neck.

She allowed herself one more shiver before pulling away. In one motion, she swept out of bed with the sheepskin wrapped around her. Balian remained on the rug at her feet, his face as barren as his naked body.

"I cannot stay in one place. You know this. Yet every time I return, you seem to forget."

"I'm struck by your beauty," he said candidly. "You cannot blame me for that."

"You are struck by delusion."

"What if I came with you this time?" he asked, a strange sincerity washing over his face. "We could join Yousef's caravan, travel in a bit of safety but keep moving as you like."

"Ha!" she let out one sharp laugh. "You will never truly leave Edirne, not for long, whether we travel with your brother or not. Besides, the invitation for you to join me has long expired. You are no longer welcome."

Balian pulled himself upright, tossing several pillows onto his lap to cover himself up. His playful smile vanished, a scowl in its place. "And what of Serap? She will feel abandoned."

Ayelet held the sheepskin up with one hand and shimmied into her blue dress with the other. When her head finally pulled free through the top, she dropped the blanket and tugged the hems so they lay straight.

"Ayelet," Balian's tone was sharp.

"Serap will be fine." She plucked stray hair from her sleeves and busied herself with tying her lyre's satchel around her waist.

"So, you will leave her without a goodbye?"

She looked up and shot him an off-hand smile. "Shall I send her off the same way as you?"

"I'm serious, Ayelet. She would never forgive you. And I will be left to pick up the pieces."

Ayelet sighed. "I'll go to see her now. Happy?"

"She's asleep."

"She won't be when I wake her."

He ground his jaw so it caught the shadows of the nearby candle. Ayelet tossed her hair over her shoulders and placed her headband on top, its silk scarf brushing her back and its cold beads her forehead.

"Thanks for an occasionally spectacular time here in Edirne," she said. And with that, she strode out of the tent, leaving the flap open so Balian would have to scramble for clothes or expose himself to the camp.

"Ayelet!" he called after her, but she marched on.

Out of earshot of Balian's cursing, she slowed. Serap slept in a small, short building on the edge of the city. The floors were dirt, and the walls crumbling cement. Spiders lived in the many cracks, and sand fell through the poorly thatched roof. She took a deep breath before pulling aside the ratty red cloth that covered the door.

Several children slept on the bare floor, sharing a communal cough. The madam who watched over the children snored quietly on a wooden cot in the corner. Ayelet crept forward, stepping over limbs and twisted torsos, then nudged Serap with her foot.

Thin, brown hair stirred, and a small nose appeared between the strands. "Ayelet?"

She held a finger to her lips and pulled Serap to her feet. Out in the dusty streets, the moon accented the little girl's hunger in sharp relief. Prominent cheekbones. Gaunt eyes. More bone than muscle from head to dirty toes. And that smile, dry lips that cracked wide at the sight of Ayelet.

"You can visit me in the daytime, you know," Serap said, rubbing sleep from her eyes with a yawn.

"Where's the fun in that?" Ayelet asked. "Besides, I had to come now. I'm leaving."

Serap's eyes shot open. "No!"

"Shhh," Ayelet chastised. "We must not wake the madam."

"You can't leave." Serap's bleeding lips curved into a frown. "You're the only one here who laughs at my jokes." Then she paused, rubbing her bare toes in the dirt. "Can't I come with you? Please? I won't be any trouble, I promise." She turned her large, sweet eyes on Ayelet, a glimmer of tears filling the edges.

For a moment, her resolve weakened and she wished to bring the girl with her. But that was selfish. Serap would never be able to stop running, sentenced to a life worse than this because one day he would find them. Maybe she'd grow too tired, or linger too long, or make a terrible mistake, and that would be the end.

"*Bu nedir?*" she chided Serap softly. "No tears. Someone must keep Balian from winding up in a ditch."

Serap sniffed. "But why must you go?"

"Because the sun never lingers in the same place. It would scorch all below it."

Serap seemed to consider her words with a wipe of her nose. "But it comes back."

Ayelet smiled gently. "It does." She knew for once that this was true. She could not bring the opal with her, not with Kadri hunting her down with some crazy ulterior motive. Anything Kadri could leverage against her would prove a liability. That meant she had to leave it here. When the seasons changed, and Kadri's band moved to the sea for fair trade and fairer weather, she would return and sell it. And if she didn't return... She crushed the thought. Returning one last time was the least and last thing she could do for the girl.

Serap nodded. "Okay. But come back soon. Balian behaved terribly for months last time you left. All he did was kick things and curse."

Ayelet laughed, then smothered her mouth to keep herself quiet. "I will." She reached around her neck and unclasped the chain, then held the locket with the opal up in the light. "You must hold on to this for me," she said, furrowing her brows to look serious. "It is what will call me home. But if I don't return—"

"You must!"

"If I *don't*—" Ayelet pushed a finger to the little girl's lips. "—you must take this to your merchant cousin, Yousef, hm? He is an honest man and will take care of it without gambling it away first." She hoped.

Serap scrunched her nose. "What's so special about the necklace? It doesn't look like much."

"The value of something depends solely on what people are willing to do to protect it. Never let yourself be deceived by looks. Watch only actions." Ayelet cast her eyes to both sides and then popped open the metal latch.

"Oha!" Serap's eyes widened. "You can't give this to me."

"I can." Ayelet snapped the locket shut. "You will keep it safe. I trust you. Just no Balian, hm?"

Serap nodded gravely.

"Good," Ayelet said and hooked the chain around her too-thin neck.

Serap wrapped her arms around Ayelet's waist, nestling her face into her dress. Ayelet slowly recoiled from Serap's tender hold and the flood of feelings it stirred within her. She had indeed lingered too long. She kissed the top of the girl's head and left her standing in the streets under the waning flicker of stars.

Ayelet passed by the gleaming Mosque of Bayezid, its great dome topped with a marble niche that pointed toward Mecca. In the intersection nearest, a wisp hovered in the dim moonlight. Ayelet slowed. While magic often lingered in the place where four streets met, it usually rested in a calm fog that whisked whichever direction the next traveler went. This one, however, darted to and fro as if waiting for something. Searching for someone. And if her history was any indication, that someone was her.

Ayelet made the sign against the Evil Eye and turned to take a different path. It didn't matter which way she went, though. Her only destination was not here. She broke into a run, hoping to change the sorrowful pounding of her heart into exertion.

Sprinting, she made it to the other side of the city after the moon had traveled a thumbs-worth in the sky. The beaded headband in her hair dripped with sweat, and heat blistered her cheeks. The gate to the east stood clear and open. She walked through, her legs warm and tired, and enjoyed the cool mountain breeze that whipped down from the towering silhouettes on the horizon.

Orange flames burst into view to her right. She stumbled back as more torches flared to her left. A group of shadowy men surrounded her, cutting off her way back to the gate. The nearest torch advanced, revealing the face of Kadri, split by the firelight, one half completely dark, the other burning with the glow of flames.

"Ayeleta," Kadri taunted. "You must work on the gods' time, for three hours, not three days have passed, and yet you leave the city."

Ayelet pinched at the gray earth through her tattered leather slippers. "I can never keep time after a few drinks. Thank you for catching me before I woke up puke-covered on a mountain trail and with an ailing headache."

"Of course." Kadri smiled, her teeth catching the flicker of light. "We are partners, are we not? I must see to your safety at all times."

A threat. Kadri's words weighed heavily on Ayelet. She would be watched from now on, morning or night. As she ate food or expelled it. If it were just humiliating, she could stomach it. Part of the traveling performer's life was making a fool of oneself to please others. But this was different. If she acquiesced now, she'd never be able to dig herself out of the dark web Kadri wove about her.

"You're quiet," Kadri said. "I wonder, is it the drink or the thought of working with me that sends you running to the mountains in the dead of night?"

Ayelet showed the amiable smile she had always used when her father threatened to cuff her for complaining too much. It took no effort, her lips knowing how to curve the second her chest felt anything but light.

"Kadri, my old friend, how could you say such a thing?"

Kadri's eyes narrowed.

"I would love nothing more than to partner with the queen of the dark market. I have only to attend some pressing business in Istanbul, first."

"We shall come with you," Kadri said, her visible teeth a warning.

"I do not want to burden such an old friend with trivial affairs as mine."

"You do not have a choice." Kadri dropped her pretense.

Ayelet, too, dropped her smile. "You do not want me. I bring trouble."

"Trouble is what I seek."

"No."

"Oh, yes." Kadri stared at her, her fiery eyes menacing in the torch's light.

They were a far cry from the gentle eyes of starlight she had seen in the marketplace. How safe that moment felt now. How strange that she should think of it.

She was not safe now, but she still could not relent. She would not be someone's slave. Not again. "I won't go with you, Kadri. Not like this."

Kadri scoffed. "You want a price for your work? You want to be paid to travel with someone as powerful as I?"

"No price could make me travel where I do not want to go."

Silence. A twitch in Kadri's left cheek. "Everyone has a price. I believe yours is burning behind you."

Ayelet fought the impulse to turn. She would not be caught off-guard by petty tricks.

Kadri sighed and waved her hand in the air. Two men with arms as thick as masts grabbed her and turned her around. Ayelet's breath caught. Smoke rose from a deadly glow over the edge of the west part of the city. From the area where Serap slept with fleas.

"What did you do?" Ayelet struggled against the tight grip of the men.

Kadri slid around to the front of her, her torch bobbing with each footstep. "I did nothing. Nadir on the other hand…"

"Slavers?" Ayelet whispered.

A fear as old as she and far older than her music sunk claws into her heart. She had left Serap behind to avoid just that fate and had brought it upon her anyway. And with the opal she had just given her? Was it lost now? Had the slavers been greedy enough to take a cheap brass necklace not knowing what was inside? And if they did, would they treat Serap better or worse for it, maybe hoping to ransom her to whoever had left it to her?

"Oops." Kadri shrugged. "Nadir told me they were headed to town. I was to tell you after our little encounter, but you fled so quickly."

"So you let it happen? There are caravan children in the homes on the west side. Families of traders, trappers, gypsies! There are children of the Bedouin, your own people!"

"I already told you I did nothing." Kadri paused and flashed her eyes. "Though I might."

Ayelet fought to bring her temper down even as it raged as a fire inside her. Yelling would get her nowhere. Her lash of anger had already revealed weakness and jeopardized any chance of a deal.

"Return Serap to me."

"Hmm?" Kadri asked.

"You asked my price," Ayelet spoke with the strange, steady confidence that always came when she found herself backed into a corner. Or a cage. Or a sour deal with a traitorous old friend who could rot in Jahannam for all she cared. "My price is the return of a young girl named Serap."

Kadri's eyes glittered above a triumphant sneer. "Do you want to hear my price in return?"

"No," Ayelet said too quickly.

"Very well. You are bound to it, regardless. Nadir, where are the slavers headed?"

"We cannot wait," Ayelet interrupted. "You must fetch her now."

"And take on the slavers as they burn and pillage? There is a reason they attack the city with impunity," Kadri said, her voice as frozen as the seas to the north. "It is because they slap their chains on both Muslims and kafir alike. Nadir?"

The wolfish face of the man emerged from the shadows and into the pool of light. "They head to the Hadrian Ruins on the south pass through the mountains and on to Istanbul."

Kadri clasped her hands together. "*Ya!* How the heavens align! You are headed there. We are headed there. And the slavers are headed there."

Ayelet closed her eyes and saw a flash of silver diamonds that brought her surprising calm. She took a deep breath. "Good fortune, indeed. Your brutes may release me now."

With a wave of Kadri's hand Ayelet was free to rotate her bruised arms. It took another thumb's worth of the moon's passage before they were on the road, Edirne at their backs and trouble to their front. The caravan she rode in carried some of Kadri's usual wares—trinkets and cloth and staples like grain, but several wagons in the back creaked under the weight of heavy brass cannons, a more brutish fare that Kadri usually stayed away from.

Kadri chatted all the way up the mountain about the increased price of agarwood and the harvest of the coming year's saffron fields as if cruel extortion had not just taken place between *old friends*. But Ayelet did not mind. It gave her a chance to sort through the mess she found herself in.

It was better to let this betrayal go for now. She expected no less of Kadri. She was human, after all. And a trader. Two knocks against her character. As long as she held up her end of the deal and returned Serap safely, Ayelet could work out the rest. She had escaped far worse in the past and would do whatever it took to keep the girl safe.

Shouts sounded from the front of the caravan. Kadri jumped out of the wagon. Ayelet's instincts told her to flee, but she hesitated. She did not yet have Serap. Instead, she jumped from the wagon. Her foot slipped on something wet and plump that squished beneath her weight. She jumped from the mess and shook her foot with a shiver. In the dark with no torch nearby, she could not make it out. But the stench filled her nostrils with the urge to vomit.

Frantic yells bloomed from various wagons in the line, and as more and more fires burst into light, the picture of carnage became clear. It was not an attack on the wagons as she had thought, but the decimation of a battle already fought before they arrived. Hunks of viscera and scales, feathers and teeth lay scattered about the earth in pools of bright green, all leading to a heap of flesh at the front of the caravan.

Ayelet picked her way to the rotting mass, careful not to ruin her other slipper, and held her nose against the putrid scent of decomposition.

Nadir ran a finger through a sloppy, scorched wound just below the broken wings of the carcass and held it up to the torch. The liquid squealed and popped near the heat, evaporating in noxious fumes. "*Kanatlı yılan.* Winged Serpents."

A jolt shot through Ayelet. She had heard stories of fanged snakes with feathery wings that blinded their prey before descending to feed. She scanned the skyline and stepped closer to Nadir. He was a cruel brute of a man. Just what she needed if monsters attacked.

"Are we close?" Kadri asked, her voice pitched with urgency.

Nadir squinted his eyes at the tree line. "The ruins lie just around the next curve in the road. We'll arrive in the ancient place before the sun."

"Good. Let's leave the beast and carry on. We must arrive before all the magic has gone to waste."

This time, Kadri sent a group of men to line the road ahead, and with every ignited torch, battle-wounded chunks of bone and muscle revealed themselves, covered in the glint of rainbow scales and bloody feathers. Whatever had taken place here was no random attack. Burns and deep perforations marred the corpses, every inch of flesh tattered. The wounds were not made by swords or arrows; it was as if the massive bodies had been ripped apart by hot irons, or something worse. The creatures numbered far too many, while not a human body was anywhere to be found. And with every step closer to the ruins, a thicker veil of white, misty magic fell across Ayelet's sight like layers of nets, one over the other until she stumbled forward, unable to see the path ahead.

Only the mangled bodies of the flying serpents penetrated the mist, their eyes glowing even in death. Ayelet's forced smile returned, tighter than ever, covering up the racing of her heart and the chill down her spine. It was not the slavers she had to worry about in this place.

CHAPTER NINE

JAHMIL

THEY ARRIVED AT THE ruins of the ancient empire when Ard's one moon was still high in the sky, yellow and cold. Columns of stone reached into the blue, dark grasses cut up by slabs of square rocks. Zamir walked at his back, dressed in armor with his obsidian sword in hand. Jahmil carried no weapon. He had not come for a fight. Besides, if there was a foe here that had managed to capture the drakontes, Zamir's sword would be less than useless against it. The only option would be to flee and return with an army.

Smells rushed through his nostrils, so thick and varied that his brain stumbled to identify them all. Ard itself—smoky and hot and wet—was so different from Qaf that no matter how many times he came to the world of humans, it still made him stumble. The musty, rotten stink of ghouls hid in the shadows, a taste of sour flesh. *Ignis fatuus.* The creatures always lurked in the dark places of the human world, clinging to existence by sucking the remains of life from the dead. Gnawing on old bones. Ghouls posed no threat to him, so susceptible were they to djinn fire, but for humans, they were to be feared alongside the greatest horrors imaginable—as strong as lions and as cruel as winter.

The final smell cut into him, rendering his hope to ash. There was no mistaking the acrid blood of drakontes. Khayin had said the cavalry had been tricked, driven like a herd of sheep through a portal into the human world, to this place. And here they had met a nameless monster, more ancient than language itself.

"The city is now a graveyard," Khayin said. "The drakontes lie in ruin."

Jahmil had been incredulous. He pressed Khayin for more information, threatening to fill his coffin with starved scarabs and bury him at sea, but the immortal traitor would say no more. Jahmil never could have made good on the threat anyway. When he closed his eyes, he could not stop himself from imagining what it would be like to be buried alive in that place of no magic. It hurt his skin and sent his stomach boiling.

The last thing he wanted was to drive the traitor deeper into madness than he already was. The fact that he could still speak or think at all was nothing short of a miracle. Jahmil made a provision that Khayin be given an ordinary cell rather than stuffed back into his coffin and that he be fed and watered. It wasn't about mercy, or so Jahmil tried to tell himself. Two more questions remained, and he may need to ask them at a moment's notice.

In spite of how angry it made him, he had hoped Khayin was lying. The drakontes could not be dead. Takisha, the cavalry commander and his own cousin, could not be dead. She was the only true ally he had left. The only friend. Her fire burned in his blood, and he would have felt her loss, no matter where she was, no matter what magic had been woven to veil her. But there are fates worse than death. He had seen that clearly when he gazed into the vast, empty eyes of the traitor.

If the drakontes were dead, if some nameless force had managed to defeat them, then not even Qadira's forces could save his fallen country from the wrath of the Vespars. If Jahmil lost his drakontes, then the war was already over. There was some small measure of comfort in that. Because if there truly were no hope left, then he could finally justify falling on his own sword.

His boots scratched on dry grass as he crept forward. Crumbling stone buildings dotted the hillside. The juts of circular columns and broken triangular roofs. A feather the size of his leg was pasted to the side of a crumbling pile of stones with sticky green blood, and more just beyond the horizon. He reached a crest of the hill and gazed down at a sprawling, semi-circular amphitheater.

The bodies of a hundred drakontes had been piled inside, perhaps even more. The snakes had been ripped to pieces, the fissures soaked in ash as if they had been torn apart by blasts of fire. Their blood pooled around them, so thick they seemed to be floating in a lake of green ooze. Congealed and cracking at the surface. Jahmil covered his mouth with his hand, his eyes bulging. He stumbled closer.

Zamir caught his arm and held him back. "*Amiri*, we must not linger."

"We have to check for survivors." Jahmil yanked free.

The ground beneath his feet trembled with a hideous squelching sound—like saliva squishing in a mouth, but much louder. His eyes widened as he watched the pile of drakontes shift and move down.

His heart froze, and his gaze swept the stones, taking in the concentric pattern, the roughly symmetrical layout. Again the horrible squelch sounded, and again the pile of dead drakontes moved down as if slowly being swallowed up.

"A nameless monster," he breathed, "more ancient than language itself."

They were not standing in a ruined Roman amphitheater. Or rather, they were not merely standing there. For the amphitheater, the statues, and the city itself were built upon the face and body of an eimlaq—the largest and most terrible of all giants. And this circle of stones was the creature's mouth, the drakontes its dinner.

Jahmil swallowed the scream that tried to build in his throat. When he looked at Zamir, the black streaks of terror flashing through his eyes confirmed that he had come to the same conclusion, for there was none other. Zamir's mouth hung agape, quivering. He stumbled over himself to scurry back up the mountain, away from two dozen rows of dull teeth.

"*Amiri*!" Zamir cried. "Come quickly!"

Jahmil put a finger to his lips and hurried along the crest of the mouth, leaping from stone to stone—from tooth to tooth—so his boots would not touch the creature's gums. He analyzed the shape of the maw, trying to decide which way was up and which was down.

He raced to the top of the highest hill and gazed down across the ruins. In the curve of a hill encircling the site, he recognized legs stretching off into the distance, buried under hundreds of years of growth. Forests lined the bend of the arms and the swell of the chest. The beast was four full *ghalwah* long, lying on its side in the valley, transforming it into a mountain. He turned back to the amphitheater, and from this vantage, he made out the outline of a face. A jutting column of stone—what he had taken for an old obelisk—was the monster's pointy nose.

The ancient humans had built these ruins on the eimlaq, not understanding that it was there. So much of their own world slipped their notice, though Jahmil could hardly begrudge their ignorance in this case. An eimlaq is a rare beast—fewer than ten were estimated to have been born since the dawn of time, with each one rising perhaps once every few millennia. He had never seen one but had heard legends of them since he was a boy. There was rumor that the city of Tel Keveh in Vespar was also built on the reclining body of such a beast. There was no mistaking the crest of the mountain, nor the twin ponds at the very edge of the ruins, glowing faintly red under an accumulation of water.

Eyes. Open eyes.

The sound came again, grinding and churning as the drakontes were swallowed up. How many had it already eaten? Had the entire force been led here so they could be fed to the eimlaq? Were his soldiers already in the creature's belly?

Was Takisha?

He clenched his fists and shook his head. It made no sense. An eimlaq is a powerful force, but this one had not moved in ages. The ground on its back had sat undisturbed for more than a thousand years and still did. The giant had not killed the drakontes; it was just a means of disposal, the reason this spot was chosen.

A trap. Whoever had brought the drakontes through from Qaf and fed them to this thing had been trying to lure him here. But why?

The sound of human voices reached his ears—shouting and fussing. He turned to see a small caravan of wagons moving along the road toward the ruins. He focused his eyes across the distance and saw an enormous man with a wolflike beard kneeling beside the stray body of a drakonte. A woman joined him and barked in his ear. Piles of golden bracelets lined each arm, her hair tied up in a mess of ribbons. Her sharp blue eyes swept the corpse, and she wetted her finger with a dab of green blood.

Another tremor rumbled beneath Jahmil's feet, this one stronger and more insistent. The eimlaq had sensed intruders. With a feast of drakontes in its belly, it must have been feeling more energetic than usual. Surely it normally survived on the occasional goat or bandit that wandered unbeknownst into its gaping jaws. Would the large meal give it enough energy to rise from its millennia-long slumber?

Jahmil turned back to the humans, and white fire erupted around his hand as he clenched a fist. Though they seemed alarmed by the corpses of the drakontes, he refused to believe they were innocent. Why were they here if they had not played some part in the slaughter? Even if they were not aware of the eimlaq, even humans were clever enough to know that ghouls lurked in ruins and all the desolate places of the world. They risked their own lives in coming here. And why would they do such a thing if they were not a part of the force that had perpetrated this abomination?

Jahmil lifted his hand to unleash a rain of fire on them but stopped cold when he saw a familiar face among them and a veil of pale blue.

Blinking, he shook his head, then refocused his eyes across the distance. Her black and ruby hair shined under her headdress with circles of beads dangling on her forehead. Her embroidered dress of blue lace and golden flowers. Full lips and sharp, penetrating eyes of gray. And hanging from her hip, the lyre that shone with the light of distant stars.

What was she doing here? He hated to imagine she had any part in this massacre, but why then was she traveling with a group of humans with auras as dingy as old mops? Had someone planted her in the market that day to charm him, to distract him? It would have been easy enough to learn about his soft spot for music.

Rage coursed through Jahmil's blood, and the fire on his fist redoubled. Before he could make up his mind about whether to unleash it, the ground under him shook violently, and he was thrown off his feet.

Jahmil rolled down the hill towards the great gaping mouth, catching himself on a tooth even as the monster swallowed what was left of its feast. The ground quaked, and the forest shifted, then tore away. A rumbling like a succession of volcanoes sounded all around, earth and dust pluming into the air to choke off the sun.

The great yawning mouth cracked and twitched, then began to ache closed.

Jahmil flung himself beyond the line of teeth moments before it crushed him into paste. His eyes scanned for Zamir and found him hanging from the long pointed nose as the creature lifted its head from its ancient pillow. He quickly recognized the form of the eimlaq—a great ifrit of fire and earth. A body of stones traced with lines of magma glowed like tangled veins, burning the forest that still clung to its chest. As its body lifted, a sharp chasm was left in its wake, glowing red. Jahmil craned his neck to see a pool of lava at the bottom—what had been the eimlaq's warm bed.

The hand ripped up from the earth with alarming speed and moved to grab him from where he crouched on the beast's shoulder. He rolled to one side, sliding down the craggy arm and nearly tumbling from the elbow to a sharp drop, the ground now eighty, now one hundred feet below.

"Jahmil Amir!" the creature bellowed his name as if from the depths of Jahannam, echoing through his skull like a sonic boom.

It swatted for him again. He latched onto the fingernail and struggled up onto the back of its hand. A hiss sounded in its throat—steam rushing through tight crags in rocks. Red fire burst from its mouth as the drakontes' blood dripped from its lips, congealing in the blast.

He clawed his way up the finger, using creases in the knuckles as grips, and scurried into the creature's palm. The giant brought its other hand in to clap and crush him like a bug.

Jahmil leapt towards the creature's torso, catching himself on the branch of a tree still stuck to its belly. His arms ached at the strain, fire igniting in his muscles. With gritted teeth, he climbed up through the trembling forest.

There was no way to fight an eimlaq. No sword, or trebuchet, or cannon could truly damage the immortal monster. The best he could hope for was to survive long enough to escape.

All he needed was a triangle.

He snatched a branch and tried to lay it across another.

"Amir!" the eimlaq bellowed again, swatting at his own chest to crush him. "Die quietly."

The trunks of great trees shattered under the blows, splintering and exploding as if struck by lightning. Fire caught leaves as the monster's molten blood splashed and sloshed, dripping from its torso to scorch the earth below.

The way down was blocked by a wide vein of shimmering lava, and the drop to the earth was far too great for djinn bones. Growling, Jahmil climbed higher, using all his strength to fling himself from one branch to the next, avoiding the crushing blows of the eimlaq, sometimes by only a foot.

When the hand came down beside him, he leapt onto it again, cleaving himself to the hard rock. The creature didn't notice him and carried on swatting at its own chest. Jahmil sailed through the air as if on the back of some horrid bird, a blur of color and fire.

The creature screamed—a sound so fierce that the ground below rumbled again. The hand paused its relentless movement, and Jahmil looked up to see Zamir clinging to the face, his obsidian sword buried in the glowing red eye like a needle.

The eye twitched, the sword moving with it. Using the hand Jahmil had latched onto, the eimlaq reached up and snatched Zamir from its face, then cast him aside as one might a speck of dust. Zamir screamed as he sailed through the air towards the forest, towards his own death. Jahmil brought up his hand and let loose a long stream of white fire, which quickened to cocoon Zamir. The fire slowed his descent, and he tumbled into a tangle of branches. It would be enough to cushion his fall. Zamir would live, though he'd sustain many scratches and maybe some broken bones.

Alone in the forest, he could find a triangle. He could get back to Ahmar and bring help if he wasn't too cowardly.

A woman's scream cut into his mind like a hot blade, and he cast his eye to where the band of humans had stood on a dirt road moments before, now a chasm of lava.

Was it her—the lyrist? The road had been swallowed up, as had many of the wagons. The bitterness of death was in the air, many of the humans having already been crushed or plunged into the fire.

Scattered men and women fled the scene. His eyes scanned for a shot of blue, but instead found the woman with the ribbons in her hair who had been flung far away from the rest by the shifting rocks. She was not running. She was scurrying from place to place, frantically trying to gather up the remains of scattered bottles. White wisps circled all around her—breaths of raw magic, and more of it than he had ever seen.

He narrowed his eyes at her, but the scream came again from far across the destroyed valley.

He turned to see a dot of blue hanging from the edge of a sharp crag, lava sloshing in the space below. An opportunistic ghoul crouched on the cliff above her, grabbing at her arms, its gnashing teeth searching for a fresh meal.

"Amir!" the beast bellowed again, and Jahmil looked up in time to roll out from under its crushing hand. As the giant's wrist curved under, he lost his grip. Panicked, his hands clawed for purchase as he plummeted towards the fire.

CHAPTER TEN

AYELET

AYELET BOLTED ACROSS MOVING earth, never knowing if her feet would land or her ankle would snap in half. Behind her, the sickly smooth head, needle-point teeth, and blade-jutting hip bones of what could only be a six-foot-tall ghoul chased, nipping and gnashing at her heels. Its drooling mouth panted like a dog being crushed to death, and its sickle-sized claws raked at passing trees.

She had only ever heard of these monsters from crazy-eyed travelers caught walking near places of death at night. Where this one appeared from, she couldn't tell, the blanket of magic still too thick to see past where she could spit. But if it came from a place of death, what did that mean? Did the caravan of slavers already arrive, torn apart by the mountain monster like the flying snakes? Even tumbling through the woods, her stomach curdled at the thought.

Was she too late to save Serap?

For now, all she could worry about was staying ahead of the ghoul's yellow and cracked teeth. It squealed and gurgled behind her, and she pushed herself faster. Air burned in her lungs, and her knees ached from unsteady landings. Even then, the earth roiled under her feet, like she was running atop a wheel. She lost her balance and tripped.

The ghoul lunged at the chance, catching the end of her foot in its jaws. She screamed, pulling her toes free from the one clean slipper. She dashed forward. The ghoul jumped for her. She dove out of its reach and skidded off the side of a cliff. She caught a root and slammed against the side, dirt and pebbles falling into her eyes.

"Jahmil Amir!" the earth beast bellowed loud enough to rattle her teeth.

She did not envy this Jahmil.

Ayelet clung to the cliff, the heat that smothered her skin hot enough to burn but not blister. Not so, if she fell into the boiling pit below. At least the heavy updraft cleared away the haze of magic, giving her an unencumbered view of the horror taking place around her. She reached to pull herself up over the edge when gnarly, stained teeth appeared above her. The creature snarled and screeched, bits of acidic phlegm flying at her face. She yelped and let go, sliding several feet down the steep side until she grabbed hold of a jutting stone carved with the relief of a naked man and a robed woman holding a baby. She gripped the stone man's chest and smirked.

The ghoul's long, flesh-slicked bones reflected the red of the lava beneath her. Jagged spikes tipped bony fingers that clawed for her over the side of the cliff. The stench of the demon's breath curdled the apricot cider still in her belly. If only the magic had done more than make her drunk.

If only she carried magic freely, like the djinn. She *had* nicked a small vial of the magic when the earth first quaked and overturned Kadri's wagon, but she wasn't sure what the white tendril would do. A drunken ghoul was no better than what she faced now. A drunken *her* while she faced the ghoul would be even worse.

Its skull appeared above her, the hollowed eyes burrowing into her own. The demon crouched low, slinking closer one bone at a time, each rib crunching as it scraped over the edge. If she let go, how far would she fall? She looked down past her dangling feet to a ledge a wagon's distance below. The jut of rock was enough for little more than her toenails. The skull gnashed its splintery teeth, dripping saliva that stung her skin.

"Amir!" the earth beast howled behind her.

Her grip weakened, sliding her an inch farther from the demon but closer to the lava pit below. She glanced over her shoulder and nearly let go in surprise. A djinn with midnight blue skin and cream robes scrambled over and under the giant's bones, only narrowly avoiding being clapped to death by massive, treed hands.

No. Ayelet squinted, squeezing the torso of rock harder. It wasn't *a* djinn. It was *the* djinn. The one she saw whenever she closed her eyes. What business had he here?

Was he the cause of the trembling, toothed mountain? And if so, why did it try to kill him?

As she watched, he fell with a scream that rivaled her own. She breathed again only when he found enough purchase to stay his fall, a cropping of loose stone that would never hold.

A flicker of turquoise and maroon caught her eye above the skeleton's sharp frame. She gasped, then choked on the sulfuric waves of heat. The only thing worse than a graveyard ghoul was a flying snake. She itched to ward against the Evil Eye but could not afford the spare hand. The serpent barreled toward her in a spiral that flashed colors in a dizzying array. It hissed, a sound that felt like a knife under fingernails. The ghoul stopped its advance, snarling over its shoulder at the magnificent beast. Just one feather was big enough to give her wings, if only she could flap hard enough.

She braced herself, convinced she was the serpent's next meal, but it flew past her and straight for the djinn. He must have seen the serpent approaching, for he kicked himself off the cliff in spectacular fashion and landed on the winged beast as it flew below. She let out a mirthless bark of laughter. He tossed opals to peasants like they were pennies, so why not own a devilish flying creature who obeyed his commands?

Ayelet released one hand and thrust it upward, searching for something to grab. No use. Instead, she slid further down. She heard once more the nail-stabbing hiss of the flying snake and strained to see over her shoulder at the executor of her fate. The djinn and his dragon snake flew directly for her. She kicked and scrambled against the side of the cliff, trying to claw her way up, but the crumbling earth refused her.

The fanged beast opened its jaw wide and dove. She screamed. In one bone-crunching snap, it plucked the ghoul from off the cliff and released it over the lava. The demon let out a cry that no human should have to hear before gurgling to its death.

Why had he saved her? She glanced again at the magnificent sight. Blue as deep as the night behind the moon sat atop a serpent that shimmered like sun on water. Even from here, she could see his silver eyes, like diamonds catching the light. It was not so bad a vision with which to meet her fate.

His serious eyes turned to her, beckoning her with but the flicker of light upon them. Her fingers shook and burned with the last of their strength. The djinn barreled closer and lifted his hands to her. His eyes shifted like the facets of a gem. *Jump*, they seemed to say. *Jump, and I will catch you.*

She swallowed hard, tempted to tune out the madness. Her only other option was to give way to fatigue and plummet to her death. At least by jumping, she remained in control of her fate. She held her breath, winced, and pushed off the cliff.

The swirling air whipped her dress and hair, and in that whirl of impending doom, she felt strangely free. Then the serpent flew beneath her, and she landed with a thud that knocked the wind from her. At once, she scrambled up its back, the sharp scales digging into her knees as she took gasping breaths. She slowed as she neared the djinn, his cream vest smeared with green and ooze.

"Hold on," he said in Arabic, his voice smooth as silk. It was not the sorrowful voice that spoke to her in the market. Every syllable commanded attention.

"To what?"

"To me," he called over the wind.

She hesitated. She had never actually touched a magical being before. On the other hand, she had only just recently consumed magic as a beverage. Ayelet bit her lip, whipped raw by the wind. Better safe than sorry. She searched for anywhere else to grab hold.

He sighed, the heaviness of his breath visible in the way his shoulders loosened for a moment before tensing back up. He reached back with both hands, grabbed hers, and pulled them forward to wrap around his waist. The kiss of moon breeze swept over her, only sweeter this time. She pressed herself into him, getting a feel for the hard body that tugged tight the fabric of his shirt. No magic or pain met her fingertips. Just the warmth and feel of a man.

"Amir!" the earth beast bellowed once more.

"*Al'ama*," the djinn cursed. "*Aikhras!*"

Lava burst from cracks in the earth like fountains in the plaza. The serpent swiveled and dipped around the molten plumes with ease. Then its magnificent wings stopped. For a breath, only the air carried them, then they dropped. She held fast to the djinn, pressing her forehead into his muscled back to keep her headband from flying away in the breeze.

From the sky where the clouds brushed by, she watched roads branching away from the mountain-like veins. She squinted and clutched the djinn's shirt tighter. Down below, a caravan of black wagons and misery fled from the ruins.

"Serap," she breathed, but the wind stole her words. She wasn't dead. As long as they hurried from the mountain fast enough... then what? She'd still be a slave, but for now, that was better than death. Wasn't it?

An absurd urge to beg the djinn to return for the girl filled her throat. But before it could escape, the monster roared behind them, and giant swaths of earth burst upward, hurtling at them with tremendous speed. Ayelet's stomach rose and flopped. She sealed her eyes shut to keep out the spinning earth, and the wind ran its invisible fingers through her hair. Then the serpent cried out. A geyser of lava caught its left wing, the white feathers now smoking with the smell of burning flesh and the worse stink of singed feathers.

"Die!" the earth beast called out. Its boulder of a hand clasped the winged snake's body just behind her and yanked.

The serpent hissed and hacked in a pathetic screech.

The djinn turned around to face her, and a breath caught in her throat. His eyes truly were diamonds. "We must jump."

She shook her head fervently. She would not follow the delusional man to her death, no matter how much his skin shone like sapphires.

Then, as the sun burst over the horizon, Ayelet had an idea. Praying the myths were true about the djinn's ability to move worlds through triangles, she grabbed the longest of the silk strands from her headband and yanked it off. Then, pressing her body once more into his, she looped the middle over the shallow horns of the serpent. She hesitated, relishing the warmth of his skin against the cool morning breeze. His thick brows rose, his stunning eyes widened. With a bite of her lip, she moved closer, quickly wrapping her legs around him as he tensed. The silk barely reached as she yanked the fabric behind her and tied the tiniest knot. A place where three lines met.

White mist at once consumed her.

She grabbed his kaftan, intertwining the fingers of one hand tightly into the soft weave that touched his chest. His hand wrapped around hers in return. Her dress and hair and the trail of silk on her headband twirled about her like dust in a storm. Then, they stilled. Powdery sparkles in shades of pink, purple, and lime green wrapped gently around her, brushing her lips and caressing her skin. She felt as if she were floating in thin air and standing on firm ground at once, and the drakonte and her silk completely disappeared.

She looked up at the man whose chest she clasped. Heat flooded her cheeks, and his skin beneath the kaftan burned as if it were fire. But she couldn't make herself let go. His gaze slid to meet her own. She inhaled a shaky breath, and his eyes flashed white and gray.

The colors and mist began to recede, and her feet landed lightly upon the prickly touch of grass. The magic dissipated into the air above her. She closed her eyes, convinced it had all been a dream. But she knew it wasn't. Even before she opened her eyes to a gray sky filled with many moons, she knew. His hand still rested upon her own, just above his heart.

The djinn tugged softly at her grasp, but she held on tight. He bent over, so they were eye to eye. A butterfly upon a flower's petal, he brought his other hand to rest upon hers. She waited for another flash of gray, but his eyes stayed crystal. He pulled his kaftan free from her clutches, lingering near her far longer than he should. His eyelashes were thick as veils, and she thought only of how they'd feel brushed against her skin.

He straightened abruptly, and her thoughts cleared, disappointment creasing her heart. There could be nothing between them, she told herself. The thought alone was absurd. She didn't even know who he was, this man who looked like he had been plucked straight from earth's bright blue sky, shining and full of magic. Still, for all her fear that he was a djinn, he had gone out of his way to save her life. And he had tossed her that opal. He couldn't be a servant of the faceless man, not with a heart like that. And if her life experiences told her anything, it was that she would not die that day, at least not by his hands. She gazed upon him as he gazed upon the foreign horizon, his lips curved in a slight frown. He turned.

"My apologies for the abrupt arrival," he said and bowed. "I am—"

"Jahmil," she finished his sentence with an arched and wary smile.

"Alamir Jahmil Abdullah ibn Almalik Bajul al-Shihalai." He tilted his head just so, his frown deepening. "How did you know?"

"It is easy to guess one's name when a mountain-sized beast bellows it into the wind." She had intentionally left off the *amir*, though. She liked him better without titles hooked upon his name.

Jahmil's eyes grew serious once more, their crystal hue flashing with hints of black and pink. The hand that had so gently touched her skin now clenched itself in a fist at his side and white fire snaked along the knuckles. How many more rumors and myths of the djinn would turn out to be true? There were many far less pleasant stories that ended poorly for humans.

Ayelet shifted uncomfortably, eyeing the smokeless flames, and put up a smile. "What was that thing?"

"An eimlaq." He watched her quietly for a moment before adding, "one of the ancients. The creation before the creation."

"And what of Edirne? Of the people who live around the mountain it destroyed? What of the slavers that were also on the mountain?"

Her stomach twisted into a snarl at the thought of the monster scooping Serap into its hungry mouth before stomping to Edirne to do the same to anyone else who fell within its tree-lined grasp.

The djinn stroked his beard and turned his gaze to the horizon once again. "Eimlaq are lazy creatures, which is lucky for djinn and humans alike. They sleep for millennia to wake up but for twenty degrees and eat. I can't imagine it will do more than search for a new bed that provides food, water, and warmth before consigning itself again to sleep."

She stared hard at the way his frown creased his sapphire skin. Perhaps they had seen the worst of the monster. She could only hope. Ayelet cleared her throat and leaned back, tucking her hands on her hips. "Well, we are free from it now, though where you've taken me is a mystery."

She cast her gaze upon their surroundings. Blackness covered most of the ground, the patch of grass where they had landed a small burst of yellow in the dreary landscape. They stood in a sparse forest of wilted trees, bark blanched a ghostly white, and leaves withered with gray. Even the sky seemed a paltry shade of gloom, its farthest edges touching mountains as black as ink.

"Is this where you come to brood?" she asked, grinning.

It was all she could do to quell her pounding heart. While she was not afraid to traverse any part of the earth, this place was anything but. Even the air smelled different, like burnt bread and unripe persimmons.

Jahmil glanced down at her before quickly looking away. "It would be a good spot."

She grinned before letting her lips fall flat, unsure if he jested. "Why did you bring me here?"

"Bring you? You're the one who invoked the three lines."

"Clever, wasn't it?" she said, crossing her arms in satisfaction.

"Foolish, more like. And arrogant." He smirked and ran fingers through his lush, dark hair. "How did you know my magic would grant your request?"

"I didn't."

He waited expectantly, the facets in his eyes too busy to see any one color.

She shrugged off his accusing stare. "Would you rather we followed your plan?"

"What plan?" he scoffed.

She steeled her expression. "Jumping from such a height would have meant my death, though perhaps you would have survived. I don't know which of the rumors about you are true."

His shoulders stiffened. "About the djinn, you mean?"

She weighed her options, trying to find the most diplomatic approach. It was like searching for a particular fish when the nets were squirming with a full day's haul. She knew nothing of him. But she also needed his help. She didn't even know where she was, and she needed to get back before the slavers sold Serap at market, or she would lose her forever. Ayelet stole a look at Jahmil. She would be honest and see what came of it.

"Some say, cast out of heaven, you are creatures of unmatched strength who are belligerent toward men." She watched his face, but it gave nothing away. "Others say you're mischievous beings and chant a prayer whenever they venture out at night so they don't break a leg."

"Is that all?" he asked, looking bored. Still, pink and gray lights danced within his eyes, and she knew he listened.

"The tales told to young ones in the hush of a storm say you eat babies."

Jahmil smirked.

"And that you steal children who stray from home."

"Everything humans say about the djinn is true." A familiar moroseness returned to his face, blue skin hardening like dried leather. "So we had better get you home."

CHAPTER ELEVEN

Jahmil

How had the human woman brought them here? Even the most powerful human sorcerers could not replicate a djinn's ability to apparate between worlds, and he had felt the Namelessness tug on his fire, which meant it was his magic that moved them. But a djinn can only apparate to places where he has been before, and he had never been to this place. This expanse of death and nothingness.

A prickly chill rushed through his blood as his eyes scanned the horizon. Withered trees of winter, cracked soil of ghostly gray. And a feeling in the air that was as oppressive as it was impossible. He looked down at his hand where weak fire encircled his knuckles like mist. Lifting his hand to his eyes, Jahmil drew the light to his palm and tried to brighten it. It pulsed once then went out. When he tried to summon a new flame, nothing would come. He felt his fire moving within his body, but it would not manifest beyond the prison of his skin.

His stomach churned and his heart dropped.

Wherever they were, he could no longer summon his fire. Which meant he could not simply slip through the veil back to Ard. They were trapped, marooned in this dead world that stretched flatly into eternity in every direction. He turned his gaze upwards to a flat gray sky. The moons of Qaf rested in the mist, assuring him that they had not fallen into some cursed third world, but they had been robbed of all their color. The bronze First Moon that lighted Qaf's days nearly as brightly as Ard's sun was like a porcelain plate left to soak in mud. Ghostly as the Maiden of Death.

These worries burned in Jahmil's soul where they should have ignited a conflagration, starting in his guts so sparks rose through his heart and liver to sear his brain with toxic smoke. But as he gazed down at the puzzling human woman who had inexplicably yanked on his magic and drawn them into the land of Qaf, another question seemed more urgent.

He turned his gaze back to the lyrist. Her headdress hung askew, locks of dark hair escaping among threads of broken beads. There was ash and dirt on her cheeks, and her dress ripped and singed at the hem.

"What is your name?"

She turned her eyes to him and smiled. "Ayelet."

The sound of her voice, lyrical and hard as a winter's dawn, clung to his skin the same as her music did his soul. He furrowed his brow, taking in the angles of her face. Whatever suspicion he had felt upon seeing her and the caravan of lowlifes arrive at the ruins had been washed away by the events of the last fifteen degrees. Many of their numbers had died, perhaps more were dying even now. If not killed by the eimlaq, then finished off by the ghouls that haunted the ruins. It was true many djinn attached little value to human life and would sacrifice their earthly allies as easily as slaughtering a lamb, but to what purpose? Their presence had not affected the eimlaq. Very little does.

Jahmil spun the rock crystal ring on his finger, wondering how the beast had reacted when they disappeared. Had it suffered a fit of temper and begun systematically smashing all the adjacent villages? Would it attack Edirne? When Ayelet had asked him what the creature would do, he had lied and said it would simply go back to sleep, for how could he know the whims of an immortal giant? It was best not to worry her.

Fear nagged at him all the same. His presence had awakened that beast. The trap seemed so obvious now, and yet he had walked into it without a second thought.

Why had Faris Khayin not warned him? Perhaps the traitor would be going back to his golden box after all.

Zamir had tried to warn him, but he was so overcautious that it was all too easy to dismiss him. But that didn't mean he wasn't right occasionally. Damn him.

Jahmil bristled. Perhaps there were drawbacks to being so prepared to die. It was making him sloppy. He reminded himself he needed to survive long enough to accomplish his goal, to restore the dignity of his people.

And then... what?

He refocused on Ayelet. Her gaze wandered over his face, as if too timid to rest on his eyes. And in that moment, he remembered the market. He had assumed she had been looking through him, unaware of his presence like the vast majority of humans, but he realized now he still had not chosen to reveal himself to her. Now that they were in Qaf, he would be visible no matter what, but on the back of the drakonte, she had seen him and touched his skin. He had been too distracted to recognize how absurd that was.

"You saw me," he said.

"Fighting the earth monster?" She scoffed. "How could I not?"

"No, in the market. You saw me." He chewed his lip. "You heard me."

She blushed and looked askance like a child caught in a lie. "You remember that?"

"That lyre of yours is difficult to forget."

She touched a hand to the pouch still resting on her hip. It glowed faintly to his eyes, but even that had dimmed since coming to this place.

"I did not think you'd care for music," she said.

"Is that something else you heard about djinn?"

"No." She looked away, her eyes trailing the tree line.

He sighed and took a few steps away, gazing at the same lifeless trees. "That is a lie. You knew I was listening. You played that song for my ears, none other."

She coughed out a barren chuckle. "Do you wish I had?"

Jahmil licked his lips and turned back to her. Did he wish that?

"Were you not frightened when you saw me?"

"By a face so sad as yours? Hardly. I was more worried about what you'd do to yourself when you left."

Her comment caught him off-guard, striking a chord that was better left unplucked. He sucked a breath through his nostrils and forced himself to chuckle. "You worried for me?"

Her eyes widened. "No."

"But we djinn eat babies, isn't that right? We carry off children in the middle of the night. We tempt good and righteous souls away from the pure path and lead them to destruction." He took a small step closer to her. "Does that not frighten you?"

"Should it? I'm not a child. I'm neither good nor righteous, and I'm already headed for destruction. What more do you wish I felt?"

Another question better left unanswered.

Jahmil refocused. "How many djinn have you known, Sayidat Ayelet? You said before you didn't even know which of the rumors about us were true, so I'm guessing even if I'm not the first djinn you've ever seen, I'm the first with whom you've spoken."

She opened her mouth to answer, but he cut her off.

"Be warned, djinn come in every color and every shade of shadow. There are those among my kind who would gleefully do everything you've described, and worse." He turned from her to glare at the smoky, lifeless sky. "You said you were headed for destruction? In what way?"

She frowned, looking him over with narrowed eyes. "What concern is it of yours? I'm but a mere human you've whisked off to this awful place. And while I did not like earth much, this place is quite dreary."

He nodded slowly. It was an awful place he'd brought them. If he'd known they were about to apparate, he could have chosen the location, but he had not thought quickly enough. He rarely did.

But no, it could not merely have been his negligence that brought them here, for he had never been here before. Perhaps she had, and he had inadvertently touched that piece of her memory to guide their fall. That was not so absurd.

"I did not whisk us here. You did. I don't know where we are. The world of djinn is equally as vast as that of *mere humans*." He lifted his hands to his eyes, opening and closing the fingers, once again trying to summon fire that refused to come. "There is no magic here."

She squinted and looked from trees to sky, then back to him. "You're right. There are more wisps of magic in my pocket than this delightful place. You know, if you wanted to spend some time alone with me, you might have chosen a better spot." She shot him a playful smile.

The corner of his mouth twitched, aching to return the smile. To flirt. He bit it all back.

"You keep wisps of magic in your pocket?"

Her face dropped. She opened her mouth, then snapped it shut, her serene smile returning. "You're welcome to see for yourself." She popped out her hip with a confidence that dared him to act.

He glanced at the curve of her leg, his fingertips pulsing to call her bluff. It would have been nothing to snatch away the small vial glowing dull white in the folds of her dress. It was imagining what lay beneath the fabric that held his gaze.

He made no move, and she smirked as if she had won. "Now, come. Show me the way home from this miserable place before I, too, turn a dreadful shade of gray."

"We can't have that." He cocked his head to one side and rubbed the back of his neck.

The atmosphere felt so close, like hot, murky water snaking into his lungs, smothering him. He tried again to summon a tiny flicker of light to the tip of one finger, what should have been as simple as taking a breath.

Nothing.

Turning his eyes to the sky, he picked out the bright pink crescent of the Second Moon on its quick easterly path. Any fool could navigate by the stars in Qaf, but they were absent, blotted out by the same nothingness that stripped the color from the land.

He narrowed his gaze at Ayelet. "*Sayidati*, I have no magic here and no way to return you to the human realm. If that truly is a wisp of raw magic in your pocket..." He trailed off, a blurry memory of a woman with ribbons in her hair coming into focus in his mind's eye. "That woman scrambling with all the jars. Is it safe to assume she is a friend of yours?"

"We're *old* friends, as she would say," Ayelet said, touching a finger to her lip. "But not dear ones. And she has crossed a line even I can't look past this time."

"I suppose that, too, is no concern of mine. But the magic. May I see it?"

Ayelet held out her hand, palm up, an expectant look on her face.

Jahmil narrowed his eyes at the lines on her hand. "I don't understand."

"Nothing but hunger is free."

He put his hands on his hips and laughed. "I think perhaps you do not fully grasp the trouble you are in. You see, I have no magic here. And if I cannot find a way to return you to the human world, then hunger will be the least of your worries."

She pouted and kept her hand out. "So you'll throw me an opal worth thousands for a bit of trite music, but you'll give me nothing for the only thing that makes you different from me?" Her hand shifted, pointing at him. "Surely you have a gold button, or a ruby paining you in your shoe. Or that ring. I would take that in exchange for what is in my pocket."

Jahmil rubbed his father's ring and shook his head. "Your music is far rarer and more beautiful than a common breath of magic." Shrugging his shoulders, he took a step towards the barren, grasping trees. "Keep your secret, if you insist. We shall walk."

Ayelet looked between her empty hand and Jahmil. At last, she clenched it into a fist and smiled far too brightly. "Then walk we shall. I have endured hunger more than half my days. How long will a rich, spoiled djinn like you last?"

"Spoiled?" He stopped in his tracks and turned to face her. "What is it you think you know about me?"

"We can start with the fact that you have two shoes and I only one." She lifted up her bare foot and wriggled her toes. "But if you must know more," she said and flashed her eyes up at him, "pay up."

He looked down at her feet—one bare and the other in a thin slipper of cheap leather—then out at the craggy terrain that sprawled towards every horizon.

"You're right." Jahmil sat down on a rock to remove his soft leather boots, then held them out to her.

A blush painted her cheeks, her fiery eyes suspicious. "I accept your trade," she said, reluctantly taking the boots from his hand. She tossed off her broken slipper, then hopped about, sliding each one on with far too much flapping. For someone who danced so gracefully, she was positively bungling.

When at last she settled, she turned to him. "Thank you."

She watched him for a long moment, an unreadable expression on her face. Then her eyebrows knit together before relaxing. "And you're spoiled because of your pet flying snake, and your fancy clothes, and the fact that you can travel anywhere you want, whenever you want."

Her words settled over him like poisonous mist. Every muscle tightened in his face and he clenched his fists.

"My *drakontes* are dead," he hissed, "as are all the obedient soldiers who were their masters. These Ahmar silks..." He flicked his vest with contempt. "They are a prison, and they are *haram*. A sin I daily commit and suffer for. And as for going wherever I want..."

He cut himself off and swallowed his next sentence.

"You go wherever you please and love whomever you please for as long as you please. And live your life in blissful obscurity free of the weight of seven and twenty thousand souls slowly crushing your bones to ash. You are the one who is spoiled, *sayidati*," he finally spat. "Not me."

Ayelet froze, her mouth half open as if she had forgotten her last retort. Then she bent down, slipped off one of the boots she had just put on, and threw it at him. It struck him lightly on the chest, then fell to his feet. With that, she turned and marched through the woods.

He watched her for a moment, her gait off kilter with one bare foot. But the sight of her bare back moving under her lace shawl softened his fury.

He pressed his face into his palm and sighed. Why had he said such things to her? Why could he never just keep his thoughts to himself?

Lifting his boot from where it lay on the ground, he turned it over in his hands. Perhaps he was asking too much. He slipped it back on, then picked up her discarded slipper, and jogged after her.

"You are a very silly woman," he called.

"I'm sure I would appear that way to someone like you," she huffed. "What are you, some noble or prince or something? I bet this is the first time you've even taken off your own shoes."

"I am a prince."

Her marching footsteps hesitated long enough for her to glance his way. "Then I think you vastly underpaid me. But I'm not convinced. What kind of prince doesn't know the way to his own castle? Or did your servants turn your feet the way they should go, too?" She turned, the beads on her headband clicking together in the silence of the woods. "Why are you so morose all the time, anyway? Don't you find it tedious?"

"Life is tedious. And I'm not morose all the time. Sometimes I'm melancholy, or even cantankerous."

"My humblest apologies," she said with a smirk.

He smirked back. "Besides, I don't have a castle."

"No castle," she said the words slowly. "No rubies. And only one shoe. If you are a prince, you're not very good at your job."

"I am..." He wasn't sure how to finish that sentence. Sighing, he looked away and held her shoe out to her. "There is no reason to suffer a naked foot. I am sorry that I upset you."

"I am sorry I let you." She took the slipper and ran a thumb over the thin, blood-stained sides before slipping it back on.

She stepped closer, leaning in so her nose was just below his chin. He breathed in her scent, rose oil and spice, and tried not to smile.

She sighed and slid to her knees, so her dress puffed up around her. Taking the silk scarf that hung from her headband, she touched his bare foot. "Up."

He lifted his foot, watching her every movement, nervous even to blink. "What is it?"

"It is kindness," she said softly. "Or pity," she added with a hint of a grin. "Whichever you prefer." She took the silk scarf and wrapped it around his foot five, six, then seven times. Taking the ends in hand, she tied a small knot and tucked it under the top edge of the fabric. "A little trick we nomads use when we're poorer than the dirt."

"You are beautiful," he said, the words tumbling from him unintended. She looked up at him, and he had to glance away so as not to forget everything. "Come."

He offered her his hand. "We follow the Bahamut winds, for they are always the sweetest."

CHAPTER TWELVE

Ayelet

THEY HAD WALKED WHAT felt like the better part of the day if she could even call it that. Only moons crossed the sky, lonely and dark with no sun to chase the first and largest moon that had settled on the horizon. More and more stony shapes appeared in the surrounding brush. Ancient ruins long forgotten and chilly with forgetting.

Only her desire to save Serap overshadowed her aching want for bread, and her slippered foot burned with blisters. She could not help but sigh. She should not have thrown the other boot at Jahmil. Why did she let him goad her so?

The memory of his kind eyes and simple gesture caught in her throat. There was no way he was a prince. Sure, he had shiny buttons and pretty language—the same elegant curls that colored the language of the faceless man and in which he had commanded she speak in his presence. An upturned nose and downturned lips, as well as a propensity to be needlessly serious, but he was also surprisingly gentle and willing to talk to a peasant.

Jahmil seemed more than willing to discuss anything other than his supposed heritage, which normally she'd find a blessing. He had even made her laugh twice with a dusting of dry humor she couldn't tell if he intended or not. But a magical ally, prince or not, was a resource she'd be foolish to waste. Though which exact resource he offered, she wasn't sure.

More opals to buy back Serap, maybe. Or the ability to walk in and out of worlds so she could just snatch Serap from the slavers' filthy hands as soon as his magic returned. Either way, she must play nice. She must find out more about him. And she must charm him into helping her save Serap. But as they talked of light-hearted nothing, she struggled to keep up with the flickering colors in his eyes. She was certain they meant something.

"So is your kingdom as lovely a place as this?" She grinned, gesturing to a gnarly tree covered in tufty white spores that looked alarmingly like ear hair.

His frown deepened, eyes darkening with purple smoke. "My homeland was so beautiful, so full of life, that should I describe it you would call me a liar."

"It would not be the first time I had thought so. But I did not take you for a quitter. If you won't describe the land you love, tell me instead of your mother."

He flinched and knitted his brow so tightly it looked painful. "My mother?"

She walked a line; she could tell by the flashes of yellow in his eyes, a color she had not yet seen. But to charm him, she needed to know him, and that meant pulling information from him one hook at a time.

"It is said that a lady can tell the true character of a man based on how he treats his mother."

He made a sound in his throat halfway between a chuckle and a groan. "The dowager Queen Zalika is resourceful, intelligent, and deserving of respect."

"What a tender relationship you must have to describe her as a history book would."

"Tender?" He chewed on one of his shock-white fingernails. "That is not a word that comes to mind. I was raised by a team of nurses. If you want tales of tenderness, I have a thousand of them. But I don't believe I even met my mother but a handful of times before I reached the age of reason."

"You've reached the age of reason?" She poked his shoulder with a giggle.

He flinched and frowned. "Nine. When a child becomes worth speaking to."

"A child is always worth speaking to," she said a little too sharply.

She took a breath to iron out her frustration. She had been seven the first time someone considered her a real person. Right before they plunged her into a dark cage filled with bad dreams.

She rubbed the lingering chill from her arms and softened her voice. "You must get all your charm from your father."

He narrowed his eyes at her as if he had just learned a secret. "What of your mother, *sayidati*? Is she a musician like yourself?"

"Can the cold breeze that wails through the cracks during winter be called a musician? For that is all she is to me. An absence in the heart when things are at their worst. Her bright spirit left this world as my dirty one entered. She'd be rather disappointed, I think."

His feet paused, and he gazed down at the earth. "It is easy to forget how closely death clings to human women as they bring life into their world. It's cruel."

She laughed. "I suppose since you don't talk to children *before the age of reason*, you wouldn't know what joy they can give and how that makes it worth it. Bringing life into this world is only cruel if that life is wasted. Do you waste the life your mother gave you?"

"*La 'atamanā*," he said in Arabic, then continued in Turkish. His accent was as smooth as wet stone, musical and gentle. "Why do you think she would be disappointed?"

"My mother or yours?" She chuckled again, this time uncomfortably. But something about this place pulled secrets from her lips. "All I've been told of my mother was that she was an honest person. The *most* honest, if the stories are true. But people do embellish. And I..." She stopped, afraid of what she was admitting and strangely giddy that she did all the same. "I am not. I think knowing that about me alone would have killed her, if my coming into this world hadn't." She swallowed the bitterness in her mouth. "Or maybe it's because I got my father's eyes. Dingy old things, aren't they?"

His lips slumped with half of a smile, and he resumed walking. "Honesty is a very difficult virtue, one that can come with dire consequences. For my part, I wish I were better at lying." He stopped and turned, then approached her until his face was only a few inches from hers. "And though you are clearly fishing, I will take the bait. Your eyes are changeable as a summer storm, a promise of rain, and a threat of fire. They gaze through me, even now."

Ayelet forced herself to breathe through the tightness in her chest. She had heard sweet nothings countless times before, but none had ever reached her so. And none had ever smelled like the glimmer of moonlight over a pond. She had grown soft since she first gazed upon his eyes in the market. Lost in a mirage that would fade the moment she returned from this strange place.

"Lying is easy." She pulled away before his intoxicating scent permeated too deep. "You simply care for no one but yourself." Then she frowned. "Or, if you're foolish, care far too much for someone else and none about yourself. But either will do the trick."

"Among my people, it is known that the eyes are where truth lives. Even a thief, or a murderer... even a human will give themselves away if you watch their eyes long enough." He held her in his gaze, the facets of his diamond eyes shimmering like freshly polished crystal. Clear, simple. Colorless. Then he turned abruptly. "But, it is very rude to force the truth from someone who would not part with it willingly."

"How noble the djinn are," she laughed through the squeamishness rising inside her throat.

He did not know her or her eyes. He could not know what she truly fished for or why she did so. And he could not hear her heart drumming in her chest whenever he got too close. But she was infernally curious.

"Come now." She slipped up onto the tips of her toes and laced her fingers through his shirt to keep her balance. "Tell me a truth and let me see what color flashes in your eyes."

"Wouldn't that be simple?" He grinned. "You're always searching for some advantage. You'd make a fair general."

She released the muslin of his shirt and strode ahead on their trailless path, careful not to let him see her frown. "I'd make a fantastic general. I know the cost and benefits of holding your ground or fleeing in defeat. And I care not for others. Isn't that a—"

Her words fell away as she pushed through the trees into a field of iridescent flowers. Against the stark white of their surroundings, they looked as if they had bloomed from the very sun and fallen like shooting stars upon the earth.

"What are these?"

Jahmil hurried into the field and plucked one blossom, a smile growing on his face like none she had ever seen. Tears sparkled at the edges of his crystal eyes. "Alyasimin," he breathed, brushing the petals with his fingertips. "I thought the Vespars had burned it all."

She took the blossom from his fingers and twirled it beneath her nose. The scent was one she didn't know, but which her body craved. Sweet, almost too much so, with hints of wood and magic. "Does this mean we're near your home?" She was at once sieged with joy and crushing disappointment.

His smile was enough of an answer. "This scent is melting the poison from my blood.." He breathed deeply and closed his eyes, tilting his face towards the sky. "I can smell the Spider's enchantment entangling the veil and holding us to this place. But with this flower, I will soon have power enough to send you home."

She followed his gaze up to stone-gray clouds. Bursts of purples, pinks, and inky greens now peeked through their defenses. "Do you have someone who waits for you?"

"Other than my mother?"

Ayelet grinned. "It is comforting to know your mother awaits your return. Shall we bring her some flowers?" She gestured to the field behind her but watched the colors in his eyes.

"If I brought her flowers, she would think I was sick." He looked back at the tangle of barren trees through which they had just come. "That must have been Vespar. Many years have passed since I last ventured there. It is not at all as I remember. Dead. Not a single living thing. Not even water. The Vespars often speak of such things, of the death of their land, but I never imagined..." Again his gaze swept the sky, then he focused on her. "The Moonless Night approaches. We must find you shelter, or you will die."

She couldn't help but giggle from deep inside her breast. "You are always so serious." Her giggles turned into a laugh that cleared her mind. "I'll be just fine. However, we must find *you* shelter and perhaps a bath. We can't have a prince return home looking worse than you do now. It would be a scandal!"

"I don't understand why you're laughing. This *is* serious. Your tender flesh cannot endure the cold."

"Ah." She nodded gravely, though giggles still shook her shoulders. "I see. It is my tender flesh you want to shelter so safely. In a dark cave, perhaps? Or under the touch of the flowers behind us? Do you plan to keep me warm?" She trailed the flower over his chest and brushed her nose against his cheek, so she could whisper in his ear. "To keep the cold from stealing secrets you seek instead?"

"A cave would be ideal, though I don't think there are any around." He shrugged, a look of confusion on his face like he wasn't a red-blooded male who a woman just draped herself over. She bit back a scowl. What color *was* his blood?

"Look at the sky, Sayidati Ayelet," he continued, unfazed. "See how the moons retreat to the horizons and none rise to take their place. Every fourteen cycles of the First Moon comes a night with none. All the heat is drained from Qaf. The Sea of Bahamut freezes, rain turns to ice, and even the lava flows of Izrak grow frost on their crusty surfaces. My body is accustomed to such cold; I make my own fire. But you, *malikat jamal*, you will die."

Ayelet sighed and stepped away from the chest that had beaten so steadily beneath her hands. Her pride and eyes stung at his refusal to acknowledge her with even a racing heartbeat. "Who is she?"

His expression twisted with bewilderment. "Who is who?"

"The woman," she said, caressing the soft, glowing petals within her hand. "The one you push us toward. The one you must be loyal to. All princes have one, or so I hear."

"You choose a strange moment for such a question, but if you must know, I am to be married in seven days to the Queen of Ahmar," he said, his voice utterly flat.

The hidden wonder bursting around her with every step and sweep of the breeze could not stop the rock that dropped into her stomach. He was taken. Of course, he was, what a stupid thing to think otherwise. No matter what she did, she would get nothing from him to help with Serap. She had wasted so much time. Had foolishly thought, for the briefest moment, that he meant his flattering words. He had played her, not the other way around, and she could not have been a more willing victim.

"Let us find shelter so I may live and return home as soon as possible. I have no more time to waste chatting with princes who take for granted even the air they breathe."

His eyes flashed bright enough to bathe the field in white light, but his voice stayed level. "What do you rush home to? Is it that man I saw you with? Is he your husband?"

"Balian?" She snorted with cold laughter. "Certainly not."

"A lover?"

"I would think that a personal matter, wouldn't you?"

"That depends on your answer."

She eyed him, wary of his sudden interest in her past. She had no plans to tell him about any of her lovers. He did not seem the type to take it well. And it would do nothing for her anyway. "He's someone I've known for a very long time. We can't help but have a history."

Jahmil raised his eyebrows. "The way he looks at you, I'd say he's in love."

"The way any man looks at me is not your concern." She jutted her chin up sharply.

"Do I appear concerned?" He shrugged his shoulders. "I'm simply making conversation."

His nonchalance caught her off-guard. How dare he pester her, flash his eyes of fire, and then say he does not care? "You're terrible at it."

He frowned, the glow from his eyes dimming and purpling where it touched the blossoms. "I pity him."

"What a polite way to call me terrible!" she said, but her shoulders shook with cool laughter. "He knows what he signed up for."

"I only mean, I can imagine what it would be like to love you."

"You mean awful?" She cracked a wry and bitter grin, willing to play his game if it meant getting home faster. She needed to nurse her pride from the bitter sting of his coldness—an impossible feat beneath his calculating eyes.

"Completely awful." He chuckled, his gaze sweeping over her face. For a foolish moment, she drank the colors in. "I've never been in love, but I know what it would be like."

"Yet more words that tumble from your mouth I don't believe at all. You do not love me."

"And yet I can see it, like the mist of a new day breaking through storm clouds..." He smiled and rubbed his finger over his lips absentmindedly. "If I loved you, nothing else would matter. Nothing in Qaf, or on Ard. Nothing in heaven. But if you were to ask me whose life was more important, yours or mine, I would say mine and you would walk away from me not knowing that you were my life. If I loved you, my tongue would be tied and words would fail me, again and again. And I would never find the right time or place to tell you, and so you would leave me."

He paused and looked past her into the distance. His smile held, but a hint of moroseness glinted in his eyes. She leaned in, wishing for more and hating herself for it.

"Yes, I can see that clearly. You would leave me even as the hottest sun abandons the desert to ice and death. You would never know the truth. And I would die every day in your absence and never love again."

The spark in his eyes returned to her, a green as bright as emeralds. She fought the heat billowing up from her chest. He should not have said that. Even her forced smile could not bear the weight. It fell, and she opened her mouth just so, trying to find something, anything to say.

With the tip of one finger, he tapped her jaw closed.

Where he touched burned hotter than her cheeks, waking her from the dangerous net his words had caught her in. They were just words, she reminded herself. His cold, steady heart did not thrum with music the way hers did when they drew near.

She swatted his hand away. "That was a lot of words to give to the breeze when you do not love me at all."

"No. I don't." He smirked and shook his head. "Thank Allah for that. You would ruin my life."

CHAPTER THIRTEEN

JAHMIL

He led her into a grove of umbrella trees, with their sparkling white leaves and shivering red blossoms. A blue-spotted anqa bird tended her nest in the heavy branches above, each of her one-pound chicks twittering for a meal. It warmed his heart to see that even under Vespar occupation, Orkeshi still burst with life.

As the Third Moon set, leaving the sky a cold canopy of reticent stars, Jahmil bent the branches of shrubs and purple palms to fashion a small shelter. With some power now surging through his veins, he was able to light smokeless fires all around Ayelet, creating a cocoon of heat to protect her from the biting cold. He could control the temperature of his fire from blazing heat to utter cold, as well as whether or not it was catching. He made a ring around her, on the ground, and nestled in the branches above her head. But it was not enough.

The Moonless Night sent the temperature plummeting far below any that ever occurred on Ard, at least not any section of the planet where human beings dared to live. Ayelet was defiant of it, but it crept into her nonetheless. In time, she had no choice but to accept his long vest to use as a blanket for her legs. When he took off his kaftan and laid it over her shoulders, exposing his skin to the elements and to her view, she had looked at him like he was insane, evil, or both. Still, the cold forced her to accept.

They didn't speak for some time, as he watched her shiver and her teeth chatter. He itched to put his arm around her, to draw her into his warmth, but worried how she might respond.

Why did he talk so much? Why could he never manage to say the right thing? And why had he not simply said *yes* when she asked if he planned to keep her warm?

It was her playful smile, the brush of her lashes, and her warm-hearted, easy attempts at flirtation that had forced him into retreat. She did not appreciate the gravity of the situation in which he found himself. This was a dream. She could never be anything more than a dream. When he sent her back to Ard, it would end. Forever. And how much colder would that moment be if he allowed himself to become accustomed to her warmth?

"The fire in your eyes does not warm me, so you may stare elsewhere," Ayelet said through chattering teeth.

He slapped a hand over his eyes so quickly that it made a noise. He had never felt nervous around a woman before. "Forgive me. I'm worried about you." His jaw twitched, tongue curling uselessly in the back of his throat. He bit it hard to bring it under control. "I could keep you warm if you would allow me to hold you."

He heard the rustle of fabric and the soft tread of feet. She knelt in front of him and pulled the hand from his eyes. "What am I to you?" she asked, a dissonant seriousness in her expression. "Why do you do this to me?"

The reflection of the pale fire glimmered in her eyes, lightning over a tempestuous sea. Fear wrapped his heart like fingers of ice. "What have I done?"

She placed her head against his chest just above his heart, sending a thrill through him he hardly recognized. After a soft sigh, she pulled back. "Nothing. I think it must be me. But I cannot let you hold me."

She stood and returned to the cold.

His heart dropped as he watched her resettle among his fire. It reached for her, longing to caress her skin with even more urgency than his fingertips. Abandoned and humiliated, Jahmil brought his hand to eye level and conjured a small flame, then rolled it over his fingers, back and forth. He glanced at Ayelet, her gaze mesmerized by the leisurely dance of fire. He touched it to his lips then blew it off his fingers so it bounced across the space and kissed her, gently melting the blue from her lips.

Her bright eyes widened as she looked up at him before quickly turning away. She pulled his kaftan tight over her shoulders and moved to get comfortable beneath it. Then, in the lonely silence of the woods, he heard the pluck of strings.

Smiling, Jahmil closed his eyes and leaned against a tree trunk. He knew this song; he had played it himself long ago on his ney, though not so skillfully.

As he listened, his heart slowed, and he filled his lungs to the brim with every breath. The slow, minor scales slithered up and down his spine, prickling with loss and longing.

"Something is aching inside of you," he said, not looking up. "Something that has nothing to do with this place. Is there someone you worry for?"

"I suppose it makes no difference if I tell you now," she said over the gentle strum of her lyre. "I have lost someone dear to me. The only person dear to me."

He opened his eyes and watched her music dance in the air, ignited by the magic of Shihala. A shifting coil of red and blue, sparkling with old starlight. He could almost make out a face inside of it. Whatever magic she kept in her pocket was nothing to the power of her music. Shihala Herself was listening and wanted to hear more.

"May I ask whom?" he said.

"A child," she said, shifting eyes rounded with sorrow from the magic of her music and onto him. "Her name is Serap."

He glanced at her, then back at the lazy river of magic. The fire barrier woven by the Spider of Karzusan stretched over all of Orkeshi, preventing normal djinn apparation. It held out Shihalan reinforcements while holding in the unfortunate refugees who had been left behind. But sitting in a field of alyasimin with Ayelet's enchanted music wafting over him and cleansing the barren hell of Vespar from his veins, Jahmil came to a horrible conclusion. He had all the power he needed to send her back.

"How did you lose her?" he asked. "Does she still live?"

Her music faltered, discordant and sour before stopping entirely. "She lives. But she will soon wish she was dead if she doesn't already. For that is the lot of those taken by slavers. I know this to be true. It is carved in my bone."

"You were a slave?" he whispered, but it was no kind of question. He saw the truth written in her eyes and heard it in the silence that had deadened her music.

Shihala was a land without slaves, where even a beggar had the right to live and die with dignity. Even Old Vespar, for all its myriad flaws, did not ascribe to the beastly practice except when it came to prisoners of war. Slavery existed in many of the other kingdoms of Qaf—Ghaluma, Jasraib, even Ahmar—but it was only upon his first sojourn to the human world that Jahmil had been exposed to it firsthand.

The experience of that day was branded on his mind. Ten years old, walking a few paces behind his father in the crowded market of Damascus. As they had passed through a market square, Jahmil had paused at the sight of a line of people chained together by their necks. They had all been dirty, some with pulsing blisters where the iron touched their skin. Some wore ragged garments, some were naked. And men in fine robes walked up and down the line, inspecting teeth and pinching skin, shouting at each other to make a good price.

Jahmil had been frightened and curious all at once. He could not look away, and his knees locked up, even as his eyes began to mist with tears. He asked his father what was happening, but he hadn't understood the explanation, not then.

"Humans are primitive," his father had explained. *"They shackle their own kind and work them like animals. They all do it. They are creatures of mud."*

His father and his mother were so similar in some things, like their outlook on Allah's worlds, yet so different in what they thought ought to be done about it.

Jahmil's gaze refocused on Ayelet, and everything in his chest twisted into knots as he imagined her chained on such a line, forced to bear it as men examined her teeth and poked at her body.

Was that why she wore such thick armor? To shield the tremendous softness in her heart from those who would steal it? For all her efforts, it leaked out through her music and smoldered in her eyes.

He stood and walked to where she was. She looked up at him as if he were a predator as he lowered himself beside her. "Let me see the alyasimin."

She pulled the blossom from within her robes, its petals crumpled and full of her warmth. "It is no longer beautiful."

"Midnight jasmine does not wither," he said, lifting the crushed flower to his eyes. "*Inshallah,* Shihala will smile upon you with Her blessings."

The black, starlike bloom of alyasimin was the flower of Shihala, the crest of his own family. It was the most common bloom in the kingdom and had no inherent power, at least not to untrained eyes. In its unassuming simplicity, it formed the perfect vessel for those who knew how to fill it. The secret of the flower was known only to the royal family of Shihala, he and his half-sister the only djinn alive who spoke its language.

After the fall of Karzusan, the Vespars had set fire to the fields that had once surrounded the summer palace, further crippling the power of Shihala's royal line. He'd brought seeds with him to Ahmar, but the sacred flower would not sprout in foreign soil. He'd thought they had been lost forever. Had they been here in Orkeshi all along? Or was it Ayelet who made them bloom, even as she had effortlessly breathed new life into the shriveled stone that had once been his heart?

He cupped the flower in his hands and brought it to his lips, then whispered a private prayer into it. When he lifted it by the stem again, all five petals straightened and thickened. Sparks of silver raced along its edges, the excess twinkling down to the earth like drops of water.

Jahmil held the bloom out to Ayelet. "It is your way home."

Her trembling fingers took hold of the stem, resting upon his.

A shrill and distant laugh cut the night, lifting the blur from his heart and lighting his mind with a sharp thrill of fear. He knew that sound—a shriek like metal scraping on glass. The cry of a bial'dabaye, the hideous werehyenas which the Vespars used to supplement their common troops. Creatures with the intelligence of a man, the ferocity of a drakonte, and a thirst for blood unmatched by any monster in the Nine Kingdoms.

It crossed his mind to go with Ayelet. To slip between the veil, re-enter the human world, and then return to Qaf in Ahmar. But if he went with her, he would just be delaying the inevitable. Every moment in her company could only make saying goodbye to her more painful. And while he now had the power to slip out of Orkeshi and into Ard through the barriers made by the Spider of Orkeshi, he did not know if even alyasmin would give him power enough to apparate back in.

"Close your eyes," he said.

"Wait." Her breath hung in the air like a cloud as a panicked look fell across her face. "You may hold me. Just let me stay with you one more moment before I meet my fate."

For the second time, his heart cracked open. He so wanted to keep her with him. A few degrees, a day. Forever.

"No." He laid his other hand atop her frozen little fingers. "You were right the first time. If I hold you now I may never let go. And then what would become of your dear one?"

Her chin quivered, from the cold or something else he could not tell. She released his vest so it fell in folds before her and slipped out of his kaftan. Then, she leaned closer and brushed her lips on his cheek. "You should laugh more," she whispered.

The soft touch sent a warm shiver through his blood. Gazing at her face, knowing he would likely never see it again, he knew there would be no more laughter.

"I will," he said.

She smiled weakly and closed her eyes.

The laugh of the bial'dabaye came again, closer. He had to be sure she was gone before the beasts descended. Holding tight to her hands, he guided her to stand. "Think of the place you need to be. The sounds of it. The taste of the air. The way you feel when you stand there. Conjure an image of what drives you to this land."

She nodded, her hands tightening beneath his.

"Now all you must do is pluck a petal and let it fall. When it hits the ground, you will be gone." He cupped the side of her face, and her eyes lifted to meet his. Every ounce of his flesh ached to draw her nearer, to kiss her lips. "Should you ever wish to return a petal will bring you back?"

She hesitated, then plucked a tender petal, letting it rest on the tip of one finger.

"*Adhhab mae Allah,*" he said and blew the petal off. As it floated to the ground, her tumultuous eyes stayed on his and did not falter even as a whirl of chilling gray smoke wrapped around her and she disappeared from sight.

The fires he'd lit to warm her all went out, plunging him into blackness. Jahmil folded into himself in the dim of the Moonless Night. He dug his fingernails into his scalp and breathed through clenched teeth.

She was gone. Gone forever, just as he knew she would be. The dream was over.

He lifted his kaftan and vest from where she'd dropped them. He was about to put them on but stopped himself. Her scent was in his clothes—roses and spice and a hint of something sweeter than he would ever taste. Part of him wanted to wrap himself in it, but it was too painful. Against his better judgment, he had allowed himself to pretend his dream could be a reality. If he was ever to recover, he had to set it aside, let it blur in the light, and be forgotten, as dreams should.

He folded his clothes and laid them back on the ground. Then he stooped over and touched the knot she had made when she wrapped his foot in her scarf. He should untie it, let it go along with everything else. Memories were of no use, mementos even less so. They only brought pain.

Thrice he tried untying the knot, but his fingers refused. He let it be.

He stepped out of the makeshift shelter of bent saplings as the First Moon rose in the northern sky—a rough, rusted sphere that filled a quarter of the heavens with its bulk. Light and heat burst over his skin, but he barely felt it. He wanted the cold to return, to cocoon him in its merciless embrace.

The cackle of the monsters came again, so close he all but tasted the rancid breath. It occurred to him to flee, but instead, he clenched a fist.

He would not run. He had given up enough this day.

CHAPTER FOURTEEN

Ayelet

The heavy mist of what must be Shihala wrapped around her once more, and the whirlwind of rippling sparkles coalesced on her skin like fingers caressing her cheek. Ayelet sealed her eyes from the wonder and wrapped her arms around her stomach, pressing in tight. Who was this djinn? He appeared like a wink in the corner of an eye and vanished just as quickly, stealing her heart with him and leaving an unquenchable thirst.

Even now, she felt his touch on her skin. His capricious eyes shifting between one color and the next as they slipped over her face and body. And his kiss. Or the fire of his kiss, lighting upon the corner of her lips with absolute warmth and a sense of yearning.

If she were wise, she would push these memories away and pretend they were but a dream. But now, alone in a cloud of magic that lived between two worlds, she let herself feel. Crouching, she pulled her knees in tight and shook with the gnawing pain of loss from which she had spent her life running.

The shimmering memories of Jahmil faded into a black as deep as the shine upon the blossom she held. She was seven again and sold into slavery to pay off her dead father's debts. And she was nine, calling out in the night for a mother she never had while tremors of demons laughed in her nightmares, their faces all the same. And she was twelve, just before fate and music marked her for their own, running from a place—a person—she so foolishly thought could be her home.

She thought she was done stupidly hoping for anything. But in the dream of Jahmil, she had faltered. And the pain was worse than all the times before because the home she wished for had never been so sweet. Because the person she longed for had never been so hopelessly out of reach.

And so hopelessly engaged. And un-human, and apparently a prince.

And so not in love with her. He said so himself. And his heart did not thrum wildly as hers did when she laid her cheek upon his chest and breathed in the scent of dusk.

Allah's mercy, she *was* stupid.

She could not laugh through her pain this time. She could not even smile.

She ran a finger along the soft petals of her flower. Each one still glowed with the magic of Shihala. Then she held up her glass bottle, so the wisp pulled down towards her. What was she to do with a breath of magic and an enchanted bloom? She twirled the petals, small galaxies of color that fit in her hand. The wisp swirled around its jar, following the movement. It was a gift from Jahmil, and she was desperate to keep it safe. She pulled the lyre from the pouch at her waist. Careful not to damage its fragile stamen, she slipped the flower into the hollow turtle shell inside.

Soft earth met her knees, and the white veil that concealed her began to fade. It was appropriate, the ending she must now face. Only a living nightmare and the harsh tug of chains could erase the pain of her tender dream. She slipped the bottle back into her pocket, then dug her nails into the dirt. She shifted one foot back, ready to run if need be.

It felt like endless time had passed since she breathed the crisp, magicless air of Türkiye. The last she saw of it was the monstrous mountain killing all in its path. The eimlaq, as Jahmil called it. Another bit of evil magic in the wrong place. If the slavers had survived, they would have had no choice but to turn back to Edirne. The mountain was all but crumbling into a fiery pit of lava when she had left, eating up every road to Istanbul. If the city still existed at all, that's where the devils would be. As such, she had chosen to appear in the ruins of a long-forgotten temple to the fickle Aphrodite, just outside the performer's camp on the west side of the city.

It was night once more, there on earth, just after dusk when the cicadas' whine begins to fade. She listened past the last of their waning chirps and heard only night. The final sliver of mist dissipated, and she stood, her eyes keen in the darkness. Through the shadows, she could see a glow in the city, whether from lights or fire, she couldn't say. Likewise, the tips of the eastern mountains were no longer visible, an ominous red-orange shimmer from where the lava must still bubble from the earth. *Allah, please let Serap survive.* She braced herself for the run to the city.

"Hold still, little human, or I'll cut your head clean off," said someone behind her. It was a woman's voice, both painfully loud and secretively quiet so chills crept up her spine.

Ayelet flinched.

"You do not follow instructions well."

Stealing a breath, Ayelet mustered her courage. "You call me human, which I am, but I've just been to the land of the djinn and come back alive. I've seen the Seven Moons traverse the sky—"

"There are eight," the woman said flatly.

Ayelet swallowed and straightened her shoulders. "—and felt the freezing death of Shihala in the hour without their light. So unless you are Iblis himself, I'd tread carefully."

"Those are powerful words coming from someone so weak," the woman finished with a guttural cough.

"I have powerful friends," she lied, knowing she'd never see Jahmil again. Emptiness consumed her.

She waited for pain, for a blow that would end her suffering, but nothing came. Ayelet turned, unsure of what would meet her eye.

In the shadows, the moon cast through the forest towered an imposing djinn. Her fiery hair shone the color of strawberry wine before fading into embers. Her skin held hints of Jahmil's blue but with whispers of green in a mesmerizing wave. She had more muscles than any sailor or soldier Ayelet had ever seen and stared at her with a confidence that would put even the best performer to shame. Her armor was in tatters, and a gash wept red blood and infection through the studded leather just under her left breast.

"You are a djinn," Ayelet said, more a fact than an accusation.

The woman snorted. "What gave it away?"

"Why do you not kill me, then?"

She leaned against a nearby tree and coughed once more, the sound coated in blood and phlegm. "Would you like me to?"

It was an odd question, considering. And one that let Ayelet know the djinn was more wounded than she let on.

"I think you should like to, except you're hurt."

The woman chuckled, a deep, throaty sound that shook the young tree branches she clung to, even as the trunk creaked under her weight. "There is truth in your words, little human. And I have not smiled in days. For that, I give you my thanks. I am Takisha Alqayid."

Ayelet smiled timidly. She hoped Takisha's temper was less fiery than Jahmil's, her eyes less flashing and fickle. Even with a wound that large, the odds of outrunning a djinn so large were like a beetle outrunning a fox. "I am Ayelet."

"Ayelet," the woman said her name like she was mulling over a mouthful of wine. "Traveler between worlds. How did you work such magic?"

"With a prayer."

The woman smirked and pushed off the tree. "You're saying *Allah* gave you the power?"

Ayelet opened her mouth to answer, but her throat squeezed tight. She did not know where the power came from. Not that she owed this hulking djinn any explanation at all. "How did you get injured?"

"Teeth... and cannons."

Ayelet grinned. "That I can see."

They stared at each other in the starlight. Then light flickered in the djinn's eyes.

"You look like a woman in need of a deal."

"*You* look like a woman in need of a deal," Ayelet countered foolishly. Why was she so keen on poking fun at creatures that might kill her? Still, the djinn did not advance. She must not think a pathetic human worth the trouble, an opportunity Ayelet would not waste. "I, however, have dire matters to attend to, so I must be on my way." Ayelet picked her way into the brambles in the forest. The sooner she was away from Shihala's troubles, the better.

"I would be a powerful ally," Takisha called behind her.

"I already have a powerful friend."

"What's the harm in making another?"

Ayelet slowed. If she garnered a favor from the djinn, she could use it to help Serap. That's why Jahmil let her go in the first place. It was why he hadn't held her tight in the dancing light of his smokeless fire. If only she had let him the first time he asked. If only. And then a new, strange, and entirely selfish thought occurred to her. If she saved Serap swiftly, would she have time to return before he married? Maybe through Takisha, or a petal from her flower?

"Ah, you're listening. Good," Takisha said. She inhaled with a snarl and spat into the trees. "As you can tell by the fact that your head remains attached to your body, I am weak from battle. Too weak even to survive the journey home. Too weak to search for my comrades, if any live. So weak, in fact, I've revealed myself to a little human to ask for help. This is an offer that will come only once. Now, show me your magic so I may know your worth. I seek to return home."

Ayelet turned and made her way back to where Takisha stood. Close up, she was even more intimidating. Each muscle flexed beneath her skin in hard coils, no part of her body smooth for the blocky shapes of power underneath. She stood taller even than Balian, whose face Ayelet had to look up to see. Taller even than Jahmil. Her wound was much deeper than Ayelet expected, as well, festering with green ooze and frothy white foam.

"And how will I know what you're worth?" Ayelet asked.

Takisha bent down. Dark eyeliner shaped her eyes beneath the fierce angle of her brows, smeared with bright green sweat. "You're a mess, little human. I'm certain any number of things I have would be of worth to you. A shoe, perhaps?" She glanced down at Ayelet's feet with a grin. Then her brows tugged together, and she looked between the boot and Ayelet. "I think I have one that would be a near-perfect match."

Ayelet blushed and rubbed her slipper over the top of Jahmil's boot, the soft leather like his touch upon her skin. "I don't need much at all," she lied through the twisting growl of her stomach. "I'm on my way to save a friend and very likely will die in the process. So unless you have the power to bring me back to life, I cannot make a deal." She bit her tongue and prayed the ploy would work. Desperate people made foolish deals, giving more than was needed not to lose hope. She hoped djinn were the same.

"If I could raise comrades from the dead, I would have armies of good men and women at my disposal." A look of fury-laced sorrow reflected in her eyes accompanied by shades of white and aubergine purple. "But to give your life for a friend is the truest sign of honor." She straightened with a groan and ran a finger under her chin. "In exchange for your magic sending me home, if indeed you have some, I will give you my sword."

"I don't know how to use that," Ayelet said flatly. She needed something more helpful than an obsidian blade too heavy to lift.

Takisha smirked. "I would accompany it. Though wounded as I am, that may be all you get."

"What if I healed you?"

"Healed me?" Takisha said, her finger rubbing away at her jaw furiously.

Ayelet pinched her toes inside Jahmil's boot to keep the lie from her face. She didn't know if the wisp of magic could heal Takisha or not.

"If you heal me, I'll lead you to victory in one battle when and where and with whomever you please. And after we win, you will send me home."

Ayelet tried to swallow, but her throat parched. She did not know if she could send Takisha home either but needed all the help she could get. Besides, the worst Takisha might do was take her life, and she already planned on losing it. For what other way would the slavers let Serap go? They had been sent by Nadir specifically to get at her. And the faceless man was in every slaver's shadow. He would never let Serap go without Ayelet in exchange. Never. And the last time she had managed to escape his grasp had taken five years of torture. Yes, her fate was all but sealed. If only she had let Jahmil hold her.

Ayelet sighed, trying not to look too eager, then challenged, "That is two favors you ask for my one."

"Then I shall make myself worthy of two."

She did not know what that meant, but the fire that burned in Takisha's eyes was enough to stay her tongue.

"We shall see," Ayelet said and stuck out her hand. Takisha's large fingers enclosed hers entirely.

After a hearty handshake that rattled her bones, Ayelet helped Takisha sit and pulled the glass bottle from her pouch.

"When I asked what magic you held, I did not think it would be a wisp in a bottle." Her throaty laugh filled the clearing of trees. "Humans are peculiar creatures."

Ayelet placed one hand on the bottom of the jar, hoping it would draw the magic down and keep it from escaping. Then, she removed the cork with a pop.

Takisha's sharp eyes watched her. "It clings to you."

Ayelet sighed with relief. The glimmer of white pooled around the glass just above her hand.

She ran her finger up to the top of the jar. Silver tendrils licked the edge, sensing escape but unwilling to flee. "Will it be enough?"

Takisha's frown was not encouraging. "We shall see."

CHAPTER FIFTEEN

JAHMIL

THE SICKLY SHINE OF the traitor's black eyes filled Jahmil's mind, along with the image inside of them. His father tumbling from the walls of Karzusan into a swarm of bial'dabaye, being torn to pieces as he screamed.

That night Jahmil had vowed to eradicate the Vespars and their monsters from the face of Qaf. Tonight he would try once again to make good on that promise.

Jahmil broke a long branch from an acacia tree and used his fire to hone one end into a point. The cry came again, sharper and closer. And then another, the beasts communicating in their shrill, barbaric language. Their legs pounded the earth, twigs snapping as they rushed closer.

Ducking into some foliage, Jahmil closed his eyes and listened. Two of the monsters, at least. Perhaps this was just a scouting party, which meant if he could silence their voices before they called for more, he might stand a chance. They were close enough now they'd be able to smell him, but what had brought them this way in the first place? The creatures made no false move as if following a string that led directly to him. Perhaps they had sensed the rush of magic Ayelet had called to this isolated place. Or perhaps, he had wandered into one of the Vespars' many invisible trip points.

It made no difference.

Two bial'dabaye burst in unison into the small clearing. Both were more than six feet long and heavily muscled with tufts of ragged, spotted fur clinging to their backs, legs, and shoulders. Their heads and faces were of hyenas, with front fangs as long as fingers and orange eyes with no pupils. They moved like animals and their knees and ankles turned like dogs, but otherwise, the bones were formed like men. Walking on all fours, they approached the shelter where moments ago Jahmil and Ayelet had taken refuge from the cold, now melting away as the First Moon rose beyond the crest of purple trees.

As one bial'dabaye bent to sniff the ground, Jahmil leapt from his hiding spot and rushed it. It turned to defend, but he buried his spear in its neck before it could move. It gurgled and thrashed, black blood foaming from its mouth.

The other bial'dabaye reared up so its manlike shoulders squared. Strapped to its hands were gloves of leather and long, steel spikes. Vespars never shied to use metal in their weapons, unlike most djinn who avoided the dangerous substance at all cost. Jahmil stood as it lunged for him, claws bared. He rolled and caught it by the crook of the arm. Spinning with the weight, he drove it to the ground and fell on top. It screamed. He punched the tender flesh of its belly, but the beast rolled aside. It found its feet and turned its jaws to face him.

Jahmil backed up, holding the spear at arm's length. He took a wide stance, knees bent, preparing himself for the beast's explosive lunge.

The monster opened its jaws wide. Its neck pulsated. It was preparing to call for its cackle. If the others heard the call, soon dozens, if not hundreds of the beasts would swarm these woods.

With a guttural cry, Jahmil pounced on the beast. It fell onto the flat of its back and he fell on top, straddling its chest. He stabbed again for the belly, but the creature caught the spear in its manlike hand, the blade cutting into the flesh of its palm. It yanked the weapon away and tossed it into the brush.

The creature's mouth yawned open, its jaws wide enough to swallow his skull in a single bite. He grabbed the fangs and pushed with all his might. They struggled, neither gaining an inch.

Jahmil opened his mouth and spat a ball of white fire into the creature's gaping throat. It choked and shivered, the strength fading from its neck.

Jahmil released the fangs and punched inside the jaws into the soft of the creature's throat. Sulfur stung at his eyes, the smell enough to draw bile to the back of his throat. He grabbed a handful of soft, slimy flesh and twisted until the light in the monster's eyes went out.

Panting for breath, Jahmil peeled himself away from the corpse. His hand was dripping with blood and yellow ooze. He shook it off, trying not to gag. Not for the first time since this excursion began, he wished he had listened to Zamir and brought along his sword.

He had cut the monster's cry short, but it was impossible to know if the cackle might still be on its way. Once again it flashed through Jahmil's mind to pull the alyasimin from his pocket and shift back to earth, leaving behind the nightmares that now called Shihala their home. His heart ached to hide from reality, to take shelter in dreams of soft eyes and gently smiling lips.

Nearly a year had passed since he'd fled the might of the conquering Vespars, and in that time he had not once returned. Had, in fact, been forbidden to return by both Queen Qadira and his own mother. But he continuously heard rumors of groups of his people still living in Shihala, hiding in the Mountains of Orkeshi, fighting a guerilla war against the invaders. And on the strength of rumor alone, every month he covertly diverted supplies from Qadira's army and dropped them by drakonte-back into Orkeshi to secret places known only to Shihalans.

He had heard nothing from the guerrillas directly. Not a scrawled letter or a whisper on the wind. Nothing.

He would not squander this serendipitous opportunity. Though he feared they would not believe it, that they would despise him for abandoning them and failing even now to come to their aid, he had to find what remained of his people. To tell them they had not been forgotten, that they were heroes to all of their scattered kinsmen. To him. And though the fruits of his labor had not yet ripened, he worked every day to find his way back to them.

Distant shrieks of more bial'dabaye circled the air, coming up the sloping hills like a tide of needles. And farther still, at the very edge of his hearing were the voices of djinn—Vespars, speaking their own bastardized, sing-song version of *lughat aljana.*

Jahmil waited, scanning the wind to find their direction, to gauge their approach. A scent of roasting meat reached his nostrils, setting his empty belly to roil. A contingency of Vespars must be encamped at the base of the hill.

Jahmil snatched his makeshift spear from the bed of midnight jasmine, and with a last glance at the jumble of trees where he and Ayelet had shared their last moments, he turned his feet uphill.

Ayelet's scarf gave scant protection to his foot, but he was thankful for it each time he stepped on a thorn or stumbled over a tree branch. Even as he listened to the hiss and whine of the bial'dabaye and the easy laughter of the Vespar soldiers, thoughts of her swirled through his mind, every word that passed between them echoing like the notes of her lyre. Everything he had said, everything he had not said and would never say. The panic on her face when she asked to stay with him but a moment longer. When he said that he could hold her and his very soul ached because it could never be so.

A hot Janu'ub wind had come out to play its mischief, rushing through the leaves so they scraped and shifted colors. He deftly wove and twisted through the understory, his steps light and silent.

When he reached the valley, the flicker of dark yellow flames bit at his eyes. Holding his breath, he peeked through the tree trunks. Scanning the tightly packed encampment, he recognized the uniforms of soldiers. The Vespars' bright white skin shone like beacons in the firelight. White hair, clean-shaven, and dark eyes that kept their secrets even when colors flashed in their djinn eyes. They wore black leather with hardened Alma bones woven over the fabric for strength and extra protection. Jahmil crept amongst the trees, summing up the rank and file. Nine campfires each with between eight and ten Vespar soldiers, and a corral of bial'dabaye—some thirty of the beasts. Jahmil gave thanks he had not sustained any bleeding injuries, as the monstrous hyenas could taste a tinge of blood from parasangs away.

Even as fear gripped his heart, a hungry grin grew on his lips. He may have been half-naked, unarmed, and exhausted, but the cry of the bial'dabaye he'd killed had gone unheeded. The Vespars didn't know he was there, and that, at least, was an advantage.

He stayed crouched in silence for another few moments, taking in every morsel of information his eyes, ears, and nose could find. It was clear they had been in the woods for some time—their bodies rank and unwashed, their morale low as supplies dwindled. He listened to the conversations of the soldiers; though it was difficult to follow individual statements in such a cacophony of chatter, the word guerilla kept coming up.

"The base at Al Abra will take years to rebuild," said one soldier, his back so close Jahmil could have speared his neck. "We ought to just set fire to Orkeshi and be done with it."

"Brilliant," another snapped sarcastically. "Burn down the forest. Are you trying to make Shihala look more like home?"

Jahmil's skin tightened, remembering the land through which he and Ayelet had come—a barren wasteland he never would have thought could exist in Qaf. Only once before had he even been to Vespar, accompanying his father on a doomed diplomatic mission that only resulted in more bloodshed. Fifteen years ago, the kingdom had looked nothing like the barren, broken hell he had seen today. Their lands had flowed with rivers, spotted by lakes of crystal. Birds of every color had filled the skies, and their strange, rectangular palaces of bright yellow stone had shone against the beauty of verdant jungles. Now, there was nothing. Nothing.

"Vespars fight without mercy or reason," his father had once said. *"They fight for their own vainglory, to bring every kingdom of Qaf under their cold white hand. The only way to stop them is to kill every last one."*

Jahmil had always believed it, as he had seen the tactics they employed. Cut and burn. Unrestrained murder of civilians—women, the elderly, even children. Conquered soldiers enslaved or fed to the bial'dabaye. They seemed to live only for destruction, their white skin painted with hot blood as they rode ever onward, ceaselessly searching for more land to steal, more loot to plunder, more innocents to exterminate.

He had heard rumor they had exhausted their own land, which had been the catalyst for their invasion. He had envisioned salinated soil worked by too many hands. A mine empty of quartz, a sea with dwindling fish. To a kingdom of such scarcity, Shihala seemed low-hanging fruit—an abundant paradise, sparsely populated and under-defended. All these years Jahmil had never questioned the Vespars' motivations. He had never cared.

It was the sky that gave him pause now. No matter how the land in Qaf changed—from the fertile land of Shihala to the deserts of Ghaluma, to the white peaks of Zabriya, the sky remained the same—an oasis of color and light bursting with stars and nebulae. Never gray, never simple. Never like the desolate sky he had seen today.

The sound of a lyre touched his ears, and for one brief and far too hopeful moment, his eyes searched for Ayelet.

An old man with dark and dusty blue skin strummed his instrument at the far end of the camp, his foot secured to a tree with a golden chain. Dancers and servants carrying goblets of wine moved among the soldiers, all of them Shihalans. These were prisoners of war: captured guerillas made into slaves. Slaves forced to serve the will of masters who reveled in filth and all that was *haram*.

A crash and a hiss of harsh laughter snatched his attention. One of the serving women had spilled some wine and was now receiving a sound beating at the hands of a soldier twice her size. Others watched and laughed as she screamed, clasping her hands over her head in a futile attempt to protect herself.

Jahmil's fists tightened as he watched the woman's blue Shihalan skin streak purple with her own blood. She was no mere slave, though that alone would be enough. She was his subject. One of the thousands of souls whose very existence gave him the right to the title of *amir*. And here she was helpless and exposed, beaten for the amusement of men so ruthless they should hardly be called djinn.

Ayelet's voice echoed through his mind. *"She will soon wish she was dead if she doesn't already. For that is the lot of those taken by slavers. I know this to be true. It is carved in my bone."*

Anger rushed Jahmil like a flash flood over the desert, but he forced it down. There is no reason with a clenched fist, and no amount of fury helps one man to stand against eighty. Only wits could win this battle. And he had to win. He could not endure turning a blind eye. Not after everything that had happened.

Jahmil lay in wait until one of the Vespar soldiers rose from his fire and stumbled towards the forest to answer the call of nature. It was not the man who had beaten the serving girl, as he had hoped, but one of the villains who had laughed at her misery.

Good enough.

Jahmil followed the man, creeping along the edge of the tree line to meet the lone soldier in a small grotto. As the Vespar relieved himself, singing in a drunken whisper, Jahmil untied the sash from his waist and crept closer until he stood a scant foot away.

If not for the bial'dabaye, he would have snatched the sword from the soldier's frog and run him through. As it stood, the deed had to be done without spilling a drop of blood or making a noise.

When the man had finished and started to turn, Jahmil wrapped the sash around his neck and twisted. The Vespar soldier struggled to grab his weapon, but he was so drunk. Jahmil scarcely had to strain his muscles.

He stripped the body and changed into the soldier's clothes. Before changing into the boots, he unwound Ayelet's scarf from his foot. It seemed strangely appropriate that the only memento he had of her would be tattered and crushed, a victim of its own utility. And yet, the silk was still soft to the touch. Still beautiful.

He tied it around his forearm and discarded the rest of his clothes.

Taking slow, deep breaths, Jahmil conjured an image in his mind of what he wanted to become. The smell, the taste, the sensation. His reason for wanting it. He called upon his fire, and it rushed over his skin as evenly as a hot wind, quickening to his will. A djinn could not make himself invisible in the land of Qaf; the best he could do was disguise himself.

His body changed, features twisting and bones shifting. It was always a little painful, enough to make him suck in a few harsh breaths. When he opened his eyes and looked down at his hands, he saw shock-white skin and dirty fingernails. He touched his cheeks to confirm and altered his features to more closely resemble the soldier who now lay forever silent on the forest bed, then laced the long, needlelike sword into the leather frog at his hip.

Jahmil took a deep breath, hunched his shoulders, and staggered into the camp.

He didn't make his way back to the fire the man had left. Fire burned in every djinn, so they did not need it to keep warm or cook food as humans did. The rainbows of fire around which the Vespar soldiers clustered were instead a matter of comradery. This practice was especially common in the military, where bonds of kinship and a sense of community are integral to the very survival of a unit. Each djinn would add their own unique flavor to the conflagration, creating something that was not of one but all. In the fire, all hearts were equal and everyone had the chance to be felt and heard, to feel themselves a part of something greater.

Vespar legions were always separated into several smaller units of no more than ten, and each unit was in constant competition with the others. The rewards for success and the punishments for failure were great. He had witnessed Vespars murder their own men over what seemed like minute mistakes and watched one unit of men feast like kings while their comrades starved. All for the sake of competition, for bringing out the best in their soldiers. And always there was the commander, upheld from all his troops—aloof and alone.

Jahmil's eyes scanned the camp until he found a man sitting on his own in the dark. No fire. No companions. His cool green eyes swept over the soldiers as he absently sharpened his long, thin sword, fashioned from the thigh bone of an Alma—the great hairy apes of the Western Desert.

He was not drinking.

Jahmil listened to the soldiers' chatter for a little while longer. These men were already on edge. Trapped in this place for Allah only knew how long, surviving on dwindling supplies. No women but a few slave girls, whom the commander had probably laid claim to. The way they grumbled and spat and shot daggers at one another with their eyes, it was clear they were already on the verge of mutiny. All they needed was a little push.

Jahmil screwed down his courage and staggered up to a fire at random and laid his hand on the shoulder of the nastiest-looking soldier in the group.

"Kemel is such a liar!" he laughed. "I can't believe you let him talk like that."

"Are you talking to me, *kalb*?" the leather-faced behemoth grunted.

"Haven't you heard what he's been saying about you?" Jahmil leaned in close and said in a loud whisper, "He's telling everyone that you're a eunuch."

The bull-like man growled, and all seven feet of him stood "He what?"

"He said it's the only explanation for the way you fight."

The man's head snapped across the camp, and Jahmil slipped away behind his back. He hurried up to another fire and leaned over between two men that were sitting very near one another.

"Now, Iqbad says you two are..." He wiggled his eyebrows and waved his hand in the air. "Is it true?"

"Who the...?" sneered one, rising to his feet.

A fight broke out on the other side of the camp, the seven-foot monster pounding another soldier, probably Kemel, into the dirt. As everyone turned to watch, Jahmil rushed to another fire. He pointed at the unit of the man getting pounded and said, "Those *abna alkilab* took twice their share of meat!"

That got every man at the fire to his feet and rushing into the fight, calling to others to join in. As more violence broke out around him, Jahmil bounced from place to place, throwing up every incendiary remark he could think of—what that one said about this one's mother, what this one said about the other one's breath, and so on, until the entire camp had erupted into a mindless brawl of drunken violence. By the time the commander deigned to step in, there was nothing he could do to settle the chain of disputes echoing through the troops. Even his sergeants were in the thick of it, throwing punches and choking on insults.

Jahmil snatched a small ax from one of the soldiers' belts and rushed to the slave woman who had earlier endured the Vespar soldier's savage beating. She huddled at the edge of the fray, the gold chain around her ankle strained as she tried to isolate herself from the violence. Jahmil skittered to her side. Her eyes snapped to him, terrified. He gazed back intently, praying she would recognize the glitter of Shihala even buried in his hideous disguise.

"*Barakat al'Shihalat 'alaykum,*" he whispered.

Her frightened eyes searched his face. "Who are you?"

"Are you with the guerillas?"

She stared in silence for another long moment before a broken smile dimpled her cheeks. Jahmil lifted his ax, and with one quick swipe freed her from her golden binds.

"Free the others," he said. "Follow the light of the Tiger Star to the grove of ash palms. I will find you. Go quickly."

Jahmil darted back into the woods and made his way back to the body of the man he had killed. While the sounds of violence raged from inside the camp, he dragged the corpse towards the rickety stables where the bial'dabaye slept.

Jahmil tied a sash around his face and hair before beginning the hideous work. He laid the corpse out with its legs and arms splayed, then working as quickly as possible, he chopped it into quarters. After the first swing, the bial'dabaye began to wake, their orange eyes flashing and noses twitching for blood. They gathered at the edge of their rickety wooden cage and watched as one of their white-skinned masters, which they had been painstakingly trained not to attack, prepared for them a feast.

He tossed the chunks of flesh to the monsters one by one, whetting their appetite for man flesh. They screamed in joy and clawed at one another, half-fed bellies desperate for a proper meal. The madness of bloodlust filled their eyes.

Jahmil opened the gate.

CHAPTER SIXTEEN

AYELET

EVEN IN THE DIM moonlight, Ayelet could see Takisha's wound was festering. Noxious foam bubbled atop the blackened gash, like a forgotten sack of carrots that had begun to liquefy.

"Let us rinse the wound before we try," Ayelet said. "There is a stream just past these ruins. Do you have something I could use to bring the water back?"

Takisha flicked the bottle in Ayelet's hands. "Shouldn't that work?"

"It won't hurt the magic?" Ayelet frowned and raised the bottle overhead so the moonlight sparkled through the wisp inside.

"Left with nowhere to go, the magic should take to the liquid, at least for a time. It makes for a strong drink and has been known to turn sprouts into trees overnight."

Ayelet's eyes widened. Takisha did not need to grow any taller. She was already halfway to a giant.

Takisha chuckled. "Don't worry. For me, it's but a taste of home."

Then another arrow of realization struck Ayelet in the back. "I drank some not three nights ago. What's it going to do to me?"

"I'd say you're past the side-effects period, so whatever already has happened is all you'll get." Takisha shook her head with a sharp grin. "What *did* it do to you?"

"I may have become a bit tipsy," Ayelet said, tilting her chin up to protect her pride.

Takisha barked out a laugh. "I'd call you a lightweight, but it sounds like you wouldn't even qualify." When she stiffened, Takisha slapped her back so she staggered forward. "Don't worry, little human, you'll be fine."

Ayelet nodded slowly, unconvinced, then took the bottle and headed into the forest. When she had passed the first large hazel tree on the edge of the clearing, the stench of rot met her nose. She turned to run when a raspy snarl snaked through the air. She screamed, stumbling back, as the brush before her writhed with the glimmer of scales.

Glowing eyes the color of cooling embers burst like flames in the dark ahead. The creature shrieked once more and lifted a broken wing.

Takisha burst past the tree, sword in hand, her face a tough mask over obvious pain. "What is it? What do you see?"

Ayelet trembled and pointed at the flying snake—no, the *drakonte*—in the brambles ahead.

"*Kun hadi*, Thueban," Takisha said and raised her hand in the air. The beast silenced, groaning as if disappointed, and slinked to the ground. Then Takisha rounded on her in one swift movement, her sword slipping below Ayelet's chin. "How do you see him?" she asked, her eyes sparking.

"I—I don't know," Ayelet said.

"You have too many tricks for a little human. Who did you say your friend was? The one powerful enough to protect you from me?"

Her breath caught as the edge of the sword pressed under her neck, nicking her skin. "Jahmil," she winced. "Jahmil Amir al Shihala."

Takisha pulled the blade from her throat and aimed it, spear-like, at her chest. The point pricked through her dress, inches away from her beating heart.

"You lie."

"I do not."

"What would he owe to the likes of you?"

"I don't know."

"But you say he is your friend. Why?"

Ayelet had nothing to say to that. She *had* said it as a lie. Still, Jahmil had saved her from the ghoul and a lava-filled death, something she had been too prideful and shocked to thank him for. And when he spoke those sweet nothings about how he could imagine loving her or when he called her eyes a storm, causing her heart to thunder in her chest, she had believed he felt *something*.

"I don't know why Jahmil does anything," said Ayelet. "He baffles me. Serious and cordial one moment, angry the next. Judgmental and... and unexpectedly kind."

Takisha's eyes narrowed, then she lowered her blade and burst out laughing.

"Why do you mock me?" Ayelet asked, humiliated at what she allowed to slip from her lips. Even Thueban in all his pain flicked his tongue out long and fast as if to laugh at her.

"I'm sorry, little human." Takisha grinned, wiping a finger under her eye. "But I can sympathize. You are not the first to be befuddled by our candid prince. Nor the first to be smitten by him."

Ayelet blushed. He had told the truth. He *was* a prince, which left no doubt he was engaged to a queen. Her humiliation deepened.

"I am not smitten," she crossed her arms and said the words around the knot in her throat.

Takisha's laughter ended abruptly, her eyes hard as obsidian. "You would be wise to make that true. It's hard enough he has to marry that spoiled *sharmouta* of a queen without you confusing him. He's one gray-eyed temptation away from abandoning his duty altogether. Not that a fling wouldn't do him some good. It would just mean the destruction of everyone else."

The word *fling* hurt her more than she expected. Apparently, she was not the only one he could imagine loving but didn't. "He does not love his queen?" she asked, petty hope and tight worry mixing in her throat.

"Can a prisoner love the rat who nightly gnaws on his neck? Her own mother could not love her. But do not pity her. There are ample reasons why and all of her own doing."

"I do not pity anyone," Ayelet said absentmindedly. Maybe Jahmil's affections were not as occupied as she thought. She scraped her teeth over her bottom lip.

"Stop your scheming, little human, or I shall have to cut you down," Takisha warned, though her threat sounded empty. Thueban didn't even rise from where he rested his head on a rotting log. Even they knew she would never see Jahmil again.

"I'm not scheming."

Thoroughly soured, she tossed the jar and caught it in her other hand. Then she spun around. "Let's get you healed."

Ayelet headed to the muddy bank of the river and tried to crush the seeds of ill-placed hope Takisha had given her with a logical list of reasons. The first and most glaring being that pursuing anything with Jahmil would supposedly mean destruction for everyone in Shihala—though, that sounded a bit dramatic.

Second, if he could not even be loyal to the woman he vowed to marry, a queen nonetheless, what did that mean of all the things he'd said to her? Probably that he had not meant them at all; that she was just another woman he trailed along in his royal wake. A vacation from his duties that he would not think of again. A *fling*.

And the last reason being that the former two points didn't matter at all. She would never see him again.

After following a craggy trail toward the babbling stream, she knelt close enough to reach the gurgling water. She pulled the magic to the bottom of the jar with her finger as she had before. Convinced it would stay put, she dipped the bottle where the river ran smooth, sheltered by a semicircle of craggy rocks.

The clear liquid splashed through the wisp. It shot up, and she barely corked the top in time to keep it inside. The magic pressed itself into the neck of the jar, so condensed it was thick as a cloud. She frowned and shook the magic. Slowly, the wisp dissipated like a drop of milk in water. This must be how Kadri infused her cider. But how did she catch the wisps in the first place, especially since she could not even see them? And where did they come from?

Ayelet returned to see Takisha leaning back against a stump, sweat upon her brow. Thueban had coiled into a rock-looking circle, his broken wing held out gingerly to the side while he breathed heavily. She looked to the bottle and back to the wounded warriors. What battle had they been fighting? The mountains to the east were hidden under the canopy of trees, but the terrifying monster lingered on the edges of her mind. It had been a drakonte that saved her from the lava and rescued Jahmil, and their feathers and scales were strewn about the road in pieces. When she had goaded him about his pet snakes, he said they were all dead, their riders with them.

Hesitant, she handed the bottle to Takisha.

"That's it?" Takisha said, swirling the water around. "You can travel the realms and see through our disguises, but to heal me, you're just handing me a wisp?" She frowned. "I do not understand you."

Ayelet squirmed. She *had* just planned to hand over the bottle and pray it worked. But she needed Takisha to see her as someone worthy of respect or she might not keep her deal. Other than her magic, what had she to offer? Juggling and quick wit would be useless here. And the only thing close to a spell she could claim she knew was a nursery rhyme meant to scare away *davalpa* monsters that ate naughty children who strayed too close to the river.

And she was pretty sure that was nonsense, anyway.

Empty of ideas, she pulled her lyre from her pouch. Takisha looked on with skeptically arched brows. When Ayelet had played for Jahmil in his circle of fire, the raggedness that creased his face had melted into a healthy glow. Maybe her gentle tune had simply raised his spirits, but it was better than nothing.

She strummed the strings, choosing a light and coaxing song about the fresh joys of spring as Takisha popped the cork and poured the shimmering liquid over her wound.

Then, she sang:

> *Kuş sesleri ovalara yayılır*
> *İnsan buna hayran olur bayılır*
> *Bal arılar çiçeklere konalar*
> *Kuzucuklar taze çimen ararlar*
> *Yeşillenmiş ağaçlarda yapraklar*
> *Amber gibi mis kokuyor topraklar.*

The sound of the birds all over the lowland
bring admirers from all over the land.
As the honey bees settle upon flowers
and grass grows for the sweet lambs,
the leaves on the trees green.
All these fragrant and fresh soils.

She felt it again, the surging of magic as she played in the market or by the fires with Jahmil, but it did not overtake her. It swelled, encircling her and Takisha. Thueban crunched in tight, pulling away from the bright white and hissing. The wisp of magic bloomed, expanding the liquid with shimmering sloshes so it overflowed from the bottle. Takisha cleaned her wound with liquid to spare, so she drank and drank three bottles worth of magic before it emptied with the lingering sound of the lyre's last chord.

Stitch by stitch, the jagged ends of her wound had sewn themselves together, then melted into one. Takisha jumped to her feet and swung her large sword in an arc over her head. "Ha!" she said, flashing her teeth in what was probably joy but which frightened Ayelet just the same. "So, this is what Jahmil sees in you. Music and a power not to be trifled with." She shoved her black blade into the scabbard on her back. "I bet he was quite taken with you, though he'd never admit it."

Ayelet ran a hand over the soft wood of her lyre, tracing the flowers and vines that coiled across the surface. "Taken enough to say loving me would ruin his life," she said with a mix of bitterness and regret.

A look of thoughtfulness crossed Takisha's face. Her brows arched and then relaxed. "That is true." Takisha turned and called her drakonte. "Thueban!"

The massive creature slithered forth, breaking branches and tumbling saplings as it approached. It was in much worse shape than Ayelet had realized. White and gray feathers bent in unforgiving angles, and a deep gash that streaked through the scales along the entire length of its body. Its wounds, too, festered, dripping green blood that hissed when it touched the ground. Takisha put out her hand, and the *drakonte* met it with its smooth nose.

"*Takun 'alā alsalam.*" Takisha raised her blade above the drakonte's head.

Ayelet gasped.

"Don't," she cried, stepping between Takisha and the beast.

"This is none of your business, little human. Thueban is hurting, and even with your healing song, I've not enough fire to transport him home, much less heal him. It is merciful to end him rather than let him suffer."

Ayelet's heart beat heavy in her chest. The creature was horrible to look at, with razor fangs the length of her legs and a flickering tongue of purple, but she could not let Takisha kill it so easily. Not when she knew how much it meant to Jahmil, how much sadness simmered in his eyes when he talked of lost soldiers.

"What if I could send him back? Would that heal him?" she asked impulsively.

"Why do you care so much?" Takisha's shrewd gaze crossed her face. "Why would you waste magic on my dying drakonte when you were so stingy with it before?"

Ayelet swallowed her first reply. "Goodwill. I need your complete loyalty if I'm to trust you in battle."

Takisha shrugged, but her narrowed eyes still looked over Ayelet with suspicion. "And how do you claim to send him home?"

Ayelet had no idea what she was thinking when she reached in and pulled the flower from her lyre. She cupped the delicate petals in her hand and gently unfolded her fingers. The blossom's glow lit the ground in a small circle around them.

Takisha nearly fell forward, her hands reaching out as if she would take it from Ayelet right then and there and disappear forever. Ayelet flinched, but Takisha kept her distance, even as her eyes drank the flower in greedily.

"*Alyasimin,*" she breathed. "How did you? I thought they were extinct. You truly did arrive on a prayer." Her eyes moved past the flower and to Ayelet. "You carry powerful gifts," Takisha said, but it did not sound like a good thing the way she inhaled the words through her teeth. She rolled her shoulders and growled, "Jahmil, you fool."

"Will it still work?" Ayelet asked, afraid to hear the answer. The temptation to flee the awfulness of earth and fall into Jahmil's arms—even if for a few days until he'd marry and be gone forever—would be far too much. She shivered.

"It will. Each petal creates a gateway between the two worlds. But Thueban cannot use it on his own." Takisha leaned back, crossing her arms over her chest with her sword still in hand.

Ayelet's heart raced like a thousand notes beating in cacophony. If she let Takisha take him home to be healed, she would probably not come back. But if she went herself... she might not come back. And Serap still wept in a slaver's cage.

Ah, she was selfish.

She *might* be able to save Serap without Takisha, but no one would save Serap without her.

"If I sent you back..." Ayelet said slowly, "would you return straight away?"

Takisha's eyes glittered, a concentrated turn to her lips. "I have the remains of an obliterated army awaiting my command, good soldiers who are lost or dying, and a prince fighting to regain his kingdom from the jaws of pure evil. What matter presses more than these?"

Ayelet faltered. He had not told her all of that. If he had, she would have shared her magic with him when he asked. But he did not trust her enough to know. The thought turned her stomach.

"I don't claim to know what Jahmil faces, but he sent me back knowing my matter cannot wait. It's—I must save a little girl, and I must do it tonight. It is a matter of life and death."

Takisha's sharp brows softened. "It was Jahmil's wish that you should do this?"

Ayelet nodded.

"Then, I can keep my oath and honor to my *amiri* at the same time. A battle when, where, and with whom you decree. On the honor of Shihala, I will take Thueban home and immediately return."

Ayelet clenched her stomach to keep the doubt in. This would be a great loss to her. Having Takisha fight against the slavers had given her hope they might succeed. But Jahmil had looked devastated about his forces. About whether he was a good prince. She ached at the memory of the haunted look that shadowed his face. If she could give him this gift, it would be worth it. Even if she could not see the color of his eyes when the drakonte returned.

"And you can take Thueban to him?" Ayelet asked. "Do you know where he will be? We were lost in the woods, in a place of ash and shadow between Shihala and the land he called Vespar."

Takisha's head jerked back. "He should not be there, that *majnun*," she snarled. "He risks everything."

With every word she said, the last of Ayelet's hopes wilted. Jahmil in danger sealed her doom. Takisha would not return. But maybe that was better. The thought of him harmed, bleeding somewhere alone, and completely enraged...

She held the alyasimin out for Takisha to pluck a petal. "Will Thueban make it?"

Takisha chuckled deep in her chest. "Entering Shihala alone will get him biting again. It may take a little longer for his wings to heal, but he'll be in fighting spirits ready to rip off the heads of the Vespars soon enough. And as soon as I help you save your little girl, I shall happily join him in tearing their skulls from their bodies and grinding them into dust."

"Do you need another petal to return?" Ayelet asked, rubbing a hand along the softly crisp edges of each petal so that silver sparkles sprinkled the ground.

"No. Keep your gifts. You shall not get another like it." Takisha put a hand on Thueban and tugged off a petal. Then she dropped it, looking directly into Ayelet's eyes before disappearing entirely.

Ayelet counted the seconds, each one making her stomach roil. The seconds turned into minutes. What had she done? What if sending Takisha back caused the death of Serap? What could she say of herself then? She was far more selfish than she had ever realized.

She fell to her knees, and a hand tapped her shoulder from behind. Ayelet whipped around and nearly fell back.

"Balian?" she asked, her voice shaking like the last leaves of fall. "What are you doing here?"

"What am *I* doing here? You can smell the mead and roasted lamb in the performer's camp from here. Edirne is my home. Something of which you never fail to remind me."

She ignored the bite in his words and flung her arms around his neck. "I have returned to save Serap. Please, will you help me?"

"*I* will save Serap," he said, shrugging her off. "What do you think I'm doing in these woods? I've been tracking the slavers to the mountain and back."

"The mountain still stands?" Ayelet asked, relieved.

"Barely," he scoffed. "It is shattered into pieces, two mountains where there once stood one. And whatever earthquake shook it sent flaming boulders to the quarters of Edirne." He flung his hand behind him in the direction of his home. Naked trees curled with embers against the moonlight. "The city is in chaos, Ayelet. All the more reason for you to run as fast and as far as you can and not look back. It's what you're good at, anyway." He flipped his hand at her with a scathing glare.

This time his words stung. "I know what the risks are for me."

"Do you?" he asked, his eyes daggers. "If Köle finds you, you will face slavery, torture, and... It would be the end of you." His face softened, and he looked away.

Her shoulders trembled when he said the devil's name. "I know what I face!" she yelled. "And I'm prepared to pay the price. My life for Serap's. It is the only price he'll take."

"I won't let you." Balian grabbed her wrist. "You blame me eternally for not protecting you last time. So, this time, I will."

"I do not need your protection, Balian. I never did. You will let me do this."

"I won't!" he cried.

"You will," boomed a voice that was not her own.

The crunch of leaves and swirl of wind sounded behind Ayelet.

Balian released her and fell back into the shadows of the trees. "*Şeytan!*" he cried, looking frantically around for the sound of the voice.

Takisha stepped forward, towering over him though he could not see. "That's not a very nice thing to call a lady of the royal court of Shihala." Her eyes flashed briefly, casting long shadows in the oblong leaves of surrounding trees. Balian's eyes nearly burst from his head. He stuttered and snarled and crawled back a few more feet, looking at Takisha as though she was made of fire and jagged teeth, but Ayelet felt lighter than snow in the breeze.

"You returned," she said breathlessly.

"I made a blood oath on the honor of Shihala." Takisha turned and bowed her head slightly. Her eyes were troubled, creased around the edges far more than when she left. Had she found Jahmil? Was he in trouble? The lightness turned into a bone-grinding weight.

Takisha turned to where Balian now knelt on the ground, a small dagger directed at her as if it could protect him from the shining sword she kept strapped to her back.

"Get up, *qut mukhif*," she pointed to Balian. "Your broad shoulders and strong lungs will be valuable in this fight."

CHAPTER SEVENTEEN

Jahmil

He raced through the trees away from the camp, but the sounds followed. Teeth tearing into flesh, the wild call of the bial'dabaye, the screams of the Vespar soldiers. Everything had gone as well as he ever could have hoped, yet his chest was heavy, slowly filling with black smoke that threatened to choke him. The magic of Shihala was whispering to him, warning him that even now, as the camp was torn apart and the brutal battle waged between the soldiers and their bial'dabaye, there were those in their rank that suspected the truth.

The commander and his eyes of sober jade.

Jahmil prayed the slaves had made it out before he'd loosed the beasts. He had given them as much time as he could.

The shape he had wrapped himself in faded as he ran. He didn't have the energy to keep it up and there was no point. So much time had passed since he'd slept. And so much had happened. His brain was swollen—pulsing between memories, realities, and fears of the future. His heart was broken, what till recently had been an empty shell was now a jumble of sharp angles. And his body had been pushed to its limit. It took everything in him just to keep moving. To run. To never stop running.

Though he longed to find the guerillas, he dared not make for the ash grove in the east where he had told the woman to bring the runaways. He could not allow them to be recaptured, not after all he had done to free them. But there was one more service he could provide—to draw the Vespars in the wrong direction and give his people their best chance of escape. And if the guerillas came to his aid, then Allah was smiling upon him.

Jahmil paused his tread and called what little energy he had left to form a fire in his palm, fanning it until it had tripled in size. Finally, he sent it rocketing into the air, and it exploded in a shower of sparks, a signal to his pursuers.

The Vespars would come for him and leave the others space to escape. Perhaps it was madness. In fact, he was certain that it was. But what did any of that matter?

He was a lousy prince, a lousy general, a lousy man. For five thousand years his family had ruled in Shihala, and because of him, his inadequacy, the land had been lost. His father had died trying to save the kingdom, fighting with honor until his last breath. Perhaps if he had stayed at his side—refused his mother's call to flee and stood his ground until the bitter end—perhaps then things might have been different.

But he had fled, leaving his people, his homeland, his father, and his best friend to suffer the cruel whims of fate. He had let it all slip through his fingers.

And today, he had let Ayelet slip through his fingers too. Nothing was safe in his hands.

The best he could do now was to sacrifice himself to the dogs of war and give some of his people a chance to escape. Death was what he had always deserved.

He heard the voices of the soldiers rushing through the woods towards him, towards his beacon. Gaining on him. The twang of a bow sounded, and he braced for the impact of the arrow, ready to throw himself into Allah's arms and accept his fate.

But the pain did not come.

A cry erupted from the trees—a familiar war song he had not heard since fleeing Shihala.

Jahmil turned towards the noise. Spackled moonlight filtered through the thick canopy, as mist flowed along the forest floor. He saw the weak outline of white-skinned Vespars, seemingly frozen in time as arrows sailed at them from the trees, piercing their flesh. Jahmil's eyes scanned the branches for the archers, anxious to see a flash of blue skin.

Nothing, and yet the song rose all around him, chanted by a dozen cracked and strained voices:

No man can outrun Fate.

When she comes,

cowards run.

I will stand my ground.

He smiled in spite of himself, the song chilling and warming all at once. Lost in the inexplicable hope of the moment, he did not see the Vespar soldier stab for his gut until it was too late.

The needlelike sword pierced him through the liver, and he stumbled. His assailant yanked out the sword, ready to pierce his body again and again, as was the Vespar way. Jahmil managed to catch the tip of the blade, but blood oozing from his gut stole the strength from his arm.

The soldier snarled and knocked him back with his thick shoulder. Jahmil fell against the trunk of a tree. The world went blurry. He felt the wind of the sword as it sailed toward his chest.

The twang of a bow. A scream. Then nothing.

He awoke in a haze—dabs of white and blue light, the faint crackle of a fire, a breath of trees. The only thing that assured him he was still alive was the throbbing pain in his guts.

"Amir?" said a voice, and a hand touched his shoulder. "*Alhamdulillah*! He's awake!"

More voices filled the air, all speaking the Shihalan dialect of *lughat aljana*—soft and yet sharp, like a well-carved knife being skillfully sharpened against a whetstone. He blinked in the light, and blurry faces came into focus. Dozens of people were crowded around him, obscuring his view of the night sky. They all looked rough. Hair hung in twists and dreadlocks. Gaunt blue faces were stained with dirt and green paint. Every eye was wreathed in shadow. And behind them, the tight canopy of the forest of Orkeshi.

They smiled at him and talked over one another. Jahmil tried to speak, but all that came out was a low, pain-filled growl.

"Get back, you rabble! Give him space to breathe." The deep voice cut the cacophony like a hot knife, and the crowd parted. Jahmil's heart lifted painfully in his chest. He knew that voice—a baritone as thick as syrup and as jagged as a saw blade. But it couldn't be.

Pale green eyes gazed down at him, glowing faintly like distant stars. A long checkmark scar marred his cheek, another scar splitting one of his dark eyebrows. Short black hair and rough stubble on a rectangular chin. And that smile—deep dimples and long crow's feet. Unpredictable and effortless warmth, which drew people to him like a magnet.

"Bakr?" Jahmil breathed. "You're alive?"

"I know." He laughed, deep and throaty. It was a sound Jahmil had missed desperately this last year when he'd assumed his best friend was dead. He thought he would never hear it again.

"Still as reckless as ever, I see," said Bakr.

Jahmil tried to sit up but hissed at the pain that shot through him.

"Don't even think about it." Bakr gently but firmly pushed him back down.

"This is impossible. I saw you die at Karzusan."

Bakr sat down beside him and laid his elbows on his knees. He looked rougher and older, though he was a few years younger than Jahmil. His sand-and-sable skin was caked in so much dirt it almost looked black, and while his cheeks were sunken, his shoulders were thicker.

"I *was* dead." He pulled down the collar of his shirt, revealing a massive scar that ran across his neck and down his chest. "I lay on the field for three days before a lilith found me and nursed me back to health."

"A lilith?" Jahmil breathed, cringing at the name of the female furies that had given the djinn their reputation for baby-eating in the human world. The creatures not only preyed on children, but they also tormented expectant mothers, sometimes smothering children even before they were born. The immortal succubi were said to be able to enslave men or murder them with nothing but a kiss, and could not be killed by any mortal weapons. True monsters, if any existed.

"A lilith *nursed* you?" asked Jahmil.

"It's a long story," he laughed. "Perhaps someday I'll have time to tell you."

"How long have you been with the guerillas?"

"I *am* the guerillas!" he shouted, then laughed again even louder so that it pounded in Jahmil's tender head. At last, his senses seemed to focus. He was lying in a bed of animal skins, his head resting on a roll of fur. His shape had returned to normal, and his skin—which had been so filthy he felt disgusted just to be alive—had been given a superficial cleanse. His chest was bare, a roll of gray fabric tied around his waist with multi-colored *bidbam* moss pressed against the wound to cleanse the blood of infection. The blue scarf Ayelet had given him was still tied around his forearm, now spackled with dots of his own blood.

He felt groggy as if someone had given him a swallow of poppy wax. Very likely.

"The slaves...?" Jahmil said, his voice gaining in strength as sleep filtered away.

"We found them," said Bakr, glaring down at him as if he were an unruly child. "They're safe."

Jahmil let his head fall back onto the furs. "And the Vespars?"

"We cleaned up what was left of the unit." Bakr patted Jahmil's shoulder roughly. "I'm not going to ask how you did it. I don't want to know. You shouldn't even be here, you magnificent idiot. You're too valuable to be risking your life in such a stupid way."

The word *valuable* stung Jahmil's ears like acid. "I should have come sooner. Especially to find you. Here. Alive." In spite of the pain, Jahmil forced himself to sit up. Bakr was half-human, with the sandy skin of the bedouin and no fire lighting his pale green eyes, but there was no mistaking the emotions that painted his expressive face.

"You have been missing from me," Bakr said and pulled him into a hug. Jahmil's stomach winced with pain, even as his heart melted. "Tell me you've been well, Jahmil. That you haven't been torturing yourself too much without me around to do it for you?"

Jahmil smiled, but couldn't bring himself to answer other than to pat his friend's back in return. "*Ana mouchtakon ilayka.*"

Large, square tents filled the space between tightly packed trees—tattered brown fabric, filthy and cracked with age under thick black trunks and bright red leaves. People of every age had gathered in a crowd around him—women with babies, the elderly. There must have been a hundred or more faces. But they all had the same look—thin, exhausted, wearing an invisible cloak of shadow. And yet, as they gazed at him, they smiled.

"How's the war going out there?" Bakr asked, though his expression was decidedly less hopeful than the gathered masses. "I noticed you didn't bring an army with you."

Jahmil lifted his gaze to address the people. "I have made an alliance with Queen Qadira al-Ahmar. Soon, I will lead her army into the Shihala."

The gathered crowd smiled at his words, but Bakr scowled. "Tell me you didn't come alone."

"Yes," he said, though it felt like a lie.

Bakr sighed and pinched the bridge of his nose. "Jahmil..."

"How many is your number?"

"Three thousand or so. We can never be all together at once. I have my forces split into twenty units."

"At least say you've received the supplies I sent."

"I expected nothing less from you." Bakr smiled, all white teeth and dimples. "And so we have never ceased to fight. I will never cease to fight."

"You have been in my thoughts every day." Jahmil clasped Bakr's hand and squeezed it hard. "I've tried many times to establish communication, but the Vespars cut every line."

"The beasts are cleverer than they look." Bakr clenched his jaw and nodded, then as if taken by a sudden storm, sadness filled his eyes. "What news of Sezan? Is she well?"

Jahmil bit the corner of his lip. He had not spoken to his younger half-sister in nearly a year, not since his mother had offered her in marriage to the King of Eastern Elm as a way of strengthening Shihala's alliance with the powerful kingdom. Not that they had ever spoken much. He and Sezan had never seen eye to eye, not even when they were babies. The only thing they had ever been able to agree on was Bakr.

If he'd known Bakr was alive, he never would have allowed Sezan to be sent away.

"She believes you dead," said Jahmil. "I will send word straight away—"

"No." Bakr glanced up at his eyes, then back at the ground. He gave a mirthless chuckle, which sounded more like death than anything he'd ever heard. "So long as the war rages, I may be dead at any moment. Why force her to mourn twice?"

Jahmil clenched his jaw, his eyes burning. "Know that I fight for you. I am still fighting."

"*Amiri*," said Bakr reproachfully. He virtually never called Jahmil by any honorific, and when he did, it was always to make a point. "*We* fight for *you*."

Jahmil shook his head quickly. "You are a hero, Bakr. You and your troops. All of you—" He lifted his gaze to the crowd. "Heroes to your people, who have been scattered to the five winds. Forgive me that I cannot give you the support you deserve."

"*Amiri*," Bakr said again, "against reason, logic, and good sense, you came alone into Orkeshi to find us, and along the way you all but single-handedly took out an entire regiment." He chuckled and shook his head. "If nothing else, I know that you fight for your people."

"I never should have left Shihala. I should have stayed at Karzusan with you—"

"And done what?" snapped Bakr, his smile curving into a smirk. "Taken on the Spider of Karzusan? Died in honor and glory, leaving your people to fend for themselves?"

Jahmil's jaw trembled, though from pain or something else he did not know.

"*Ya'ish al'amir!*" someone shouted in the crowd, and then the call was echoed back by every voice in unison. *Long live the prince!*

"You have been missing from me," said Bakr again, then he rose to his feet and called out in his deep, powerful voice. "*Ya'ish almalik Jahmil!*"

Long live King Jahmil!

The call echoed through the people, through the very trees, back and forth like anxious waves rolling in to meet the sand. It set every hair on his body on edge, and his bones trembled.

He heard their defiant cry, saw the joy and determination on their faces when they looked at him, and guilt crashed over him with the force of a cyclone. He was wounded, exhausted, barely breathing—an empty shell of the man he should have been. The man his father had been. The man Bakr still was. And yet, for no reason at all but the weight of his name and the quality of his blood, he embodied the hope of so many people.

What seemed like mere moments before, stumbling through the jungle as the Vespars dogged his every step, he had been ready for his life to end. To be free of the admiration, the expectation, the responsibility. Now, that distant, cynical hope for death seemed like the greatest sin he had ever committed. No matter how much pain it caused him or how he longed to simply lie down and give up the fight, there were too many people depending on him. There was no way out of this war for him, not even the sweet kiss of death. He had to keep fighting.

Music began to play, and people began to dance. Traditional patriotic music—songs that had been sung for five thousand years in Shihala before it was lost. They brought an unexpected swelling of pride to his chest. The songs were still being sung, the old ways preserved by those left behind.

And to see Bakr again. Alive, and strong, and fighting, just like he had always fought. Laughing as easily as he had always laughed. It made his heart beat louder, more vigorously.

A woman with black tattoos on her face, a checkered scarf draped over her hair, and flowers tied to her skirt made her way toward him through the crowd. A healer. She handed a wooden goblet to Bakr, who in turn passed it to Jahmil. Deep blue magic spilled from the sides in mist. He knew this drink. Cobalt potion—precious and rare, its healing powers unmatched by anything on Qaf or Ard.

"Drink, my friend," said Bakr, smiling. "Drink of Shihala and be whole again."

Jahmil thanked the medicine woman and lifted the goblet to his lips. He'd taken but one swallow when a flash of white filled the camp. Startled, he spilled some potion on his arm as he moved to shield his eyes. The music ceased and people scattered, scrambling for their weapons.

When he looked back, he balked at the creature that now filled the camp.

It was a drakonte—its scales shimmering like the light of a nebula. The stink of its blood hit his nostrils.

Slightly healed from the mouthful of cobalt's bliss, Jahmil peeled himself from the ground and stumbled closer. It made no sense. It was impossible to slip through the veil into Orkeshi. At least, without alyasimin. He had tried every means to do just that so many times, but the Vespar spiders had woven such a tight web. But there was no arguing with the massive body that now filled the guerillas' camp, its great purple tongue flicking at the leaves of fire trees. Not just any drakonte, but Takisha's own beloved.

"Thueban?" Jahmil said, stumbling closer.

The wounded beast gave a pitiful *orgle*, its head slumping to one side.

"*Ibn khal*?" Her deep voice filled the space as thoroughly as the bulk of the drakonte. Then he caught sight of her face peeking from around the head of the beast.

His chest lightened so quickly that it stung. "Takisha?"

"Jahmil, you utter fool. What are you thinking, coming to Orkeshi? And alone?"

"Not alone," said Bakr, stepping up beside him.

"Bakr?" she breathed, shocked white and golden happiness brightening her lime-green eyes. "My lion. Can it be true?"

His smile brightened. "I live, *qamari*. Again and again."

"Two years dead and still you shine as brightly as Ard's sun..."

"What happened to you, Takisha?" Jahmil cut in before Bakr and his compulsive flirting could get out of hand. "Where are the rest of the drakontes?"

"The short answer to both is *I don't know*," she said, her eyes still drinking in Bakr like a dehydrated elephant. Her jaw tightened and she turned to Jahmil. "I will give you the long answer after I fulfill my most recent blood oath."

"Takisha!"

"There is no time. See Thueban is taken care of. And get your ridiculous self out of this hyena's den and back to Ahmar where you belong!"

"You don't order me around," Jahmil spat. "Stand and answer."

She snatched the half-empty goblet of magic from his hand and drank it down in one massive gulp, then tossed the cup aside and let out a long, satisfied belch that echoed down the mountain.

"Just what I needed." She reached out and ran her fingers lightly over Bakr's chest as if confirming he was really there, then she dropped a petal of alyasimin and disappeared back through the veil, leaving nothing but the faint smell of sulfur in her wake.

CHAPTER EIGHTEEN

Ayelet

Ayelet and Balian snuck their way through the city, dodging between pools of shadow as they neared where the slavers had set up camp. Takisha flew overhead as a white-throated kingfisher, the feathers on her back and wings as blue-green and shimmering as her normal skin, and her beak and talons the same ruby-red as her hair.

Though Takisha had looked somewhat healed before she vanished, she had returned lustrously glowing. The power of Shihala. The more Ayelet learned about the wondrous place, with its leaves the color of dewy rainbows and its sky pure swaths of merging stars, the more a hardness filled her heart. It was a world Jahmil would never leave. He was devoted. To the people, yes, but also to the place.

Balian had been right about Edirne; the streets crawled with utter chaos. Raging fires still burned in corners, dark red against the boring black sky. And where flames did not lick up the thatched roofs of homes, torches lit the street to make it look like sunset, not the dead of night. Mothers wept. Children fled. And angry fathers with bloodshot eyes took up their sickles, not knowing whom to fight. Twice, they had seen a band of slavers patrolling the streets, looking for things—or people—to steal. And twice ice ran up Ayelet's spine and lingered on her lips.

"This is mad," Balian huffed as they squeezed into a small space between buildings. "You shouldn't be here."

"As you've said a thousand times already."

"And I'll say it a thousand more."

The crowd of shadows that they hid from passed, and Ayelet tumbled back out into the street to get away from Balian's pestering. Then a voice rang from around the corner, too familiar to be of comfort, that of an old friend she had never wanted to see again. She scooted back, her heels catching the hems of her dress as she crawled behind a barrel of musty grain.

Kadri appeared at the end of the street, barking orders at her men with Nadir on her heels.

"Quickly," she hissed, kicking an abandoned palanquin out of her way.

Behind her, a rough, wooden wagon creaked through the narrow streets. Row after row of bottled wisps were piled high upon each other, the bed so full, three men on each end were required to move it. Even then, their muscles strained, and the highest bottles teetered to and fro, pulling anxiously against their tethers.

"If you allow those *kahrolası* slavers to steal our magic without paying," Kadri growled, "I will enslave you myself to make up the debt."

The group rolled closer until the wheel of the wagon sank into the muddy road. Their progress halted as the slurping muck sucked the wheels down farther. Takisha, still in bird form, alighted on the tallest corked jar, trilling deeply. Ayelet couldn't help but agree. The number of wisps on that cart alone was absurd. Had capturing all that magic been what quelled the mountain and put the eimlaq back to rest? Or had it wandered off to crush another city, the jars of magic a mere drip of its massive stores?

Kadri seethed and threw her arms up in the air. "We survived the teeth of an awakened giant to be slowed by wet dirt? The irony is laughable." She kicked the barrel Ayelet hid behind, sending her heart into her throat. "I shall kill the spy who misinformed us. There was to be magic at those ruins under the half phase of the moon, not a murderous beast."

"Patience," Nadir said in his gruff voice. "We gathered more magic than we thought possible even without your *little instrument*."

Kadri huffed dramatically and leaned her back against the barrel, propping herself up on her elbows. The tips of her beaded and frizzy hair spilled over the top. Ayelet prayed Balian would take her lead and not reveal himself.

"If she had just waited three days…" Kadri complained. "After yesterday's disaster, Köle will rip the flesh from our bones if we miss a shipment. He's been using up magic like it is but grass in the field."

Ayelet felt as though she had plunged into the frigid depths of the northern sea. Köle. Icicles filled her heart, all stabbing inward. Her fears had been confirmed. The people who had taken Serap were not just the usual moralless, degenerate wastes of humankind that made up the slavers—they were pure evil. The last twitching breath of someone dying in pain. The cold chuckle of cruelty one feels in their heart when misfortune has finally ended them. This was her former master, Köle. And now, he had magic. She gasped, and Kadri quieted.

Then Balian burst from the crack behind her. "Kadri," he crooned, "I thought I heard you. I figured you'd be about, capitalizing on everyone's distress."

Kadri pulled herself up, and the beads of her hair disappeared from Ayelet's view. "Ballık? No, Stalian was it?" Kadri asked, her voice half-mocking and entirely serious.

"Balian," he grinned widely, not missing a beat. "Ayelet's *nişanlı.*"

Fiancé? Ayelet stifled the sound of her choking. The absurdity of his claim grounded her once more in the present.

"You tease," Kadri said. "Ayelet will settle for no one and no place. That is part of her poisonous charm."

"*Yok canım,*" Balian tsked. "You underestimate my charm."

Kadri's voice could cut through ice. "I'm not sure I do."

"She is done with her games. No more hide and seek. I am enough for her to stay."

Ayelet heard the sorrow in his words, nearly imperceptible. But she could not linger on that, for he had given his signal for her to run—*hide and seek*—just as he did when they were young.

It seemed reckless to run when Kadri stood less than a yard away. No, it *was* reckless. She refused to budge.

"Where is she, then?" Kadri asked, her words smooth as silk and soaked in oil. "Your *nişanlı?*"

Takisha glided over from the jars and onto the awning above Ayelet's head. Her blackened eyes peered down at her past the wood. She chirped expectantly.

"By the southern gates," Balian lied. "Trying to recruit people for the cause you would not help her with."

"She told you of that?" Nadir said, breaking his silence. "Did she tell you what she was up to?"

"Does the breeze inform the rock which way it will blow? Ayelet is a free spirit, she does not tell me much of anything."

Nadir grunted. Takisha chirped once more, her head bobbing in the direction of an alleyway across from Ayelet.

"I thought you said she did not play games anymore," Kadri said, still fishing.

"Ah." Balian chuckled. "Freedom is never a game, queen. Though perhaps she should trust her partners more and go when they tell her to."

Ayelet grimaced. He pushed her to go. He pushed her to stay. Pushing, pushing. Always pushing. He had no right. But Takisha chirped once more, dipping her head to the right over and over. She trusted Balian as far as she could throw her slipper. But Takisha was different. Maybe Shihala still clouded her mind, or maybe Jahmil had been right about the eyes of the djinn, but Ayelet was beginning to trust her. She had returned, after all, to honor her oath.

Ayelet pressed her thumb to her head to ward against the Evil Eye and sprinted into the streets.

"Ayelet!" Kadri cried over the pelter of her feet.

She did not stop, shimmying between the wagon and the stone wall in the direction Takisha led. A torrent of yelling broke out behind her, and she heard Balian cry with pain. She did not stop running. From Balian and the slavers, she never would. The guilt only made her run faster.

Takisha appeared, gliding just ahead and leading the way. Then one of Kadri's men broke free from the narrow streets and rushed toward her. She hastened her pace, but the lopsided run of only one boot slowed her progress. He grabbed for her shawl, grazing the muslin with his thick fingers.

Takisha swooped around and whistled low, but Ayelet shook her head. She was asking if this was the battle to fight, Ayelet was sure of it. And despite the disgusting pant of the brute's breath and the certainty that if he laid his hands on her, he would beat her with his heavy fists, she could not take the risk. There was a much bigger battle to fight ahead, and she would get Takisha's help for only one.

She skidded into an adjoining street filled with emptied market stalls. Strips of fabric littered the dirt road in bursts of colors like the jasmine field, only much less bright. Her whole world was much less bright since she had left Jahmil. Like a sunny day turned overcast with rain that never comes.

The brute, at last, achieved his goal, yanking her dress back in a snarling knot. She swung around and punched him in the eye. His head jerked back, but he did not let go. She had only enraged him. He grabbed her right arm, his fingers pressing into her flesh hard enough to bruise bone. She swung her left fist in an uppercut so his jaw clamped together with an audible snap.

This time he released her, pulling back with a mouthful of blood. She spun and ran, but he was on her again, this time tackling her to the ground. He grinned and licked his bloody lips, revealing glimpses of blackened teeth. Then he pinned her arms down and grabbed at her clothes with feverish perverseness.

Takisha swooped overhead, dive-bombing the man's face. He cried and fell back, swatting at a being he would never catch. Ayelet squirmed out from his hold and rammed her heel into his groin. He doubled over, crying like an infant brought fresh into the world. Ayelet wiped the sweat from her eyes and scooted out of his reach.

Takisha was not so kind. She swooped, again and again, pecking the man's lips and eyes so they bled. In the flurry of blue-flamed commotion, Ayelet swore she saw the bird's talons lengthen and sharpen and its eyes glow with fire. Even its crimson beak elongated to become a mini spear, sharp and meant for eviscerating. Only when he lay utterly destroyed, his hands still holding his crotch and his face streaming with bloody tears and flecks of flesh did Takisha leave him be.

Ayelet stared at the carnage. At the kingfisher and its radiant wings. What being had she made a deal with? Fear shot through her body, cold and quick. Her one battle was over, wasted on this *piç*. She spat to the side and wiped her mouth. If she couldn't even take on one hired man, how could she take on twenty? Or fifty? She covered her eyes and moaned.

Takisha alighted upon the ground, hopping on little ruby-red feet. She nudged Ayelet's ankle, just below the "K" shaped scar she got when she was seven. She nudged her again and then chirped. The despair in Ayelet's chest eased.

"Thank you," she said, tempted to brush her finger over the little bird's feathers. She refrained, certain the hulking form of Takisha would punch her in the nose if she tried.

Feet pummeled the earth behind her, and she turned, exhausted at the thought of another fight when so many more lay ahead.

Balian pelted around the corner, his eyes wide under a purpling shiner and his lips quirked up in a grin. "Incoming," he cried and spun on his heels. He waited for the sound of grunting breaths, then kicked his leg up so it landed on the brute's chest just as he rounded the corner.

The man stumbled back, the breath knocked from his lungs. Balian kicked him again in the stomach so he landed on the earth. The man groaned and did not get up.

"Come," Balian said and wiped back the slick hair that stuck to his forehead. "We're almost there."

Takisha took to flight, and Ayelet brushed herself off before finding her feet. They jogged down increasingly dark and filthy streets, once more hiding at any sign of trouble. Then Balian put a finger to his lips and eased around the corner of a dingy storefront with ratty curtains. Ayelet followed as Takisha swooped overhead to check around back. She trilled twice. Two slavers. And three more Ayelet could see through the roughly cut window.

Takisha flew back, morphing into her warrior self in a puff of white smoke. She didn't even wince, drawing her shoulders back in a sign of strength as the mist faded and her impressive and bare body revealed itself. Balian blushed and reached into his satchel. Pulling out her heavy armor and leather gear, he kept his eyes averted, then dropped them at her feet and turned.

Ayelet smiled sadly. While Takisha's presence increased their odds of getting Serap out alive, it did nothing to improve her fortunes. Köle would know she was here. She didn't know how, but he always did, just as a bee knows the way to its hive. If he was here, he probably felt her now. The thought terrified her and ate at her mind. Balian had been right. She should not have come. She should have cared only for herself, for that was all she was good at.

"Ready, little human?" Takisha asked, laying a comforting hand on Ayelet's shoulders.

Ayelet felt the thrum of magic in the iridescent fingers that now offered her strength. Good idea or not, she was here and she would fight.

She nodded. "Let us save Serap."

CHAPTER NINETEEN

JAHMIL

IF TAKISHA WEREN'T HIS cousin, Jahmil would have had her flogged. After leaving him thinking she was dead for half a month, she turns up and refuses to explain anything before popping back out of existence.

Maybe he ought to flog her anyway.

Fury boiled in his blood at her evasiveness, yet he could not help the fact that he trusted her. Even after everything she had done or failed to do. He didn't know which because she had told him nothing. What was she hiding, and who had she sworn a blood oath to? She was *his* sworn commander. It felt like a betrayal.

Takisha was right about one thing, though. He had lingered in Orkeshi long enough. He had to get back to Ahmar, to hear the intel from all his commanders and brief them on all he had learned. More than anything else, he had to find out the truth of the barren desert the Vespar homeland had become. What had happened to it, and more importantly, could it happen somewhere else?

The medicine woman who had given him the cobalt potion worked her wonders on Thueban. Given enough time, Shihala may have healed him on its own, but Jahmil did not have days to wait.

When the massive drakonte was well enough to fly, Jahmil said his goodbyes to Bakr and the guerillas. It hurt to leave his old friend again so quickly after learning that he lived, without any time to spend catching up and just being alive together. But it was a good pain, a pain of knowing that such things might wait in the future.

Thueban could have carried a dozen djinn on his muscular back, but when Jahmil offered, no one was prepared to leave.

"It's too late for that," Bakr said, his eyes as playful as his smile as he gazed up at Jahmil, perched on Thueban's back. "And don't you dare come back here. I don't want to see you again until King Jahmil calls us to celebrate his victory at Karzusan Palace!"

"*Ya'ish almalik Jahmil!*" They chanted, as Thueban reared up on his hindquarters and shot up into the sky like a cannon. The snake's cry cut the air, the wind rushing over them in hot, hurried gasps.

King Jahmil. He'd always known he would be king someday, provided he lived that long, but to hear the words felt strange. He felt certain his mother would not be well pleased by their sound.

The *Darab Altibana* had risen in the western sky, a splash of stars so thick it looked like a stream of milk spread over crystal. It lighted his ascent into the heavens, Thueban's scales shimmering like fire and his massive wings stretching twenty feet in either direction so they blotted out the light of the Fourth Moon. The Vespars would be able to see the massive drakonte, of course. And they would have heard its ear-splitting cry, which carried like thunder. They would know someone from Shihala had come and spoken to the guerillas. They would make guesses about what information had been relayed, what supplies may have been given.

Let them writhe.

Thueban flew high above the clouds, well out of range of any possible attack. The Vespars had their own flying forces—large bats that could carry a single rider over short distances, or spear ships and fortifications with their blood-red claws. But they were no match for a drakonte and could not reach the clouds on the wing even without a rider, let alone sail above them so high that ice licked at their bellies.

From such a high vantage, Jahmil saw only the faint sparkle of lakes and rivers, the churning mists of the mountains. He caught a glimpse of wide, dead-looking earth to the south and realized the forest of Diyu had been clear-cut, leaving barren death where verdant life had once thrived. Logic told him to investigate, to fly closer and gauge the extent of the damage, but his heart couldn't take it. He didn't want to know.

While it had always had a small population, in terms of land, Shihala was one of the largest of the Nine Kingdoms. And while Thueban was a strong flyer, he was not especially swift. He glided lazily on high currents, his body waving like a whip to take full advantage of the wind. At such great heights, he was able to soar by keeping his wings outstretched while only occasionally flapping.

Their destination was Ain Khuleel, a city on the border of Vespar-occupied Shihala and Ahmar, where Takisha and the drakonte had fought the fateful battle that sent them into oblivion. For weeks Jahmil had been trying to find answers, and no one—not his system of spies and messengers, nor his moles in Qadira's army, nor Takisha herself—had satisfactorily answered a single question. So he would go to the city and find the truth for himself, come hell, or fire, or death. He was finished asking the same question and getting nothing but empty wind as a reply.

Jahmil rested against Thueban, absorbing the heat of his fiery body as frozen winds whipped around him in circles. He watched the slow shift of clouds in the sea of stars and moons. His mind drifted from place and time, away from the moment into something that resembled eternity as much as it did oblivion.

The notes of her lyre filled his mind and dispersed throughout his body like ink in water. They filled him to the brim while leaving him empty. The old song she had played. The last song, which he had heard so many times. Which he had played himself when nights were lighter and the future teemed with possibility. Taken by the wind, he sang so only he could hear:

Your eyes have a voice.
Such nervous fragility.
Eternity in every breath.
How the first summer would open,
leaf by leaf.

With a skillful touch,

deeper than all roses.

No one, not even the rain,

has such hands as yours.

If any actual tears formed in his eyes, they were whipped away by the icy wind before they could fall.

He felt the shift in gravity as Thueban began his descent. They landed in a field of purple grass and tall black brambles with spines as long as a man's arm and sharp as needles. Thueban lowered his head and Jahmil rolled off, landing on his bare feet on the stringy grass.

Bakr had offered him shoes and a coat, but Jahmil did not want to take anything from them. They needed every stitch of fabric, every inch of leather. He kept the rough shirt and pants they provided and gave them the boots and leathers he had stolen from the Vespars, not only because he knew they could find a good use for them, but because he could not show himself in public wearing Vespar-made clothing. Better to be filthy and barefoot. Better to be naked than caught dead dressed as the enemy in a place like Ain Khuleel, a border city that constantly suffered their assaults.

The city bloomed before him, its walls unbreached. Unblemished. He had heard no report from the battle that supposedly had taken place there, but had assumed it had been horrific. Nothing but a rain of brimstone would have succeeded in defeating the drakontes. And yet the building on the horizon looked freshly hewn of new stone.

Perhaps Thueban had taken them to the wrong place.

He turned to the snake. "This can't be right."

Thueban hissed, his huge purple tongue twitching. He pushed Jahmil with his sharp, triangular nose and he stumbled.

"Oh, calm down, you sensitive thing." Jahmil laid his hand on the tip of the snake's nose. "I'm only saying, look at this city. It's perfect."

Again, Thueban let loose a long, disapproving hiss and pushed him forward, harder this time. He staggered, catching himself from tumbling into the deadly brambles. The sleeve of his shirt caught on a thorn and was ripped clean off, opening a line of blood on his bicep.

"Look what you've done, you fool snake!" He snatched the sleeve from where it hung in the brambles. He turned it over in his hands, but that was all there was.

Panic gripped his heart. Ayelet's scarf—everything he had left of her—was missing.

He fell to his knees in the sticky grass to search for it, the flash of white fire from his eyes illuminating every detail.

Nothing. Bakr's people would not have been fool enough to have taken it and discarded it, thinking it had no meaning. Would they?

Hands clenched into fists, a scream broke from his lips enough to shake not only his body but innocent wisps playing in the breeze. Panting, he touched his arm where the scarf had been, then froze at the strange texture of his skin.

Jahmil opened his eyes and lifted his arm to examine it. The scarf was gone, but wrapped around the upper part of his forearm—exactly where he had tied the scarf—were the twisted serifs of a black tattoo. He had never seen the design, let alone seen it etched on his own skin. But he knew what it was. As well as he knew his own name, he knew what it was. And what it meant.

The Covenant of Shihala, a physical manifestation of the bond between two souls. Not a marriage, nothing so common and bureaucratic. Not even a promise. A rare symbol, and unequivocally permanent. The power of Shihala had put it there and no force of man, djinn, or angels could remove it. It happened when a soul met its partner—those souls that have partners.

Jahmil narrowed his eyes at the black markings. They were still shifting like shallow rivers on his skin, searching for their final path. The writing meant nothing. Not yet.

"No," he breathed, grabbing at the design. "No, Shihala. You don't understand."

She had made a mistake, he was certain. As much as his heart secretly yearned for her, he could no more enter into the Covenant with Ayelet than he could throw off the yoke of his position. And what would Qadira say when she saw the mark of another woman etched into his skin?

It had to be a mistake.

Even as he thought it, he repented his arrogance. Shihala did not make mistakes.

Though his heart still thrummed, he ran his fingertips over the rough marks, feeling their movement. "What do You know that I do not?" he whispered.

There would be no answer. Not from Shihala, the silent mistress of all knowings. The undercurrent which rules the lives of all Her people yet shows Herself to no one. Shihala had understood what it meant to him, even if he did not fully understand. After all, what was Ayelet? A whisper of sunlight on moon-kissed shores. He hardly knew her. They had exchanged a few words and shared but one night together.

An immaculate kiss of fire.

What did he have of her but memories of music? Eyes that saw what no one else had ever bothered to look for? Fragility like a fresh summer bud, and a skillful touch. Kindness, or pity.

What did he know of her, or she of him? No more than the clouds can know of the moon. No more than the sun can describe the stars.

But here it was, his hopeless dream, written on his skin as if the scar on his heart were not enough.

By Allah, why had he let her go? He didn't remember anymore. Some misplaced sense of nobility? Or mere resignation?

No. He had let her go because he feared what may have happened had he held on. To her, to himself. To everyone who looked to him with hope in their eyes and cried *long live the king.*

His eyes burned, so he closed them and sank deeper on his knees in the prickly grass. A warm wind rushed over him, and he breathed in the scent of charcoal and silence.

The tattoo under his fingers pulsed with his heart. Not in time, but in harmony. And then a whisper rose all around him, cocooning him in a sound that chilled the heat of his blood and stopped all music dead. Gentle and soft, a whisper. And yet there was so much pain in it.

A child's pain. Weeping in darkness, hopeless and alone.

He looked up, searching for the owner of the voice, but there was only him and Thueban. The city stood on the horizon, indifferent and much too far away for any such gentle, broken noise to be heard from within its walls.

He lifted the tattoo to his eyes and the sound intensified, rising in volume and clarity. A message from Shihala. A message about Ayelet.

Jahmil closed his eyes and focused on it, trying to listen beyond the dissonance into something deeper.

An echo. The smell of iron. Whatever the message meant, he could feel the silks of the veil wrapped around him. It was coming from beyond the limits of Qaf. The human world.

Was Ayelet in trouble? He wouldn't doubt it.

Jahmil snapped his eyes to Thueban. "Fly to the City of Pearls, to my mother. I will meet you."

The drakonte gave an ear-splitting whine of disapproval.

His eyes flashed as he straightened to stand. "You think because I suffer Takisha's insolence, I will endure yours?" His fists ignited with fire. "Go. Now."

Thueban stared at him for a few more moments with his impassive, unreadable eyes of sunset, then groaned sadly and shook his head. He reared back and rocketed up into the air, leaving Jahmil alone in a field of thorns.

The sobs radiated through the tattoo, touching his ears and every other piece of him. He closed his eyes and fell through the veil like a stone through wet paper into Ard. The Covenant guided him through the white namelessness that rested between worlds, and he came out the other side crouched and quiet. Ready.

Dull pain radiated through his skin. Jahmil opened his eyes.

He was surrounded by curtains of irons—walls and even a ceiling fashioned of thick bars of the horrible metal. Only the ground was safe, soft dirt under his feet. He rested his fingertips in the safety of the filthy sand.

Usually, when he came into the human world, his eyes would sting with light, but it was painfully dark in this place. A few thin strips of sunlight peeked through holes in the walls where time or rot had worn away a patch of adobe that clung to thick wooden beams.

Weeping reached his ears, and he turned, his heart filled with the dread of seeing Ayelet in such a place, yet hopeful for her all the same. Instead he found himself looking at a small girl locked in an iron cage. She sat in the corner of the small cell, pressed against the bars with her knees drawn to her chest. She was clothed in rags, her black hair hanging like a dingy curtain over her face. The scent of blood wafted at him from her corner, as well as the sting of salt.

Who was she, he wondered. Again his fingers went to the Covenant, where the lines were swirling more quickly than before, searching for their final path. He was here for Ayelet, that was all he knew for certain. Shihala was challenging him to choose his path.

I have lost someone dear to me, Ayelet had said. *The only person dear to me.*

Jahmil's eyes swept up and down the hall. There were four cells in the space, but all sat empty except for the girl. The smell assaulted his senses, even as the throb of iron burned like hot sand. And worst of all, the sound of the child weeping. The pain in her voice echoed through his head until his temples were pulsing. Someone so small, shivering in the dark with such truths already carved on her bones. Ayelet had called her Serap.

There was no way into the cell but through the iron, and no way out. But he had to get to her, even as the world fell apart around him. The suffering of a kingdom set against the nightmares of one child, and yet there was no clear winner. Neither could be tolerated. And if this was Ayelet's dear one...

He knew that his natural form was alarming, if not terrifying, to most humans. He had to choose a better form before revealing himself.

Jahmil closed his eyes and took a few slow breaths. His hands and feet became paws, his ears lengthening into tall triangles. Thick black fur sprung from every inch of his skin, and he shrank. His clothes fell away as a swishy, slinky tail grew.

The only part of him he could not change was his eyes. No magic would alter them, which was half the reason Jahmil preferred to appear as a cat in the human world, should he allow himself to be seen at all. Everyone already expected cats to have ethereal eyes.

The agate circle he wore pierced through one ear had stayed with him as a cat, which was odd enough. Jahmil pawed through the pile of clothes on the floor until he found his father's ring, then fiddled with it a bit until he was able to slip it onto his tiny, furry wrist.

The bars would still be a tight squeeze, but like walking across hot coals with bare feet—the pain would be quick, the damage minimal.

Jahmil announced himself with a meow and leaped between the bars. Heat like acid licked at his skin, singing the fur on his sides. His back leg touched the bar as he pulled through, burning so quickly that it blistered. He fell into the dirt and rolled back and forth, searching for any comfort.

The child gasped and sat up quickly. There were bruises on her face, her large brown eyes red from tears. Jahmil sat down and scratched his ear, then tilted his head and meowed.

The fear in her eyes faded, replaced by confusion. "How did you get in here, kitty?"

He flicked his tail a few times and slinked closer.

"You should go," she said, her gaze lifting along a wooden beam in one corner to a small opening in the ceiling. "I would leave if I were you."

Tiny, trembling fingers reached for him. He pressed his face against her dirty palm. When her fingers touched his fur, she giggled even through her thick tears.

He hopped up in her lap and pushed his face against hers a few times until she scratched his ears. When he started to purr, she wrapped her arms around him and squeezed a little too tight. Her tears redoubled, and she cried into his fur, hugging him and stroking him. He purred and rubbed his little face against her chin, catching every tear that fell.

After some time, she gained control over her crying and wiped her nose. "My name is Serap. Do you have a name?"

So it was her—Ayelet's dear one. She had said the girl had been taken by slavers and that had been enough, but he had never expected this. This iron cell looked more like a prison for a murderer than quarters for a slave.

He wished he could speak when he was in animal form. It would have made things simpler. But he didn't want to frighten her—not by appearing as his ordinary self, and certainly not by shapeshifting in front of her.

"I'm going to call you Meyan," she said, patting the soft fur between his ears, "because you're black and you're sweet."

He licked her palm, then rolled over her hand so she would pet him again. She giggled, exactly as he had hoped. He climbed up on her lap again and pushed his front paws against her chest and leaned back to look at her face.

"Oh, Meyan! What pretty eyes you have."

He meowed and hopped from her lap to the floor, scanning for a way out. The heat from the iron was already making him dizzy, stealing the strength from his weary bones.

"I've looked, there isn't a way out," said Serap, slowly pulling herself up onto shaky feet. "Besides, even if we did get out of this room, we couldn't get past the guards. Well, maybe you could."

He wanted to ask her how many guards there were, how many fellow prisoners, where they were taking her, and what kind of work she was expected to perform. What had happened to her since being taken by these monsters?

"Meow," he said.

Serap bent over and scooped him up into her arms. "Where *did* you come from, Meyan?" She walked to the bars, her huge brown eyes scanning for breaks in the wall or a hole in the floor. Of course, there was nothing. He'd slipped into this prison from another world, and that seemed the only logical way out.

Jahmil climbed up onto Serap's shoulder and put his paws on the dingy cream and purple scarf wrapped over her hair.

"Deh!" she cried, giggling. "Stop it, Meyan. What are you doing?"

He got his claws into the fabric and hopped down, taking the scarf with him. She yelped as it was torn free from her hair, bringing a few strays along with it.

"No." She wagged her finger at him then lunged playfully. "Bad kitty. Give that back."

He skipped to one corner of the room, where a large, exposed wooden beam held up a weak spot in the ceiling. Biting the fabric in his tiny white fangs, he used his claws to climb the beam and hooked the fabric over a rusted nail, careful to keep his twitching nose from touching the iron.

"Bad kitty," she said again, reaching for the scarf.

He rushed to her and rubbed against her ankle, meowing insistently.

"You want to play, is that it?" Serap grabbed the end of the scarf and waved it in front of his face.

He snatched up the scarf and carried it across the room, letting the fabric rest on the ground so it formed a small, billowy triangle with the earth and the wood. He meowed again, gesturing with his head for her to go through.

Serap grabbed the scarf and waved it in front of him again. "Silly kitty."

Jahmil sighed and batted for it, but she kept pulling it back.

"Meow," he cried and leaped up, snatching the end from her hand. He dragged it back to the other side of the room to make a triangle then looked up at her with pleading eyes and nodded his head toward the opening. "Meow?"

"You have got to be the weirdest cat I have ever met." She looked at her scarf, then back at him. "I don't know this game."

He meowed and pushed at her ankle with his nose. He lowered down on his belly and crawled across the floor, trying to show her.

"You want me to crawl under it?"

"Meow!" He hopped up and did a quick backflip.

She laughed and shook her head. "Why?"

He pushed against her ankle again, then got up on his hind legs, front paws reaching up. Begging.

Again, she did a double take, then wrinkled her nose at him. "You're not an ordinary cat, are you?"

"Meow."

She bit her lip nervously, then got down on her knees. She swallowed hard and set her hands on the dirt. He scurried closer and hopped onto her back, leaning his face over one of her shoulders.

"I don't know why," she said, "but I trust you."

Serap crawled under the scarf. He dug his claws into the fabric of her dress, holding tight to her with might and magic, as a cloud of white mist encircled them.

CHAPTER TWENTY

AYELET

The first several times Takisha cracked a bone or ran her sword through a man with an unmistakable gurgling sound, Ayelet's stomach twisted. A slave for six years, she had grown accustomed to the sounds of misery that lay in the reedy thrash of whips and the constant whimpering of abused persons: women, children, and men alike. Horrendous, but familiar. This was different. The cacophony of battle was foreign to her, and she now understood why men who returned from war came back with glazed eyes and belligerent tempers.

Was a lifetime of battles why Jahmil's temper ran so hot?

Even so, there was a rhythm to fighting she hadn't known existed. A silent drum everyone moved to in time, not knowing if they would live or die. Ayelet heard the beating, too; her muscles knew what to do while her mind pulled back from the horror. It was a heavy, incessant sound that overcame the sense of humanity and called to the primal.

Their advance progressed easily through the first layers of the slavers' defenses. With Takisha rejuvenated, she could remain invisible, slicing men as if from nowhere. She was far too good a tactician and void enough of pride to forgo such an immediate advantage, even if it was a slaughter. It so terrified Balian that he could only walk from one hallway to the next, his jaw agape and his eyes painfully wide. But as they worked their way deeper into the complex of buildings, a veil of wisps descended, becoming thicker and thicker.

Soon, men began to cry out, reciting prayers from the Quran or crossing chests with ornate hand movements to ward against the red-haired *seytan* approaching them. For her part, Takisha seemed to enjoy this much more. Her face had changed from rote and bored, if not slightly pained, to animated. Her grin could scare a wolf from its dinner if her incredible size and bulging muscles did not do the trick.

"What exactly are we fighting?" Takisha asked as she held a man by his hair and plunged her sword into his chest with a screaming squish. "Why can they see me when I haven't revealed myself?"

"I don't know," Ayelet answered. "But the air is heavy with magic. Would that aid them in seeing past your enchantment?"

Takisha pulled her sword from the man, leaving him to crumple, and sniffed at the air. "You're right, little human. The magic of Qaf is nearly as thick here as at home, only chaotic, unusable, and unformed. That may be what's allowing these pathetic humans to see me. Can you see all magic?" She looked impressed.

"I wouldn't know if there's magic I haven't seen. But djinn and wisps have yet to leave my sight since I was given the gift of my lyre."

"Really?" Balian asked, still dazed from Takisha's prowess. "You never told me you could see djinn." His eyes refocused with a watery look of betrayal.

"I got my lyre after you chose to stay in Edirne and left me to wander on my own. I did not see it as your business to know after that."

He glowered at her, twirling his knife in his hand.

"Maybe I should have taken a better look at your instrument." Takisha frowned.

Ayelet placed a hand protectively over her pouch, a movement Takisha's sharp eyes registered.

The stalwart cries of suicidal men approached rapidly from a heavy door on the right. Takisha's intense gaze swept away from Ayelet's face, and she released a breath she hadn't realized she held.

"Our fight continues. How many more rooms must we coat in their blood?" Takisha sounded irritated, anxious, though not for fear of winning the fight.

Ayelet was sure she worried for Jahmil. For those she cared about who were lost. The same worry threaded itself through Ayelet, making it painful to breathe. Jahmil. Serap. The worry intensified, snaking its way inside her heart and filling it up with pulp. Even if Jahmil returned safely to his kingdom, and even if she was able to free Serap and hold her once more in her arms, there was no future with either. She hadn't told Balian or Takisha, but if Köle let them in far enough to save the girl, it was only because he understood what Ayelet was offering. Serap would leave. She would stay. A life for a life. A homecoming.

"I'd say one or two more rooms through this door to make our way to the stairs," Balian said and shrugged. "Then we must decide if we go up or down and hope to find Serap."

Takisha scratched at her smooth, rounded cheek. "While I do love hurling men out of windows, I find evil lurks closer to the ground."

Ayelet nodded, memories and logic warring in her head. Balian cast a worried gaze her way, and she forced herself to smile, though each time it felt impossibly harder. "Yes, as I recall, they kept the worst of their actions in the dark where no one but them could see."

That was not all they kept in the dark.

Balian twirled his knife once more and then stuck it in the leather sleeve on his belt. The grunts of men grew louder, and soon they would arrive, but his eyes were on her. "You should stay here, guard the stairs. Takisha and I can go farther."

Ayelet widened her temporary smile. "I'm sorry, Balian, but your chance to come to my rescue passed long ago. There is nothing you can do to save me."

And if the wisps were any indication, she knew what she said was true. The air had always felt thick around the curtain of red that hid her master's shadows; now she knew why. Perhaps Köle had always been collecting magic. Using it to abuse and warp. It would explain why whenever a wisp showed up, he soon followed. Either way, the sludge-like whirl of misty wind could only mean one thing. Köle had just been here. Perhaps he was here even now.

Balian's anxious eyes turned ugly and hurt.

"No more talking," Takisha boomed. "I haven't any more time to spare on this maze of infidels. We all go down together and kill anything we find that isn't a child."

She kicked the door down, splintering pieces of wood that shattered like daggers into the men behind. Their boisterous chants turned into calls of alarm, and the small group of slavers regrouped on the far side of the room. They huddled with swords pointed out and a small, rounded cane shield in front.

Takisha stymied Ayelet's advance, pushing her and Balian behind her with one gruff shove. She brought her clenched fist to the front, and a lime-green light brighter than any sun flashed into the room. The men cried out as their corneas burned. When the surge of magic faded, they lay on the ground clawing at the floorboards and mumbling in frantic whispers that they were blind.

Ayelet worked past them, almost pitying their pathetic writhing. But she was more concerned with Takisha's brazen use of magic. The warrior was no longer holding back, even being reckless. If her zeal to return to Jahmil was enough to waste her strength, then his position was far worse than Ayelet had thought.

They arrived at the stairs, light filtering in shades of orange from the floor above and an eating blackness shadowing the way to the basement. Balian jumped to the front, insisting that he go first. Ayelet let him. She had no desire to descend into her nightmares.

Takisha snorted behind her, rubbing her nose with the back of her blood-speckled hand. "It reeks of iron in that pit."

"It reeks of iron on your hand." Ayelet poked a dried spot of blood.

"Not like this, little human." She showed no fear, but her eyes were narrowed and her mouth grim.

"Stay," Ayelet said, bolstering her voice so it sounded like a command. "Most of the men have already come to block the way. If Balian and I need help, we will call. Then you can barrel down and cut off more sheads."

Takisha eyed her defiantly, but already the tension in her face began to ease. "One word and I'm down there. So don't let *qut mukhif* squeal at a rat."

"I heard that," Balian mumbled from the dark below.

Ayelet smiled, and it almost felt real. "No guarantees."

She took a few steps into the dark and found Balian waiting for her. What little light filtered down reflected on his serious eyes. Only Jahmil's had ever looked grimmer. But Balian did not fight her this time, and in a moment of weakness, she grabbed the back of his shirt and let him lead her down the stairs.

Murky bursts of shadow and light crossed her mind as dark memories descended. It did not matter that this was not the same prison Köle had kept her in; the feeling was the same, like a hand of cold fire reaching down her throat and crushing her heart into coal. The wisps were thinner down here, only a few circling overhead. Silence held the air in captivity, and she feared even breathing would manifest a monster.

The dungeon—for what else would she call such an iron-shackled place?—consisted of metal coverings and bars, with only the dirt beneath her feet and a few slapdash wooden beams as the exception, and even they were smoothed to an ominous shine.

Balian put a finger to his lips in a completely unneeded warning. They crept forward and reached a split in the paths. Ayelet released his shirt and pushed him one way while she turned for the other. He shook his head fervently. She pushed him again with a glare, only tiptoeing down her hallway when she was sure he would not turn back. She did not want to be alone, but neither did Serap. *Inşallah*, the faster they searched the prison, the faster they would find her.

When they parted ways, the wisps stayed with her, swirling conspiratorially overhead. She reached up once to touch one, and the wisp pulled just out of reach. Then it reconsidered, twirling around her finger like mist around rocks at the bottom of a waterfall. She entered a section of cells, each dingier and more rusted than the last.

"Serap?" she tried to say, but it came out scratchy and misshapen. She cleared her throat and called again, "Serap?"

Dry quiet met her ears; not even the sound of gnawing rats whispered from the corners. She pushed on, one foot forced in front of the other and dragging through the dirt. Nothing. Each cell was ghostly empty through its narrow mottled bars. But why? Hadn't the slavers taken a fresh group of children just the night before? The cells should be teeming with whimpers and tearful, wide eyes.

Ayelet peered into each one as she passed, just in case a child hid in silence for fear of being beaten. Some cells held tufts of mangled hair while others held worse: red blood and a rotted green ooze pooled in the cracks. What had Köle been doing to the children in this place? He had always been an exceptionally cruel master, putting his captives through hellish bouts of bizarre torture. It was no wonder she had nightmares of his faceless cruelty commanding his hordes of same-faced monsters who laughed while she slept.

She shuddered so hard her bones hurt, and she turned from the wretched sight. When she reached the end of the row, she gasped.

A light purplish blue scarf with dingy ends draped from a beam to the floor. The same scarf Serap had worn every day since Ayelet had returned to Edirne and given it to her as a gift. She flung herself at the bars, straining as she reached inside.

"Serap? Serap!"

But no one answered. The wisps moved from her and blew around the thin fabric so the scarf's ragged ends brushed together in the breeze. Nothing. Again. No one hid beneath its frayed threads.

"Serap!" she screamed, not caring who or what heard in the heavens or earth below.

Balian tumbled into the other end of the hallway, tripping over himself as he hastened to her. Takisha was on his heels, squeezing herself close and ducking low, her uneasy eyes darting between Ayelet and the tangle of iron that could sear her flesh. When Balian's eyes lighted on Serap's scarf, he too threw himself against the metal stays.

"Where is she?" he flipped on Ayelet. "Where did they take her?"

"They're not here," Takisha said. "There's no way they can be. We've checked this dungeon, and I traversed the upstairs. There are no children here. Are you sure this was the right place?"

"I'm sure," Balian snapped. "That's her scarf right there." His trembling finger pointed to the patchwork of dingy creams and purples still fluttering with wisps. His extended hand morphed into a clenched fist. "They were not to move the children until tomorrow. That's what my source said. He swore on his life." Balian kicked the bars hard enough to break a toe. He seethed. "I will kill him."

"Where are they going?" Takisha asked. "Maybe we can ambush them?"

Balian dropped his hand to his side, his shoulders hunched. "I don't know."

"To the sea," Ayelet spoke just loud enough to hear above Balian's heavy breathing. "Köle will take them to the sea."

"Then let's go," Takisha urged, scooting carefully back the way they had come.

"Two dozen roads lead to the southern sea and two dozen more to the northern," Ayelet said, the very effort drawing the last of her strength. "We will never find her in time."

Ayelet sank, the dips and folds of her dress pooling in the space between her knees. All this work. All this running and death, and for what? She had been too late. Serap was gone. She was a failure, and her caring for the girl had done nothing at all to save her. *Nothing*. Caring for people never did. It only brought suffering. Köle had let her come this far just to take Serap away and watch her suffer.

Twice, Balian tried to raise her after his fits of fury subsided, but she would not move. She had lost everything. Had given everything—her dream of Jahmil and her path to freedom, she had even been willing to give her life—and it still wasn't enough.

Any physical pain she had ever endured paled in comparison to this.

Eventually, Takisha's patience thinned, and she hefted her over her shoulder and dragged her back to the light. It didn't matter. No amount of sun could reach her soul. She might as well have died.

CHAPTER TWENTY-ONE

JAHMIL

They arrived in his apartments in a flash of light sparked with silver. As his senses focused, he heard the girl making a deep keening sound, and his blood froze. Ayelet was special in so many ways. Perhaps he couldn't bring any other humans to Qaf. Had he hurt her?

He hopped down from her back, his cat tail swishing in concern. But as she lifted her face, he realized she wasn't crying or moaning in pain. She was laughing.

"*Oha*! Meyan!" She snatched him from the floor and hugged him close, her eyes dazzling at the suddenly luxurious surroundings. "You are not an ordinary cat at all!"

The sound of her giggles trickled into him like warm honey. No wonder Ayelet was taken with this girl.

"Where are we, Meyan? Is this where you live?"

He nodded, then wriggled out of her arms and scampered behind a lacquered changing screen in the corner. He shed his fur in a small pile on the carpet and quickly morphed into his own skin. Jahmil spat out the ring he'd been holding in his cheek and wiped it on a towel before shoving it back on his finger. Then he snatched a robe from a hook and pulled it on. When all six feet of him stepped out from behind the screen, Serap gasped and scurried back, tripping over bare little feet.

"Who are you?" she demanded.

"Do not be afraid, Serap," he said, approaching gingerly. "I won't hurt you."

She wrinkled her nose, gazing into his eyes. "Meyan?"

"I prefer Jahmil if you don't mind."

"You're a djinn."

He smiled and nodded slowly.

"What is going on? Why did you come get me from the prison? Why did you bring me here?" She wrapped her arms over her chest and stepped back until her ragged little frame was pressed against a wall. "Are you going to eat me?"

"Curse the fool who started that rumor." Chuckling, he shook his head. "I'm a friend of Ayelet."

"Ayelet?" Her face brightened. "You know Ayelet? Is she here?"

"No. But I will take you back to her soon."

A hundred emotions played across the little girl's eyes in such quick succession. He could see them like shades of shadow, but without the aid of djinn colors, it was impossible to keep track. "What is this place?"

He looked back and forth at his bedroom, realizing how strange it must seem to her. The massive bed draped in silk, the lush white and cerulean carpets, the pool of crystal water, and chandeliers of starlight hanging from the vaulted ceiling.

It was strange to him, too.

"This is my apartment." He shrugged. "And you, Anisa Serap, are my honored guest."

He lifted a porcelain bell from a table and rang it. A moment later, a woman hurried into the room. She was one of his few personal servants, a Shihalan, who oversaw his household. A smile burst across her face when she saw him.

"Prince Jahmil!" she cried, rushing past Serap as if she were not there. "You're home! I did not see you come in."

"Waiola, will you please draw a bath for my young friend? And have some food prepared, something fit for human consumption. She also needs a healing draught."

Waiola looked over at Serap and sneered as if finding something a dog left behind on the bottom of her shoe. "Yes, *Amiri*, but I do not understand. Who is this human child?"

She said the word human with so much disdain that it made him chuckle.

"Never mind that. Just do as I ask."

Bowing, Waiola headed for the door, but then she hesitated and turned slowly. "Your mother has been searching for you ceaselessly. She asked to be informed the moment you arrived."

He suppressed a groan. "I need some time to compose myself and will call upon the queen in my own time."

"Yes, *Amiri*. Except..."

As she trailed off, he narrowed his eyes impatiently.

"Queen Zalika bade me remind you, in case you forgot..." She exhaled a nervous little breath. "Though, of course, you would not forget..."

"Out with it."

"The rehearsal for your wedding ceremony is in one hundred degrees, *Amiri*."

He groaned and waved her out. Of course, he had forgotten. How could he be expected to remember such a pointless bit of pageantry weighed against everything else in his mind?

When Waiola left the room, shutting the door firmly behind her, Serap took a few quick steps closer to him. "*Amir?*" She scrunched her nose at the Arabic word, then continued in Turkish. "Did she just call you a prince?"

He rubbed his eyebrows with his thumb and forefinger. "That's right."

Serap folded her arms and jutted out one bony hip. "How do you know Ayelet, exactly? I thought she would have told me if she knew a djinn prince that could transform himself into a cat." She looked a little wounded, as if Ayelet had betrayed her.

"Our acquaintance is a fairly recent development. I'm sure she planned to tell you when she saw you next."

He went down on his knees to look at her straight. She had a ring of bruised red flesh around one eye and a cut on her lip. Her cheeks were sunken with hunger, her limbs little more than skin and bone. He was certain if it weren't for the loose kaftan she wore, he would have been able to count every rib.

A sad smile cracked her thin lips, her oversized eyes moving from place to place, unsure where to rest.

Waiola returned and took Serap to have a bath and to find her some clean clothes. His own skin was so caked in filth, his hands and feet black where his bare paws had brushed the filthy floor of Serap's prison. Under normal circumstances, he bathed once, sometimes twice each day. He shuddered to think how long it had been now.

He didn't want to go to the palace hammam, afraid to be spotted and forced back into intrigue before he was ready. So he called his masseur and had all the supplies brought to his room. First, he went into his private hot room—a smaller replica of the one in the palace hammam—made of marble and jade, with long, carved benches flanking all sides of a central heating source. Jahmil lay there in his towel for eight or nine degrees until his body was coated in sweat and a sheen of cool fire, the impurities of the last few days dripping from every pore.

As he lay, Jahmil examined the swirling lines of the Covenant etched into his forearm. If anything, it was darker than it had been before he went to find Serap. But that only made sense. It had called to him, and he had responded like a faithful dog. When faced with Ayelet and the one thing in Allah's worlds that mattered to her, what choice did he have in that? Still, as beautiful as the lines were, their every twist and curve was mocking him. He'd never heard of the mark forming on a djinn who wasn't a Shihalan, let alone someone who wasn't even a djinn. And he barely knew her.

The words he'd spoken to Ayelet during their dreamlike stroll through the nightmarish landscape of Vespar echoed in his ears like the whispers of a cruel ghost.

If I loved you, he had said. *If.*

His masseur returned, interrupting Jahmil's ruminations. He was a man of few words and many pounds, who washed all but the most tender inches of his body with a sandpapery cloth. Jahmil was horrified by the amount of dirt that slithered down the drain. The masseur had to fetch a clean rag eight times before he was finished scrubbing, then rinsed him in cold water, and gave him a massage that was equal parts painful and therapeutic. When it was over, and perfumed oil had been applied to his skin and hair, Jahmil felt like a raw lump of fresh clay.

The masseur eyed the tattoo on his arm and gave it extra attention. But no amount of scouring could make a difference. Would anything?

Jahmil dressed in a clean kaftan and loose white şalvar then made his way to the dining room, where he found Serap waiting for him. Though, if not for her bright brown eyes, he may not have recognized her.

She too had been scrubbed clean, and he cringed, imagining how black the water must have been when they rinsed her. Her hair, what a scant few degrees ago had looked like tendrils of oil-soaked black rope, now hung around her face in shiny brown ringlets. She was wearing a dress of bright green silk with billowy sleeves and a transparent veil over her hair. It seemed Waiola had already administered the healing potion. The swelling and cuts were gone, Serap's face bright and sprinkled with golden freckles.

She didn't notice him as he stepped closer, for she was so thoroughly engaged in shoving every morsel of food into her little mouth. A warm sensation swelled in his chest as he watched her eat. How long had it been since she'd had a proper meal? Had she ever had one?

His stomach growled, reminding him he'd gone far too long without eating, too.

"Good evening, *anisa saghira*," he said, settling onto the sloping divan across from her and setting his feet on the ottoman. "How are you feeling?"

She looked up at him and tried to answer, but her mouth was so stuffed with baklava, it was incomprehensible.

"Never mind." He waved a hand and took a bite of a lamb-stuffed *poğaça*. He bent to fill their glasses with pomegranate juice. "Try not to eat too quickly. An empty stomach can turn if it gets overstuffed."

She swallowed hard and took several long gulps of juice. "How would you know?"

Jahmil laughed and shook his head. Yes, this one definitely belonged to Ayelet.

"So, how do you know Ayelet?" he asked. "Are you family?"

"Sort of. Not really. No. She used to live with my cousin Balian's family."

"Ah. Good ol' Balian." Jahmil took a sip of juice to cleanse the sour taste in his mouth. "I don't know much about Ayelet before she... I mean." He laughed at himself. "I don't know much about her. How'd she come to live with Balian's family?"

"My uncle Ahmet was friends with her father, I think. After he died, Ayelet was in a spice farm for a while, and then they took her in."

"On a spice farm…" he said, images of human beings chained like chattel resting on the corners of his mind. He tried to force out the imagining of Ayelet in their ranks, but it came all the same.

He set the *poğaças* back on the tray. He had lost his appetite.

"How old was she when her father died?"

She chewed on her lip. "Six, I think. She doesn't really talk about it, not to me anyway. I know she was a slave, though, because she has that mark on her leg. I don't know for how long. And then Balian's family took her in, and I think she was twelve when she ran away from home that time. That's what he said, I think."

Jahmil furrowed his brow. "Why did she run away?"

"I've only ever heard rumors."

"What sort of rumors?"

"Why are you so interested?" She squished her face in confusion, then a light dawned in her eyes that Jahmil felt certain was an entirely negative thing. "Oh, I get it."

He rolled his eyes, but couldn't deny the smile tugging on his lips. "What kind of rumors?"

"I heard Toulin… she was my aunt… I heard her say once that Ahmet, my uncle, had made a deal to trade Ayelet back to the man that used to own her."

His lips parted, her words picking up substance as they tumbled through his brain like a mudslide. "Her fosters tried to sell her back into slavery?"

"That's what I heard." She took a bite out of an unpeeled orange like it was an apple, then spat it back out into her hand. "These are nasty."

Jahmil took the fruit from her. He peeled it, sectioned it, then piled the fruit on her plate.

She picked up a section and bit into it, then smiled. "*Oha!* That's much better."

He smiled at the girl, but the lump in his heart made it fade into nothing. "After such a betrayal, she still talks to Balian? To you?"

"After Ahmet and Toulin died, Ayelet started showing up back in Edirne. I mean, I wasn't even alive back when all that stuff happened, so…"

"Is he a good man?"

She stuffed her mouth with six more sections of orange and answered from around them. "Who?"

"Your cousin."

"Balian? He's fine. He gambles a lot." She swallowed, but that look filled her eyes again as if she had remembered something very important. "But *you* mean is he good for Ayelet?"

"Well, I mean…" he stammered. "I suppose that is what I mean."

"Ayelet's too much for him." She swallowed another big gulp of juice, then crawled forward on the divan to gaze at his eyes, her tongue stuck between her teeth in a mischievous smile. "Besides, why would she want somebody like him when she could have somebody like you?"

"I've been asking myself that same question," he muttered, then his eyes went wide.

He should not have said that.

"*Allahalla!*" the little girl cried. "Now I get it. You're in love with her!"

"No, I'm not."

"Yes, you are. Look at you. I can tell. I'm very good at these kinds of things. Everybody says so." She pointed to her chest proudly. "I'm the one who figured out Khalid al-Musa was having an affair with the innkeeper's wife. But I didn't tell anybody. I never tell anybody anything."

He cocked a brow at her. "Clearly."

"Does she love you too? *Maşallah!* I hope she loves you too."

"Why? You don't know me."

Serap put a hand on her hip, which only succeeded in making her look awkward, tucked as she was on the overstuffed divan. "I know you're a magical prince that came to the rescue of a human slave girl. What else do I need to know?"

He shook his head. "My dear Serap, things are not as simple as they may seem."

"Adults always make things so complicated. If you love her and she loves you, then you should just shut up and get married."

He laughed so hard, he spat out his juice. He slapped down the goblet and covered his eyes with his hands, leaning far back in the cushions.

"We'll come live with you in your palace," Serap continued. "I'm coming, by the way. Me and Ayelet are a package deal."

"Are you now?" He chuckled, not looking up at her.

"And then we can all go on quests together. Princes like to go on quests, right?"

He leaned forward and set his chin on a fist, meeting her glittering eyes. "Sometimes we do."

"That's perfect. Ayelet would love that." She reached across the space and poked him in the ribs. "Are you shy? Is that why you haven't told her? Because I can tell her if you want me to. I don't mind. Let me tell her."

"Don't even think about it," he said, and he meant it, but his tone was gentle. "Listen, Serap, adults don't just *make* things complicated. Things *are* complicated. And you are clearly a very smart girl, so I think you already know that nobody can just run around doing whatever they like. There are consequences for our actions. People who depend on us. No person can afford to think of nothing but their own happiness, especially not me."

Sighing, he looked down at his lap. He sounded like his mother. His shoulders hunched. Had he really sunk so low?

"Love is not a luxury that I can afford," he sighed.

Serap folded into herself, and for the first time since he'd come into the dining room, he saw a glimmer of the sadness in her eyes that had threatened to consume him when he'd found her in that cell.

He turned away to gaze out of the window, but his fingers were tracing his forearm. He could almost feel the lines of tattoo moving under the satin, mocking him and goading him on all at once. "Even if I did feel something new, real, and unlike anything when I looked in her eyes. Even if my heart keeps screaming that there will never be another moment like the first time she smiled at me. It's just my scourge to bear."

Serap didn't speak for a moment. He glanced back to see her pushing her lips to one side of her face and then the other, considering him with overly serious eyes. "Maybe you could buy it on credit."

"Buy what on credit?"

"You said you couldn't afford love. Well, sometimes when we can't afford something, a shopkeeper will let Balian buy it on credit. So maybe you could do that."

"That which is bought on credit must always be paid back with interest." He chuckled and chewed on his thumbnail. "But maybe I could."

Serap swiped a big piece of rolled baklava off the table and stuffed it in her cheek. "You're kind of depressing, but I like you."

"I like you too, *anisa saghira*." He laced his fingers together and gazed at her over his knuckles. "Now, if you're done eating, we should get you back to Ayelet."

CHAPTER TWENTY-TWO

Ayelet

Ayelet sat next to the roaring fire, the chill on her skin impervious to its licking warmth. Balian had placed her there amongst her fellow performers at camp in hopes the bright music might help lift her spirits. After all, it seemed everyone had reason to celebrate, and cider flowed freely. The sultan—*Alhamdulillah! Praise God!*—had sent his emissaries to aid the people in their disaster with bread for all who had a hand to take it. And performers, with their sleight of hand and skills in misdirection, had multiple hands each.

But the music shattered like glass in her ears. Where had the slavers taken Serap? There were so many paths to the sea, and the trading boats were far worse than Istanbul. One would cast Serap somewhere across the Ottoman Empire, the other would cast her somewhere across the continents.

She had just wasted her best chance of saving Serap. And Takisha would no longer be at her side when she needed to fight again. She had been kind enough, in her boisterous, blunt way, to go with Balian to try to find which way the slavers had gone. But after that, she would return to Jahmil, another person Ayelet would never see again. Maybe, at least, he could put her to better use. He deserved happiness far more than she.

Ayelet groaned and rubbed the fire from her eyes. She poked at the loaf of bread by her side, knowing she should eat. Even considering her life of hunger, three days without food pushed her limits. She would not be able to save Serap if she passed out from weakness. Then again, she probably would not be able to save Serap at all.

The musicians at the front put down their instruments and took up cups in their place. Ayelet, drunk on misery, couldn't be more glad. She did not have the heart to dance. She did, however, have the heart to play. She pulled out her lyre. The glow of the jasmine radiated gently inside and she held it close, inhaling the impossible scent of Shihala. Then she placed it below her chin and stood.

The surrounding dancers cheered, and wrapped in the safety of her music, she dreamed she saw Jahmil standing in the back just as he had that first day. Eyes like crystal. Skin like the sky and impossibly tall. She expected the music to pour forth from her fingers in a harrowing dirge, but the melody was light. A wistfulness plucked from deep inside when she thought of all the things she didn't know about him and the few things she did, and how it didn't matter at all because she knew he was kind. And loyal. And honest.

She held his eyes, this mirage of Jahmil, as the music took on a mind of its own. But before she could drink him in and drown in the memory, a familiar voice called through the crowd.

"Ayelet!"

The muddy brown of the gathered crowd parted, and a streak of bright green peeled toward her. The girl's smile was impossible, but Ayelet recognized her wide, shining eyes.

"Serap?" Her voice trembled as her music came to an abrupt halt.

She wiped an arm across her eyes and blinked twice. Unlike all the other things she'd lost, this wasn't a mirage. She dropped her lyre on the ground and embraced her. And even though she was dressed in simple finery and her hair curled tighter than she'd ever seen, she smelled like Serap and honey and home.

"Serap, Serap," she nearly cried, pushing hair from her face. "Where have you—How did you—How are you here? I came for you, but you were gone!"

"He told me you were looking for me."

"Who told you? Balian? Is he back already?"

"No." She laughed, louder and healthier than Ayelet had ever heard before. She pushed Ayelet's shoulder playfully. "I cannot believe you didn't tell me about him! I'm angry with you."

Ayelet pressed Serap's jasmine-smelling hair against her chest tightly before pulling back and looking at her. "I don't know *what* you're talking about, but I'm too glad to see you to care. Who on earth would I not tell you about?"

"Oh, I don't know. Bright blue. Kind of shy. Can turn himself into a cat." Again, she let loose that giggle. "Who do you think came and got me away from the slavers?"

Ayelet jumped to her feet to stare once more at the back of the crowd. She had been certain he wasn't really there, a figment of her desperation, but if Serap was telling the truth—and there was no way she'd come up with a story as crazy as that—he must be real, too.

She scanned the faces, her heart screaming louder than the beating drums. Gone? She looked to Serap, almost too scared to ask. "He brought you here? Is he here now? Will he—Did he talk about me?" She felt foolish even saying the words.

"I'm not allowed to say anything." She mimed a key turning in her lips.

She pinched Serap's rosy cheeks in her hand so her lips puckered. "It's what I've always loved about you, but I'm Ayelet. The giver of bread and laugher at jokes. Break your secret for me?"

"I don't know…" She chewed on her cheek. "Have you seen this dress?"

Ayelet gave her a once over and sighed. "It is beautiful. And he is clever, buying your silence. But we are family. Er, sort of."

Serap's eyes darted from side to side before she waved her closer. "All right. But don't tell him I told you. He said—"

"I knew I couldn't trust you." A deep, melodious voice came from over her shoulder.

Ayelet dropped her hold on Serap's cheeks and shoved her hands behind her back like a child caught playing in the mud. "Jahmil?" she asked stupidly.

"Good evening, *sayidati*." He smiled, lifting his hand to ask for hers. She gave it, and he kissed her knuckles.

She froze, afraid that if she moved he would disappear. He shone far brighter than the day in the market like the nearby fire knew his power and bolstered his might. And while she was still dressed in her shredded, blood-stained garments, his skin was polished and smelled of dew and his clothes were clean, crisp, and fresh. She rubbed her slipper over the boot she still wore, ashamed for the first time of how she looked. Serap elbowed her with a goofy smile.

"What are you doing here?" Ayelet asked clumsily. "And with my Serap?"

"Forgive me." He looked down at her feet, then back up to meet her eyes. His were dusted in copper and a blue so deep it nearly matched his skin. "I did not understand the gravity of your situation before. I should have offered my help."

The formality of his address brought a smile to her lips, and the music of the party broke the bubble she had been lost in. "Yes, you should have. But you're not very good about thinking of others. I'm certain your servants do that for you as well."

"Not very well, it seems." He laughed—really laughed—and shook his head. "If I had known a little more about this one—" His eyes brushed Serap. "—I would have known the kind of trouble she could get herself into."

Serap scowled playfully, and Ayelet chuckled. "She's learned from the best, unfortunately." Then a thought crossed her mind, and she poked his chest. "A little warning would have been nice. I had to barge in there with scant help, killing whoever and whatever, just to get inside and find her gone. I thought I had lost her forever."

He frowned and tightened his fingers around hers. His skin was as warm as a midsummer evening. "Forgive me. As you may have guessed, I did not have a plan. My servants had the afternoon off."

She bit back a smile. "That's the second time you've not had a plan and played with my heart." She blushed, and trying to cover her slip of honesty, teased him instead. "It was a good thing Balian was there to help me."

His smile cooled, but did not fade. He brushed her hair behind her shoulder. "I am thankful for anything that makes your life easier. Even him."

Ayelet regretted even the smallest slip in a smile that so rarely came. Serap elbowed her once more, and putting a hand to the side of her mouth so Jahmil wouldn't hear, whispered conspiratorially, "He's not a fan of Balian too much."

Ayelet giggled. "Neither am I," she said loud enough for him to hear. "He seems a fan of yours, though. What finery he's showered upon you! And your breath smells of baklava. I'm beginning to wonder if you're the queen he spends so much time with."

"As always, you are determined to cause trouble," he teased. "Don't you find it tedious?"

"Life is tedious." She grinned, brushing his shirt as if dust lay there, happy just to touch him. "But not always. Sometimes I cause mischief. Or lucky happenstances."

Again he laughed, this time so much that his shoulders shook. "My humblest apologies."

A warmth spread through her at the sight of him happy. No, not happy. Joyous. Light. Even elated. What had changed that he was able to put aside his burdens and just be?

She let his laugh die down naturally, wanting him to have every chuckle and sharp inhale in case his joy was fleeting. When at last he'd found his breath, she playfully furrowed her brows. "While I appreciate the apology, I can't *give* you my forgiveness. Only hunger is free." She held out her hand and flashed him her eyes. "So, what have you to offer?"

He lifted one eyebrow. "I see you expect I would come to your party empty-handed, but I'm afraid I shall have to disappoint you." He reached into the pocket of his vest and took out a small wooden box inlaid with emeralds and mother-of-pearl. "Someone told me you were fond of opals."

She hesitated, afraid that if she touched the beautiful box, it would turn to dust.

"Oh, come on already," Serap interjected, taking the box from his hand and putting it in hers.

Ayelet smiled shyly and opened the lid. Inside, a dozen small opals shone in shades of blue and green, pastel pink shimmers carving their way like waves upon the sea. A necklace, held together by links of porcelain.

She clamped her jaw and the box shut and abruptly handed it back to Jahmil. "I cannot take that."

It would hurt too much, having something so perfect to haunt her memories when he disappeared once more.

"I will!" cried Serap.

"Oh, why don't you go do something with yourself?" said Jahmil, then he turned back to Ayelet with serious eyes—shimmering in shades of gold and purple. "I don't expect anything in return. I just thought…"

The joy in his eyes was fading too quickly. She snatched the box back and held it close to her chest. "I love it," she said and bit her bottom lip. "But you'll have to help me put it on. I don't know if you noticed, but I can be a clutz."

"The most graceful clutz I've ever met." He lifted the necklace from the case and stepped up behind her. Moving her hair to one side, he clasped it around her throat, his fingers gently brushing her skin. "It belonged to my grandmother," he said, pulling her hair back into place.

She bit her lip harder, forcing herself not to shiver under the warmth of his hand and the cool of the necklace. She touched a smooth stone and felt the weight of each opal upon her chest.

"She told me that I…" He smiled and shook his head. "She used to say it brought her glad dreams. Serap tells me you sometimes do not sleep very well."

Ayelet turned and ran a finger over his cheek and soft, trimmed beard. Ever since Köle had found her, night had brought perpetual hauntings, and she desperately sought an escape from the torment, taking in one lover or the next because she was too afraid to be alone. That was until she saw Jahmil. Now, when the nightmares came in what little sleep she stole, shining crystals helped ease the fear and chase away the darkness.

"I shall be the best-dressed in any bed," she said and smiled to cut the heaviness. She did not know what to do with him, with his gifts and gentle words, knowing he would not be there tomorrow. "I have something to give you, too."

He furrowed his brow. "Should I be worried?"

She slapped his chest lightly, fighting the urge to linger. "Do you want the gift or not?"

"Of course, I do."

She leaned against him, slipping her arm around his waist and looking up. "Come a little closer, please."

He still looked suspicious, but smiled and drew nearer.

His thick eyelashes framed starry eyes, and she could feel the warmth of his skin so close. She was tempted to close the gap, to breathe him in and never let go. But if she did so now, the agony would be far greater when he was gone. Instead, she popped her back foot up behind her and removed his boot. Still holding him close, she slipped it into his free hand. "I believe this is yours."

Sighing, he shook his head. "I cannot in good conscience take it back."

"It is a gift," she said resolutely, pulling back and furrowing her brows.

He laughed and shook his head. "A gift from the hands of Sayidat Ayelet." He lifted the boot reverentially towards the moon. "In that case, I shall wear it with pride." He tied the laces around his neck and let the boot dangle on his chest. "Does it suit me?"

She giggled, struck by his playfulness. "Now, you'll be the best-dressed in any bed."

He laced his arm around her waist and drew her closer. "Quite a pair we'll make."

She blushed and let herself believe his words, even if just for this moment. To hope that maybe, just maybe, he would stay with her. Then she paused, tugging on her lip. "But if my gift is too much, you may always give my scarf back in return."

He rubbed his arm and shook his head. "I'm afraid that is one thing I cannot part with."

"Then you can honor me with a dance," she said and held out her hands. "Though I heard a rumor that djinn are terribly flat-footed."

"Only because we are unaccustomed to dancing on the ground." He took the boot from around his neck and set it down. "I'll leave my present here, if you don't mind." He took her hand and pulled her quickly to his chest.

She let out a tiny gasp before cutting it short. Ah, why was she so foolish? This was a wretched idea. But she didn't pull away. She would stay with him like this until he cast her off once more, leaving her to miss every moment with him and love the beautiful pain.

As he led her out into the crowd, she saw Serap staring at them from the edge of the circle. She clapped her hands and wiggled her eyebrows.

A blush crept up Ayelet's cheeks, and she shooed her away behind his back. "What *did* you do to charm Serap so?" she asked as the musicians tuned their instruments for the next song.

"Honestly?" he said, slipping his hand around the small of her back. "I think it was the food."

"I'm glad you're not this charming all the time." She chuckled, savoring the feel of his hand upon her skin. "I'm not sure I could handle it."

"It would be exhausting," he agreed.

She grinned as a ballad started up, smooth and slow with an off-beat wail of desert mystery. "Indeed. The good news is, I have seen you cranky. And I liked you then, too." She took hold of his arms and looked up expectantly. "I hope you know how to lead. I shouldn't like to dance with your servant."

"Nor should I. I complain every time he asks, but it makes him happy."

The music picked up, and he spun her out onto the floor, his movements fast and sure, precise with the rhythm. As the beat picked up, she was left with little time to think, following and not following. Moving together as easily as if it had been practiced. Whenever she looked up at his face, his gaze was fixed on hers, his crystal eyes shimmering with the reflection of the firelight. And in that moment, nothing else mattered. Not her hunger or her past or even what would come tomorrow.

And only when the last notes twinged to rest did her utter elation fade. It was not just Jahmil's eyes alone that watched her. The crowd looked on, awestruck by the effortless spinning of a lone woman dancing under the stars, leaning on nothing, lifted as if by the wind. And among those faces, Balian's and Takisha's, each with their own look of fire.

It seemed Jahmil had not yet noticed, for he set his forehead against hers and whispered, "Is my servant a satisfactory dancer?"

She turned her head away so he would not feel the heat on her cheeks. "He makes my heart yearn for things it should not." And foolishly, recklessly, knowing Takisha and Balian watched, she leaned in and kissed Jahmil softly on the lips. "Please be sure to give him that... for me."

Jahmil sighed, his eyes falling closed. He lifted her chin closer. "I have a terrible memory. Tell me again."

"*Al'ama* Jahmil!" Takisha thundered. "What do you think you are doing?"

Ayelet pulled away, throwing her arms in front of him as if she could do anything. The time had come for a reckoning, and she did not regret a second.

CHAPTER TWENTY-THREE

Jahmil

Jahmil stood, shoulders hunched exactly as they had been when she kissed him. His head snapped to one side to look at Takisha. His eyes narrowed, gaze shifting between the imposing warrior and the bedraggled figure of Balian slack-jawed at her side.

He lifted his arm and pointed at them. "No."

"Get away from that little human this instant!" Takisha thundered. "Do you not know what this might do?"

"I said no." He snatched Ayelet's hand, then dragged her off in the opposite direction, parting the crowd as they went.

"Jahmil." Ayelet tugged at his hand, jogging to keep up with the speedy clip of feet. "You're going too fast."

He looked back at her, struggling in her ill-fitting slipper and bare foot. But they were nearly to the edge of the crowd. The tree line rose in the distance like an oasis of darkness and silence. So close.

He picked up Ayelet and threw her over one shoulder, then quickened his pace. She struggled at first, then gave in, clinging tightly to him.

He ran until they were concealed in the forest, carefully dodging through the branches so nothing but the soft feather of leaves touched her skin. When he was satisfied they were far enough away, he set her down.

"Jahmil..." she started to say, his name light on her heavy breath.

"I'm sorry. I'm sorry," he whispered, then he shook his head and pulled her close. "No, I'm not sorry."

He cupped the sides of her face and drew her lips so close that he could almost taste them. Ayelet hesitated, then urgently grasped his cheeks and pulled him into a kiss. His blood surged, and his fire flared. He had to focus to keep it cool and smooth, warm enough to tingle where his hands caressed her skin, but not hot enough to burn. Her lips on his were everything he had hoped they would be. Nothing in his past compared to it, and surely nothing in his future, if not her. The smell of her filled his senses, the softness of her skin. He wrapped his arms around her, pulling her closer, wishing their bodies would melt together and cease to exist in the world.

He pressed her against the trunk of a tree. She looped her legs around his back. After a moment, he broke off the kiss so that he could taste her neck, her shoulder, her collarbone. Her gentle moan in his ear shivered through his blood like lightning. His hand slipped under her skirts and tightened on the firm, satiny flesh of her thigh.

He knew this was going to happen. He'd warned her. He'd warned himself. *If I loved you, nothing else would matter. Nothing in Qaf or on Ard. Nothing in heaven.*

That was what he had said, and while he had meant it to sound merely flirtatious, no words had ever been truer. He had never been very good at following his own advice. Curse and bless his honesty. Shihala had called his bluff as easily as clouds make rain. There was no going back now.

The crash of a tree branch sounded through his mind and heart like a scream.

"Jahmil!"

Takisha. She was following them, inserting herself into the situation as if it were any of her business. Perhaps it was, but that didn't matter either. Nothing in Qaf or on Ard.

Ayelet flinched and drew in a harsh breath. He set her feet on the ground and wrapped his arms around her protectively. "Don't be frightened. She won't hurt you."

"I've seen what she can do," Ayelet whispered, and the fear in her face helped him to wrangle some control over his frantically beating heart. "The splash damage will be bad enough."

"What do you mean?" He narrowed his eyes. "You've met her before?"

She nodded, but her gaze kept flinching back to the shivering tree line.

"I'll go calm her before she brings down the entire forest." He ran his hand over Ayelet's cheek, stealing another moment to drink in the storms in her eyes. "Such eyes you have, *sayidati*."

She smiled, and he couldn't resist a moment longer. He kissed her, breathing in her scent. Sweeter than alyasmin, and rarer still. His tongue slipped into her mouth, and he pulled her closer to his chest.

A tree teetered nearby and crashed to the ground with an ear-splitting thud. "Jahmil!"

Ayelet flinched again, her shoulders shrinking.

He pushed back the hair that had fallen over her eyes. "She can be a bit insistent, can't she?"

Ayelet managed a small grin. "This I know well. And she's protective of you, too. You had better go, but please—" Her breath caught as he ran a finger under his jaw. "—don't forget about me here in the brush. Okay?"

"I could never forget you, not if I lived for another thousand years." He kissed her again, meaning for it to be nothing more than a peck and unable to stop himself from lingering.

"I will set this entire forest ablaze!" thundered Takisha.

"I will return, this I swear to you," he said and stepped back, but his hand was still clinging to hers. Their fingers slowly untangled as he pulled away. Then, with a final lingering glance in her direction, he took off through the forest towards the sound of crashing trees.

His feet did not seem to touch the earth. Rather, he floated over the tangled brush as if leaping on clouds. And his smile was so wide it was painful. The most exquisite pain.

Nothing else mattered. He had given Ayelet his grandmother's necklace, and while nobody in two worlds, including Ayelet, knew what that meant, it was everything to him. The moment he pulled that box from his pocket and offered it to her, he had made his choice. And his choice was Ayelet, now and forever. She was written on his skin and on his soul. She wore the symbol of everything good that was left in his heart. He would not marry Qadira. Shihala had all but forbidden it. Ayelet was his future, his truth. She and only she was the honorable path.

Honor. The feeling was like fresh mountain air filling up his lungs. At last, a taste of honor.

When he showed Takisha the Covenant on his arm, she would understand. She may have been only half-Shihalan, her father hailing from the Valley of Giants, but half was more than enough. To go against his heart was to go against the Will of Shihala. And that was tantamount to betrayal, if not blasphemy.

He spied Takisha through a break in the trees, her muscles rippling and shimmering bright green in the moonlight. When he called out to her, there was unexpected laughter on his breath. "Calm down, you great hulking beast. I'm here."

She turned on him, white fire so bright in her eyes it was like being stared down by the sun. "Have you completely lost your mind?"

He crossed his arms over his chest and laughed. "You're the one threatening to burn down a forest."

She snarled like a bull and clenched her fists, pale green fire erupting from her hands. She marched closer. "Djinn are everywhere, you fool. And you have one of the most recognizable faces in Qaf. If word of this night gets back to Qadira..."

"So what if it does?"

Her eyes widened, and she snorted steam from her nostrils. "What did you say?"

"I am no longer willing to pay the promised price to secure an allegiance with Ahmar."

A laugh broke from her chest that sounded like screaming. "I was gone from you but two weeks, and you have nearly succeeded in destroying everything we have worked so hard for!"

"Why should I capitulate?" he said, his heart filled with such bravery as he had not felt since the fall of Karzusan. All he had to do was think of Ayelet and he felt as tall as Takisha. Taller, in fact. "The brightest of Qadira's generals already recognize that my leadership is their only chance against the Vespars. My knowledge of their tactics, the terrain of Shihala."

"You can't be saying you want to call off the wedding."

"I will call upon the forces I have collected and lead them away from Ahmar. They are loyal to me. I know they are."

"It is not enough!"

"Let the Vespars fall on Qadira. Let her be ousted from her palace and left in rags and see how she comes crawling, begging for *my* help, scrambling to swallow any scraps *I* feel like tossing her way."

"It is not enough," she said again, emphasizing each word.

"It is the more difficult path, I grant you. But it is the one I have chosen, and you will tread it with me."

"You would risk the future of Shihala for some filthy, irrelevant human!"

Jahmil's eyes flashed, the warmth in his chest Ayelet had planted quickly erupting into white-hot fire. "Choose your words carefully, *Alqayid*. I am your amir and there is a limit to how much insolence I am prepared to tolerate, even from you."

"Clearly your lust has rendered you deaf, dumb, and blind!" Takisha drew the massive obsidian sword from the holster on her back. "I will restore you to your senses, one way or another."

His hand instinctively went to his hip, but his sword was not there. He had not come here tonight with the intent of fighting. From now on, he was determined to carry the heavy, miserable hunk of stone everywhere, no matter what he was expecting. He had intended to show her the Covenant, to convince her that he was not acting merely upon his own will but that of Shihala Herself. But why should he? As Bakr had so plainly put it, *he* was the amir. The people followed *him*. Fought for *him*. Rallied around *him*. This was his decision and his alone. And he would be damned if he was going to cajole his own commanders into following his orders.

Takisha swung her sword in a few quick circles, the weight swooshing through the night air. "I don't want to hurt you, Jahmil, but I will drag you back to Ahmar by the hair if you make me."

He took a long breath and put back his shoulders. "I will not marry Qadira."

She growled, baring her teeth even as she turned her head aside. "Jahmil, there is nothing saying you could not have your little human in time. Once Qadira's lust for you cools, you can take Ayelet as your mistress—"

"How dare you?" he hissed, the last of his good mood falling away like autumn leaves in a gust of winter wind. "You imagine I do not know what is at stake? That I would change the course of our entire nation for the sake of lust?"

She scoffed. "What else is there?"

Jahmil pulled back his shoulders. "Ayelet will be my queen, or no one shall be. I've made my decision. And if you cannot abide by it, then I shall dismiss you from my service."

"Curse your passion! And your vanity!"

Without warning, she lunged at him, bringing her sword down in an overhanded arc as if to split him in twain. He dodged to one side, and the massive sword buried itself in the dirt, leaving a rift in the earth. Dust exploded, and he coughed, even as her sword whirled towards him again.

This was not like any other time he had ever come up against Takisha. She was not holding back. Jahmil was an excellent fighter, but he had never been any match for Takisha. After all, it was she who taught him to fight when he was a young boy—to hold a sword, to throw a fist, to fire an arrow. Tactics and combat he had learned from his father. He could outwit her in any war game, but in melee, he stood no chance. Even Bakr had never won a sparring match against Takisha. She was the daughter of giants, a berserker. The fury shining in her eyes only made her faster and more precise. At seven-and-a-half feet tall, she outweighed him by over a hundred pounds, every inch of her body corded in muscle as hard as river stones. Yet, she moved quicker on her feet and landed her blows with absolute precision.

And he had no weapon, no knowledge of the terrain. Not a single trick up his sleeve.

"Takisha! Stop this!"

In desperation, he shot a few fireballs at her face, but they splashed harmlessly like water. He turned and tried to run. She kicked the thick trunk of a massive acacia, and it crashed in front of him, showering him with splinters and blocking his path. He scrambled through the prickly branches. She snatched him by the back of his shirt and yanked him back.

"Unhand me!" he cried.

She punched him in the face, the force of it like a stone falling from heaven. His vision blurred, and he tasted blood. Another blow came, and another. She pounded his face, his ribs, his stomach. Then she picked him up and snapped him over her knee as if trying to break up firewood and let him fall limply to the ground.

The pain still running up his legs was the only thing that reassured him she hadn't literally broken him in half. Moaning and twisting on the earth, Jahmil coughed out a lungful of blood. She lifted him up like a sack of wheat and tossed him over one hulking shoulder. He tried to struggle, but she punched him in the guts again. He spat out another mouthful of dark blood.

Using her one free hand, Takisha downed another tree. It crashed against one that was still standing, forming a triangle. A way back to Qaf.

"No," he moaned, blinking through the blood and lightning in his vision. At the far end of the clearing, he saw a flash of bright green and two large brown eyes twinkling with fright as they watched, unblinking.

"Serap," he rasped. "Tell Ayelet..."

But that was all he managed to say before Takisha carted him through the portal and the white winds of Qaf enclosed him. The rush of the mist hit his already swimming mind, and he fell unconscious.

CHAPTER TWENTY-FOUR

Ayelet

Ayelet waited for Jahmil until the moon arched high in the sky and fell back behind the bay laurel and pistachio trees.

When he first left, Takisha's yelling had been thunderous. But after some muddled arguing, things had fallen suddenly silent, replaced by the croak of frogs and the dry rustling of cricket wings. She had been tempted to check on Jahmil, but Takisha's murderous eyes at the campfire burned brightly in her memory.

She wouldn't hurt him, right? Her amir?

Trusting in Jahmil's promise to return, Ayelet lay back in the brush where Jahmil had kissed her, remembering his touch and the brazen, coppery color of his eyes. His nearness—his intensity—hadn't felt like any lover before, and none ever would again. But as the night waxed and waned, the tie of affection she felt toward him began to knot.

Unable to lie another second alone in the cool air, she sat up and brushed the leaves from her hair. She had never waited so long for anyone in her life; she had never trusted anyone to return. Even now, she fought to keep the sap of doubt from sticking to her mind. She reached for the solace of her lyre and gasped. Patting her waist and dress frantically, she jumped to her feet.

Where? The camp! She had dropped it to embrace Serap and never picked it up.

An emptiness took hold of her. She had not once let it out of her sight since the peddler gave it to her, his keen eyes haunting as he told her strange words. She grasped at her throat as though she were missing her voice, then glanced back into the dark of the woods. If Jahmil returned to find her gone, would he search for her? She had to assume it so; without her lyre, she had little to offer the shining prince of Shihala. It was clear her gift had been what drew him near in the beginning, and just before she had called him spoiled, he had said as much.

Your music is far rarer and more beautiful than a common breath of magic.

She was not so certain she meant anything without it.

Even worse, her only way back to Shihala lay cradled inside.

She adjusted her skirts and flew to the camp. When she entered the warm circle around the fire, she scanned the packed earth for where it lay. The crowd had thinned, dancers and musicians alike turning in for slumber so only a few clusters of men and women stood talking in hushed whispers. She scoured over and under logs, throwing mugs and barrels aside as her panic increased.

"Ayelet."

She refused to stop her search so Balian could berate her.

"What were you thinking?" he asked, grabbing her arm and spinning her to face him.

She ripped herself from him, but he grabbed both her wrists. "I'm thinking I've lost my lyre and need to get it back."

"There will be other lyres."

She shook her head at him, mouth agape, unable to respond to such ignorant stupidity.

He took her silence as permission to proceed. "What were you *doing,* behaving so absurdly in camp? Do you know how many are whispering already?"

"Am I absurd to dance alone with the moonlight?"

"You were floating through the air on the way into the woods!" He barked a cold laugh. "Or do you also tussle in the brush with moonlight, cheeks red and skirts in disarray?"

She froze.

"You're a disgrace," he spat. "A complete and utter fool."

"I'm only a fool if I feel ashamed, and I do not." She struggled to pull her wrists free, but he brought them together, crisscrossing her hands and forcing her still.

"What *do* you feel for the creature, then?" Balian's eyes blazed despite the dying fire behind her. "Fascination? Obsession? Or are you so hellbent on running from your problems that you've decided to make a deal with a djinn, hoping to leave earth entirely?"

"And what if I have?" she asked defiantly.

His eyes widened. "No human has ever trusted their fate to a djinn and walked away unscathed."

"I did just that with Takisha."

He glowered, his fingers constricting like snakes on her wrists. "What did he make you promise him for bringing Serap back? Hm? Your affections?"

"Don't be ridiculous," she scoffed.

"Then he spoils you with risible gifts for no reason?" he asked, jutting his chin at the necklace draped around her throat. "Are you bought so easily? I mean, by Allah, Ayelet. That could buy a lifetime of food for everyone in this camp. It looks absurd resting upon you in your filth."

Ayelet burned with shame for the second time that night. "Does a man need a reason to spoil a woman? Don't envy Jahmil for providing what you never could."

"*Jahmil?*" Balian snarled like a starved dog. "You speak so informally of someone who would entrap you? Trading one slave master for another is no better. Just because he's magical and a ridiculous shade of blue doesn't make his intentions for you any different."

The embers smoldering inside her ignited. She kicked his shin so hard pain ricocheted through her bare foot. Then she yanked her hands free. "How dare you," she growled in a whisper. "How dare you even compare Jahmil to that—that— "

He glared at her unapologetically, and she spat at his feet.

Balian clenched his fist so hard it trembled and took a shaky breath. "He will hurt you, Ayelet. He will destroy you."

"More than you already did?"

He held his ground, wincing only slightly at the grievance of which they rarely spoke but of which she never would let him forget. "I've said I'm sorry a thousand times."

"Your parents tried to sell me back into slavery while you stood by to watch it happen! You could apologize for all of eternity and it would never be enough."

"That's not fair," he said gruffly. "I didn't think them capable of such a thing."

"I told you they were." She glared at him, feeling fire and showing ice. "Ahmet had already taken his payment. But you did not believe me."

"I was twelve." He dropped his gaze and whispered bitterly, "So you'd rather trust a demonic being than forgive me?"

"Yes."

"You're more a fool than I thought." He shook his head and turned. "I hope trading away your life is worth the cost."

Her blood hissed inside her. "The only thing we've traded is a boot and some words!"

She waved him away and resumed her search, throwing aside everything in her path with furious abandon. Unlike Balian, who took and never gave, Jahmil had asked for nothing in return; he had always given freely. It was she who kept demanding things from him. She laid a hand upon her opal necklace, stroking the smooth cool of each perfect bead. He had asked for nothing.

At last, she spied something under the splintered legs of a broken stool. Something soft and leather and an autumn's brown. She lifted the boot with ginger fingers, brushing off stray dust and a spot of cider. She ran a thumb over the stitching. He would come back. She shoved her foot inside the leather and wriggled her toes freely. He had to for his boot.

"Ayelet!" her name blew on the wind.

She looked up to see a few disinterested heads turn before resuming their muted chatter.

"Ayelet!" the voice came again, sweet and simple, but high-pitched with distress.

"Serap?" Ayelet cast her gaze around once more and spied Serap racing from the woods. She hesitated only enough to sweep the camp once more for her lyre, then ran to meet her. "Are you okay?" She knelt and ran a hand through Serap's curls over and over. "Is everything okay?"

"I'm okay," she said between short gasps. "It's Jahmil."

"What's wrong?" Ayelet jumped to her feet. Her heart struggled to beat under the weight of the opals.

"He—" Serap took another dramatic breath.

"He what?" Ayelet asked, resisting the urge to shake the poor girl's shoulders.

"A *basty* or a ghost must have come because Jahmil was flinging all around, fighting with something I couldn't see and getting hurt really bad."

"Takisha." Ayelet groaned.

If the little girl couldn't see the djinn, that's exactly what it would have looked like. Like her dance with no one in the moonlight. What had the warrior done?

Serap wiped her forehead, leaving a streak of sweat on her brand-new dress, and opened her mouth to speak when a haunting sound slithered through the air. A sound Ayelet knew by heart, though it had never played so ghastly. She whipped around.

"Ayeleta," Kadri said, accenting each syllable in a sing-songy voice. She clumsily strummed the strings of Ayelet's lyre as a group of her men made a semicircle behind her. "It's Allah's blessing that we keep running into each other."

Ayelet pushed Serap behind her. "What do you want, Kadri?"

"No banter between old friends this time?" Kadri put a hand to her chest in a dramatic flair. "I'm hurt."

Ayelet forced her shaking shoulders to still so Serap would not fear. "We did not part on the best of terms."

"Ah." Kadri nodded knowingly. "I see, you're still hung up on all that messy business from the other day. I don't see why; it seems everything turned out well in the end."

"Does a girl sold into slavery and a mountain being rent into twain sound well to you? What about a field of dead snakes and Edirne in flames?"

"You don't think *I'm* responsible for all that, do you?" Kadri asked. "Even as the Queen of Black Trade, you give me too much credit."

"I think you're skirt-deep in everything that's happened," Ayelet challenged, tired of her games. "We headed to those ruins so you could collect more magic, and lo-and-behold, a giant eimlaq shows up with more power than this earth has ever seen and blows a mountain apart."

"That was *not*—" Kadri held up a hand to stop herself. "I admit, the mountain fiasco did not go as planned. But it wasn't a suicide mission. In fact, if we had gone in three days as you had promised, I'm confident we wouldn't have been in any danger at all, but you ran and forced my hand. Regardless—" He flicked her fingers to the side. "—I had no intention of letting you come to harm."

"Just Serap?"

Kadri's smile tightened, and she plucked a string on Ayelet's lyre so it twanged pitifully. "This is a beautiful instrument."

"It's also mine," Ayelet said, her heart seizing every time Kadri jostled the delicate pegs.

"And I will give it back when you come with me," Kadri said. "Minus the flower, of course." She held her hand, palm up, to the side. A servant hurried forward from the huddled group of men and handed her the glowing jasmine.

The air in Ayelet's body disintegrated like wisps in water. The only thing keeping her from screaming was the too-easy smile she had carved onto her face. "They're like sand where they come from, stretching as far as the eye can see. A common flower, if not pretty."

"My Ayeleta, there is nothing common about this flower."

"Give me back my lyre," she said through clenched teeth. She would bash it over the fake queen's head and take back her path to Jahmil.

Kadri brushed the precious petals beneath her chin. "I will after you come with me."

"Not in a thousand moons would I be caught traveling with you."

Kadri's smile wilted. "Don't you get tired of this runaround, Ayelet? You are coming with me, and you don't have a choice." She waved her hand, and several men emerged from the nearby woods to surround her and Serap in a moment of infuriating déjà vu. "The only question you should be asking is if you want to come willingly or by force. And so you're fully informed before you glibly brush me off, the little girl will be paying the price for the second."

Serap flinched behind her, and Ayelet seethed. "I would rather die than let me or Serap go to the sea and be sold to Köle."

Kadri winced at his name. "I was not aware you knew of our benefactor."

"One cannot truly know of what lies behind smoke and shadows. But he's been chasing me for nigh a decade; you're just the new ugly face of his operations."

"That must be why he knows so much of you." Kadri paused, tilting her head so the moon glinted off her beaded hair. "It's all rather pitiful if you ask me. He speaks of you like a doting father does an errant daughter, and for the life of me, I can't tell why. Aside from your ability to pluck a few strings—" She hefted the lyre above her head. "—I don't see anything at all worth caring for."

Thinking of the faceless cruelty inflicted by Köle's unseen hands spilled an aching chill over her bones. He would never let her be.

"Know that by the time he is done with you, you will wish you were dead," Ayelet warned. She had a mind to make a run at Kadri and rip out her wrapped braids so Serap would have a chance to escape, but the girl's quivering body, pressed against her back, softened her impulse. "I will come. Just leave the girl be."

Kadri beamed as if she had won a sitting with the sultan. "Splendid."

With another wave of her pretentious little hand, one of Kadri's brutes wrapped his hulking arms around Ayelet, dragging her into the woods at a pace that made her trip over clumps of grass and rodent holes. She dug her nails into his wrists until he grabbed her other arm and yanked them both painfully high. She closed her eyes and pictured Jahmil's steely gaze, his firm resolve as he dragged her away from Takisha and Balian, determined to protect her, to have a moment alone with her. In those precious minutes in the woods, she had felt he would have given everything for her.

Everything.

And asked nothing in return.

He would return. Whatever kerfuffle took place between him and Takisha surely meant nothing, and he would soon find his way back and save her from this nightmare. He had a flair for dramatic, last-minute rescues, anyway, she reasoned half-heartedly. She was certain he would return. He had to.

She let herself believe it with all she had left and cried into the woods, "Jahmil! Jahmil, help me!"

It surprised her that the words did not taste bitter, that the need for him did not fill her with shame or fear. She continued her calls, hoping the wind would carry them to the other end of the forest, or Shihala, or wherever it was Jahmil had vanished.

"Quiet!" The man shook her arms so they popped in their sockets.

She stumbled over the brambles and tried again, "Jahmil, you said you would not forget!"

But shame and doubt had already begun creeping their way back in when a glimmer of white shone through the wild maples and scruffy date palms. Her breath caught, then the misty white thinned into two wisps trailing behind them through the darkness. She stretched her nose forward to try to reach one, and it brushed her skin like the kiss of morning dew upon a blade of grass.

Serap screamed somewhere past them in the dark. The wisps recoiled as Ayelet thrashed wildly, digging her heels into the damp earth and kicking at the back of her captor's knees.

"You said you'd leave her be!" she screamed into the breeze, no longer able to see the camp through the thickening forest.

Kadri's fading voice carried all the way from the clearing. "A good trader knows when she'll need collateral. Now, stop all the yelling. You'll scare away the magic."

CHAPTER TWENTY-FIVE

Jahmil

"Amiri?" The voice funneled towards him as if from the clouds. He twitched, pain wrapping around every muscle. "Your Highness?"

Jahmil blinked in soft candlelight. The ceiling above twisted in geometric patterns of gold, copper, and bronze. A mere trick of his vision, as he gazed up at the complex design. A blob of light blue reposed in the corner.

"Zamir?" he groaned, turning his gaze to the figure seated on the edge of his bed. "Where am I?"

"You are safe, *Amiri*. We are in Ahmar."

He pushed himself up slowly, a dozen silken pillows strewn about him. He lay in a giant circular bed draped in furs that shivered in tones of gray as if being blown by the wind, though the air was still.

Rubbing open palms over his stomach and chest, Jahmil groaned. He'd already been healed considerably; much of the pain that remained was the stiffness that always came with magical treatments. "What happened?"

Zamir looked down at his lap before answering. "Takisha appeared in the main atrium of the palace with your broken body draped over her shoulder. She told everybody that you had forced her to beat some sense into you."

He tried to sigh, but it came out as a growl as memories of what had happened bubbled in his brain. One word seared at his vocal cords like a drop of acid. "Traitor."

"Qadira has already punished her."

"Punished her?"

Zamir's eyes darted across the room, down his lap, and then back again, making the rounds to look at everything except Jahmil. His bottom lip quivered.

Jahmil touched his wrist, forcing him to focus. "Zamir, what did Qadira do?"

"Takisha was given fifty lashes and sent to Ashkult."

"What?" He snapped straight up, every muscle in his body tensing. "Qadira has no authority to do such a thing."

"Given the state Takisha brought you back in, I dare say Qadira was not only justified in punishing her but showed tremendous restraint. You are the crown prince, soon to be the king. No one has the right to lay their hands on you."

True enough, Jahmil thought. And certainly, Takisha deserved a good flogging. But that was to come only on his authority, not Qadira's. Her days of meddling in Shihala's business were supposed to be over. And yet here he was, laid out like a slug, while the Queen of Ahmar meddled freely in his affairs.

His blood boiled, and he clenched a fist, white fire rising like mist on his knuckles. "How long have I been unconscious?"

"Ninety degrees, *Amiri*."

"That's all?" He pushed Zamir out of the way and rolled out of bed. Only when he was standing in the center of the room, skin tightening in the cold, did he realize he wasn't wearing any clothes. He scanned the room, but he had never been there before, had never even seen it. "What is this place?"

"These are your mother's bed chambers."

He flinched. "Why?"

"She wanted you to have the benefit of her personal care."

A cold chill raced down his back. His mother had never cared for him personally. "Where are my clothes?"

Zamir shook his head. "Forgive me, *Amiri*. Queen Zalika and Queen Qadira agreed you needed to remain in the palace until you are full well again."

"They plan to keep me trapped by keeping me naked?" Jahmil's heart thrashed in his chest, breath pulsing in his lungs. He couldn't decide who to be angry with or for what reason. Takisha for beating him so brutally. Qadira for punishing her. His mother for trying to trap him. Or Zamir for going along with everything.

And what was Ayelet going to think? Serap had made it clear that she had difficulty trusting anyone. Would she believe he had abandoned her?

He had to get back to her. To explain what happened. Tell her the truth of everything he had decided and why it had made Takisha so angry.

He marched to the wardrobe on one wall and yanked it open. Empty. He checked the chest at the end of the bed. Nothing.

"This is insane," he snarled, slapping the lid closed. His eyes darted around the room once again before coming to rest on Zamir. Or more precisely, on Zamir's perfectly pressed yellow kaftan with shiny sapphire buttons. "Give me your clothes."

"I'm sorry, *Amiri*?"

"Don't be sorry." He snapped his fingers. "Take off your clothes and give them to me."

Zamir stood and backed away, his hand nervously fiddling with the keyhole-shaped neckline of his kaftan. "I'm afraid I can't do that."

"Are you disobeying me?"

His jaw quivered. "Queen Zalika explicitly forbade it."

"Dowager Queen Zalika signed away all of her authority." Jahmil cracked his neck hard to one side. "And I am warning you, Zamir. I will tackle you and tear your clothes off, and it will not be a pleasant memory for either of us."

"*Amiri*, please." He backed towards the door.

Jahmil advanced after him. "One last chance."

"*Amiri!*" Zamir turned and raced away. Jahmil lunged for him, but he yanked open the door and slipped out, the fabric of his shirt slipping through Jahmil's fingers. Jahmil was about to go into the hall after him, but the sound of half a dozen voices rushed over him, and he pulled back.

He was in his mother's quarters in Qadira's harem, a massive complex of buildings that housed the apartments for all her important officials' spouses and families. He heard young children in the hall as well as old women.

Jahmil snarled and slammed the door shut. Naked and trapped, his muscles pulsating with rage, he searched the room for any stitch of fabric. He touched the curtains, then yanked back his fingers at the sting of metal. Golden chainmail, enough to dull fire and burn flesh like the naked sun. The bed was so massive that trying to use one of the blankets would result in a garment far too large to even walk in. Besides, there were no sheets, only thick furs.

Better than nothing, he decided, but when he tried to rip them into smaller pieces, it was impossible, and when he tried to tie them around his waist or even gather them over his shoulders, they kept falling apart into individual hairs. The fabric must have been enchanted so that it refused to be clothing.

Grinding his teeth, he tore open a pillow to use the case to at least make himself some braies, but the moment the stitches ripped, the entire pillow popped into nothing like a puff of cloud. The same happened if he held the pillow up to cover himself; it puffed out of existence. An illusion.

There wasn't a single stitch of usable fabric in the entire room.

He tried to open the door a crack to call out to someone in the hall, to ask them to find him a tailor or a seamstress, but the door would not simply crack open. Every time he tried, it flew all the way open, and then there was no way to hide except to slam it shut again.

Jahmil paced back and forth like a caged animal. At the beginning of last night, he had rather hoped he would wake up naked this morning. But not in his mother's room, and not with Zamir.

If he had been anywhere else, it would have been easier to work up the courage to walk out of the door, nudity or not. But not in the harem, not with dowager countesses and small children everywhere.

His only option was to slip back to earth and pray that nobody who could see him would see him before he found some clothes. He closed his eyes and reached for the veil between worlds.

Nothing happened. If anything, the room seemed to shrink. Qadira, his mother, or both had cast a powerful net over the room—not unlike the Spider webs that covered Vespar—to keep him from slipping through to Ard.

He was trapped.

He lifted his arms and tried to shapeshift into a cat so he could slink out, but again nothing happened. His magic was useless. At last, his gaze turned to the gold curtains. Not merely an ostentatious fashion statement. How much more gold was hidden in this room unseen, embedded in the very walls?

A furious shout bubbled up from his guts, and he punched a hole in the wall. But there was nothing on the other side. Just more wood, more magic.

Jahmil grabbed his hair and pulled, a painful scream frothing in his chest. The next time he saw Zamir, he was going to break his jaw, and possibly much more.

As he paced, the minutes stretching intolerably, the anger came at him in waves. Takisha had betrayed him; he'd never thought it was possible. At first, that was all he could think. Then an unwelcome whisper broke through the surface.

From her perspective, he had betrayed her. She couldn't understand why he had changed his mind. *He* wasn't entirely sure why. The Covenant, yes. But there was more than that. Something about seeing Bakr again—hearing that loud, halting laughter that in the past had always reminded him not to take everything so seriously. Or perhaps it was Serap's innocent analysis of the situation that cut down to the heart of the matter, leaving no fat to chew on. Or perhaps it had been Ayelet herself, the way she looked at him. Her smile, her kiss, the silent question that he now knew she would never be able to ask any more than he could frankly answer.

But she had to know the truth by now. Didn't she?

He had promised to come back to her. And if that meant he had to walk naked through the harem, in front of the entire court of Ahmar...

He walked to the door and gripped the handle, but his arm trembled. He swallowed hard and rolled his shoulders. How far would he have to walk before he reached a place where he could slip back to Ard? Fifty paces? A hundred? How many old women and small children could he possibly startle at such a distance?

"Do it. Do it, Jahmil. Do it." He started to turn the handle, but fear flashed through his guts and he pulled away. "*La'anaha Allah!*"

He clapped his hands and rubbed them together quickly, popping his neck from side to side. "For Ayelet," he said, and marched back towards the door.

As he reached for the handle again, it turned and was drawn open. On instinct, he ducked behind the edge of the wardrobe to hide.

His mother stepped inside and shut the door behind her before folding her hands together and lifting her brow to regard him. "Are you feeling better, *abnay*?

"What in Allah's name is the matter with you, woman?" he spat, straightening to face her while keeping his bottom half hidden behind the dresser. "Is this some kind of joke?"

"Of course not." She cocked her head to one side. "Just a very effective way to contain a respectable man." She hurried across the room towards him, coming around the side of the dresser. He wanted to hide, but there was nothing but his hands. Impossibly insufficient.

She looked him up and down, then hardened her jaw and slapped him across the face. She was a small woman but had always known how to throw a hit. His neck snapped back.

"Where have you been?" she demanded.

Jahmil touched his lip, gathering a trickle of blood on his fingertip. His eyes flashed to hers.

"With less than a week until the wedding, you're galavanting around the Nine Kingdoms and Allah only knows where else, with some...? What? Can you even call such a creature a woman?"

"Do not speak to me about her." He clenched his teeth and his fists. "My personal affairs are none of your business."

"I think you will find every bit of you is my business," she snapped, her eyes sweeping over his body. A sensation like ants crawling over his flesh forced his shoulders to hunch. "Do you know the situation you left me in?"

He snarled and then took a slow breath. "If you can't be trusted to handle the goings on here while I am away, then I truly do not understand your purpose anymore."

Her eyes flashed with yellow and white lightning, so fast and bright that a tiny clap of thunder sounded behind him. He had not seen her so angry in years, not since he had fought against her desire to flee the unwinnable battle of Karzusan. His instinct was to recoil, but thinking of Ayelet, he put back his shoulders and refused to turn away.

"You must pacify Qadira," she said.

Jahmil smirked in spite of himself. "I beg your pardon?"

"She is getting on my last nerve, Jahmil. Three days in a row she has come into my apartments and moaned the degrees away, asking every pointless question about you. Your refusal to bed her has backfired and caused her to become obsessed."

"You're out of your league, old woman."

"Nothing has ever been denied her before. She has never had to wait for anything. And no man has ever dared refuse her. You should see how she pines for you, how she raged when you missed the rehearsal."

He laughed coldly. "Let her eat her own heart."

She slapped him again. He growled and clenched his back teeth.

"What happens when Qadira tires of you and decides to call off the match?" Her cold fingers latched onto his arm. The ants marched faster, and again the urge to recoil congealed the meager contents of his stomach. "What exactly do you bring to the table that couldn't be brought by any prince in the Nine Kingdoms, or so much more in fact? You said yourself Jahmil, all you are is a good name and rich blood. Do you know how easily that is replaced?"

"Make up your mind, Mother. Is she dangerously obsessed or about to cast me off?"

His mother laid her hand on his chest, leaning around his shoulder to gaze up into his eyes. He stood a foot taller than her, broader, thicker, stronger. But her touch fell on him like a chill.

"You must sleep with her tonight," she said.

"Never."

"You do not have the luxury of love, *abnay*. Do you imagine for a moment that you would even be here if I only ever lay with men that I loved?"

He exhaled sharply and turned to look at her, but her face was as flat as ever. She never said anything she didn't mean. Not to him. In his heart, he had always known his parents did not love each other, that there wasn't even any affection between them. But to hear her say it out loud and so matter-of-factly was more difficult than he would have expected.

He was even more startled when his mother brushed the side of his face with one hand, a far gentler touch than he had felt from her in years. Perhaps it would have even had the power to melt him had he not been trapped and naked and biting at the bit like a caged *namur*.

"I do not know where your soul acquired such romance, Jahmil. Certainly not from your father or me." She sighed and cast her eyes down. "Qadira can sense it in you, as any woman could. It has arrested her interest, and she longs to feel it directed at her."

He laughed at the absurdity of her argument. "It doesn't work that way."

"And why not? If you are to be king, you must be the master of all you see, including yourself. Particularly yourself."

She turned away and glided to the end of the room, where she took a small, ivory-inlaid box from within her robes. She set it on the table and removed the emerald catch. She took from it a bottle, twisted to a point at the end like a bolt of lightning. Black liquid sloshed inside.

"I can help you, Jahmil," she said, showing him the barest hint of a smile. "I can make this easier for you."

Tremors licked up his spine. "What is that?"

"I can clear your mind of the human that has clouded it. She is a vandal, stealing her way into your heart, and now, she slices it apart, piece by piece." She lifted the bottle. "This can evict her forever."

Her words hit him like a blast of cold air. He took a step back. "No."

"My son, I understand why you said what you did to Takisha about calling off the wedding. You are under a lot of pressure and you were speaking from a place of anger."

"Those words were not spoken in anger." His eyes flicked to the swirling tattoo on his arm, then back to her. "You do not speak for Shihala. She speaks for Herself."

"If you do not marry Qadira, our race is already extinct. Only you can save our people." She turned to him.

Her diamond eyes swam in shades of deep purple sorrow. They had only brought him so much pain once before—the night she screamed at him that his father and all his friends were already dead. The night she had convinced him to flee from the crumbling remains of Karzusan, even as Vespar's Spiders blasted through the walls of his childhood home and stole everything he had ever held dear. Ever since then, he could never look at her face without feeling the flames on his neck, without hatred bubbling in his gut.

"I understand how difficult it is," she said, "when you have this hunger of new love gnawing away at you like a viper searching for the kill. This bottle can take the pain away and allow you to focus on the task at hand."

He shook his head. "I want my pain."

She uncorked the bottle. "It is making you sloppy, Jahmil. I wish I could simply wash away this useless aspect of your personality that longs to love." Grimacing, she shook her head. "You are so handsome, my son. If only you learned to wield that weapon as it is meant to be wielded."

"I have enough weapons."

The door opened, and several soldiers marched inside, each with full armor and muscles to make a stone wall envious.

"What is the meaning of this?" he growled, backing even further into a corner.

"I'm not asking you to give up love," his mother said, casting her gaze at him over one shoulder. "You may keep your poetry, provided it is directed at the right person. After the forgetting potion has a chance to take effect, I will have a love potion prepared. Qadira will have to administer it herself, so you may gaze into her eyes while it takes effect." She looked down at her feet and shook her head. "Seeing the doubt and defiance in you, I should have done this months ago. In that regard, I must take my own portion of responsibility for the situation." She turned to the guards. "Seize him."

The guards rushed him. He punched one in the face and kicked the feet out from under another, but their number quickly overwhelmed him. They pinned his arms to his sides. The hard leather of their armor scraped against his naked body, causing a thousand tiny abrasions.

"Let go of me!" he shouted, yanking at his captors' steel grasp. "I will do as you ask. I will go to Qadira tonight."

She pressed her lips together and shook her head. "She doesn't simply want your body, Jahmil. She wants your heart. Your soul."

"That was not part of the agreement," he spat. "It would be a lie. An illusion."

"Love always is. Like a mirage in the hot desert, it appears in a flash and tempts our minds, only to evaporate with the first touch of cold." She sighed and shook her head. "Is such a fantasy worth giving up everything we have worked so hard to achieve?"

"Is the Covenant of Shihala a fantasy?" he hissed, yanking against his captors.

Her gaze dropped to the mark on his arm—the twisting black tattoo that spoke the truth more completely than he ever could.

"That is unfortunate, but it is not yet fully formed. Once you forget about the human and swallow Qadira's love potion, it should shift to reflect the proper choice." She sighed. "And if it does not, I will pay to have a permanent illusion woven over it."

"That is treason!" He shook his head quickly, struggling against the eight hands that held him captive.

"Qadira and I have amended the contract of trothplight to include this stipulation. Cast aside your desire for all others—" She lifted the potion. "—and cleave yourself to the queen, or there will be no wedding."

"I won't see Ayelet again, I swear. But please, do not make me forget her."

She lifted the bottle and began to chant words that made no sense but stabbed at him like iron claws. White light flashed through his senses, blinding him. Muting him. A guard snatched his face and forced his mouth open, then his mother poured the vile liquid down his throat. His nose and mouth were held shut until he swallowed, then everything went black.

CHAPTER TWENTY-SIX

Ayelet

Ayelet moved through the sculpted archways of lost ruins as she had many times in her nightmares. If only this were one, now.

Nadir led her through the rustle of dry leaves and down pitted stairways until the cool of the earth was all that touched her skin. She knew what came next, what lingered past the faceless marble statues and cracked stone walls. Endless torture. Cuts on her skin that never killed. Burns on her feet that never healed. Suffocation. Just enough pain and torture to wish she were dead, to yearn for it, but never reach it. Then darkness. Isolation. Only the cruel laughter of demon-filled dreams and the hiss of rats for weeks and weeks until it started all over again.

And why?

For something Köle searched for in her that she had always failed to give. Yet, Köle was the only one who had ever consistently been there for her, whether she wanted it or not. Ironic. She ran a finger over a passing pillar and pulled it away covered in chalky white dust, strangely calm.

No, she was not calm.

She was nothing, the empty vastness she recoiled into as a child and had only begun to peek out from, having not learned her lesson. A day had passed, her pleadings to Jahmil having fallen on deaf ears and chirping woods. If he were to come, it would be now. The last minute before she'd be lost forever. After all, he had promised.

But he would not—the muted ache in her belly told her that. Maybe djinn and humans were alike. Untrustworthy. And it did not bother her one way or the other, or so she lied to herself. She could not let it, or else the one-faced demons would know and find her and laugh cruelly as they destroyed that part of her, along with everything else. Serap, too, she pushed from her mind, chained to the decaying pillars above with a group of other children. Köle cared nothing for physical possessions, so it was possible little Serap still held onto the opal in her necklace, a little symbol of her love and hope, even if it could not bring her a brighter future if she was not free.

Nadir's heavy footfalls echoed as they entered deeper into the ancient temple of a false god long lost to human memory. The shiver of wind whispered through the hallways, faint enough for one to think they had heard nothing at all but still check the corners of the room for ghosts.

Köle was no ghost; she could feel him in the altar room ahead and hear his labored breathing. A writhing sea of wisps clung to the root-cracked stones overhead, one or two dipping down every so often to brush her cheek or tousle her hair until she stood in the center of the roughly-hewn floor.

"My Ada," Köle rasped an 'h' sound out before the 'a' with a hoarse breath.

Needles pricked from her skin inward, over and over in waves of pain. It had not been long enough since she'd heard her birth name. Not since the gods gave her the lyre and marked her their instrument, their *ayelet*. Eternity would not be long enough.

"Ada," Köle rasped again. "Come where I can see you." An ironic statement, since he hid perpetually behind a curtain and she had never once seen him. Even as a child, when he called her to him often, red velvet and a cold, cutting voice were all she knew him as.

Her footsteps struck the earth like heavy bags of grain. She locked her eyes on the pocked wall above the familiar scarlet curtain. Wisps swirled in eddies on every inch of stone, blurring the dark spots on the wall and the faces of armless statues, before leaving them clear again.

"You have the look of your mother," he said with detestation. "Except for your eyes."

A wisp broke free from the whirlpools of magic and swept by to brush her hair.

"*Eawdatu!*" Köle snarled, and the wisp shrunk away. "You've picked up nasty habits while you were away," he said brittlely, like glass being ground beneath a boot.

She continued her stare past the curtain.

"Look at me when I'm talking to you!" Köle's voice shook the room with a flash of orange light that burst from behind the edges of the trembling velvet.

She slid her empty gaze down each dusty crack and onto the folds of the curtain.

"Do you know why you're here?" he asked, tainting each 'h' with a guttural hack and exhaling far too much before every word. He did not wait for an answer. "Because you're mine and are finally ready to do what you were born to do. To do what I've painstakingly raised you up to do."

She blinked slowly.

"You give me nothing?" he hissed, crushing shards of glass once more. "You dare look at me with those deadened eyes? Where is your fear?"

When she did not respond, another flash of orange lit the room, and the curtain shook so hard the little metal hooks clinked. A sliver of darkness appeared on one side. Her mind stirred, and her eyes snapped to attention. Never once in all the years she'd been with Köle had he shown himself more than a brush of ghostly white hidden in the black.

"Perhaps you have been away for too long. Has the cruel world given you a perverted sense of hope, child? Have you come to believe you're worth anything without me?"

Ayelet kept her eyes trained on the open slit, wishing to see anything that would make him more tangible and less like the faceless man of her nightmares.

He hissed and ripped the curtain closed with a pinch of the fabric. "Nadir!" Köle screeched in a whisper. "Bring Kadri to me."

Only the occasional sigh of a lively wisp broke the oppressive silence as they waited.

"Yes, Köle?" Kadri asked, bowing low into the room like the demon of a man was the sultan himself. The confidence that previously coated her words like oil had dried, leaving a squeak.

"Give her the lyre," he commanded.

Kadri fumbled as she patted her skirts.

His irritated growl stirred up a squall in the wisps overhead. "Now!"

Kadri ripped the instrument free, as delicate with the fine craftsmanship as a child is with the neck of a baby bird, and shoved it into Ayelet's hands. Ayelet flicked her gaze to the smooth wood and back up. Köle hated music. It was, as he had said once while he had her brutally lashed for another child humming, "the whine of souls who never learned to shut up."

"Play," he breathed.

She ran a finger up and down the length of one of the rough strings. Her music was not his. It was the first thing she had made her own after she ran from him, and it was the only thing that had ever truly been hers, the only whole piece of her left. She pulled back her finger and dropped her hand so the lyre hung limply at her sides.

"Play," he snarled again. "So you can know what I've done for you and what you must do for me."

"I'd rather die," she said flatly.

Köle howled in outrage. The orange of angry fire flashed from the curtain and onto the ceiling, blasting apart the wisps, which fell upon the ground like rain. "You rake at me, you snarking, nasty little girl. Nadir, lock her up until I can look upon her without wanting to spit. Perhaps some time with the rats and her memories will remind her who she must serve."

Nadir's hairy knuckles looped around her arm and dragged her from the room.

Kadri followed behind, a jumpy skip in her step. "Do you want us all to die, Ayelet? Is that your plan?"

Ayelet gripped the neck of her lyre tightly, finding strength with its weight once more in her hand. A few stray wisps broke free from the red-curtained room and followed, grasping at the lyre with tiny tendril hands. "If you don't want to die at the hands of Köle, I suggest you run."

"Like you did?" Kadri asked bitterly.

"Exactly."

Kadri scowled. "That's not a long-term option that works for me."

"It is your only option," Ayelet said flatly.

As they walked through shadowy passageways carved with ancient prayers, a wailing sound, shrill and shrieking, echoed faintly from rooms she could not see. Each cry brushed against her ears like razors, sending chills up her spine and back down again. She worried the ghastly screams would scare the wisps away, but they lingered like shadows in the sky. She had begun to take comfort in them, in a strange way, a familiar sight far away from the home she never had. A sight she always knew would return, unlike people. Or djinn.

Her mind began to slip towards Jahmil, a stir of tender warmth before smoldering to ash in a pit of shame. Was she a fool to trust him, as Balian said?

"Where are we?" she asked, allowing herself to be escorted like a goat toward the milking stand to be sucked dry by icy hands. It was better to be near Nadir's wolfish eyes than to be alone in this place.

"The ruins of Sihar," he grunted.

"Or so Köle says," Kadri huffed. "It's in the middle of nowhere to the south of Edirne, not a trade route in sight. What does he think my business will subsist on if there's nothing and no one to barter with?"

Ayelet inhaled the musty air and let out a resigned sigh. "I'm certain he doesn't care."

"Well, he should," Kadri snapped at nobody in particular. "He may provide the magic, but the cider and jars all have to be found and paid for."

"Köle provides the magic?" Ayelet couldn't help her curiosity. "Does it come from him?" Then, a sneaking dread ran nails down her neck. She shot an uneasy look at the wisps twirling playfully above, the ones she had just begun to trust. "Does it work for him? Does it spy?"

"Don't be naïve," Nadir brushed her off.

He tightened his grip and shoved her around a corner into a hallway with an iron-grated door at the end. Mottled metal flowers that wilted with rust carved their way from one end to the next, so the room could see out and everyone else could see in. Past that lay a ratty, moth-eaten blanket, three lit and already dying candles, and a small bowl of bread and cheese.

"I've told you once already that magic is not a creature," Nadir said. "It has no mind of its own, and it certainly doesn't work *for* anyone, it is worked *by* them through various tools, like fire or an instrument." He pulled open the gate. "And it does not come from any being. It comes from a place."

He finished his patronizing lecture and cast her inside the room, locking the orangey iron behind her with a heavy copper key. Three melting candles lit the small space just enough to see the filth clinging to every inch of the walls.

The two turned to leave her, and Ayelet pushed herself against the door, reaching through the twining metal. "Kadri."

She hesitated, glancing over her shoulder with a cocked brow as Nadir disappeared in the dark.

"What is the magic being used for?" Ayelet whispered with an anxious glance upward. Nadir's speech had done nothing to convince her the wisps were not Köle's spies.

Kadri's shoulders slumped in a sigh. "I don't know."

"You must know something."

"Must I?" Kadri quipped, tight-lipped.

"Please?" Ayelet asked pitifully, the last play in her paltry hand of cards. "For an old friend?"

Kadri seemed to mull it over, chewing her cheek so hard her jaw shook, then she held out her hand.

"What?"

"Nothing in life is free," said Kadri, and her eyes glittered in the candlelight.

Ayelet couldn't help but smirk. It did not feel so good being on the receiving end of such trite condescension. Maybe that's why Jahmil had not returned.

"I'm a prisoner in a ruin." Ayelet laughed bitterly, the cold sound echoing off even colder walls. "What is it you think I might have?"

"Your necklace." Her eyes caught the dying candlelight with a mixture of greed and malice. "Köle forbade us from taking anything that belonged to you, but he said nothing against you giving me things."

Ayelet's hand shot to her throat. Her gift from Jahmil, a family heirloom from his grandmother. His words rushed through her like a moonlit breeze. *She used to say it brought her glad dreams. Serap tells me you sometimes do not sleep very well.*

She clenched a fist over the opals. "No deal."

Kadri smirked. "Fine, no deal. I hope those cold stones bring you comfort while you sleep. I have seen several rats."

With that, Kadri and the soft yellow glow of her candlelight faded from view. Not even the wisps had stayed behind. Ayelet turned, pressing her back into the jagged flowers that acted as sentinels for her cruel fate.

She was home.

Already the three candles had melted down to stubs. Soon it would be completely dark. She pressed her thumb to her head and stifled a whimper as she slid to the floor. *Please, Allah, let me have glad dreams.*

CHAPTER TWENTY-SEVEN

JAHMIL

Summoned to Qadira's quarters with no time to purchase a new present, Jahmil fell back on his stash. Whenever he was on Ard, he would pick up something for just such an occasion. Qadira loved all things Ardish, which was lucky because he couldn't afford the kind of jewelry she bought for herself in Ahmar's cosmopolitan hubs like Al Manidat. He tried to make each gift seem deliberate and thoughtful to distract from the fact that they were really just cheap.

He rifled through the bottom drawer of his jewelry chest and took out a string of blue glass beads he'd picked up in Edirne when last he was there. As he turned away, closing the box absently, something flashed through him. He opened the lid again and searched through the oddments.

Gone. No, it couldn't be gone. His grandmother's necklace and the only thing he had left of the gentle-hearted, wise-cracking old battleaxe. A memory flashed before him of her lying in twists of sweaty sheets, her thin hands trembling as she unclasped it from her neck and placed it in his hands. How her eyes had sparkled as she rasped the words, "For your queen."

Jahmil's hands clenched into fists. He never would have misplaced it, never would have moved it. Someone had stolen it, and he immediately suspected his mother. The necklace, while beautiful, was just a chain of common opals, not worth much weighed as raw gain. But his mother knew what it had meant to his grandmother, what it meant to him.

She had always hated her mother-in-law. Zalika blamed her for Jahmil's useless *tendency towards passion.* But would she have been cruel enough to give it to Qadira? Imagining that cold witch wearing his grandmother's necklace ignited such fury in his blood that his vision blurred.

"*Amiri?*" Zamir's voice called from the door.

Jahmil clenched his teeth, the flames in his eyes flickering on the wall. He tucked in his kaftan and yanked out the cuffs to peek out from under his dark red jacket. "Where is my grandmother's necklace?"

Zamir's jaw trembled before he set it. "It was taken to be cleaned, Your Highness."

"Cleaned?" he growled. "Cleaned to what purpose?"

"Forgive me." Zamir bowed deeply. "Waiola noticed it was looking a bit dingy and asked for permission to take it to a jeweler. I told her it was alright. I will get it back straight away."

Jahmil narrowed his eyes and approached Zamir, searching his expression. Zamir turned his gaze downward, but not before he saw it. The pink shine at the backs of his irises. He was lying. But why? Had he stolen it?

"Zamir," Jahmil said, unable to help the sharpness in his voice. "Are you telling me the truth?"

"Of course, *Amiri.*"

He took a deep breath and loosened his fists. His mother must have gotten to Zamir, yet again. Zamir could no longer be trusted, not even with simple things.

"Forget it," he spat. "Just be certain it is placed back where it belongs."

"Yes, *Amiri.*"

Jahmil slipped by Zamir into the hall, running a hand through his freshly oiled hair as he went. There was too much energy in his blood, so although he knew it would leave him with a sheen of sweat on his brow, he forwent the carriage and ran the distance from his apartments at the far end of the complex to the palace proper. He knew from experience that when he was feeling this way, destructive fires burning just beneath the surface of his skin, he was liable to make stupid decisions. It was better to appear before Qadira a little disheveled than with forks of hatred hot on his tongue.

An ear-splitting shriek cut into him as he passed by the royal stables. He knew that voice, if one could call such a hideous sound a voice. Thueban. Jahmil's heart lifted, thinking Takisha had finally returned, but then something dark drove him back down. Foggy, half-formed memories tumbled through his mind. Fighting with Takisha in the woods outside Edirne. She had beaten him bloody, cracked his ribs. Had she broken his back? He couldn't remember what they were fighting about.

But he did remember what Zamir had said happened to her. Qadira had her flogged and sent to Ashkult Prison. Panic ripped through his veins, thinking of his cousin in that horrific place. Even if she had beaten him savagely, she did not deserve such a reprimand. He had to get to her.

He stumbled over thoughts of Zamir. Something about being naked and threatening to tackle Zamir to the ground to tear off his clothes as well...

Jahmil put a hand to his forehead to check if perhaps his fire was burning too hot. He wasn't thinking clearly.

His forehead was cool, and that meant he had no excuse not to answer Qadira's summons. Before he could do anything, he had to go dance for her like the slave he was. He ran the rest of the way to the palace, but the exercise only added energy to his frantically thrashing heart.

Qadira's eunuch led him to her chambers but did not follow Jahmil inside, as he always had before, but shut the door behind him. Candles burned on every surface and in the massive chandelier hanging from the ceiling. But the flames were all low, all steady as moonlight.

"Jahmil?" she called from behind the screen that separated the rest of the massive chamber from her bed, her voice sticky sweet. "Is that you?"

"Yes, *malikati*."

"Come here, *habibi*. Let me see you."

He closed his eyes and bit his lip, stifling the sound of his sigh, and walked around the screen.

Qadira lay in a bed of silk pillows, her long black hair carefully strewn about her, red flowers threaded into it. Her purple skin looked shiny and shimmery, her makeup impeccable—dark eyes, thick red lips, lashes like black curtains. She was wearing a tiny brassiere decorated with so many diamonds that it glowed and a transparent skirt, slit up both hips so her legs hung out. One leg was drawn up over the other, her hip jutting up into the air. He'd never seen so much of her, but she looked pretty much how he figured she would look.

A stone dropped in his stomach. Had it already come to this? Did he not have a few days left until the wedding? Where had the time gone?

"My queen," he said, bowing stiffly. "You sent for me."

"Come close." She beckoned him with one long red fingernail.

He stepped up to the side of the bed. She patted the sheets beside her. His stomach roiled at her indecency, but he sat down.

Looking down at his lap, he shook his head. "*Malikati...*"

"Shh." She sat up and pressed her honey-scented finger to his lips. "I know what you're going to say."

"I doubt it."

"Don't worry. I've come around to your way of thinking. The longer we wait, the sweeter the eventual release will be." She leaned across him, her body so close he felt its heat. She grabbed the small box from his hand—his offering. He held his breath, waiting for her to open it, inspect it, and let him know if it was acceptable. Instead, she set it down on her nightstand. "Thank you for this."

"You didn't even look at it." He chuckled dryly.

"You missed our wedding rehearsal."

His eyes tried to widen. He crushed them into slits. Had he really done something so foolish? And why?

Bakr's bright jade eyes presented in his mind. Jahmil took a deep breath, drawing strength from them as ever he had. "Forgive me. I found myself in Orkeshi and I could not allow the opportunity to go to waste. The guerillas there..."

"Shh." She laid her finger on his lips again. "What have I told you about discussing war in my bedroom?"

His brow furrowed. "Forgive me, *malikati*."

"Perhaps I will. Perhaps I will not." She licked her lips.

"I need to speak with you about Takisha."

"My decision is final, and I will not suffer the name of that traitor to be uttered in my presence."

"But did she tell you why she—?"

"As if there is any justification for laying her hands on my fiancé." She stroked his cheek with the back of her hand. "You look thirsty. Allow me to offer you refreshment."

"Thank you," he breathed, chewing on his anger and then swallowing it. She leaned over to the far side of her bed, exposing the line of her back. Jahmil realized he was drumming his fingers and shoved his hand in his jacket pocket.

When she turned back to him, she had a strange bottle in her hand, the liquid inside shimmering bright red like fresh blood. She poured all of it into his goblet and smiled. "I had it brewed especially for you."

He swirled the concoction, watching the thick liquid slosh up the sides of his cup. "What is it?"

"Don't worry. It's not alcohol. I know you're a stickler, *Amiri*." She winked and crawled across the bed closer to him and pressed her palm against his chest, her gaze piercing into him.

She had never looked at him like that, with such intensity of thought. The skin around her eyes was tight while they were wide, hopeful with pale blue sparkles. And her lips were smiling, but the inner corners of her eyebrows were drawn up as if she was worried about something.

Jahmil glanced at the liquid, taking but a moment to weigh his options. She wouldn't be so foolish as to try to deceive him so blatantly... would she?

"You look radiant tonight," he said, setting the drink on her nightstand without turning his gaze from her. A glimmer of white panic touched her eyes.

"Thank you." She flashed a quick smile. "Aren't you going to try your drink?"

"That is not what I thirst for." Jahmil snatched her by the shoulders and pushed her down on the bed, coming down on top of her with a soft growl.

"Jahmil," she breathed, her lower lip trembling. Her skin broke out in goosebumps, and her breath quickened. "What are you doing?"

"Do you know how difficult it has been for me to resist you these last months?" He inhaled as he brushed his lips over her neck. "Do you take pleasure in tormenting me?"

He grabbed her wrists and gently guided them to either side of her head, pinning them to the pillows. He kissed her quickly, then nibbled down her neck, between her breasts, and over her stomach. "I cannot wait any longer."

He ripped off the gauzy fabric of her skirt, revealing stringy, bejeweled underwear that matched her brassiere.

She let out a little scream that morphed into a startled giggle. He ran his hands over her legs, her body twisting under his touch. He kissed her thigh and hip, then moved back up her stomach. As he raised up to kiss her lips again, he knocked the goblet resting on the nightstand with his elbow. It wobbled, then fell to the ground and shattered.

"Oh no!" she cried, shooting up.

He sat back, his eyes sweeping over the gelatinous liquid soaking into the carpet. "Oops."

"You fool," she chided him. "That is very rare and difficult to replace."

"Forgive me." He dropped his head into his hands as he scrambled to his feet. "I don't know what came over me."

"Wait!" She hurried to the edge of the bed, her teeth on her bottom lip as she reached for his hand. "You don't have to go."

He shook his head. "No, I must go." He looked into her eyes, conjuring severity in his expression. "I should not have grabbed you like that."

"It's fine. I don't mind."

"No. It was wrong," he said, breathing heavily. He punched his thigh. "We must wait until we are married. Forgive me, my queen."

"Jahmil!" she called after him, but he hurried from her room as quickly as his legs would carry him, then out of the palace. As he passed a soldier standing guard beyond the door, he called out to him, "Have Thueban saddled and ready to fly. Now."

The guard saluted and hurried off to fulfill his orders. Jahmil hocked a big wad of spit on the sparkling stones and clawed at his tongue with his fingernails.

A love potion! How stupid did she think he was? Or how stupid did his mother hope he was?

On the upside, after practicing in the mirror practically every night for the last several years, he was finally becoming a better liar. He'd even managed to conjure rosy lust in his eyes when he was running his lips over Qadira, though it went against his every instinct. Another woman had been in his mind then, someone with gray eyes and skin like satin. Fiction, of course. But a surprisingly effective one.

The great drakonte was brought, and Jahmil climbed on behind his massive triangular head and urged him into the air. As the cold wind whipped over him, Jahmil's frantic mind began to focus. It made no sense. Why had Takisha attacked him? He couldn't imagine anything in Qaf or Ard that might make her do such a thing. Perhaps she had given him a concussion, and that was why his temples throbbed every time he tried to think back on it.

Either way, she was suffering for it now, trapped in Ashkult Prison. The fires of Jahannam could compete with the horrors she may be facing, but his memories were fighting against his sympathy. Blood in his mouth and the crack of bone as she mercilessly attacked. With no memory of what had provoked it, it was impossible to say if Qadira's punishment was justified, light, or harsh. What he did know was that he was not satisfied with letting Qadira or anyone else make the decision for him.

He had no choice. He had to go to Ashkult and force Takisha to explain her actions.

CHAPTER TWENTY-EIGHT

Ayelet

Ayelet's eyes darted rapidly to and fro underneath her dark lids until she jolted up from the cell floor. Her heart beat like a bendir drum, and a shiver lingered on her lips. She clenched her fist around the opals. What strange power did they hold? For she had not dreamed of Köle and his one-faced demons, but of Jahmil.

She lay back down and banged her head against the dusty stone, trying to quell her racing pulse with deep gulps of stale air. She felt his hand caressing her stomach, gliding down her thigh. The weight of his body wrapped around hers as he whispered against her skin like a moonlit breeze, and her sigh in reply. The dream had ended as abruptly as it had started, leaving her wanting more. So much more. When she knew she'd never have it.

Maybe it had been a nightmare.

She groaned and hit her head so hard, little bursts of light dappled her eyes despite the oppressive dark. It had finally happened. She had gone insane. Trapped in the dungeon of a hidden madman with Serap suffering somewhere nearby, she still thought only of impossible dreams, of herself. Balian was right. She was a fool.

She pressed her chilled hands over her face, massaging them into her eyes. She dreamed of a man from a different world. A man who left her trembling in the brush and burning for more but who did not come to rescue her when she so shamefully cried for help. A man who was a djinn. A prince. And that was all. She punched the earth. Her void of nothing was far better than this. Still, she left on the necklace and found her finger wandering gently over her lips.

Now that she had awakened, she realized the mournful shrieks from before had found their way to her cell. She stood and pressed herself into the back corner so nothing could sneak up on her and so she could listen for rats. Or worse.

A metallic crack broke the darkened silence. She yelped. Then cringed and waited. Nothing. Had Nadir or Kadri come to take her back to Köle? What time was it?

"Hello?" she asked the silence.

Another sound, clinking and brittle, scratched at the dark. Rats. It had to be. She lifted her slippered foot so they would not chew it, grateful for Jahmil's boot on the other. No. Her boot, she realized with a sinking stomach. He would not come to fetch it. Not from this place.

The sound of grating metal continued, muffling the distant shrieks. She bent slowly to the earth, still balanced on one leg, and picked up her lyre. If the awful sounds that skittered up and down her spine would not stop, she would play over them. She tucked the instrument under her chin, needing no light to lay her fingers precisely where they should go on the strings.

She took a breath to play and then stopped. She had always used her music to lure people and djinn in. But she did not want to entice anything to come closer in this squalid place. She knit her brows together and tapped her hand on her skirts. Not a single song came to mind for repelling. Not one melody for pushing back or sending away. She had never needed one before because she had always been the one to leave.

She raked her fingernails over the strings with a growl of frustration and startled a wisp she had not seen by the iron door. It recoiled into a tight cloud that hovered at shoulder height.

"Are you spying on me?" She narrowed her eyes with suspicion. The wisp stayed scrunched up, like a ball of translucent silk that had been suspended in midair. "Is *he* spying on me *through* you?"

No change. Of course not. She was now as crazy as Nadir, talking to the sky as if someone or something would reply. She reached her hand out, and the wisp unfolded, gliding over and weaving itself in and out of her fingers. Then it returned to the door and vanished. She frowned. Had that been why she did not see it sooner?

Ayelet lowered her slippered foot and inched her way forward. Blind, she waved her free hand in front of her until she felt the cold iron of the door. Guessing where the wisp had disappeared, she ran her fingers side to side until she found a spire-shaped keyhole. She crouched low, hoping to spy a glimmer of white.

The breath of magic had thinned itself to the width of spider's silk and cast a sparkling web around the lock's mechanics like a nest. It undulated gently as if waiting for something. She stared back expectantly.

"Well don't look at me," she said when nothing happened.

She sighed. If Nadir was right, the wisps weren't evil. They just were. And if they were just a resource like water or air or livestock, then maybe she could put them to work for her. They seemed to like her well enough, which was far better than any master she'd had to serve.

She squinted, then poked the lock. When that did nothing, she tried swirling her finger around in hopes the wisp would follow and pop the lock open. It made no sense. But magic never did. She fiddled futilely until frustration boiled under her skin.

"I want out," she yelled at the wisp. Didn't Köle chase the magic back with his voice when she stood before him? "Open!" she commanded.

Ayelet banged the metal with her fist and cried out, sucking the sting from the side of her fingers and spitting when she remembered where they'd been. She lifted her lyre and plucked out three angry chords in quick succession over and over, mixing and improvising until the music tumbled out in a scurried melody. As she played, the lock began to glow white.

Hadn't Nadir mentioned instruments?

Relief filled her, and her fingers slowed, but so did the wisps. She bit her tongue hard and plucked through the pain. More mists of magic appeared down the hallway, yanking and pulling at each other's formless bodies to get to her cell first. She closed her eyes and waited for the impact of the wall of wisps, but they threw themselves into the lock instead. The copper keyhole burst. Shards of metal flew across the room, several cutting her cheek as she ducked for cover. When the final bits of debris had pitter-pattered to the earth, she peeked out from over her lyre, which she had recklessly thrown up in her defense.

Eyes wide, she surveyed the damage.

"Oops," Ayelet whispered.

Had her music really caused the wisps to blow up the lock? She shuddered. A final trickle of wisps pulled into her room, illuminating the sharp and broken angles of what used to be the door. What *had* Köle turned her into?

She toed the jagged pieces, stepping over them gingerly before sprinting down the hall. Though where she rushed to was a mystery. Turn after turn took her in the loops of a maze, and the only time she knew she was making progress was when the wailing and gnashing of teeth grew louder. Each time, she would spin on her heels and run anywhere else but there. And each time, the trail of wisps trailing above her would grow thicker by one or two.

On the seventh loop of that infernal temple, she acknowledged defeat. With a swipe at her forehead to keep the sweat from her eyes, she faced the darkest hallway from which the torment leaked. Afraid to go where she could not see, she put up her fingers and waited, holding her breath. Two little wisps seeped down through a crack in the ceiling, following overgrown roots that the forest had used to reclaim the temple. They circled her wrist, then hovered helpfully, lighting the way a few paces ahead. She smiled.

Steeling herself, she made her way past ancient texts and empty doorways, waving a finger at dark corners to be lit by her wisps. With every step, it became clearer that children made the horrible sounds. Children, and something terrible that snarled and snapped its teeth.

Memories of her own childhood soaked into her heart and sent shivers down her spine. It didn't help that as she progressed, the veil of white around her grew heavier, obscuring more than it revealed. At last, she turned down a hallway illuminated by the orange glow of an unseen fire where shadows flickered with exaggerated features. Abnormally long legs, hunched and hairy backs, and fangs far too sharp and large for a human's mouth.

The same-faced demons appeared in her mind, mocking and cruel and pushing her to do something, something, though she never knew what, and always at the behest of faceless Köle. She raised her hand again, unable to keep her fear from pouring into the call for more wisps. They obliged, a halo of seven circling protectively around her. She braced herself for what she would see when a throat-searing snarl rent the air. Not in front of her, but behind.

Ayelet twisted, a dead-end at her back as a creature from her nightmares crawled forward on mangy legs. Its orange eyes glowed, untarnished by pupil or humanity and infinitely cold. Eyes that sought to kill. The hideous, hyena-faced beast lumbered toward her, back curled at an unnatural angle, like a man bent over to walk on all fours. It snarled, flinging putrid, green saliva in her direction, scattering her thin shield of wisps.

Fear ran through her, icy cold down her back, while adrenaline coursed through her veins, hot on her cheeks. She flung herself at the side wall and tried to make an escape around it. Its giant fangs chomped at her arm, and she recoiled, her spirits frantically spinning around her. She turned and ran through the archway. The creature nipped at her heels, shrieking in anger.

Desperate, Ayelet pushed her legs harder, running past cells filled with the wide, frightened eyes of children. Her gaze darted frantically over the faces, both terrified and relieved that none of them were Serap. She wanted to turn, to force wisps into the locks and break them free, but she could not do so if she were dead. She spied an empty cage at the end of the hallway, its back wall stacked with jars of magic.

Allah'a şükür! Praise Allah! If she could throw herself inside and shut the bars behind her, she might have a chance. She sprinted so fast, her hips popped. The bones ached in her knees.

A force hit her back, sharp and stinking of death. The creature had caught up. Ayelet screamed, crawling forward as it raked her skin with its claws. Pain shredded her senses along with the flesh on her calf. She would not escape this. With every snap of the creature's drooling fangs, the children in the dungeon cried out in pain and utter horror. Ayelet stopped reaching and turned.

She twisted her back to face the monster, its too-long tongue licking at her hungrily. She punched it hard in the nose. It growled out a laugh. Her physical strength would never be enough. She would never be enough. But maybe the magic would be. Stoking her desperation, she reached past the creature's ears and called an eddy of wisps down to her. They hit her fist with a flash that lit the room like lightning. The beast fell forward against her. She kicked hard at its chest with a grunt and scraped herself free.

Ayelet eyed the magic that frantically reached for her inside the glass jars. It was not what she needed. She would not kill it with an explosion—the thought of the beast tearing into pieces and coating the room made her stomach turn. But when she called magic from above to fight the monster, a wisp had snaked out of its ear, too. Whatever the thing was, it was made of magic, or else soaked in it. She would suck it dry.

Instead of running, she took the offensive and threw herself at the beast, clinging to the oily tufts of fur on its back. With a mixture of yearning and fear, she called the wisps to only her. White flooded the room. The creature writhed beneath her as magic seeped from its ears and eyes and nose. When its snarls dropped to agonized whimpers and its swiping claws began to twitch, she tumbled off.

Then watched in horror as the demon's fiery eyes faded into those of Serap.

CHAPTER TWENTY-NINE

JAHMIL

THE MOMENT THUEBAN TOUCHED ground on the white shores of Buhayrat Alzaybiq, Jahmil realized why Zamir had looked so pale when he returned from collecting Khayin. He could hardly imagine the spineless fusspot being able to stand on these gloomy shores and gaze across the heavy white mist, let alone dare to go across. Very likely, he had delegated the task.

Perhaps Jahmil should have done the same.

The surface of the lake shone like a mirror. No wind, no movement. Someone who didn't know better may have thought they could walk across, but that would have been a dire mistake. For the waters of Buhayrat Alzaybiq were not water at all, but a thousand square parasangs of poisonous quicksilver. Perhaps a human could have wandered in, even floated on the freezing, dense liquid, then realized their mistake and rushed back to shore with minimal damage, but for a djinn, the liquid metal was worse than acid, worse even than iron. A single drop landing on a hand or foot would mean permanent amputation. A splash to the face or torso would inevitably bring slow and excruciating death.

Worse than that, to be in the presence of quicksilver was to be without magic. Compared to this place, the barren homeland of the Vespars felt downright welcoming. The sky was awash in flat white clouds that bathed the land in smokey iridescence. No moons, no stars, no sprays of nebulas. Situated at the heart of Qaf and shrouded in perpetual moonlessness, it was the coldest, most isolated, most hostile land in all the Nine Kingdoms or the wastelands beyond.

Legend had it that Allah created the lake of quicksilver from the tears of a great wali, *sadiq Allah*, whose name now was lost to history. It was no longer known who had originally braved the quicksilver to build the prison at the center, on a lone island of razor-sharp lava stone. The structure had stood for ten thousand years. It rose like the coiled body of a black eimlaq at the center of the lake, a misshapen lump of stone and concrete. The only way to know for certain it even was a building was the occasional rectangular slit of a window.

The walls were built to the very edge of the island so no flying creature would have any space to land, let alone the massive Thueban. The only way to the prison was by ferry, and there was only one ferry.

Jahmil spotted a shack sitting back a few hundred feet from the shore, tiny, slanted, and made of porous black stone. His heart beat faster as he approached gingerly. The ferryman of Ashkult was almost as infamous as the prison itself. An immortal warrior who, like Khayin, had braved the great Bahamut Sea to seek favor from the Eternal One. They said his eyes held the secrets of the ages, that the eggs of sacred tze birds grew from the rough leather of his back, and his legs were encased in impenetrable glass, protecting him from the swell of Alzaybiq's waters.

Jahmil's hands were sweaty, but his feet were frozen in his boots. He had never experienced such cold.

A strange memory came to him of huddling in the shelter of trees during the last Moonless Night, lighting white fires all around himself, removing his shirt. He wrinkled his nose at it. None of those things made the slightest bit of sense.

When he reached the ferryman's shack, he hesitated, but the door was yanked open before he had a chance to knock. Jahmil's breath caught in his throat as he prepared to meet the face of the Nameless Ferryman, but his eyes scanned the empty doorway for several seconds before finally glancing down. The creature was four feet tall with long, coarse black hairs twisting from his head, chin, ears, and arms. He wore a rough gray robe, belted at the waist with what looked like mooring line. His skin was deep red, crispy, and patched with shadows.

The tiny hairy man groaned, scratched his butt, and went back into the hut, leaving the door dangling. Jahmil was wondering if he was supposed to follow when the ferryman returned, a worn leather book in one hand, a quill in the other, and tiny half-moon glasses perched on his lumpy, carrot-like nose. "Dropping off or picking up?"

Jahmil bit his lip. Part of him was anxious to say *picking up*, but the brutal, unprovoked thrashing he had endured at Takisha's hands made the words stick in his throat. "I'm here to visit."

The ferryman swiped off his glasses in contempt. "There are no visitors at Ashkult."

"Call it interrogation then."

"Hmm." He put his glasses back on. "Name?"

"Alamir Jahmil Abdullah ibn Almalik Bajul al-Shihalai."

The ferryman ran the quill up and down the page. "Nope."

Jahmil's eye twitched. "Nope?"

"You're not on the list. Go away." He started to slam the door, but Jahmil wedged his foot in the frame.

"How does one get on your list?"

The hairy little man stuck out his hand, palm up. A disconcerting sense of déjà vu raced up Jahmil's spine, but he shook it off.

He didn't have any money, let alone enough to bribe his way into Ashkult. Everything of any real value belonged to Qadira, and she never gave him spending money. It was in her interest to keep him poor and dependent on her. He was nothing more than a gilded slave who didn't even own the clothes he was standing in.

With a sigh, Jahmil took the ring of white rock crystal from his finger. His father had given it to him on his seventeenth birthday, symbolizing his official recognition of the heir to the throne. What till that moment had been an assumption based on blood had become a conscious determination and unbreakable promise. It was also the only memento Jahmil had of his father—a reminder of the man he was and the future that was stolen from him.

But King Bajul had never placed any significance on trinkets, only on action. Only on results. The ring itself had no real meaning. Unlike his grandmother's necklace.

He sighed and passed it to the ferryman.

Meaty fingers wrapped it up. "Jahmil Amir, is it?" He scribbled in his book. "Come on, then."

He waddled out of the hut into the gray mist, Jahmil at his heels. As they approached the lake, he saw the small boat resting in the silver. Nothing special—a paddle, a haul, a seat. He didn't know what he had been expecting, but this wasn't it.

Jahmil climbed aboard carefully to avoid rocking the small vessel. "Is it really so simple to get into Ashkult?"

"It's a prison," the ferryman replied, taking up his post at the back and picking up his paddle. "Getting out is the hard part."

As the boat crawled across the lake, Jahmil kept to the middle of his seat, arms folded and shoulders turned in. Quicksilver sloshed against the high sides of the small boat. They moved so slowly it was excruciating, not simply because every tiny ripple of the lake was a promise of torture. His brain was swirling with unfinished thoughts like a hurricane bumping up against a brick wall.

After what felt like a full cycle of the Third Moon, the prison finally rose through the mist. When they were close, the ferryman threw a rope around one of several sharp stalagmites and drew the boat closer, arm over arm.

Jahmil stood uneasily. He had to take a moment to screw down his courage before leaping across the space to land on a sharp stone. His gaze swept up the twists of towers, weather-beaten, and smooth as obsidian. He mounted a long, twisting staircase leading up from the shore.

More red men awaited him at the top, though they could not have been more different from the tiny, hairy boatman. The guards embodied the very ideal of Ghaluman soldiers, every one of them at least a handspan taller than Jahmil and corded in muscle that shined in tones of ruby and burgundy under their sparse leather armor. They asked for his name, his purpose, the name of the prisoner he wished to interrogate, and the date of admittance. They patted him down to be sure he was unarmed and took his purse when they found it, though it was empty. They also unstrung the laces from his boots.

When they were satisfied, a tremendously lumpy red prison guard led him into the building. He was so tall his bald head nearly scraped the stone ceiling. Jahmil's eyes struggled to adjust to the dimness, nothing but torches burning with smokey fire to light the way. The stench was more subtle than he would have expected. Musty like a cave, yet metallic like a doctor's surgery left to fester.

He was brought to a small chamber with three four-inch-wide slitted windows and left alone, while the guard went to fetch Takisha. As he waited, he walked to the window and gazed out at the formless whiteness of the lake. This was the only view prisoners at Ashkult were ever afforded. He tried not to imagine what it would be like to be trapped in this cell for months, years, even a lifetime. No outside contact, minimal contact with other prisoners. No books, no music. Nothing but that white, unchanging sky and its constant light.

Would it not have been more humane to execute them?

The door shifted, startling him. Red men shuffled in, and at their backs was a great, hulking, blue-green behemoth. She stood shoulder to shoulder with the Ghaluman behemoths but had never looked so small. A golden collar was tightened around her neck, affixed with long rods that the guards used to guide her like an animal. Her ankles and wrists were in manacles. All her hair had been shaved off. Black circles clung to her under-eyes. When her gaze landed on him, he braced himself for the ferocity he had seen the night she snapped his back over her knee. Instead, she smiled so sadly that hairline fractures tore open his heart.

"What are you doing here?" she asked as the red men led her to a chair of gold and forced her to sit.

He couldn't bear to look at her. He turned to the widows, trying to rein in the tremendous sympathy growing in his chest that threatened to steal away with all his anger. "Why, Takisha? Why did you attack me?"

"What do you mean *why*?" She drew her dark eyebrows together. "You mean you don't remember?"

"All I remember is you attacking me for no reason, and then taking me back to Ahmar so my mother and Qadira could punish you for it." He rubbed a hand over his beard and shook his head. "Did you hit your head harder than usual at Ain Khuleel?"

"So Zalika took care of it." She scoffed and jutted out her chin. "It was worth it then."

"Took care of what?"

"You've come back to your senses."

He narrowed his eyes. "When had I ever lost them?"

"Are you going to marry Qadira?"

"You know I am. What sort of question…?"

She reached for him. Jahmil flinched, and a guard yanked her back against the corrosive chair. "I still have not told you what happened at the battle."

Her words ignited his mind like a spark set to dry grass. "Were all the drakontes killed by the eimlaq?"

"Not the eimlaq." She shook her head, black haze pooling in her eyes. "Köle still lives."

Her words entered his blood and transformed into slush, slugging through his veins painfully. "What did you say?"

Her face did not change, shimmering green eyes boring into him.

"That's not possible," he stammered. "He died at Rananbar. Everybody knows…"

"Jahmil, listen to me. I saw him. He was there. Whatever happened to him at Rananbar, it left him scarred, but alive."

"All right." He shook his head hard, trying to settle the new information into its place. "So what if he is?"

"He is allied with humans." She shook her head, then refocused her eyes on his. "They were at Ain Khuleel fighting alongside the Vespars. Humans with machines unlike anything I've ever seen. Great iron bombards. Not merely flashes of fire, but iron hurtling through the sky, cutting through everything. Cannon fire. It ripped down the walls at Ain Khuleel and tore through the flesh of our drakontes like tissue paper."

Jahmil shook his head again. "But I've been to the city. I saw it. It was perfect."

"An illusion left to delay your response. The city was flattened. Five hundred drakontes and riders lost their lives. And then…"

Jahmil leaned closer, the shadows in her lime-green eyes sending a chill through his blood. "Takisha?"

"Köle. He has control over some great power source. He used it to send the dead and injured to feed the eimlaq. I don't know what happened to the rest. I ordered them to flee. Perhaps Köle got to them, too."

Jahmil shook his head hard. "But why?"

"I thought it was to lure you there to kill you."

He almost laughed. "Surely there are simpler ways to kill me."

"It wasn't just about killing you, *ibn khali*. It was about raising the eimlaq. I see that now."

"To what purpose?"

"There is something there, under the eimlaq. In the fire of the earth. I felt it. The great wound is a door to Qaf, a door through which raw magic may be drawn and stolen. The eimlaq was blocking the path, and now it is open."

"*What* is open?"

"I don't know. But we must find out."

Jahmil folded his fingers together and took a deep breath. "Takisha, if I release you from this place, do you swear you will not attack me again?"

Her upper lip curled in defiance. "Provided that you maintain your senses."

"That is not good enough," he spat. "Even if I lose them again, whatever that means. You must promise."

She growled and bared her teeth. "Provided you swear to heed my counsel."

"No." He shook his head. "I make the decisions and you follow orders. Swear it on Shihala or I shall leave you here to rot."

She was silent for a long time, spittle foaming at the edges of her mouth. "I will follow you into Jahannam, *Amiri*."

Jahmil nodded, satisfied. "Now, tell me why you attacked me."

"You were about to throw away everything we have worked for. Your resolve was growing weak. I had to beat some sense into you." Her eyes darkened, and she lowered her voice. "You are the only one who can save Shihala. I know that in my soul. I cannot let you fail."

He shook his head slowly, but now was not the moment for doubt. "Then you must trust in me, even if you disagree with me." She opened her mouth to rebut, but he cut her off. "You must stand by my decisions even if they seem senseless."

She bowed her head. "I swear on Shihala, I will not question you again."

He looked up at the guards. "She is coming with me."

"That's fine," one said, then he turned to the others and said something in a crude, guttural language. "But there will be no refunds on the price of her tenure."

"Keep it," Jahmil scoffed. "Burn it for all I care."

The guard gave a cold, drakonte smile. "I will lead you both to the ferry."

"Not yet. Take her now, but there is one more prisoner I must speak with."

Takisha's eyes snapped up. "Jahmil?"

He did not answer, and Takisha was led from the room, leaving Jahmil alone for a long while. As everything she had said tumbled through his mind, he absently lifted his sleeve and began to play with some roughly textured skin on his upper forearm that was aching him. Lost in thought, it took him some time to bother to look down at it.

He had expected to see a rash or a leftover abrasion, but instead, a shifting black tattoo met his eyes. He'd never seen it before. The lines were thick at some points and thin at the ends like fine calligraphy, but they meant nothing. They swelled and disappeared like clouds on a warm summer day. And when he touched them, he felt something he couldn't explain. Storm clouds on a rough sea. His chest burned with heat, painful and beautiful all at once. The shrillest highs and deepest lows of an instrument expertly played.

Where had it come from? Had this been a consequence of him losing his senses? It looked eerily like the mark formed when one entered into the Covenant of Shihala, but that couldn't be right. No matter what Qadira or his mother tried to force upon him, Shihala would never confirm a Covenant between him and the queen he despised with every breath.

Whatever the mark was, the more he pondered it, the more vague fascination twisted into cold, iron lumps. Like shards of metal piercing supple skin. Broken promises.

The door banged open again, and Jahmil pushed down his sleeve.

A cloaked figure was led inside, the same collar affixed to his neck that Takisha had worn, and forced to sit in the same stinging, golden chair. Outside of Ashkult, gold was often used on prisoners to dampen their magic and make certain they could not escape. But it was redundant here; the cold glimmer of the lake chased away every wisp in a hundred *marhalah*. The only purpose of the golden chair was to cause the prisoner pain.

"You lied to me, Khayin," said Jahmil, rising to his feet to pace back to the tiny window. "You tried to send me to my death."

"Yet you're still alive." The creature under the hood chuckled cruelly. "And you found your drakontes, didn't you?"

"Only some. Our deal is void unless you lead me to the rest."

"Are you certain that's how you want to use your second question?"

Jahmil's eyes twitched, and he turned to regard the creature. "It is not a second question, merely a reiteration of the first."

"Are you sure you don't want to ask me about your grandmother's necklace?"

Jahmil's pulse skipped and changed its rhythm. "How do you know about that? There is no magic here."

"There is magic here, *amir*." Khayin tapped his forehead. "And there." He pointed one long, bony finger at Jahmil's forearm. "It is amazing, isn't it? How ordinary things in the right hands and under the right circumstances can become so extraordinary. And how extraordinary things can be leached and squeezed into nothing."

"*Bihaqi alsama',*" Jahmil cursed. "Must you always speak in riddles?"

"I want to tell you a story, *Amir*."

"I do not want to hear your story. I want you to answer my question."

"It's a story of two princes fighting to save their kingdoms at any cost, and a lost little girl who was the only one that could help them."

CHAPTER THIRTY

Ayelet

Ayelet fell back, putting the back of her hand to her mouth to hold in a scream. The body of the beast still twitched, and its mangled jaws moaned, but its shape began to morph. The dingy claws shrunk a size, and the patches of green-gray fur receded or sloughed off entirely. And while the hyena-like jaws still held fangs that protruded in odd angles, the skin behind them softened, pinkened, clinging to bones that snapped into a shape distinctly more human. What she thought was a metal collar embedded in the creature's flesh loosened until it dangled around the shrinking neck. The locket with the opal inside.

And then there were those eyes.

Ayelet would recognize Serap's sweet brown eyes anywhere.

As the wisps she had freed from the beast flew helter-skelter into the air, the shrunken figure stopped twitching. She wiped the spit from her mouth, but her hand shook so hard it merely smeared her spittle around. She sniffed and then retched at the stink of boiling blood.

"Serap?" Ayelet exhaled when she could at last breathe. She reached for its muzzle, or where she thought Serap's tender cheek might be.

The creature snarled, a wimpy and pathetic attempt to keep her back. She clenched her fist and fought her revulsion by staring at its eyes. Serap's eyes. She had almost destroyed the only person she had ever wanted to protect. Ayelet set a shaking hand on a tuft of greasy green fur and tried not to breathe in as she stroked back and forth.

Then she stopped, tugged the hair up, and realized it wasn't fur at all. It was the shredded green fabric of Serap's new dress. Her heart stung.

"There, there, little Serap. I can see it's you."

Serap whimpered a guttural cry. Ayelet shivered.

Köle was using magic to create monsters. But what for? She tried to control her frothing anger. For now, she must help Serap. She crouched closer to the ground to look into Serap's eyes. If she focused with all her might, she could see a swirl of silver in the white, but she didn't dare call it out with her hands. Not when she barely knew what to do with the wisps and not when fear soaked every part of her mind. She neither wanted to blow Serap apart nor drain her completely. This would take a finer touch.

Ayelet sat back and pulled out her lyre. She adjusted the pegs with a few twangs to find the perfect pitch for this contaminated place. A pitch the complete opposite, warm and bright and full of hope. She stroked a chord, satisfied. Then she sang, her fingers following the tune she had played at Kadri's camp, the tune she could swear her mother sang to her in her dreams.

Dandini dandini danadan
A moon was born from a mother's womb
spared from all harm
and protected from the evil eye.

Dandini dandini danadan
A moon has called her children home
to keep them safe
and bring them to fulfillment.

The magic slithered out from Serap like a rivulet of water being sucked into dry earth. But soon a torrent of wisps poured out, bursting from ears, nose, throat, and a patchy wound upon her back. They coalesced into a chaotic whirlwind overhead, bumping and pulling at each other as one by one they began to dissipate into the walls and ceiling around them. The body shrank. The festering ceased. And the monster's maw melted back into Serap's gentle face.

Still, Ayelet played on, not wanting any hint of magic to remain to corrupt again. When she was sure the last tendrils of wisp were free, she exhaled a final chord. Then, she crawled forward on hands and knees and scooted her folded legs under Serap's sweat-soaked head. Her fragile body shivered, covered only in the tattered remains of her dress. Ayelet hummed, waiting for her to wake as she painstakingly tied each frayed end of the dress to the next to make a semblance of something to shield her tiny body from the cold and eyes alike. Memories of Serap's scarf, of her own, flooded her mind, and she paused, touching a hand to her boot.

"Aye-let?" Serap whispered. Her brows knit together and parted just as quickly. She nuzzled her face into Ayelet's blue skirt. "I had a terrible dream of a man with no face and demons with all the same one." Her body quivered, and she coughed out green spit.

Ayelet wiped the corners of her mouth. She knew those dreams. They used to be hers.

"Hush, hush," she said gently. "It will do no good to linger. We must get you out of here."

Serap turned her head weakly from one side to the other, her wide eyes searching those of the other children. "You must get us out."

The "us" wrapped tight around her, vines choking a tree. Serap was right. She could no sooner leave the children here than she could burn her lyre and jump in after it. She stifled a groan. Honor came with a great sense of burden, and an even greater sense of guilt. Perhaps that was why Jahmil looked so miserable. Perhaps that was why he broke his promise. She had tried to lighten his burden and had only been throwing boulders on top. Takisha had warned her. He should be as free from her as these children should be from Köle.

She smoothed her face and stoked her resolve. A fine general. That's what Jahmil had said she could be, and while she was certain he had been just a bit patronizing, he had also been right. She felt magic billow into her mind like fog over the city. In the haze, she saw the answer to her troubles as if written in stars.

Ayelet scooped up Serap and tucked her away behind the jars of magic in the empty cell. "Be quiet," she gently scolded Serap. Then she turned to the room of whimpering children. "All of you, be quiet. I will come back for you as the sun does for the morning, but you must stay put. The slavers are still above ground and will snatch little children who stray."

Serap opened her mouth to argue, but Ayelet pursed her lips with a shake of her head, then strode off into the dark. She did not try to find her way out of the maze this time but went into the hallway that led to the children. This job did not require any fine handiwork, and she left her lyre tied to her waist.

With a hand raised, she pulled some wisps to her and scanned the ceiling. When she found the vine-filled cracks the wisps had seeped through before, she stopped and called more magic. Over and over, she ran a waterfall of magic through the hairline fractures and bigger fissures. The force was enough to knock away dust and debris, loosening large stones that soon came crashing down. She continued her torrent of erosion, careful to lead away from the room with the children's cells until holes the size of entire blocks cut into the ceiling. The sun's white light filtered down, its welcome warmth kissing her skin.

When at last there were enough blocks to climb and room enough to fit through, she yanked free a particularly thick set of scraggly roots and pulled her body up through a jagged hole. She squeezed herself through on elbows and knees. Then stood and surveyed the room. Empty, of course, though not for long. She did not know how often the temple crumbled on its own. Kadri and Nadir may be upon her soon.

Then she smirked. On the pillar to her left, a long streak marked the dust where her finger swept through it earlier. She was not far from Köle at all.

Following the footprints that dappled the dusty floor like sunshine through leaves, she arrived at the room with the red curtain faster than she could have hoped. This time, she did not bottle up her fear. If Köle wanted to see it, she would let him. And her anger with it. She burst into the room, picking up speed until she was running full kilter toward the shadows where he hid. She stopped abruptly, grabbed a fistful of silky fabric, and ripped it off with all her strength.

She inhaled sharply. Empty.

A deep cry erupted from her throat. She threw the red upon the ground and raised her hands into the air.

"Köle!" she yelled, sending the wisps into a tizzy. "Show yourself!"

A hand grabbed her shoulder. White as ice and cracked as parched earth, it sent thrills of lightning through her blood. The tattered nails were a black far darker than abyss and shattered unevenly in sharp crags.

Köle cackled softly. "I knew there was more to you than your human flesh." His gargled chuckle grew to fill the room.

She ripped herself away and pressed her palms to her ears to keep out the bone-scratching sound. Oh, how she wanted to turn. To see the faceless face that had tormented her dreams, her reality. But oh, how she feared what she would find.

"Ada, Ada." His breathy voice snaked across her skin. "Turn and be embraced."

Köle's voice was like a thousand forks scraping down her spine. She had already embraced a monster today. But no innocent child hid inside the demon behind her. Still, facing him was the reason she had come. To fight him. To fight for herself. She pressed a hand to where her lyre hung on her hip and spun.

Her breath caught in her throat. He was not the shadowy, ugly man she had expected. Nor was he a scaly serpent draped in human flesh. Thick white hair. Black eyes. The same ghost-white skin. But besides the dry cracks that spread across his face like shattered glass and the hint of sparkle to his skin, he looked unequivocally normal. Even handsome, if you could tolerate the bottomless pit of his eyes.

He grinned, each tooth outlined in shadows. They were yellow, the color of ivory tusks that had aged through the years. He, however, did not look aged. Not as much as she had suspected of a man marked white by the Evil Eye.

Köle opened his arms wide, the folds of plum-colored robes draping his thin frame. Gold thread, dirtied by the squalor of ruins, wove its way around the hems, unfolding upon the chest in a crest that matched her ankle.

She sucked in tiny gasps of air and took a step back. "I have not come to embrace you," she said, surprised the words came out loud enough to hear. Emboldened, she straightened her back and tried for Jahmil's haughty disregard when he had warned her she was in danger. He would know how to deal with someone like this, had he deigned to come and do so himself. Which he had not. She did not need him, though. Memory was enough.

Cruel humor sparked in Köle's eye. "And what have you come to do, my Ada?"

"Fight you."

His breathy laughter caught nearby wisps, trailing them along in a flurry that broke only when it hit the wall. Ayelet held her breath against the olfactory onslaught of decaying teeth and a strange hint of basil and persimmon. He placed a hand on his chin and leaned in intently. "And what has made you find your courage after all these years?"

She ground her teeth over the next words, trying to make them taste less acrid. "What you're doing to those children is despicable."

The humor in his eyes dimmed so they resembled two lumps of coal with a heavy ring of yellow shining in the center. He raised his brows and waved the hand at his chin for her to continue.

"I've come to make sure you stop torturing them. Stop turning them into horrible creatures for your own sick pleasure."

He smiled that shadowy, ivory smile. "You wish me... to stop... because what I do is despicable?"

She nodded once, then lifted her gaze defiantly. She should just call the wisps now, but being in the presence of her tormentor set her resolve on slippery, cracking ground. She should do it. She should do it. Why couldn't she do it?

"And what else would you consider despicable, my Ada?" The skin around her eyes tightened at his question. He continued, "Killing men? Or is that not so grievous because their bones have had more time to grow? What about women?" he asked, reaching for her.

She recoiled, what was left of her false confidence evaporating with every word.

"For I have suffered the loss of all of these and thousands of children, more!" His voice thundered, sending orange flashes among the wisps, lightning behind clouds.

Her shoulders slumped as she folded into herself. "Do not place your evils on others. They are yours alone to bear."

Köle chuckled softly, and his continual, cruel mirth unsettled her. Why must he smile so?

"Mine alone to bear? A war is fought on two sides, Ada. And to this I want you to listen well, for you will see it, too, and soon enough. When one kingdom succeeds, another must fail."

Dread filled her as she remembered the first part of the warning spoken by the peddler when she was twelve. *Music, the folly. Magic, the call. When one kingdom rises, another must fall.* Haunting, too, was the same hardened look in Jahmil's eyes when he spoke of war and duty.

"But we digress," Köle said on an inhale. "You have come to destroy me unless I stop my *despicable* ways. And yet, the bial'dabaye are invaluable in the war I fight. If I cease to create them from your precious human children, I would be ruined. So go ahead, strike me down."

She tightened her hand on her lyre, and two wisps broke free from the eddy above and brushed through her hair. A bemused chuckle broke from Köle's throat.

Her lungs and chest squeezed, the memory of each of the children's soulful eyes knotting it tighter and tighter. She felt this to be a trap with every inch of her being but could see no other way out. And still, she could not raise her hand, too terrified of what would befall her at his merciless whims. She was a coward. A coward who could still save the children.

"Let's make a deal," she whispered.

He sneered. "A deal? And what is it you offer for the souls of such pathetic little humans?"

She tried to take a deep breath, but it felt shallow and weak. "I will do as you ask. I will play my lyre."

"What are you really offering?" He did not chuckle this time, his coal-like eyes scrutinizing.

She shuddered.

"Say it." His voice was the hiss of water in fire.

Ayelet clenched her shaking hands so hard her bones ached. She had spent her whole life hiding and running, never having a family or finding love so she could be free from Köle. And never in eternity, not on Ard or Qaf as Jahmil would say, had she ever dreamt she'd willingly utter the most wretched words on the planet. But no one would come to save her. Just as no one ever had before. And so the words slit her tongue as they fell from her mouth.

"I will give you me."

CHAPTER THIRTY-ONE

Jahmil

He didn't realize how long he had been with Khayin until he left the interrogation chamber. Thirty degrees had passed listening to his infernal story. It was utter nonsense. Every word that came from the traitor's mouth was at most a half-truth, if not an outright lie.

So why had he stayed to listen? And why were Khayin's words twisting in his guts like poison? Perhaps it was proof of the magic in Khayin's mind that Jahmil was questioning everything he had ever known, even though he didn't believe a word of it.

He didn't believe a word of it.

And no matter how Khayin pestered him, he hadn't asked about his grandmother's necklace. He was certain if he had, the horrible little goblin would have simply said, "Waiola took it to be cleaned," and he would have wasted his second question on nothing.

Takisha was in the boat, still chained like an animal. But a bundle of her possessions had been loaded in the front, the hilt of her obsidian sword hanging over the side, causing the small boat to dip off-center. When Jahmil entered, he repositioned the sword, even as the reckless ferryman pushed out in a dangerously high slosh of quicksilver. What had he to worry about with his glass legs and immortal flesh?

Jahmil said nothing to Takisha. He was prepared to forgive her, but he would never trust her again. It wasn't as simple as a handshake or a promise. From now on, he would always be looking over his shoulder, nervous that should he make a choice she disagreed with, she would fly off the handle. Other than when they were sparring, he had never raised a hand to her. And he never would have, not only because he knew she could crush him like a worm, but because he had more respect for her than that. In fact, he had more respect for everyone than that. As much as he liked to threaten to flog his officers, he never actually did it. He had always looked down on nobles who beat their servants or commanders who flogged their soldiers. If you must hit a person to make them loyal, then they are not loyal and never can be.

It pained his heart, but there was nothing else for it. He could not travel with her. He was confident in her loyalty to Shihala, so she could still be of use, but not serving at his side. Never again.

He heaved a sigh of relief when they reached the shores of Buhayrat Alzaybiq and his feet were again on solid ground. Takisha raced to Thueban and stroked his nose, even as the beast pushed against her. The show of tenderness brought a smile to his lips, but it changed nothing.

"Are you prepared to fly?" he asked.

"Always." Takisha did not turn. "What is in your mind?"

Khayin's warnings were on the tip of his tongue, but he bit them back. He would not disseminate the information until he had confirmed it.

It was all nonsense. And yet, when he had been standing in Vespar, a vacuum of magic all around him, he had felt it. But there had to be another explanation. Khayin's lies were too horrible to be true.

"How well do you know the terrain of Vespar?" he asked.

At last, she faced him, her expression knotted with confusion. "I have not been there in nigh fifteen years."

"Do you know the city of Tel Keveh?"

She shook her head.

"On the far coast of Vespar, nestled in the Shamaal Range under the shadow of ash palms. It was once a large city, home to the miners who harvested obsidian from the mountains. I do not know what has become of it now, but they say that is where the plague began. The beginning of the end of Vespar."

"I can't fly to the heart of Vespar," said Takisha, her incredulity doing nothing to mask her fear. "Did you bring me from Ashkult just to see me murdered by the enemy?"

"You will meet no resistance. There is not a soul left living in Vespar."

"Has something changed that I am unaware of?"

He paused, unsure how to answer. There was much they were both unaware of, but that meant nothing had changed. "Vespar has been empty for years. Why do you suppose they attacked Shihala so ruthlessly?"

"I don't understand."

"Nor did I until I was standing in that land." He lifted his gaze to focus on her eyes. "The city of Tel Keveh is a series of concentric circles, and at its center is the Shrine of Nasim."

"The what?"

"The Eimlaq of Wind. I need you to go there and tell me if Nasim still sleeps or if the shrine has been ripped open."

At last, a wave of understanding seemed to crash over Takisha. She moved closer. "You suspect another door?"

He met her eyes and did not answer.

"Where will I meet you again? I cannot go back to Ahmar."

He clenched his teeth and drew in a breath. "I will speak with Qadira about your return as soon as possible. Until then, wait for me in Vespar."

"But you said it was a wasteland."

He lifted his eyebrows. "You were perhaps hoping I would send you to a hammam?"

She bowed. "Yes, *Amiri*."

The formality made him cringe. She never called him that, never bowed to him. Perhaps it was her way of apologizing. Or perhaps, she was acknowledging that things between them could never be the same.

Normally, she would have asked him where he was going, but that was none of her business anymore. Takisha mounted Thueban and guided him up into the air without even a word of goodbye. It was painful, but also the way things had to be. Particularly because no matter how he pressed her, she still refused to give any further explanation of their altercation other than *he had lost his senses.*

She was lying to him, just like everyone else. There wasn't a soul alive that he could trust.

He watched the drakonte disappear into the mists of night, then closed his eyes and slipped through the veil to Ard, back to the ruined valley where he had met the great Eimlaq of Fire. A cloud of scentless white swirled around him. As it cleared, he found himself gazing at a pale orange, cloudless sky, the sun sinking beyond the horizon. The heat always made him a little dizzy, but like blood rushing to his head, it passed quickly. He blinked, and his eyes focused on what had once been ruins—the place where he had found the mangled bodies of his drakontes being sucked into merciless, gaping jaws.

The surge of magma between two craggy mountains had cooled to a lazy slosh of black ash. All the fires had gone out, the forest a tangled, blackened caricature of itself. He hopped down onto a triangular shelf of land jutting out over the sluggish sea of embers. He paced, his boots silent on the packed dirt, as his eyes scanned for a faint memory. He wasn't certain what he was looking for until he found it. Would he be able to feel the door Takisha spoke of? And if he could, was there any way to use it to lead him to Köle?

As he paced, he noticed a tattered yellow ribbon twisting in the wind, caught on the brambles of a scorched bush. He snatched it with two fingers, lifted it to his eyes, and found a single long, brown hair tangled up with it. Pulling the hair free, he let the wind catch the ribbon and carry it off.

He remembered the woman it belonged to. She had been there on the day of the eimlaq attack, standing at the head of a caravan of lowlife humans. He had suspected they were involved in the murder of his drakontes, but he had not attacked them. He couldn't remember why.

Jahmil scratched his itchy forearm.

He remembered looking down on this piece of land and seeing this yellow ribbon as he battled with the giant.. He remembered a heavy headdress of bronze coins, a gown of thick, patterned brocade. The human woman inside had held glass jars brimming with something no human should have had access to—raw, unrefined magic stolen from the land of Qaf. Stolen from...

He couldn't even finish the thought. Khayin was a liar, and his story was impossible.

As he gazed at the hair, turning it this way and that so the sun would catch the golden highlights, an image of the woman's face came into focus. Blue eyes that somehow seemed dark, as if always turned away from the source of light. Dark eyebrows. A small, upturned nose. Pale, fleshy lips that always smiled and yet never did.

"Kadri," her name fell from his lips even as he discovered it. At that moment, he caught her scent on the wind—campfire smoke and apricots. The faintest tinge of someone else's blood. She was close.

Jahmil lifted his arms to the sky and shifted his form. His clothes fell in a pile as he shrank rapidly. His mouth and nose elongated into a curved, golden beak. Feathers sprang from every inch of his body except his feet; his toenails grew and sharpened into long talons. Small black spots formed on his brown wings as black flight feathers grew to full length.

His eyes searched for his crystal ring before he remembered he'd paid it to the ferryman to gain access to Takisha. One less thing to worry about, he supposed. But the earring he'd been wearing sat atop the pile of clothes. The falcon didn't have any skin on its ear for the stone to hold onto. He lost more jewelry this way.

He shrugged, then set his feet wide, flattened his back, and spread his wings. With a burst of energy, he took to the air. The bird's-eye view of the decimated mountain allowed him to discern an outline of where the eimlaq had lain, on its side, arms stretched out, head tilted towards the surface so it could breathe. And eat.

He flew into the light of the falling sun, catching gusts of hot wind and gliding to reserve his energy. He passed over Edirne, which he saw had been considerably damaged by fire and rock, though it didn't look as though the eimlaq had attacked, the destruction more likely just the consequence of its initial extraction from the earth.

Khayin's theory had made sense of that too, why the drakontes had been fed to the eimlaq, why the beast had wanted to kill him. The drakontes had been more than a lure; they had been the promised price—what Köle Amir had given the giant to inspire it to rise from its sleep and attack him.

It was a good plan, and it should have worked. What had gone wrong? Why couldn't Jahmil remember how he had escaped?

His keen falcon's eyes found their quarry—a circle of tents, a low-burning campfire. The glint of bronze and ribbons. Jahmil dove nearer and alighted on a branch just beyond the fire. More ruins sprawled about them. High stone archways and worn statues, many of them armless, legless. Faceless.

The woman, Kadri, was seated at the fire. As he watched her, the sun finished its descent, and the cold of the cloudless sky swept in and wrapped around her. She scooted closer to the flames and rubbed her arms for warmth. A man with a roughly shorn beard and an expression on his face like he had just swallowed a bee approached Kadri. They spoke in close whispers before he rushed away.

She used a stick to draw in the soft earth. Jahmil flew down to a lower branch for a closer look. Arabic numerals, figures. She stared at them with fixed concentration, but they meant nothing to him.

Her dark eyes flinched and looked at him. Immediately her expression changed, a cold smile sliding onto her lips. "Hello there..." she said and slithered closer. "Aren't you pretty?"

He had a distinct feeling she was about to grab him and shove him into a cage. She was a person who never looked at anything—not animals, or even humans—without weighing its value in raw coin.

He flew up to a safer distance.

She reached into a bag at her side and took out a hunk of salted pork and held it out to him. "Come over here, you stupid bird. I know somebody who would pay five hundred *akçe* for a bird like you. At least for your feathers."

She offered the pork higher and made a clicking noise like she was trying to call over a cat. He rolled his neck and glared at her.

"Who needs you, anyway?" she said, stuffing the pork back in her bag. "Pretty soon, I won't need anybody."

She wiped away the calculations she'd written in the dirt with her foot, picked up her stick, and jabbed the dying fire.

A distant shriek filled the night—long, high-pitched, and unmistakable. A bial'dabaye. There was nothing else that made such a noise. But that was impossible. The bial'dabaye were creatures of Qaf, not Ard. Hadn't Takisha said Köle had allied himself with humans? Did that mean the nightmare creatures were expanding their territory? He cringed at the thought.

Kadri cringed herself, then chased it away with a quiet laugh. "Not much longer."

He watched her for some time longer, and she knew he was watching her. Every now and then she would glance up at the tree and give a disappointed little sigh, then turn back to the fire. As the night became cold, she left the fire and went into her tent. The camp had gone dead silent, but for the occasional distant shriek of a bial'dabaye. He was desperate to go investigate but forced himself to be patient. He would deal with Kadri first. There was yet time.

Wasn't there?

He waited until he heard the soft sound of snoring, then flew down from the tree and crept into the tent.

She slept alone on a raised cot draped in leopard skins. In the corner, several jars of white magic were piled on top of one another, wisps darting back and forth inside. They shivered with excitement and reached for him. He'd never seen a wisp exhibit such behavior.

Jahmil changed back into himself and snatched a lamb skin from an open chest to tie around his waist. A curved *khanjar* dagger rested on Kadri's pillow near her face, the blade clouding with her every exhalation. Jahmil wrapped his hand in one of many scarves left hanging from the ceiling and picked up the small, steel weapon.

Jahmil sat down on the edge of the cot and set the edge of the dagger against her throat. Her eyelids twitched and then peeled open. When her gaze focused on his face, she froze.

"Show me your hands," he said, his voice low and cold.

Her eyes stayed fixed on his as she lifted her hands over the top of the blanket. "*Bismillah,*" she breathed. "Djinn."

"I have questions for you, *'imra'at shaba.*" He flicked the dagger so she felt its cold. "And I need you to try, against your nature, to be honest."

She managed to smirk despite the blade to her throat. "I've already made a deal with a djinn."

"Who?"

"Whoever pays the highest."

He pressed the blade more firmly against her throat. "Why do you protect him?"

"I'm trying to protect myself," she said, a worry in her voice that had not been there before.

"Then might I suggest being more helpful."

She narrowed her eyes. Licked her lips. Then hissed, "Köle."

Jahmil's breath froze, but his fingers tightened on the hilt. "Is he here?"

"I'm a merchant, not his nursemaid."

He glanced at the shimmering bottles in the corner. "You trade magic?"

Her eyes glinted. "And sometimes a cannon or two."

"Where did you get the magic?"

She ran her tongue over her bottom lip and glanced once more at his blade. "The mountain outside of Edirne."

"Köle sent you there?"

"Yes," she said in almost a snarl. "And he forgot to mention the earth beast and its dinner of disgusting dead snakes. I lost half my people. Maybe more."

"Yet you still trade with him?"

"I'll trade with whoever I need to in order to stay alive and get my dues."

Jahmil smirked. "I need you to tell me where he is, or I'm afraid your trading days are over."

"Are you always this charming?" She flashed an uneasy smile.

"Exhausting, isn't it?" He returned her smile. "Answer the question."

She shook her head tightly. "What he'll do to me if I tell you is far more frightening than your little blade."

"*Your* little blade," he corrected. "How would he know it was you who told me?"

"The only other people who know anything about his little magical forays are Nadir and Ayelet. And he needs both of them far more than me."

"Why? Who are they?"

Kadri considered his words. "Nadir is a genie catcher who also sometimes catches people. And Ayelet…" Her face soured. "Is a musical hack Köle dotes on. Now, will you please remove the blade from my throat?"

The scream of a bial'dabaye cut the night, louder than before and yet no closer. It twisted like bone spurs through his blood, but he didn't move his eyes from Kadri. "Köle cannot torture you if you are dead."

Kadri lifted her chin and breathed in. "You're just as cruel as he is, did you know?"

"Business is business."

"Right. What's a human life to any of you djinn? Fine, I'll tell you something useful. But when you break up the party, you have to leave me and my men alone. And you must get rid of Ayelet. Do we have a deal?"

"I've no grudge against you or your men, provided you are open to seeking out a new employer. But this Ayelet? What harm has she done?"

"To me? Or to Köle? Or to whoever the stupid people of Shihala are? There are too many grievances to count."

An enemy of the people of Shihala was all he needed to hear. Kadri was right. What did he care about a single human life?

"Consider her gone," he said, then he lifted his brow expectantly.

"Köle will be here tomorrow night. But know that he plans something big. He's been saving most of his magic."

"I don't suppose you can provide any more details than *something big*?"

She glared. "No. I cannot."

"Very well." He stood and flung the dagger at the floor. "If you are here tomorrow night when I come for him, I cannot be responsible for what may happen to you or your men. And if you capture any more magic in glass jars, I will not bother to wake you when I return to slit your throat."

White fire exploded from his hands, and he hurtled it at the stack of jars in the corner. The glass exploded into shards and Kadri screamed, ducking down for cover. The wisps hovered momentarily, then rushed away all in one direction as if they had very urgent business to attend to. It was strange, but Jahmil didn't stand around considering it. They were free, and that was all that mattered.

He made himself invisible and rushed into the woods, disappearing back to Qaf under a slant of broken branches. He wanted to go investigate the bial'dabaye, but given everything he heard, there was no reason to assume anything other than the worst. He would send back trained spies to try to gain an understanding of Köle's troops and supplies. Tomorrow night was approaching fast, and he had to get back to Ahmar to plan his offensive.

CHAPTER THIRTY-TWO

Ayelet

Ayelet needed no escort on her way to free the children. There was no point. She knew staying was the only way to ensure Köle stopped his harrowing torture. And Köle knew she knew this. What troubled her the most was why.

Why did Köle make these monsters?

He said they were invaluable to the war he was fighting. She thought of his cold rage when he spoke of lost women and children. The embroidered emblem on his robes. Maybe he was fighting to get a kingdom back, doing whatever it took in that flippant way rulers did to keep their pride, regardless of who it hurt. But if he was a king, what kingdom rose when his fell? And from whom was he trying to take it back?

The whole exchange nipped at and fed on her. *Human* children, he had said. And the glimmer of his skin. The opacity of his eyes and the flashes of orange thunder. She shook, the air suddenly frigid.

Köle was no man.

He was a djinn! The chill leaked through her bones. She had been stupid to not see it before. He had been by her side through every torture, watching a knife's length away as she broke, and she hadn't been able to see him. Not before her lyre. Her stomach coiled into a ball and stuck in her throat at the thought.

It lodged itself further into her chest, and she struggled to breathe. Was Köle fighting the same war as Jahmil? Did they fight in an alliance together?

No.

Jahmil Amir may have chosen his queen and kingdom over her when he left her to Köle, but he had honor. What was her one soul to his thousands? She would not have come back for herself, either. Not if she had a beautiful home like Shihala and people who loved her. Besides, he did not know she had been taken by slavers, right? Or he would be here now, white fire flashing, even if he did not love her. And the way he tended to Serap... he would die before he used children as fodder in a war.

The knot in her throat burst out as she yelped in horror. If Köle fought *against* Jahmil, that meant all the monsters he was killing—She clapped a hand over her mouth so hard it hurt.

She had to stop him.

She ran until she reached the cells, praying magic would keep her heart from bursting. The children cried out as she arrived, reaching their grubby little hands through the bars to pull at her dress. Someone had returned for them. A gift she could give that was never given to her.

She hurried and burst the locks on the cells, Köle refusing to give her a key so she'd be forced to use her magic once more. The frightened little ones huddled in a group in the center, afraid to move without her as she tended to Serap. She lay in the corner, sweat still soaking her forehead and clothes as if the magic had been a fever that just broke.

"Can you walk?" Ayelet asked, pulling Serap to her feet.

Her little chin wobbled, but she nodded.

"Can you sneak?"

Her eyes lit up, and a brush of color came to her cheeks. She nodded again.

Ayelet lowered her voice. "Kadri took from me a flower. I need your help to get it back."

"The pretty one with only three petals?" Serap asked, conspiracy shining in her eyes.

"The very one. I'm certain she keeps it on her person, tucked in the hidden folds of her dress. If I distract her, could you steal it for me?" Ayelet asked.

Though she had tried to keep Serap free from the dirtier tricks the caravan dabbled in, steering her more toward the honest work of acrobatics, little could stop hungry fingers from swiping unwatched bread. And the sweet little miscreant was a natural.

"What does the flower do?" Serap pushed herself up.

Ayelet narrowed her eyes. "Why must it do anything?"

"Why else would you want me to steal it?" Serap raised a thin brow. "It comes from Jahmil's land, doesn't it? I saw all sorts of glowing plants outside his window. Everything there is magic."

She bit her tongue. She had forgotten Serap's sojourn into Jahmil's land. Into his very room. The envy streaming through her veins was laughable. "Do you remember that place? Jahmil's rooms and his windows?"

Serap nodded. "Have *you* been there?" She wriggled her eyebrows with a look that said she knew far too much.

"No, of course not." Ayelet pushed the girl's squirming brows back down with two fingers, wishing she could quench the heat in her cheeks. It would do nothing to change the fact that he did not come back. "Once I have the flower, you will take a petal and think of that place and nowhere else. Think of what you smelled and saw and—"

"Ate?" Serap licked her lips.

Ayelet smiled. "Yes, and ate. Think only of that and drop the petal, and when you open your eyes, you will be there. Hide. Wait for Jahmil to return and then tell him what happened to you. He needs to know that—" She cut herself off, not wanting to alarm her. "He just needs to know. Will you do that for me?"

"Got it," she said, confidence adding a glow to her face. "But why won't you come with me? I know he'll want to see you."

Ayelet dropped her gaze and traced the shadowy bumps that ran across the dungeon floor. "I am not so sure he will. Besides, I must make sure no more children are brought here ever again."

"He would want to. See you, that is," Serap said, dipping her head to look Ayelet in the eye. She grinned, puffed her cheeks, and then blew out the air. "So much tasty food. And maybe I'll get a new dress!" she added brightly, tugging at the shredded green strips of what had been her beautiful gown.

"Yes," Ayelet said through the squeeze in her chest. He would not begrudge Serap the care he afforded her last time. She knew he cared for the girl despite whatever his feelings were for her.

"Now, up. It's time to pick a flower."

Ayelet led the group of children into the campground from the hole she had blasted in the temple. Two little girls fell to the earth and rolled in the dry leaves while the others beamed hopefully at the sky. She grinned at their innocence and how quickly they could brush off horror. Then her smile fell. Kadri's men were packing up camp, taking everything from the billowy tents to the unused firewood.

Kadri rounded the side of a wagon and started. She rushed towards Ayelet, raising her hand in the air so her men gathered with her. "How did you get out?"

Ayelet smirked. "You are not the only one who can make deals with Köle." Just saying the words made her sick.

"He freed you?" Kadri's eyes widened, then shot down to slits.

"I'm out here, aren't I?" she said.

Kadri scowled and waved her men away just in time for Serap to slip behind the wagon.

"Where are you going?" Ayelet asked.

"Wherever I want."

The words stung more than she expected. "To Edirne?"

Kadri sighed, and Serap eased a bit closer. "Yes, to Edirne. I recently lost some cargo and must replace it."

"It's not like the queen of black trade to lose any cargo," Ayelet said, poking the badger.

Kadri clapped her hands together and squeezed her palms. What little civility she had mustered faded entirely. "Go ahead and be smug, instrument Ayelet. You only ruined everything I've worked for."

"What have I done to you?"

Kadri bared her teeth, spit collecting in the corners of her mouth as she yelled, "Existed!" She released her palms and shoved Ayelet. "I was doing fine with my trade. Great, even. Then I hear rumors of someone looking for an *instrument of the gods*. A whisperer of winds. A mover of magic. A deceiver of djinn. Alliterations abound concerning you for whatever reason. I mean, what does all that even mean? But I knew what people said about you. I decided to check out the man who put up the offer of a reward."

"Köle."

"Yes, Köle. Obviously Köle. Anyway, being a good trader—"

"The best," Ayelet said and smiled sweetly. From the corner of her eye, she watched Serap loop her arms over a large spoked wheel and twist so her legs slipped up and over the edge in a backward somersault. Then she squeezed between the barrels on the wagon behind Kadri. Her bony arm reached out but fell short of its mark.

Kadri glared. "I kept what I knew about you to myself. I didn't want to trade you in for bread when I could get rubies."

"So generous of you." Ayelet leaned forward in a bow, and Kadri stepped back, closer to Serap.

Another glare. "It turned out Nadir was already working with him, figuring out ways to put magic into water and things and people."

Serap's tiny fingers slipped into a fold just behind the beaded tail of Kadri's headdress. Then pulled away empty-handed.

Ayelet sighed, catching the twisted casualness with which Kadri said *people*. "How do you put magic into a living thing?"

"You force it into their blood or something." Kadri shrugged.

So, that's how they turned Serap. The smell of limes and dates that hung in the breeze turned rancid in her nose. She swallowed a mouthful of spit. "In the same way you make your cider?"

"Right, but grosser. And don't even talk to me about the cider. I was going to make a fortune off that."

"Was? Did you run out of apricots?"

"No," Kadri said bitterly. Then her smile turned coy. "I lost it in a deal."

Curiosity needled her, but she needed to know more about Kadri's business with Köle. Serap reached forward again.

"Why is Köle putting magic in children?"

"Because he was trying to make another you or something. I don't know. But it didn't work because they weren't 'marked' or whatever and instead, the magic created those monsters. So he just started shipping them off to some strange land."

"Strange land?" A queasy feeling settled over her. "Which one? Do you know the name?" *Please, Allah, let it not be Shihala.* And yet, she felt certain it was.

"Why does everyone keep asking me about Köle?" Kadri cried, flinging her hands in the air. "I can't even get a night's rest anymore."

All the arm-flailing had Serap in retreat.

"So why is it my fault that you lost everything?" Ayelet asked, trying to refocus her temper. "Sounds like you just made a poor business decision."

"Because he found out where you were."

Serap's fingers lingered, shifting as softly as the breeze in Kadri's pockets.

Ayelet frowned. "He always does."

"Well, I didn't know that, did I?" she snapped. "Then he changed the terms of our deal. Find you. Get you. Bring you to the mountain to collect the magic. He said you knew how to call it, control it, so Nadir could put it in the bottles. He said he wanted to see what you were capable of."

Serap's hand slipped out of a fold and into another. *Did she even have the flower?*

Ayelet let out a soft growl. "I didn't do anything."

"Yeah, I noticed." Kadri poked her hard in the chest, stepping away and back again so Serap was left dangling and then scurrying out of the way. "We were obliterated! I even tested you at camp with Nadir. You pulled the magic, just like Köle said you could, and Nadir's prayer got it in the bottles. But when it mattered? Nothing! I lost all my cargo but the magic, most of my men—" She stopped and snorted. "And then I went back to Köle without you, and he took the rest."

"What do you mean he took the rest?"

"I mean everything I own from here to Ankara. Gone. Poof. I don't know how he did it. All the weapons I stockpiled, the money, the jewels, the gold. A whole fleet of cannons I won gambling with the sultan's çorbacı. My reputation—only my oldest acquaintances and those owing bleeding favors will deal with me now. Only you mattered to Köle, and because you wouldn't do a favor for an old friend, I lost it all."

Sympathy almost sunk its hooks into Ayelet, when Serap's sneaky hands pulled away with the alyasimin, its petals clumped but still glowing.

"Take the children," Ayelet said.

"Excuse me?" Kadri scowled incredulously.

"You want to better your reputation? Take the children back. You will be a hero to their families. And the ones that don't have families will be indebted to you." If she could have offered the children a better way back than a cruel merchant, she would have. She'd have to rely on the hope that Köle had burned Kadri badly enough that she wouldn't turn right around and try to make a deal. It was thin and far more hopeful than she usually allowed herself, but sending Serap to Jahmil was risky enough. She imagined his face as thirty filthy children made a mess of his room and almost chuckled at the thought.

Kadri's eyes narrowed slowly. "Give me the necklace."

"What?" Ayelet's heart froze as her hand flashed up to the opals around her neck.

"You want me to take care of the little brats and make sure they don't die here in Köle's woods, pay me with the necklace."

"No."

"Fine by me." Kadri sneered and turned to leave.

"Wait." Ayelet clenched her teeth. "Wait." Her hand squeezed around the beads hard enough to imprint them on her skin.

Why was she still fighting against her fate, pretending there was hope for her and Jahmil when she knew there could be none? And at the expense of innocent little children who had suffered some of the same tortures she had. She slid her fingers around the back to unclasp the necklace but couldn't do it. She couldn't give up the hopeless dream. Her eyes flickered to Serap and an idea caught like tinder.

"Someone as fallen as you has no right to ask for the entire necklace. I will, however, trade you one opal."

Kadri sneered. "One opal to watch over at least forty sticky hands? You're out of your mind."

Ayelet tilted her chin with another telling glance at Serap, who clasped her hands around her locket with wide eyes and shook her head. Ayelet gave the tiniest nod. Serap shook her head even harder.

"It's not about the opal, Kadri," Ayelet said, speaking half to Serap. "It's about righting wrongs, honor, and good business. Those little children are innocent in all this, and as much as I'd like to, I can't save them by myself. I have to stay here. But you can help get them away from here. You're the only one who can." Ayelet swallowed the sticky heat in her throat and softened her eyes for Serap.

Kadri twitched. So did Serap, before her shoulders slouched. She popped the opal free and slid it into Kadri's nearest pocket.

"Fine. On my honor as the Queen of Black Trade, I'll get the miscreants away from Köle for an opal." Kadri stuck out her hand.

"Not one of these," Ayelet cupped the necklace close to her skin. "Check your left pocket."

Kadri shoved a hand in and pulled Jahmil's first gift out so the soft blues glinted in the light. She held it up, squinting suspiciously between it and Ayelet. Then she shrugged. "I hate you, by the way." She waved her hand in the air, and a servant popped up as if from nowhere. "Round up the children. The ones who can walk, will. Throw the others in with the empty bottles."

"I hope to see you again, soon," Ayelet said as cheerfully as she could muster. Then something in the woods caught her eye.

"I know you will not," Kadri said, that coy smile appearing once more. "Have a good night."

Ayelet waved her away half-heartedly, attempting to ignore the great hollow chunk that now took up a good part of her heart. She squinted into the brush at the edge of camp as Kadri slunk away, yelling orders at her men. Serap waited for her nearby.

And Jahmil needed to know the horror of what Köle was doing. But something was off. She needed to make sure the children would be safe.

She hedged her way into the woods, circling about from the backside. She spied the bay laurel where the movement had come from. She inched forward, then ripped back a bush. Empty.

Then a cold knife pressed against her throat.

"*Yuh!*"

Relief poured over her like water in a bath. "Balian!" she whisper-yelled, pushing his arm away and spinning around. "What are you doing here?"

"Tracking slavers, like I always do. What are you doing here?"

"Getting enslaved, like I always do."

The joke hurt too much for either of them to smile. Then a gentle hand poked her from behind. "Ta-da!" Serap said, popping around Ayelet's waist. "I got it!" Her eyes flicked to Balian, and she scowled. "What's he doing here?"

"Little rug-rat," he said, pulling her to him and rumpling her hair. Then he took a good look at her, and his face paled. "What happened to you?"

"Ayelet and I were taken after your big fight, and then we were dragged through the forest, and—"

"*Yeter,*" Ayelet chided. "You can fill him in later. Right now you have somewhere else to be."

Balian's face scrunched with suspicion. "Where exactly?"

"A magic la—"

Ayelet smacked her hand over Serap's mouth, but it was too late.

"Magic?" Balian accused. "You're sending her to that djinn? Why?"

She sighed. "Because he needs to know what's happening here."

"Since when does he care about slavers and children?"

"He rescued Serap," Ayelet reminded him flatly.

Balian grabbed Serap's wrist. "I'm not letting her go."

Ayelet squeezed her eyes shut, took a breath to calm herself, and then opened them. "She has to."

She turned to look at Serap, ignoring Balian's angry twitching. "Go. Jahmil will take care of you. And if he gives you any guff about me sending you to Shihala, tell him he forgot his boot."

She pulled off the soft leather, running her finger up the sides. She could let go of him. She had to. And now, he would know she had and wouldn't feel guilty—if he at all did—for breaking his promise when he chose to stay. She was releasing him from his word, from the heat of his skin and the urgency in his eyes that had led her to believe he cared for her when he so clearly did not. He would not need to see her ever again. And she would not expect it. She brushed the opals around her throat, a thin dressing for the humiliation and rage and hurt that bubbled closely under the surface.

Ayelet sighed and slipped the boot onto Serap's foot. He would return, she knew, but for the children, not for her.

"And—" She stopped, indulging in the last of her foolish dreams. "And tell him thank you for the glad dreams."

"No," Balian cut her off. "Go yourself. Don't send a child to a demon to do your dirty work for you."

"Oh, he's not a demon, Balian," Serap interjected. "He's a djinn. And he's really nice, and he gave me this dress—well it *was* a dress—and fed me baklava. I told you this at camp, remember?"

Balian looked like every word was a needle in his eye. "You're not going!"

"Balian," Ayelet tried to reason.

Then Serap plucked a petal from the alyasimin, winked at Ayelet, and dropped it.

They both disappeared in a puff of smoke, leaving Ayelet alone in the forest with her mouth agape. She slid a hand up to her mouth and giggled despite herself. Balian in Jahmil's bedroom would be a disaster.

Ayelet stood to return to the ruins when a pain nipped at her ankle without the boot to protect it. She reached down to brush away the offending stick or bramble but felt only rough skin. She hiked the hem of her dress. The "K" scar was changing, its ends curling longer, its jagged, white flesh turning dark, like henna. She threw her skirt back down and hurried down the steps. Whatever new form of torture Köle now inflicted upon her, it stung of magic and eternity.

CHAPTER THIRTY-THREE

Jahmil

Jahmil sat in his chambers all through the evening, poring over tactical maps, reports from his generals, and holding briefings with his spies. That he had to direct the war effort while hiding in his bedroom rather than openly calling his commanders to a war room was not merely inconvenient. It was an insult he was not prepared to tolerate for much longer. How many lives had to be lost before Qadira would give him full control of her military? He wished he could move the stupid wedding up to tomorrow morning so his hands would no longer be tied by her ridiculous caprice.

The Spider of Karzusan had broken the line at Fahdal, and he and his army of elite soldiers were making streaks across the land, murdering and burning everything that lay in their path. He estimated civilian casualties to be at least a thousand, possibly much higher. Jahmil's attempts to bolster the defenses and evacuate the borderlands had no doubt saved tenfold more than had been lost. But as expected, Ahmar's scattered and woefully underprepared army was crumpling like tissue paper.

He had only sent Takisha off some ninety degrees before, yet he was already anxious that no word had yet been returned of the state of Tel Keveh. If she could even find Tel Keveh. Once again, he felt trapped in inertia until he heard from her, until the truth—or more accurately the lie—of Khayin's ridiculous story could be confirmed.

"Once upon a time there were two princes," the horrid little goblin had said, as they sat in the black, lifeless room in Ashkult. "One ruled in a Land of White and the second in a Land of Blue. Their kingdoms had been at near-constant war for hundreds of years so that even in times of peace they were locked in constant competition. Neither prince did anything without considering how it would affect the other. Their education, their training, their families, and their very religion, were all directed at one another like naked blades. Finding the advantage was all that mattered, regardless of the cost. And for many years they were evenly matched, every victory balanced with a defeat. Both proclaimed their love of their own people, but neither truly cared how those people suffered from the constant warfare, the insecurity, the hatred that their royal rivalry fomented. All that mattered was victory."

"Why do you evade me, Khayin?" Jamil demanded.

"And then the Blue Prince stumbled upon an advantage, brought to him by a knight errant who had traveled to the edges of Qaf and learned the secrets of eternity. But the knight spoke without thinking. He too had believed that the Land of Blue must triumph—that only victory was worth having, not peace. He had discovered there was a way—a quick and simple way—to destroy the Land of White from the inside out, to be free forever from what he saw as the tyranny of the White. The knight had uncovered a way to drain the White of its life force, its magic."

"Just say Vespar, for the love of Allah. You are not fooling anyone."

"Under a cover of secrecy, the Blue Prince and the knight errant stole away into the Land of White, to a City of Circles. There did they find Nasim, the Eimlaq of Wind. And there did they and one hundred strong soldiers slay the beast. And when the body disintegrated, it left a gaping hole in the fabric of the Land of White. It was the reckoning—the Death of Magic. And without magic, the people of White began to decompose while still living."

"The Tel Keveh plague..." Jahmil cut himself short and shook his head. "Are you trying to tell me that you and my father...? You are a liar."

"Everything in the Land of White withered and died. Crops failed. Livestock starved. Pestilence and famine swept the land. The People of White cried out in pain and desperation. The White Prince, not knowing it was the Blue Prince that had caused this suffering, even humbled himself before him, begging for assistance to save his people."

"It was a trick," Jahmil said, remembering when the King of Vespar had come to Shihala and taken the knee before his father, asking for a truce. For shelter for his people. His father had scoffed at him and had him thrown out by his collar.

"They are liars, Jahmil," he had said. *"All of them. Liars. They will sneak into Shihala like termites and eat Her up from the inside out."*

"The Blue Prince sent him away in shame," Khayin continued, "and laughed as more and more of the People of White died of plague, of poverty, of the gradual desertification of what had once been their paradise. They died by the thousands. By the tens of thousands. And the Blue Prince rejoiced in their suffering, so assured was he of his victory."

Jahmil snapped the pencil in his hand. It wasn't true. His father had loved his people and would have done anything to protect them, but he never would have resorted to the tactics of which Khayin accused him. No honorable man would attack the peasantry by afflicting them with plague and famine, draining the very life force from their homeland. No leader worthy of the name could do as the Blue Prince, with the aid of his knight errant, had done in Khayin's hideous work of fiction. The King of Shihala would never have been so callous. Khayin was just trying to get into his head, to hurt him.

But then what *had* happened in Vespar? Why was it so dead? A natural process? The greed and cruelty of its own rulers?

The hatred of the Blue Prince.

It wasn't true. It couldn't be true.

And then there was the promise of the girl who was, according to Khayin, his only hope. *"Strange and beautiful,"* Khayin had called her. *"A creature carved of bone that is destined to become the Savior of Vespar, and the undoing of the new Prince of Shihala."*

That part of the tale made even less sense than the rest. Jahmil tried to dismiss it, but thoughts of the strange and beautiful lingered at the back of his brain like hungry flies. Still, Khayin's story, the desolation he'd seen in Vespar, and the rumors that for years had been circulating about the plague and the Death of Magic, gave Jahmil pause. His parents had always told him to give no credence to the titterings of the peasants, but clearly, the Vespars had not become nomadic warlords overnight and thrown everything they had at Shihala without provocation. There was one person that might be able to tell him the truth.

The last thing he wanted was to speak to his mother. Every time he thought of her, bile pooled in the back of his throat. He felt exposed and trapped, like a shaved prisoner at Ashkult forced into a golden chair. But regardless of how opposed he was to speaking to his mother at the moment, he had no choice. He had to ask her what she knew, if anything, about the barren land of Vespar. *Inshallah*, she would be able to put his mind at ease.

He stood and put on his boots. He was about to slip from the room when a flash came from over his shoulder. He turned to see black and gray mist swirling at the center of his room, silver sparks shimmering within.

Alyasmin. But who...?

He narrowed his eyes as two figures slowly came into focus. One was a small girl with dirt on her face and loose ringlets, a tattered green dress hanging from her skeletal frame. He knew her even before her sparkling brown eyes came into focus. Serap, a girl he had rescued from a horrible iron cage. The other person was even dirtier, with shaggy brown hair hanging in his angry and frightened eyes.

The luckiest man alive, Jahmil thought, and then wondered why.

"Jahmil!" the girl cried and tried to rush towards him, but the man snatched her by the arm.

"Stay away from us!" the man warned, lifting his hand to warn him away.

Jahmil chuckled. "An odd greeting from a man who just materialized in my bedroom. Uninvited, I might add."

"Jahmil, where have you been?" said Serap. "Ayelet thinks you abandoned her. I've tried to explain, but nobody will give me a chance to—"

"Don't speak to it," Balian hissed, yanking her back. "Send us back now, demon. *Bismillah!*"

"*Bismillah*?" Jahmil narrowed his eyes at the strange, angry, inexplicably *lucky* man. "Who *are* you?"

"Balian, let go of my arm! You're hurting me," said Serap. She kicked him in the shin, and he loosened his grasp enough for her to rush across the room and scurry behind Jahmil.

She snatched Jahmil's hand. "You have to come back with us."

"Come where? How did you even get here?"

"Ayelet sent me. She needs you."

"This demon is the last thing Ayelet needs," the man said.

"Ayelet?" Jahmil lifted a brow, searching his memory. The hack musician Kadri had spoken of, was that not her name? The enemy of Shihala. "What should such a person want with me? Does she want to negotiate? And how does she have the power of alyasmin?"

"I knew it," hissed Balian. "See, Serap? He's had his way with her and forgotten her already. I warned her this would happen. Only pain can come from dealing with djinn. They are evil."

"If you're certain I am evil, perhaps you should watch your tongue," spat Jahmil, but then his mind tumbled backward. "Did you say I had my way with her?"

Serap yanked on his hand with both of hers. "That's not true. You're in love with her."

"In love?" He chuckled. "I should think not."

"What's wrong with you?" Her voice cracked as if brimming with tears. "You wouldn't just forget. Not you. Not Ayelet."

"Djinn are not capable of love," said Balian in a low voice that sounded much more confident and threatening than he looked.

Jahmil lowered himself to his knees so he could look at Serap straight. She gazed back with massive eyes of sparkling brown—as honest as any he had ever seen. He searched for the lie in them, but there was nothing but integrity, tinged with anxiety and fear.

His gaze shifted down to her feet, awkwardly clad in one torn silk slipper and one large leather boot. "Where did you get my shoe?"

"You don't know what has been happening to us," she said, and finally the façade holding her together broke, and the tears welling in her eyes spilled onto her cheeks. Her shoulders drew up and shook horribly. She fell in a coil against his chest, sobbing and sniffling. He held her close and stroked her dirty hair.

Jahmil looked past her shoulder up at Balian. The hatred in his eyes was palpable. The fear and mistrust. And yet, there was more than that. It did not take a djinn to recognize the Evil Eye. Balian was envious of him. Perhaps even jealous.

And why shouldn't he be? The question was, why did Jahmil return the sentiment?

"Ayelet told me to tell you that she is having glad dreams," said Serap, wiping her nose on her sleeve.

Jahmil smiled, mostly for the little girl's benefit. He didn't know why he should care about this Ayelet or her dreams.

"Is Waiola here?" asked Serap.

"Would you like me to call her for you?"

She nodded. "I feel disgusting."

"I wasn't going to say anything." He smiled and stroked the side of her face. "Would you like me to have some food brought?"

"Yes," she snapped, cutting off the end of his sentence.

"Serap," the man warned. He took a step forward as if to grab for her, but when Jahmil turned his gaze on him, he froze in place.

He called Waiola. When the large, plushy nurse saw Serap, she wrapped her up in a big squishy hug and led her out of the room to help her get cleaned up. Balian tried to protest, but it was as if his feet were glued to the spot. Which was lucky, Jahmil supposed, since they were so filthy he didn't want them trodding all over his carpet.

"Where is she taking her?" Balian demanded.

"Please relax, my friend. I promise no harm will come to your cousin."

"I am not your friend. And how do you know she's my cousin?"

Jahmil stroked his beard, considering this. "You know, I'm not certain. Can I get you anything? Tea? Pastry? Complimentary delousing?"

"There is no time for this!" Balian shouted. "I must get back to Ayelet. She needs me."

"If she needs you so, then why did she send you here?"

"Because she is delusional," he murmured.

"She works for Köle, isn't that right?"

Balian scoffed. "She is his slave."

"A slave?" The word stuck in Jahmil's throat.

Everything these people were saying made no sense. Ayelet, a musician, a slave, an enemy of Shihala. And yet if Serap was to be believed he was in love with her. But how could he love someone he had never met? And why would he...?

Jahmil stumbled over his next thought. He had lost his senses, that was what Takisha had said. His resolve had been weak, and he had been ready to give up everything. And now pieces of his past were missing, woven with half-formed memories that made no sense. Could Ayelet be the missing piece? Had he taken leave of his senses and fallen in love with one of Köle's sycophants? Perhaps Köle had sent her to him with that very purpose in mind. To seduce him, to convince him that she loved him, and trick him into destroying himself.

He cringed with humiliation, and his hand went instinctively to stroke the tattoo on his forearm. Had he been so lonely, so desperate for connection that he fell for such an underhanded trick? Had been so deceived that Shihala Herself had tried to warn him with the twisting fabrication of a so-called Covenant?

It made sense of everything. This woman had come to him and manipulated him into loving her, and he must have fallen for her every deception. And then, recognizing his mistake, he had found a spell to make himself forget her. To ease the pain and shame she had left on his soul so he could focus on more important matters. He had plucked the memory of the duplicitous vixen from his mind and from his heart. But perhaps she didn't know that. Perhaps she believed she still had a hold over him. That was why she had sent little Serap—to play on his heartstrings. This Ayelet wielded a child like a weapon against his compassion. For if he had loved her, surely she knew about his soft heart, that compulsive tenderness that both his parents had always despised, and which he even now worked to correct.

But why send Balian?

His gaze shifted to the filthy man standing in the center of his bedroom, hands clenched in fists. It had to be another ploy.

"How do you know Ayelet?" Jahmil asked.

"Never mind how I know her. She has nothing to do with you anymore. She doesn't need your help." He snarled and stomped closer, at last finding his courage. "You think you can buy her with your magic? Your necklace of opals? For all your money, your charms, and your honey-soaked words, she chose me. Do you understand, demon? She is mine. Not yours."

Jahmil's heart stumbled. "I gave her a necklace of opals?"

"You used every trick at your disposal to try to charm her," he sneered.

That was what had happened to his grandmother's necklace. He had given it away to this spy. This coldhearted, manipulative seductress called Ayelet. Rage and disgrace flooded his blood, urging him to tighten his fists and lash out at Balian. To become the monster the human kept accusing him of being.

Jahmil clenched his teeth and forced down his anger. Hurting Balian would do no good. Ayelet was the one who deserved his fury. And tonight when he returned with his army to crash Köle's big event, he would show her the consequences of deceiving him.

CHAPTER THIRTY-FOUR

Ayelet

Ayelet brushed her arm to keep away the chill. Now that the wails and shrieking had vanished from the temple, she could feel the magic of the place. No wonder so many wisps swirled in the gulf of Köle's altar room. If she held very still, she could feel it in the floor beneath her, the tiniest tremble of surging power.

She rubbed her arm harder, remembering the eimlaq. Something about the whole affair felt off, like one flat note in an otherwise perfect chord. If she had been brought there by Kadri to collect magic, why were all the dead drakontes everywhere? Why had Jahmil been there? And why, if Köle wanted her alive so badly, did he almost kill her with a ghoul and lava and a raging eimlaq?

"Ada," Köle's voice snapped as if from nowhere. A wisp spiraled around the corner, carrying his next command with it. "Come."

She sighed and absentmindedly touched a hand to the opals on her necklace. While her immediate fear of Köle had begun to fade with the absence of her nightmares and the strange kinship she felt to the bodiless wisps, she was still his slave. And knowing the evils he inflicted on children—an involuntary convulsion racked her shoulders—whatever he wanted her to play her music for would be far worse. The only way he'd give up his soldiers in war was if he thought there was another way to win it. But there was only so much she could do. Only so much she could give before she had given everything. She simply wasn't enough.

"Ada," another wisp of words whipped by, irritated this time.

She called a bit of magic to her and sent it on its way, no message included. None was needed. They both knew what this was.

She forced her feet forward, the soft pad of leather slipper and bare foot the only sound as she took her time arriving for torture. She felt exposed without Jahmil's shoe protecting her scar.

Köle was her home now, and in a strange way, she had always known he would be. That he would find her and bring her back. He watched her with wisps and loved her through torture. The usual deadness smothered her heart, and Kadri's words about Köle testing her came to mind. Almost killing her to test her limits was exactly something he would do.

As a child, Köle would put her through any number of terrors. He'd thrown her in a room of hyenas once. A pit full of vipers. Starved and tied her in the desert as vultures circled overhead. Had a rock tied to her foot and then had her thrown into the sea. And had her drink terrible drinks she had been sure were poison. Though she now wondered differently. And every time, he'd send another slave to save her, if she could even call it that, just before death, searching, searching for the fear in her eyes. And if he thought there was enough, he'd tell her to pull herself together.

A trite condescension from anyone, and one she could see irony in now. Or maybe it wasn't mere irony. Köle did everything for a reason.

She entered the red-curtained altar room and strode to the middle, where the line of light was cut sharply by darkness. Köle rested at the front of the room, sitting atop the altar, his robes draping grandly over the sides.

"Köle," she said, blank-faced.

He did not bother to hide any longer, not that he could with her anymore, and it seemed almost as if his stark white skin sucked up the dust. But she did not find it ugly, his black-on-white features, his dark eyes that flickered with tiny dots of color. She found it alarmingly familiar... like how a baby knows the scent of its mother before ever seeing her face. But the recognition she felt towards him was more than a twisted sense of parenthood. This djinn was so similar to Jahmil in his powers and princehood and overwhelming desire for justice. In the look Jahmil sometimes got in his eye when speaking of duty.

Was Köle the outcome of unfulfilled passion? Of blame? Was Köle Jahmil's future if the war did not end?

"You brought your lyre?" he asked.

The lack of repulsion unsettled her as she pulled out the smooth wood and rough strings.

"Play for me."

She sighed again, cringing at the oily dryness in his voice that rubbed against her ears like flakes of dead skin. It was the last piece of her she had kept from his emptiness. Playing for him felt like sealing her doom. But so had giving up Jahmil's boot. The two halves of her heart would now be complete in death.

"What would you have me play? You look like a dirge kind of person. Shall I play a dirge?"

"Look into my eyes and play what you see."

She slipped her eyes around every nook and crevice, statue and curtain in the room before sliding her gaze up to meet his. She expected a shot of ice in her veins that would make her recoil but instead found a chilly sea. Pain, like Jahmil's, but more desperate. A sense of loss. *The weight of seven and twenty thousand souls slowly crushing your bones to ash.*

She flicked her eyes away, then took up her lyre and played a song she had never heard before. A song that did not come from her, one so terrible and aching that her fingers hurt just to play it. The wisps responded, rising up in thunderous waves from every crack in the floor. Köle cackled, then jutted a hand out and stopped her mid-strum.

"Beautiful girl," he said, and the words felt slimy. He had never once called her anything less than pitiful. Compliments were worse. "Don't waste. Don't waste."

"I don't think you're going to run out of wisps if that's your concern," she said flatly.

He grinned. "No, *we* will not run out of magic, that's true. But I want tonight to be remembered forever. I want all that shines to dim in the blink of a star. All at once. It is the only way they'll know it was me. The only way they'll cower."

"The only way who will?"

"Shihala," he breathed out the word until every last drop of air had been expelled from his lungs.

She snapped her head up. "What are you doing to Shihala?"

"The same thing they did to me. To me and my people."

"What has Jahmil ever done to anyone?" A sneaky little thought crossed her mind about his fiancée queen and what he might, in fact, be doing to her. She ran her tongue over her teeth so hard it hurt.

"Ah, the incompetent little prince who thinks he can rule as king when he has no kingdom to rule."

If Jahmil were here, his fist would be on fire. This time she bit her cheek until she tasted blood. She'd gotten rid of the boot. The memories should have gone with it.

"I ask again, what has Jahmil done to you?"

"Why do you speak his name without even the 'amir'?"

Her eyes widened.

"You are familiar with him." His airy voice did not sound angry, and that made it all the worse. Köle chuckled deep in his chest. "It is only right for those in positions of power to be drawn to the one marked by fate. Someone as weak as that pathetic amir wouldn't be able to help himself."

"He did not search me out because of any stupid mark," she snapped. "We met by chance. Fate."

Köle's eyes were slits. "Either he is ignorant or you are." Then he leaned back.

"Ignorant of what?" Ayelet asked, her throat squeezing over the words.

"Amir Jahmil fights for a kingdom that destroyed the Vespar lands. *My* lands. When his father was young and impetuous and caught up in trying to be the best, the mere existence of the Vespars ate at him. When he'd had enough of our prosperity, he opened a hole in the heart of our land and sucked the magic out of it, bit by bit, from the air, the land... the people. When we were all but ruined, I insisted we fight back, but my father banished me for heresy and chose to grovel, instead. The kingdom was lost. The people died or turned horrid and cruel. Then he died, too."

"So, now you plan to take over both kingdoms and rule them, instead?"

"If there's any kingdom left to rule when I am done."

"Good luck."

"I do not need luck."

She smirked. "Jahmil will do anything for his kingdom."

His smile cut like the tip of a dagger through tender skin. "You grow fond of him."

She looked away, ashamed that she still felt that way. Ashamed it was so obvious, and that she was so weak. And ashamed that someone as heartless as Köle read it on her face so easily.

He reached out and touched the cool opals around her neck. "I see this troubles you." He pouted sympathetically. "As it should. It should. You must not get close to him. Too much rides on everything he does for you to be of any consequence to him. Even this necklace you wear, thinking it some grand gift from him no doubt, is worth nothing on Qaf."

She dropped her gaze.

"Ah, Ada, Ada. He used you so cruelly. I can see it in your eyes. You felt him close, but now you are with me and he is nowhere to be found. He does not know what a precious gift he turned away so heartlessly."

She tightened her grip around her lyre so that one of the pegs stabbed between her fingers, and she focused on that pain.

"But do not worry. I think you shall find he is not the amir you think he is."

"I try not to think of him at all." She adjusted her skirts as if trying to brush Köle's words from them. She slid her lyre away, flashing for a moment the gentle glow of the alyasimin, then hastily covered it up.

Köle chuckled, then gasped.

She flinched when he reached for her, shielding her pouch. He lunged, not for her waist, but for her leg.

He screamed and pulled her ankle up so she fell onto her back. Rage speckled the white of his skin, storm clouds on a winter's day. "What is this?"

Her elbow rang with pain that trickled up into her forehead. "I don't know," she groaned, not sure which part of herself to nurse first. She glanced at the ankle he held in his leathery hands.

The "K" of her scar had turned black, making the surrounding skin look as white as the moon. It no longer held its shape, curling around the back of her leg and onto the other side in symbols and rows that grew increasingly complex.

"I don't know," she whispered again.

"When did it start? Tell me exactly."

"Earlier today, in the woods." She twisted her tongue inside her mouth to keep from saying more. She couldn't tell him about the alyasimin. About Serap and Balian and their trip to Shihala.

"You lie!"

The wisps in the room twisted together in a funnel that sucked rock and debris toward the sky.

"I do not," she yelled over the roaring wind that now whipped her hair. Each dark strand lashed her face so it stung, and her headband pulled away, lost to the magic. "I do not. I was in the woods, getting rid of everything from Amir Jahmil. He broke a promise to me. He broke a promise and I—I hate him for it."

The whirlwind dissipated in one breath. Rocks and leaves and her headband fell limply to the ground with a clatter. She winced as pebbles rained down on her head.

"You hate him?" He smiled, but his eyes were suspicious slits of permeating black.

"I do." Her lip trembled, and she bit it. "He swore he'd return for me. He promised. But he chose his kingdom instead. He always chooses his kingdom. I should have known. Why would anyone choose me?"

Köle cackled once more. "See? See! He only cares about Shihala. That place. The power he can wield over it. You were nothing to him. And he is nothing to me." His sharp eyes found her face, and this time, she did not cringe. "But you are something to me."

Ayelet gripped her elbow, pushing the bruise so the pain would distract her from his terrible words.

"Do not worry, my Ada. Do not worry. He will not forget you when he sees you next."

She lay her head down on the dirty floor and stared at the pool of wisps overhead. They shimmered like eyes she wished to see. Eyes she wished she didn't. She didn't really hate Jahmil for leaving her. She didn't blame him for the same thing she unforgivingly held over Balian for years. For leaving her to the slavers, to Köle, so he could keep his home... Did she?

Her stomach twisted in answer, and she wondered if whatever Köle planned for her that night would be when she saw Jahmil next. She thought, briefly, to warn him. To use one of the last two petals to whisk to Shihala and tell him everything. But she had already sent Serap. Hours had passed, and he still had not come. Perhaps he *would* give up anything to save his kingdom. Perhaps anything was too much.

CHAPTER THIRTY-FIVE

Jahmil

The void of Tel Keveh is impenetrable darkness, rivaled only by Ashkult. Perhaps it is even worse because it is nothing. No quicksilver. No clouds. No remote place designed for punishment. It is nothing where something used to be, and the nothing stretches in every direction as far as the eye can see. There is not a single soul left in Vespar. Not a person, an animal, a ghoul. Not a lilith or even the whisper of a fire sprite. I knew the Vespar kingdom had suffered hardships, but this is beyond anything I could have imagined. Worse still, it is spreading into Shihala. I can see it from Thueban's back, the nothingness nipping at the crest of Orkeshi.

It is death, Jahmil. Eternal death. What are you going to do about it?

After reading Takisha's message, Jahmil set a flame to it and dropped it. It was consumed before it hit the ground.

He should not have been surprised. Takisha had found what the traitor had said would be there, to give his lies more bite. And yet, the cold teeth of doubt gnawing at his underbelly seemed even sharper.

The goal had always been to drive the Vespars out of Shihala, to send them back to where they came from. Now that he knew the land they came from was incapable of supporting life, what did it mean to drive the Vespars out? To send not just the entire army, but all the civilians who had settled in Shihala back to Vespar was not merely an act of war. It would be genocide.

As he had these thoughts, he ran his fingers absently over the twists of black on his forearm. They seemed darker now and more excitable, swirling around his arm like leaves caught in a high breeze. And when he touched them, something swelled inside of him he never would have expected.

Was it pity? Pity for the blood-soaked hordes that had attacked his homeland, murdered all his friends, cut and burned his land, viciously slaughtered his kinfolk, and sent his father tumbling to his death in the jaws of a pack of flesh-hungry hyenas.

Or pity for displaced souls, hungry stomachs, and bare feet. Pity for refugees. Pity even for wisps of free magic trapped in jars like slaves.

A lost little girl was the key to everything, that was what Khayin had said. The marked one. The *instrument* whose song could soothe the soul of one prince and burn the hatred of the other. But who was she? Was there even any point in looking for such a person, or was she just an invention of the traitor's duplicitous mind? A distraction from an actual solution. A fantasy.

The tattoo rippled under his touch, and his thoughts wandered aimlessly through Khayin's lies until they came to rest on old, half-forgotten memories. Memories of the one and only time he had met Alamir Köle al-Vespar.

Summer, seventeen years ago. The year Jahmil turned nine and reached the age of reason. The most recent war between the two kingdoms was drawing to a close, as both sides agreed to meet and discuss a peace treaty. Jahmil had seen and experienced nothing of the war and knew nothing more of it than what games and anecdotes could teach. This was long before he had stood at the edge of battle, his blood rushing in his ears as the enemy charged at full speed. Long before he made his first kill. Long before he had held the bloody, twitching body of one of his comrades as they died, calling out to Allah in strangled gasps.

The peace talks were overseen by Qadira's mother, Queen Mahreen. Jahmil's father, King Bajul, and Köle's father, King Harduk, had agreed to meet at a neutral place high in the north where the lands of Ahmar, Vespar, and Shihala met. The city was called Rananbar.

It was the first time Jahmil's father had brought him along on a diplomatic mission. He remembered being both excited and nervous. He had never spent any time alone with his father before that trip, only ever allowed to come home during the occasional festival, and even then he was largely ignored. The trip to Rananbar had been a chance to prove himself, to show that he wasn't just a silly child. Though, of course, that was exactly what he had been.

The garden at Rananbar had been beautiful, with its long reflecting pool running down the middle, flanked on both sides by flowers from all over Qaf. He had been sitting on a stone bench playing clumsy measures on the ney that his Aunt Sabra had given him for his birthday when the Crown Prince of Vespar strode into the space.

Köle Amir had been in his twenties then, perhaps early thirties. His shock-white skin was as smooth as crystal, utterly frictionless as if even light refused to cling to it. He wore his white hair in a deliberately disheveled coiffure and sported a short, squarish beard on his long chin. His dark eyes shimmered in tones of yellow, copper, and blue as they swept the gardens and came to settle on Jahmil. Something about his penetrating gaze sent shivers down Jahmil's spine.

He hadn't recognized the expression at the time, as no one had ever shown it to him before. He felt certain that if he went back, he would know precisely what to call it: loathing.

Nervous, Jahmil stood and offered a small bow. "Köle Amir."

"Is this what passes for royalty in Shihala?" The tall, immaculately costumed prince snorted and jutted out his chin. "Pathetic."

Rage flooded Jahmil at the insult. He clenched his fists, but his fire had not yet come in. "How dare you speak to me like that?"

Köle had laughed and yanked the flute out of his hand. "And is this what passes for training in your so-called kingdom?"

"Give that back!" Jahmil reached for it, but the tall, solid prince held it beyond his reach.

"You waste your time squeaking on a peasant's flute while affairs of state fly over your head." He laughed and chucked the ney into the shimmering water.

Jahmil lunged, but Köle shoved his shoulder, knocking him to the flat of his back. "I bet you've never even held a sword, have you?"

"Stop it," Jahmil said, trying to get to his feet.

Köle kicked him back to the ground. "Someday soon, our fathers will both be dead. When that day comes, do you intend to defend your kingdom with a song?"

"We are at peace."

Köle threw his head back and laughed. "The Great Kingdom of Vespar and the so-called Sovereignty of Shihala have been at war for a thousand years, *al'amir alsaghir*. Do you imagine a few pieces of paper will ever be able to change that? Your father is just buying time because he knows our forces are superior. I am Vespar, as glorious as the First Moon, and you are Shihala, weak and shivering in my shadow."

"What you're saying is treason," Jahmil hissed.

"Treason?" Köle kicked him in the face so hard that his nose split with a geyser of blood. He tumbled over himself in the flowers and covered his head.

A loud clank hit the ground. Jahmil looked up and saw a sword lying in the flower bed beside him.

"Pick up the sword," Köle commanded.

Tears sprang to Jahmil's eyes. He fought to hold them back. He rolled to his hands and feet, then straightened to a stand. "I do not want to fight you."

"Nobody cares what you want, *al'amir alsaghir*. Least of all me." He drew a second sword from the frog at his hip, long and thin and made of bone like all Vespar swords. "Pick it up."

"No."

The Vespar prince snarled and punched him in the face with the butt of his sword. Jahmil stumbled back, blood pooling in his mouth.

"Pick it up!" Köle snapped. "Before I run you through on principle."

"We don't have to fight." Jahmil scurried back, stumbling over the flower beds. "There can be peace."

Köle lunged at him, the point of the blade aiming square for his chest. Jahmil dodged, but his feet were off-balance. He fell, catching himself on one hand.

Köle kicked him in the guts and he rolled back, choking and spitting. "Weakness will not save you."

Jahmil rolled onto his back in time to see Köle lift his sword high with both hands. He snatched a fistful of dirt from the flower bed and threw it at his eyes. Köle let out a low growl and took a step back, but quickly refocused. He stabbed down.

Rolling narrowly out of the way, Jahmil struggled to his feet and raced for the sword in the flower bed. Heavy, slow footfalls dogged him. He snatched up the sword and lifted it, turning in time to catch a swipe, which came with so much force it drove him to the dirt.

Köle stabbed down. The needlelike blade pierced the flesh of Jahmil's shoulder, through muscle and beyond bone to come out the other side. Jahmil screamed in pain. Köle yanked out the blade and readied a second strike.

Desperate, Jahmil rushed back, rolling over the edge of the reflecting pool. The blade missed piercing him by a finger's width.

As he struggled to find his feet, sharp, blinding pain in his leg drove him to the ground. He looked down at the narrow of white blade sticking out through the front of his thigh.

Köle drew his blade back, and Jahmil fell to his knees. The sword shook in his hand. He lacked the strength to rise.

"The guards and everyone else have been given the evening off as a show of good faith between our two peaceful kingdoms, but if you scream loud enough, surely your servants will come. Go on and scream, *al'amir alsaghir*," said Köle, looming over him like an eclipse. "Prove the inferiority of Shihalan blood once and for all."

Jahmil gritted his teeth. Fury tingled in his good arm. With eyes clenched shut, he let out a scream and used what was left of his strength to swipe the blade backward in a high arc.

Köle hissed and stepped back. Silence fell over them. Nothing but the gentle whoosh of water in the calm fountain. Jahmil opened his eyes and took in the long line of red on Köle's white trousers, his upper right thigh slit open.

His eyes widened, the tease of pride at the edges of his mouth. Guards and servants rushed into the garden from the far end, screaming and calling to them, but none of it meant anything. All he could see was Köle.

Thin white lips curled into a cruel grin, yet his eyes had changed. They were clear now, shimmering black like starlit waters. "I could have killed you tonight," he whispered, his voice low and tight. "Someday, I will. Perhaps you'll even grow to manhood first."

That had been the end of the peace talks. When Jahmil's father learned what had happened, he demanded Köle be sent to Ashkult to pay for his crime, but of course, the King of Vespar refused. The kings quarreled, then led their troops into the field, where the Battle of Al'atfalyu was fought the very next day. Both sides took heavy casualties. There was no winner.

Jahmil wondered now if there ever could be.

He refocused in the dim light of his bedroom, that muggy night of seventeen years past still glimmering in the backs of his eyes. He tightened the leather cuff over his forearm. He'd mustered his troops—technically Qadira's troops as his own were still inexplicably missing—just outside the city limit. One thousand strong and loyal soldiers who heeded only his word. Not Qadira. Not his mother. Not any other force of djinn or humans. After seventeen years, he would finally get an opportunity for a rematch, and no amount of pity or hope for peace could stay his hand from cutting Köle down like the dog he was.

"Jahmil?" A tiny voice hit his ears, and he turned with a scowl.

"Serap?" His expression softened. "What are you doing here? I told you to remain in quarters."

She stepped shyly into the room. Her hair was done in two braids hanging down by her ears from under a yellow headdress, her gown the same sunny cascade of color. "Are you going to Ayelet?"

The question stung, and he didn't want to answer. Against all his instincts, he trusted Serap's brown eyes. There was no lie in them, had never been. If she was being used as a spy, it was unwittingly.

He glanced out of the large, ivory-trimmed window at the heavens, gauging the time by the stars. A scant fifteen degrees before the sun set in Edirne, on the ruins where Köle made his sickly nest. Still, a twist of curiosity was in his guts.

He walked to Serap and knelt down in front of her to meet her eyes. "I do not know Ayelet."

"I know." She chewed on her lip and looked down. "But I wish you could just believe me."

"Believe what, *anisa*?"

"That when you looked in her eyes you felt something new, and real, and unlike anything you had ever known."

Jahmil drew his brow together. Unexpectedly, her words hit him like cool water rushing over sun-kissed skin. "I said that?"

She nodded quickly. "You said there could never be another moment like the first time she smiled at you."

Jahmil's breath caught in his throat. He tried to shake his head and tell her that she was wrong, but nothing would come out.

He never would have said such things. He had never felt such things. And if he had felt them... could he ever have gotten rid of them? Even if she had deceived him, could he ever have thrown away such exquisite pain as the one that burned in his heart now, just from being told what he may once have felt for some mysterious, impossible creature called Ayelet?

"I don't know what's wrong with you," said Serap, "but she needs you right now. And if you don't do anything to help her, I don't think..." She looked down and wiped away a tear with the back of her sleeve. "I don't think she'll ever let anybody near her ever again."

He smiled sadly and touched her cheek with the knuckles of his gloved hand.

"Promise me you'll give her a chance to smile at you," said Serap, eyes twinkling in the moonlight. "And if she does, promise me you'll listen to whatever it makes you feel."

He watched her silently for a long moment, allowing her request to pool in his mind. The child was wise beyond her short years; he saw that clearly. And her request was not so much to ask. In fact, he was curious himself, though it shamed him.

Jahmil nodded, then rose to stand. "You must stay here. Out of harm's way."

She nodded, a mixture of guilt and relief playing across her features. "Are you taking Balian with you?"

"Of course." He smiled and rolled his shoulders in his thick leather armor. "It only seems fair I give him his opportunity at a daring rescue. Besides—" Jahmil picked up his heavy obsidian sword and threaded it into his belt. "—he's spreading dirt all over my bed chambers."

CHAPTER THIRTY-SIX

Ayelet

Ayelet rubbed her ankle nervously. The flicker of black itched beneath her skin and plucked at her vessels. But that's not why she fidgeted. Köle had gathered her up to the ruins on the surface of the thickly forested hill. Ridged columns rose up between weathered blocks and faded reliefs of victims being slaughtered in battle, of warriors doing the slaughtering.

"Wait," Köle had told her. "Wait."

He had made her change into a brocaded purple robe similar to his, with a simple white dress underneath. And for all she hated Köle, the fabric was soft and smelled of persimmons. Her mind drifted to the dead Vespar lands. Had the loss of magic taken its sweet scent with it? She rubbed her nose against the delicate fabric and pushed its hem over her swirling scar. The sun hovered low and large to the west, shadows of clouds disappearing when they crossed its light. A flash of starlit eyes crossed her mind, and she smothered it with the ash.

"Happy now?" she called to Jahmil, though she knew he could not hear. "With your queen, and your fancy clothes, and your flying snakes? You're welcome for Thueban, by the way."

She bit her lip to keep the sting from her eyes. Then she dropped her gaze to the weedy grass beneath her feet and breathed in the tangy air.

"If you plan to come for me…" she whispered. "It is the last moment. I don't know what to do. I can't let Köle take the children. And I can't let you kill them. If there's another way to save the children without sucking the magic from Shihala, come and tell me now."

She raised her face to the sky and closed her eyes. The chirp of crickets and call of sandgrouse piped through the rustle of leaves. She sighed and used her shame to crush her moment of weakness.

Humans lived without magic each and every day, she tried to reason. The djinn could get by just as well. They didn't need their apparitions and glowing flowers and skies that reflected the realms of the universe to live. They needed food and water and air. Same as humans. And all those things could be found on earth. Sucking the magic from Shihala didn't have to mean the death of the Shihalan people. The kings of Qaf would just have to let go of their precious kingdoms and come live with everyone else. She just needed to slow the pull of magic enough to give them time to escape.

She blinked and saw the deadness of Vespar when she first arrived in Qaf. Heard Köle's words as he described how Jahmil's father had sucked the magic from the land… and the people. Guilt and ugliness ate at her heart. If Jahmil had just come for her as he promised, she wouldn't have to decide between humans and djinn. But that was the choice he had made. She clutched as tightly to that flimsy excuse as she did to the folds of her dress.

Ayelet swept her eyes across the hill. Nadir had spent the better part of the day stomping around the ruins, placing charms and empty bottles with strange, frothing liquids inside every nook and cranny. A thick whip hung spiraled at his waist, and she rolled her shoulders at the familiar sight of terror. But he wasn't the only busy one.

Scores of wisps flew around the camp as Köle used them to set up a terrifying barrage of weapons. Kadri hadn't lied when she said he had taken everything. Siege cannons and super-sized bombards had been nestled away in the trees, and lines of blades had been laid out on the grass as if they had been forgotten there by careless soldiers. What did Köle think would be coming? Or worse, who?

But she knew the answer, even if she couldn't bear to think of it.

"Move," Nadir huffed, shoving her shoulder as he tried to pull a crate out from under her.

She smirked and obliged. "You plan to catch the magic of an entire world in your tiny bottles?"

"As much as I can," he said without looking up. "Would you rather it go into this world uncontained? We do not want those creatures coming here."

"Why not? They're not all monsters."

"And what of the ones that are?"

She frowned, and Köle emerged from the ruins of the temple steps. "The sun sets. Bring out your lyre."

Ayelet did as he asked, but her fingers brushed the tips of the jasmine in the folds of her dress. She hesitated. One last chance to run. To drop a petal and be free. Of the horrid responsibility to suck the magic from Qaf. Of her promise to save the children. Of Jahmil.

She stroked the delicate softness of the flower once more before pulling out her lyre. She strummed it, plucking out strings and tuning the pegs until they sang together. Satisfied, she dragged herself up a set of columns, steadying herself with an occasional wisp. An arch crossed between two of the pillars, and she climbed atop it.

The magic would come from the earth—she could feel it pulling there—and she wanted a steady foundation away from it so she could focus on what she must do. Pull the magic slowly, so the djinn would have time to escape and save the children, and then demolish a world.

Great. Just great.

The sun had just kissed the horizon when she raised her lyre. She twanged a single note, and three wisps swirled up from the earth, entangled in a braid before thinning into the sky. Then she plucked two notes. Two dozen wisps grew from the earth, forming shimmering white trees that faded just as quickly into the breeze. She scowled. So much difference between one note and two. If she started playing, how would she be able to control it?

"Pull yourself together," Köle hissed. "You must feel something for the magic to respond. Channel your hatred for Jahmil."

She winced and rubbed her one tattered slipper over the sting in her scar, tempted to throw the useless thing across the ruins.

"Play," Köle hissed. "The silver of the moon will help call the wisps. I will open the hole into the other world, and you will pull the magic. All of it. So that Shihala will suffer the same fate they inflicted on Vespar and so all the rest of Qaf who just sat by and watched will get what they deserve." His voice dropped down to a menacing whisper. "For every drop you fail to draw, I will make a thousand bial'dabaye for Jahmil Amir to slay. And the first one I'll turn is the little girl we found you with."

"She is not on earth to find," Ayelet said, the prick of thorns racing across her chest.

"Then she will die with the rest tonight," he sneered.

A bone-aching chill splashed over her, making her lips tremble. Jahmil would not let that happen. But if he was here, fighting the battle, who would save her then? Balian?

She focused harder as she plucked a few more notes, trying with everything to pull just enough wisps to catch the leaves or move the magic in a square. She was still terrible at it, but with Serap on her mind, the wisps were beginning to be more than just a flood of power.

"Enough!" Köle howled. "Play!"

Ayelet took a deep breath. She did not even ward off the Evil Eye. What was the point when the world of djinn was to exist no more? Then she began her tune, rapid, staccato notes flurrying in succession to get the wisps in a churn. When a great, shimmering funnel of magic whirled around the ruins with her at the center, she slowed the melody. And without thought, she shifted to a solemn thrum—the song she had played for Jahmil in the market.

Had he only been drawn to her because of her power? Because of the music he said was far rarer and more beautiful than a common breath of magic?

As she played each note, her ankle burning beneath her robe, she could not believe it was true. Not when he wanted to save Shihala more than anything else. More than her. If he had known her power, he would not have left her. But he had not known. And since she never told him how she felt, he, thinking he was nothing to her and she was nothing to him, left.

She closed her eyes and cherished the gentle smile he gave her when he thought she could not see. This song was not about her hate for Jahmil. It was a song of yearning, and the wisps took up her broken heart and pulled themselves into it.

White shimmers shot up from the earth, turning the funnel into a dome that encased the ruins and sucked magic from its center. The ground trembled, and, one by one, ancient columns and blocks of stone disappeared into a gaping white hole. Through groaning cracks shone what must be the majestic expanse of Shihala's skies, untainted by magicless clouds.

Jahmil had been right. She would not have believed him. She gave herself to the ache in her heart, and in the tender way of the non-living wisps, they swirled around her, billowing her hair and whipping her robes. Occasionally, a glittering tendril would wipe an errant tear from her cheek, and she would smile sadly.

A crack sounded. She looked to the sky and saw only the moon. Then, a gulf of wisps broke the lines as an army burst through the center of the hole. They climbed as if out of a pit, though she could see nothing beneath their hands. And with a terrible screech that startled her from her music, a flying serpent flew up to the stars. Thueban. She stumbled over her notes. Thueban with Jahmil on his back.

Köle, still hovering behind her, placed a dry hand around her neck and squeezed enough to hurt. "Focus," he growled with a breathy snarl.

She did focus. On how the moonlight whispered across his azure skin. On how the dark leather of his armor widened his broad shoulders. On his oh-so-serious eyes, flashing white. By the fire in his fists, she knew he was not there for her. He was there to stop her.

His eyes flashed at the scene below, drawing lightning from the sky. He yelled a command in Arabic, and another surge of soldiers rose from the depths of Shihala. They advanced on her and Köle, sprinting over the abandoned ruins, eager to end her.

How foolish she and her master must look. Two lone beings in a field with an army approaching. She glanced over her shoulder at Köle, barely able to play with her shaking fingers.

He sneered.

With the whip of his hand, a firework of wisps shot into the trees. Trunks snapped. Branches swayed and crashed to the earth, and then a quiet *thwang*. A ball of iron hurtled through the sky, welding fissures like scars. She yelped when it almost hit Thueban, who glittered in the moon and gave an angry shriek. Instead, the mass of metal exploded into the earth. Bits of iron flew into the faces and bodies of the advancing djinn soldiers. Searing screams broke through her melody. Shimmering embers of red flashed wherever metal touched skin and ate away at the soldiers' flesh.

She turned her head, unable to watch. Her fingers tripped over the next few notes. Köle's hand sneaked up her neck once more. A warning.

Leaving behind their fallen comrades, Jahmil's army continued forward. She searched the sky, hoping, praying that Jahmil would look at her. Really look at her and know she would do anything to stop this if she could think of a way. His eyes sparked, and he did look her way. Their gazes met. And he hurtled toward her, sword drawn on Thueban's back. Köle staggered with haste across a fallen column behind her to an arch farther away, leaving her on her own.

Why, Jahmil? Why do you come to slay me with a sword in hand when the last thing you held was me? Don't you care at all why I stand here with my lyre? Don't you want to understand?

Arm-long teeth gaped before her, ready to snap. She played a terrible streak of music so awful that wisps nearby burst into sparks, but Thueban still advanced. Like a comet from the sky, Jahmil descended with him, ready to kill her. She braced herself, tossing her lyre up in defense when Thueban jutted to the side at the last second. She felt a heavy blow that shook her bones, then the lick of the drakonte's tongue and an *urgle* of recognition as it passed.

Jahmil cursed. She unsealed her eyes and saw his fiery fists.

Ayelet wiped the stinging saliva from her face. What had just happened? Then, her world shattered to gray. Her lyre lay in two splintered pieces in her hands, only the strings holding it together in a warped and mangled web. She felt as if her body had been split in twain with it, and only the ugly half was left. Then her horror deepened. She was not playing any music, but the wisps still pulled magic from Shihala. Another cannonball exploded in the sky.

Thueban snarled and rolled, dropping Jahmil from his back into the field of soldiers below.

Why, Jahmil? Why?

Köle raised his hands and a torrent of magic hurled forward, sweeping up the abandoned swords from the grass. He clenched his fist, and the wisps swarmed together into a tight whirlwind, the blades glinting like the moon on water as they swept ferociously in the twisting wind. He sneered and pushed the eviscerating whirlwind toward Jahmil, who stumbled to his feet.

Ayelet cried out. She reached forward and yanked back so hard her shoulders popped.

The whirlwind dissipated in one breath. Knives fell from the sky, and the soldiers below scattered, advancing to where she stood on the top of the ruins.

Where was Jahmil? And had he been aiming for her lyre or her heart? She could still feel the spark of his kiss on her lips under moonlit trees. Hear his promise to never forget her. And yet, it felt as if he really had. Why else would he attempt to slay her when words would be enough? Or had he never truly known her and assumed she was the villain? A betrayer that had laid a snare so she could destroy his kingdom?

Either way, he had destroyed the most precious part of her to save what was most precious to him.

Her chest stung as much as if he had found his mark. She had to find him. She scanned the fields for Jahmil but couldn't see him in the sea of blue men fighting for their lives. So many djinn in this human plane. A soldier approached. He looked no more than twenty, his face resolute and pained.

"Please," she said, backing up.

His eyes faltered, a purplish-black shine of regret swimming in his irises. He crossed one column. Then two.

"Please."

Then a guttural, screeching cry broke the air and sliced through her. Nasty hyena creatures burst from the bowels of the ruins, Nadir driving them forward with his whip. More children. How many more?

She shot a horrified look to Köle, who returned her stare, his face cruel and smooth. He knew she had stopped the whirlwind. And he would make her pay. One of the snarling beasts broke from the pack that attacked screaming soldiers and raced towards the young man who held a knife toward her. The creature ripped into his neck as he cried for Allah, for Shihala, and for his mother. He raised his blade to slice its throat.

"No!" she cried and jumped between them.

The obsidian dagger raked her arm as she pushed the creature to the ground and focused on its eyes. The soldier fell limp behind her, legs twitching, but there was nothing she could do to save him. Instead, she focused on the monstrous child. She wanted to rip the magic from it, to get the poison out of the child's blood, but she had no lyre to guide the wisps out. She had only half herself.

Ayelet dumped the broken instrument on the ground as the beast whimpered pitifully beside her. If she pulled too hard, if the wisps felt her raw pain from the way Jahmil had looked at her—not just as if he didn't know her, but with contempt—the child would die, and she wouldn't be able to live with herself. But she couldn't let the child live and die this way either.

She took a shuddering breath, unsure what to do with her hands. She decided to place them on the beast's face as she had with Serap. It jerked from her touch, and she flinched. So she hummed, instead. Slow and gentle and sweet, until, just as slowly, the creature let her near. She stroked mangy hair instead of her beautiful lyre, plucked oily fur in place of strings. The wisps snaked out from the blood-licked mouth in a trickle that turned into a stream. Encouraged, her hum turned to the soft lullaby of the moon and the Evil Eye.

Pupils returned, and the fiery eyes cleared. The body twitched and snapped with awful crackles until, at last, it morphed back into a child.

Ayelet sighed with relief and broke her eyes free from the shaking body of a little boy covered only in scraps of fabric. And in the dark night above the tiny, worn body, she spied eyes of diamonds. He knelt in the grass before her with a hand to his mouth and eyes of horror.

"Jahmil!"

CHAPTER THIRTY-SEVEN

JAHMIL

ALL THE STRENGTH WENT from Jahmil's legs, and he fell, catching himself on his hands. Muscles ossified while bones melted into liquid. Freezing quicksilver raced through his veins and into his brain, scalding his thoughts. Acid in his mouth. The little boy trembled, filthy and naked but for the scraps of fabric that clung to his skin like cobwebs. His ragged flesh worn away on his knees and elbows.

Was it an illusion? A trick played on his mind to stay his blade and make him weak? It had to be. What he was seeing defiled logic and memory in a breath. It couldn't be real.

Another bial'dabaye stalked closer, its orange, lifeless eyes glaring at the helpless morsel standing fixed before it. The upper lip curled, pink foam dripping from the horrid lips. It drew back on its legs, preparing to leap on the boy and tear into its easy meal.

The woman screamed. On instinct, Jahmil leaped forward and caught the boy in his arms seconds before the creature could tear into him. Claws and teeth slammed into his back, catching on his armor. He rolled aside and threw back an elbow to catch the beast in the maw, holding tight to the boy with the other arm.

When he looked up again, the woman—Ayelet—was reaching her fingers towards the creature, drawing magic from it as she had the boy a moment before. Such eyes she had. Even in the whirl of battle, the horror of the moment, the perfect storm of her gaze seized his heart like a boat caught in a cyclone.

The bial'dabaye fell on its back and began to twitch violently. Once again, Jahmil watched in horror as the creature shriveled, its fur fell away, and a girl, no more than sixteen, was left shivering in the dust in its place, blood streaming from her nose where he had hit her.

He looked up at Ayelet to find her watching him. The expression on her face was impossible to interpret. Sadness, desperation, disgust, anger, hatred, fear. All of that and none of it. And something else he didn't have the presence of mind to understand.

His gaze swept the battlefield. Suddenly nothing was the same. Where before he would have seen his troops pressing their advantage, battling back Köle's monsters with bravery and precision, now all he saw were men with armor attacking children. And what should have been the intimidating image of a man whipping the backs of flesh-eating bial'dabaye, driving them forward into his ranks, now looked to him like a slave market.

Had every bial'dabaye he'd ever faced held a trembling human inside of it? It was too horrible to believe.

He spotted one of his soldiers nearby, lifting his sword to drive it into the great, muscular back of a snarling bial'dabaye.

"No!" Jahmil shouted, lifting his arm as he stumbled forward.

The soldier drew back, and the snarling creature sunk its teeth into the man's hip. He raised his blade and then brought it down. The bial'dabaye screamed and then was silent.

"Fall back!" Jahmil shouted.

His soldiers had made it to the center of the fray. They were winning. Though Köle was nowhere to be seen, how easy it would have been to cut through the remaining bial'dabaye. To behead Ayelet and put an end to all of this. But suddenly it was unthinkable, knowing what he now knew. And seeing whatever he had seen in her eyes.

"Fall back!" he called again, pushing himself up on legs of concrete.

He left his sword on the ground—dreadful, heavy. Horrible.

"Retreat to Qaf! *Tarajae!*"

The call echoed through the commanders. As Jahmil himself turned to run, the shriek of one of the creatures hit close to his ear. The beast leaped on him—nine feet and three hundred pounds of pure muscle. Its claws penetrated his leather breastplate, cutting into the flesh beneath. He struggled and swung his fists at the monster, trying to get away. Teeth sunk into his thigh.

Jahmil pulled the dagger from the scabbard on his belt and lifted it, but when he looked at the slobbering monster chewing on his leg, his blood coating its muzzle, he saw a trembling boy. A bleeding girl. He also saw the fury of fate come to collect its due. His death for all the harm he had caused.

He screamed and his head fell back. Another shriek. A second monster fell on him, slobbering jaws biting at his neck. He brought up his arm to defend himself, and the creature's teeth sank through the leather into his flesh.

"*Astaghfirullah!*" he screamed through the white-hot pain threatening to consume his senses, and then all of him. *Allah, forgive me.* He had to get out. He couldn't let himself die here like this, no matter how justified. No matter how it tore at his soul. His hand tightened around his dagger.

A voice filled his ears, soft and brimming with gentleness. Blurry eyes peeled up, and he saw before him white whispers of magic rising from the bodies of the monsters, and beyond them, eyes of gray, flickering with inconstant light like the skies of Shihala.

The creatures transformed—a girl with whip marks on her back and a boy, shaking furiously in the dirt. Jahmil tried to lift his bones from the filth, but they would not move. He was frozen.

A shock of cannon fire sounded, and something exploded overhead like an orange skyflower, filling his vision. He turned his gaze to the last of his men disappearing from this world back into Qaf. They had left him, as he had ordered them to. Though likely they did not realize that he had fallen. The sky filled with a dark cloud, and then tiny dots of black began to rain down. Only when they touched his skin, searing into him like hot embers, did he realize they were iron filings.

A blast of wind overtook him, chasing away the horrid dust. He opened his eyes again and there she was. Ayelet, shining like starlight as white magic shifted in clouds all around her. He opened his mouth to speak, but it was so full of blood. He turned his face and coughed weakly.

She knelt at his side, an alyasmin flower in her hand with only two petals still clinging to the fragile pistil.

"Ada!" a voice called, loud and furious and taunting. "Do not tempt your master."

Jahmil recognized the voice as if from a dream, and yet he was certain. Köle was near. His chest tightened, and he pushed himself up on his elbows. Now was his chance.

But one look at Ayelet stilled his every thought. Fear flashed across her features. Then she turned her eyes back to him. She laid a hand on his chest and smiled sadly, then she plucked a petal and let it fall.

White wind warped around them. Black and gray mist followed quickly. Even caught in a storm of iron, the power of Shihala was enough. It caught them in its hands with a soft grip and pulled them through to the other side.

For a split second, they were alone together in the space between worlds. The tremendous pain in his body fell away, along with the tortured beat of his broken heart, and all he could see was her. Ruby-black hair whipping around her in the furious breeze. Soft hazel wood skin. Delicate coral lips. And such eyes, gazing into his as if they understood a secret he hadn't known he'd been keeping.

His forearm tingled. He tightened his fingers around her hand.

The spell was broken the moment they arrived in Qaf. All the pain flooded back in an instant. The tears in his chest, missing flesh on his leg and arm. The sensation of acid on his skin. He screamed and his head fell back, the rush of agony overwhelming his senses.

Ayelet tightened her grip on his hand as he shook. His teeth clenched so tightly his tongue bled, muscles pulsating. He heard her voice again, though closer than before. Weak and cracked as if with smoke. Tired and trembling.

She sang:

Dandini dandini danadan
A moon was born from a mother's womb
spared from all harm
and protected from the evil eye.

Calming magic rushed into his body as if carried on her breath. The wisps burrowed into the claw and teeth marks, swept over the burns left by the iron. They attached themselves to his skin and then melted into it. The relief of pain was instant. Actual healing would take much longer.

Looking up at her from the flat of his back, her gentle gaze and her kindness were too much for him to bear, even if he didn't understand why she was offering them. She'd brought him away from the battle, and without the bombards blasting above and the sound of snarls resounding in his ears, everything he had seen began to crash over him like the relentless waves of a frozen ocean.

All the energy drained from his bones, and he let himself go limp. He wished the ground would swallow him up, cleanse him with the fires of Jahannam. For the moment he saw the bial'dabaye transform into the figure of a tattered, broken child he had known that the only fate he could be bound for was eternal fire. When he died, the book Allah placed in his left hand would be written in the blood of children.

He rubbed his arms—the bite marks, the scratches. The wounds given him by the children, so much less than he deserved. He wanted to dig his fingernails into them, to draw from them as much blood as possible. To give some small reparation for all he had taken, and tasted, and delighted in since the war began.

But even punishing himself was an act of cruelty against the human children. His guilt was of no value to them and did nothing to ease their suffering. Putting aside the dozen bial'dabaye he had killed with his own hands, how many thousands had been killed by his soldiers? Innocent souls inside the monsters and innocent souls fighting the monsters. Fighting, always fighting. Always a sword in hand and death at the end. A lifetime soaked in blood and ignited by the fires of hatred.

"Jahmil?" she breathed, and her fingers touched his shoulder.

"Why did you save me?" He raked his fingernails through his hair and forced himself to sit up and meet her eyes. "You must not yet know how evil I truly am. For I hide under layers of lies and false intentions so nobody can predict me. And it's impossible for anybody to draw the truth from my eyes because I myself cannot differentiate between truth and lies."

Ayelet said nothing, and he could not look at her. Not at her eyes of kindness and pity, which he deserved no more than any cold-blooded murderer. But why was she looking at him like that, anyway? What right did she have to look at him like that?

His mother came into his mind at that moment, though he did not know why. Karzusan. The torn expression on her face as he stood, wounded in his left side and desperately trying to charge back into the swarm of bial'dabaye to rescue his father. He couldn't remember what she had said that finally convinced him to flee. It had been her expression, her eyes, silently begging him not to go. Not to fight, but to flee.

To flee and survive for another day.

And then a tear had slipped out, a single silver tear—the first and last he ever saw on her cheek—which he knew she had shed only for him. Her need to protect him, to push him to do all the work that she believed was good and necessary.

He realized in that moment that he loved her.

The children transformed into monsters by the Vespars—no, by Köle—they had mothers shedding not one tear for them, but thousands. Crying until their eyes should bleed and never knowing what happened to their dear ones. Or perhaps they were slaves—orphans with nobody to cry for them.

Ayelet was a slave, too. That was what Balian had said. A slave of the cruelest man Jahmil had ever known. Somehow, the thought gave him the courage to look up at her again.

CHAPTER THIRTY-EIGHT

AYELET

For once, Ayelet had not intended to run away. To leave the children to Köle's cruelty or Shihala to the gaping hole of magic.

At least, every last living soldier had disappeared from the field and the bial'dabaye—the children—were no longer in harm's way or harming others. This was a moment to think. A breath to feel. To suffer. The eye of a storm before it all came collapsing together. For she did not know if Köle still pulled wisps through the gap. Or if, with none of her anguish to draw them, they had stopped.

She had to go back. Had to return to face her fate with cowardly Köle, who had slipped to safety as Jahmil's men had pressed. She should have returned already, but...

She was selfish.

Jahmil sat on the ground before her, a crumpled version of his former self, in an opulent room with lavishly high ceilings. Bowls of sweet-smelling fruit sat on every table, and plump pillows covered a bed big enough to sleep four bears. The air tasted of honey, and the shiny, purple leaves of a tree peeked through one of the windows.

His room? She frowned. It was so bare of personal effects, it might as well have been empty. But what did it matter, anyway?

She touched a hand to her opal necklace and turned her eyes to Jahmil. His lush hair and thick eyelashes were now soaked with sweat and tears. He had lashed out at her when they first appeared, then turned his head and refused to see her. Flash after flash of his look of torment when the child transformed tumbled across her vision. It was as if he had not known. And she knew, even now, he was adding guilt, child by child, to the weight of seven and twenty thousand souls that slowly crushed his bones to ash.

She had tried to warn him. To give him time to prepare by sending Serap. What happened? Her heart ached. If Jahmil could look at her with such raw contempt, if he could aim his sword at her heart, what might he have done with Serap? Or did she never make it here? And where was Balian? But blanketing all these questions was another.

Why, Jahmil? Why do you not love me?

At last, his shoulder stirred, and she yearned to both caress his cheek and hit him. But he had suffered enough, and he did not care to know her. She smiled weakly, the last defense she had against disappearing entirely. But her heart was not in it. It never was. His brows knit together, and his face plunged into misery.

She still held the alyasimin in one hand, its last petal tempting her in the dusky light of Shihala. If he did not want to see her, she should go. It was what she was best at. But she could not leave him in this place. Not like this.

"Jahmil Amir," she said. The stiff greeting lay like wool on her tongue and dried up her next words. She started over. "This is not your fault."

He looked up at her and shook his head. "What do you know of the things I have done? Of how many sins lay on my head?"

"I do not know." She sighed. "But I do not think that numbers matter. I think only you do."

He pressed his palm against the side of his face and shook his head. "Who are you to me?"

A soft, sad smile slipped from her lips at the same words she had once asked him. "No one, I guess."

The lie burned her tongue. But he had left before she could tell him otherwise in the woods. And now, he pretended like he didn't even know her. She tucked a strand of hair behind her ear.

"I know what you are to your people, though. And to the Vespars. You are hope. Because once you knew the monsters were children, you stopped fighting. You feel such deep remorse. You give everything for your kingdom, for innocent lives." She reached a hand for his, then remembered the look of sheer contempt in his eyes on the battlefield and dropped it. "That is enough."

He closed his eyes and shook his head defiantly. "Is that why I made myself forget you? Because I loved you, and to you, I am no one?"

Pain filled up every part of her tired body. "You forgot me?" She bit her lip so it would not shake. "You forgot me."

He was still trembling, breath short and heavy. Wincing with pain, he pulled himself to his knees to look at her straight. "I do not know what happened. Serap tells me that I loved you, and yet until tonight I had never seen you. Takisha nearly killed me..."

"Thank Allah Serap is okay, that she made it to see you. But what do you mean Takisha tried to kill you?" A flicker of anger struck inside before her misery snuffed it out once more.

"She broke my back," he said. "She said I had lost my senses. And I think that was your doing."

Hope and anger swirled dangerously inside her, and she caught sight of a wisp outside the window. She had to control herself or she'd suck the magic from Shihala right there. "If you wanted to forget me so badly..." She inhaled a shaky breath. "If you were beaten..." She didn't know which trail to follow. "You're so selfish!"

"Selfish?" He furrowed his brow. "Perhaps, I am. But please, tell me why. Why would I want to forget you? Did you hurt me? Do you hate me? Were you using me? Did I have my way with you?"

"Have your way with—" She dug her nails into her palm. "You couldn't even manage that."

"Then I'm a fool and a coward, too." He cut himself short and looked down at the floor. "Did I love you?"

Ayelet sighed. "If you loved me, nothing else would matter. Nothing in Qaf or on Ard." The words he had said to her during their frozen night together fell from her lips like a forgotten song. She bit her lip. "I loved you."

He moved closer to her and clasped one of her hands in his, his gaze fixed on her face. "I failed you, didn't I?"

The sorrow she had pushed deep down welled up inside her. "I told you not to forget about me... in the brush, I told you." Her eyes widened with the shameful sting of tears. "And that's exactly what you did. You danced with me... you kissed me, made me foolish enough to believe in hope. And then you left me. To *Köle*. You are worse than Balian."

He clenched his teeth, chest heaving with every harsh breath. "If I loved you, I never would have made myself forget you. No matter what happened. Even if I died for it."

"But you did forget me." The question she ached to ask ever since he had left twisted on her tongue. Twice she bit it back, tasting the salt from her tears. "So, why? Why didn't you love me?"

"You are wearing my grandmother's necklace."

Of course. He would never give her a straight answer. She touched a hand to the smooth opals and smiled wistfully. Bitterly. "You gave it to me so I would have glad dreams." She hesitated, fingers shaking.

"It does do that." He watched her in silence for a moment, his gaze shifting between the necklace and her eyes. "Did I tell you that it is all I have left of her? That she pressed it into my hands as she lay dying so that one day I could give it to the woman that I would make my queen? Or was I hopeless and evasive and simply said it would give you glad dreams?"

"When are you not hopeless and evasive?" she asked, allowing a tiny smile. "And it gave me the best dreams when I needed them the most... But you would not make me your queen. You are engaged, and Takisha said it would destroy everything. Even you said—"

"As if everything is not already destroyed!" he shouted, capped with a hopeless laugh, and splayed his arms to the side. "As if Qadira and her money could fix the desolation in Vespar. As if any army could end this war. I will die before I marry her."

"Then perhaps we should be getting back so there is something left to save." Ayelet turned away from his anger, tracing the pristine lines of the marble floor.

"Tonight's battle is at an end. Every new moon brings another. What difference does it make?"

"If this necklace was meant to be for your queen, that means you proposed to me, didn't tell me you proposed to me, and then forgot you proposed to me. Perhaps you did not believe even then that fate would allow us to be." Ayelet sighed and forced her eyes to his. "Which is all the more reason you cannot marry someone you do not remember. Don't you realize this?"

"And why not, if Shihala decrees it?"

Pools blurred her vision. "What am I to you?" She trembled, repeating the words back to him. "Why do you do this to me?"

"You are the woman I chose to be my queen, whether or not that was wise." He chewed on his lip and looked away. "No. I would not have administered the potion myself, even if you were a coldhearted seductress. I am not one to part with pain so easily. Someone stole you from me. Probably my mother." He ran his fingers softly over his own cheek. "Do you want me to leave you alone?"

What was she to say to that? Already, his politically trained mind was hunting for answers and trying to solve riddles, while hers still clung to memories. Memories he no longer had.

"Such eyes you have, Ayelet." He shook his head sadly. "They gaze through me."

"Even when you think I cannot see." She brushed a finger through his hair and then pulled back. She stood and took a step away. The abyss of loss already twined its way from her heart and out to her limbs, pulling her fingers into a fist. "Perhaps you have been given a mercy."

"You mean that you should abandon me?"

"I mean to spare you... and myself."

He scoffed. "You never loved me."

"Do not say that…" Her shoulders shook, from misery or growing anger she wasn't sure. "You cannot say that to me. I am the only one who has said I care! You never did. And—" Wounded rage won out in her exhausted mind. "You cannot marry someone you do not remember!"

He chuckled, a dead, horrible sound. "Then I will marry no one. I'm not fit for it. I will lay down here and die. Shihala can find a prince who is better at his job to fight Her wars."

The roaring anger in Ayelet flicked out with irritation. "Good. Fine. Don't marry anyone. Then there will be no one to shatter when you leave them to the slavers!" She took off her one slipper and threw it at him, satisfied when he flinched weakly where it hit. "And if you do not fight for Shihala, I will be left to do it on my own. So do not come back someday and call me spoiled when it is clear it is you who is."

"What do you want from me?"

"To get better servants."

"You despise me, don't you?"

She laughed, her hurt flaking into bitterness. "See? You don't even know to what I refer. You think only of yourself. Of how this is hurting you. Have you ever thought I would not want to marry someone who cannot remember me because I cannot bear to be forgotten?"

He set his jaw and stared at her fixedly, his shoulders rolling down as his back straightened. The spray of wild colors that had been rushing through his eyes stilled in an instant, so only clear diamond remained. "Then remind me."

His words hit her. She could barely breathe. She took short, angry, desperate breaths, afraid of what she might show him and afraid of what would happen if she didn't. She marched over to him with clenched fists and knelt, so her lips were a mere breath from his. Then she lay a hand on his heart to see if she felt something. Anything.

His heart thrashed so hard and so fast she could feel its heat. She leaned in and kissed him.

Wisps spilled into the room, pulling her dress and tugging her hair. They wrapped around Jahmil, too, shimmering against his already sparkling skin and dancing in his eyes. She felt his heat and yearning, an urgency that guided his every movement, just as it had when he had carried her into the woods. She pulled back and cast her gaze sideways, afraid the kiss and the wisps and the magical connection had all been for naught.

He pressed his forehead against hers, his hand weaving into her hair. "I'm sorry. I have a terrible memory," he whispered, eyes still closed. "Tell me again."

A grin spilled from her lips, and the tears she cried this time were filled with relief. She kissed him once more, then pulled away and punched him right in the heart. "Don't you ever forget me again. My heart cannot bear to be away from you."

CHAPTER THIRTY-NINE

JAHMIL

As the last of the fog cleared from his mind, Jahmil kissed her hair, her forehead, and squeezed her tightly. "Forgive me. I never would have... What has Köle done to you?"

She pulled away from him, shadows as dark as ghouls stalking the frozen night in her eyes. Her mouth hitched into a sad smile. "Everything."

His heart froze and shattered in an instant, and heat pricked at his eyes. "Please don't say everything." He wiped back her tears and kissed her forehead again. "This is all my fault. What does he want with you? What is he trying to make you do?"

She looked away, and the loss in her eyes, even for all the darkness inside of him, was as profound as any pain he had ever known. "He asks me to call on Shihala's magic. To drain it away from Qaf. To let it free on earth so your land will be as desolate as Vespar. So your heart will be as black as his." She flipped her hands over and back, flexing her fingers as if searching for the phantom of her broken lyre.

How could he have done that to her? From the cold perspective of a general on the field, it had been strictly necessary. It had even occurred to him at the time, with his memories clouded by sticky black magic, to run her through and be done with it. Only the words of gentle Serap had stayed his hand. He owed her his life for that.

"I am not Ayelet," she said in a cracked voice, and his face lifted again to hers. "I am Ada. I am marked. An instrument. An *ayelet*. Köle says—" She bit her lip hard enough to bleed and clamped her mouth shut.

He touched her chin, lifting her gaze. "You are beautiful, whatever your name is."

"Do you—" She steeled her gaze, her muscles clenching under his touch. "In the market. The day you gave me the opal. I drew you with my music, did I not? And then held you with the magic that hides in my eyes?" She grasped his jaw and pulled him close, searching for the truth in his face. "Tell me the truth."

Jahmil wanted to kiss her. To dance with her. To take her in his arms and run away with her to a place where none of this mattered and would never matter again.

"Yes," he said at last, "and no. The draw of your music is indescribable, and your eyes hide many secrets. But it was your laughter that made me want to be near you. Your dreamy expression that made me long to know your thoughts. And your swift, yet inexplicably clumsy little feet that made me want to dance with you. I cannot think of anything about you that did not draw me in." He shrugged. "Maybe Balian."

She furrowed her brows. "So, you would feel the same about me if I never played the lyre again?"

"It would be a shame." He sighed. "But if the lyre brings you pain, I will smash every lyre from Al Madinat to Bengal."

"You have already broken the only one I want to play." She shot him a dirty look, but the soft smile had returned to her eyes. "And still you will not tell me how you really feel." She pulled away and shook her head in resignation.

"You are a very silly woman."

"Nuh-uh. I am not falling for your tricks this time."

He dropped his gaze to the floor, trying to find the right words and knowing that there were none. He was tongue-tied for her. "Do you remember how I said loving you would ruin my life?"

"Not my favorite memory," she said, but she laid a soft hand on his chest.

"Will you *please* ruin my life?"

Pink spilled across her cheeks, spreading slowly. She coughed out a small giggle. "You want me to ruin your life *more?*"

"Every single night." He lifted her hand to his lips and kissed her knuckles. "I want you to destroy all of them."

She grinned conspiratorially. Then her smile fell. "Jahmil. I must go back."

"No. I won't let you."

"I know you will. You know as well as I that you have to."

"But what do you plan to do?" he asked, wrinkling the skin around his eyes. "You cannot drain Shihala."

"I will not hurt your precious home," she said with a sigh. "But I must save the children. And when they are free from magic..."

"You don't understand. There are thousands more. Thousands upon thousands of bial'dabaye here in Qaf. If every one of them was once a human child..."

"I understand perfectly, Jahmil," she snipped before releasing a heavy sigh. She reached for his hand and placed it over her heart. "Please tell me you do, too."

"I understand that we cannot let Köle do to Shihala what my—" He flicked his gaze to the side, phantoms dancing before him, mocking him. Khayin had once again been telling the truth, that much was clear as the night of the Eight Moons now. He could no longer deny it.

"What my father did to Vespar," he managed to say aloud. "I want to keep you here where it is safe, but nowhere is safe, is it? Not in Qaf, and not on Ard should so much magic overflow to that land. Djinn need magic to live, but humans can only hold so much before their minds are torn to pieces." He glanced at her and smirked. "Well, most humans, anyway."

"Which is why I must go back." She dropped her gaze as if trying to hide a sadness that he could taste through his very pores. "The only way to save Shihala is to stop Köle. And the only way to kill Köle is to take his magic. And I am the only one who can do that. I will suck him dry even if I die in the process, so he can never hurt Serap or anyone else again." She traced a cool finger across his brows and down his cheek. "And so he can never make your eyes as black as his." She pulled the alyasimin from her robes.

"I'll go with you."

"No."

He snarled. "Why are you so stubborn?"

"Perhaps, it is because you have two shoes when I have none." She tried to smile playfully.

"*Aya!*" he cried. "Such shoes I will buy you!"

"Or perhaps," she whispered and placed a hand on his cheek, "it is because Köle cannot be stopped by a sword."

He laid his hand on the back of her neck and kissed her. When he pulled away, his tattered sleeve fell back to reveal the inky tattoo swirled upon his skin, undecided which way it should turn. She glanced at it, then rubbed her foot against her ankle and slid her gaze back to his.

"You are bullheaded and too brazen," he said. "But I trust you."

She sighed, tugging his soft beard. "If the chasm between worlds is not still open, you will need to find a way to open it from your side."

A horrible taste had formed in his mouth, and he swallowed hard. There was only one solution to this problem. He'd seen that for some time now, though he had been unwilling to admit it to himself. The very idea was a betrayal of everything his father had ever stood for. But given what his father had done, perhaps he was the traitor. For Shihala never would have asked one of Her children to do anything so cruel.

He was the Blue Prince now, and as he gazed at Ayelet, he knew she was the girl who could help him. If only he could find the courage to guide her to do what needed to be done.

"Shihala cannot thrive while Her sister withers," he said at last. "You must push the magic to Vespar. It is the only way." Jahmil stilled his breath and looked up at Ayelet's eyes. "Do you trust me?"

***

He let her go again, but this time he was determined that it would be the last. He watched as the magic of alyasimin wrapped around her, whisking her back into the fire from which she had only just been plucked. He wanted to leap into the mists and follow her, whether she wanted him there or not. But she was right. Köle would not be defeated by a sword any more than the problem with the Vespars would be solved by raising an army.

It was Köle that had first forced him to lift a sword that night in the gardens of Rananbar. He had convinced him that the only way to defend himself, to protect Shihala and her people, was with a naked blade in his fist. But he had never wanted to lift it. As a warrior of Shihala, he was supposed to carry it with him everywhere. As Takisha did, as Bakr did. As his father had. The black blade should have been his constant companion. But he always managed to leave it behind. With the eimlaq, with Takisha, even with the Vespar camp, he had not brought a sword.

He had always told himself that it was because it was bulky. After all, Shihalan swords were double-bladed, carved from pure obsidian, stretched as long as a man's shoulders, and weighed as much as a small boulder. But Jahmil had been training with them all his life. His shoulders and arms were hard as rocks, lending him more than enough strength to wield the cumbersome weapon and do it well. He was a professional soldier, a general who had trained his entire life to fight and win battles. To fill his father's shoes as the protector of Shihala. To fight and never stop fighting. But he didn't like the way it felt in his hand.

He had left his heavy, blood-stained weapon in the grass outside Köle's temple of one-faced demons, and there it would lay until it crumbled into dust. Jahmil would never lift it again.

In the quiet of his room, empty without Ayelet and more full than ever for her having been there, Jahmil closed his eyes, prostrated himself, and prayed a dua.

"*Alhamdulillah,*" he said, and then he asked for forgiveness.

Forgiveness for never questioning the origin of the bial'dabaye.

Forgiveness for never caring what had happened in the land of Vespar.

Forgiveness for forgetting that his duty was not to the people of Shihala, but to every soul, human and djinn. Ayelet was right about that, too. The numbers did not matter. For whoever kills an innocent it shall be as if he has killed all of mankind, and whoever saves an innocent it shall be as if he saved all of mankind. There were many children left in those horrible circumstances, forced to kill and be killed in a war that did not concern them. The only way to save them was to put an end to the conflict that had been raging between Shihala and Vespar for a thousand years.

It was his father that had taught him to hate the enemy. He could see that clearly now. And he could also see why his father had been so quick to dismiss the cruelty of the human slave markets.

"They are creatures of mud," his father had said. Not people. He spoke the same way of the Vespars. *"They are disease-infested rats that profane everything they touch. All of Qaf would be better without them."*

Finally, Jahmil prayed for Ayelet. For her protection, for her success. For her. She was the one Khayin had spoken of. The lost girl whose song could quell the millennium-old fire that scorched the lands of Shihala and Vespar.

Even with all his memories back where they belonged, he still didn't understand exactly what it was about her. He may never find the words to explain it, even to himself. All he knew was he wanted to be near it, to nurture it and protect it. Or die trying.

The wisps Ayelet had implanted in his wounds were slowly working their miracles. He felt strong enough to stand, though he still hobbled. It could be days before he was fully well again, but he did not have the luxury to lie down and wait. He stripped off his armor and changed into simple white clothes. No gems, no embroidery. Nothing that set him apart. He put on shoes and then took them off again. He would do nothing to put himself above her. Barefoot, he found an old walking stick and hobbled towards his bedroom door, when something caught his eye and he paused.

Dusty and neglected, his ney sat on its velvet pillow in the corner. In the empty luxury that was his surroundings, the simple wooden flute was the only thing that belonged to him. To a time before the sword of Vespar cut into his flesh and the scream of Shihala filled his every thought. He picked it up and put his fingers to the stops, strange and uncomfortable, a half-remembered dream. He shook his head, but still slipped the flute into his belt before making his way outside to the bailey.

Thueban was gone. He would have to slip through the veil to Orkeshi and then make his way from there to Tel Keveh, the city of the sleeping eimlaq. The city where his father had written the doom of all of Vespar and Shihala. But he didn't have the power to make the trip on his own. He needed help from someone who had a strong connection to Shihala, who loved Her as much as he did, and who had the power of royal blood in their veins.

Jahmil called for a horse and trotted across the plaza towards the harem, but when he was only halfway there, he saw his mother's carriage coming in the opposite direction. He dismounted and waited, leaning against the horse's neck and breathing hard as the silk-draped coach pulled up beside him. The door slapped open and his mother stepped out. She approached quickly in rustling skirts of white silk and black satin, her serious eyes of diamond sweeping over him.

"Jahmil, what were you thinking?" she admonished, but he wasn't listening. He was gazing into her eyes, watching the flickering vibrancy she concealed in their depths. "First you lead an army into Ard without my approval, and then you force it to retreat and stay behind alone?"

"Don't worry, Mother," he said, smiling softly down at her. "I'm all right."

Her expression tightened, and a shiver of pale blue flashed in her eyes. She regrouped. "And what is this I hear about you running off on Qadira? I told you, you have to..."

"I'm not going to marry Qadira."

Her face tightened with anger, but he kept his gaze on her eyes. Fear lived there, always. Fear and worry. A pathological obsession with the welfare of her kingdom. The future of her people. The weight of it all pressed down on her, squeezing every moment of joy from her life. All of her life. But there was something else there, too. A whisper of the blackness Ayelet spoke of, the determination of Köle. The belief that she had to do whatever was necessary to save her people.

He'd never noticed it before, and that fact alone broke his heart.

"Jahmil," she said, scolding. "We have talked about this time and again."

"I know. And I forgive you."

Her jaw twitched. "I beg your pardon?"

"I forgive you for what you did to me. I understand why you thought you needed to." He hobbled closer, laid one hand on the back of her shoulder, and kissed her forehead.

She flinched. "Did you hit your head?" She went up on her tiptoes and scanned his hair for a wound.

He laughed and stepped back. "I need your help, Mother. I need to get to Orkeshi."

"Orkeshi," she sneered then shook her head hard. "You never should have gone there in the first place! You absolutely cannot return."

"Do you know about what Father did in Vespar?"

"Excuse me?"

"He and Khayin drained the magic from the land. They are the reason it is dead. They were trying to kill all the Vespars, but they only succeeded in destroying the land, driving the people to fight their way out to maintain their very existence."

"That is the stupidest thing I have ever heard in my life!" she cried, her eyes as clear as a winter wind. "Your father never did anything to those viruses they would not have done first."

"That makes no difference." Jahmil shook his head, even as relief crashed over him. She was not involved and so he could still trust her. "He did it. And now Köle Amir is trying to do the same to Shihala."

"*Allah yahmini*!" she cried, then she spat on the ground and pressed her thumb against her forehead to ward off the Evil Eye. "That viper is dead."

"No," said Jahmil, his voice low and somber. "He is on Ard, mounting his attack against Shihala. Against all of Qaf."

Black mist pooled in her eyes, blotting out the other colors. "Is that why you took the army...?" She pressed a hand over her mouth and shook her head. "You fool! Why did you not tell me?"

"I am telling you now." He forced a smile. "We have a chance to end all of this. To stop the war and return home, but I have to get to Vespar now. Will you help me?"

"Even if I used every trick I know, I don't have the power to send an army to Orkeshi."

"Not an army. Just me."

Her eyes snapped to meet his. "Are you out of your mind? You'll be dead in two minutes."

"Why do you refuse to trust me?"

"Because the last time I trusted someone, he lost me our kingdom and turned our people into exiles!" she snapped, then turned away from him.

As he watched her shoulders heave with every breath, he realized he had been wrong all this time. His father had not been the outstanding leader, the savior of the people, the martyr to his cause. He had been a jingoist and a warmonger. A simple general with no desire in his heart other than to win the next battle, to dominate his enemy, to expand his lands. Honor, glory, victory, and all that senseless poetry.

It had been his mother who ruled the people, his mother who cleaned up every mess, his mother who sacrificed every piece of herself to the cause she believed in. She had even been willing to lay aside her crown and swallow her pride in the hopes that Qadira could rescue the kingdom and restore the people to their homes.

"I love you, Mother," he said.

She craned her neck to gaze at him over her shoulder, eyes wild with flickers of lightning and as wide as the First Moon. "You truly have lost your mind."

"It comes and goes," he said, cracking a smile. "If this works, we won't need Qadira anymore. You won't have to be a dowager, and I won't have to be king, at least not yet. You were a good queen. You cared about your people more than you did your lands. That's why you made us flee, even though fools like me called you a coward and hated you for it. We are all alive because of you."

Her jaw quivered almost imperceptibly before she managed to set it. "You have been behaving like a spoiled little brat."

"I know."

"It is good to hear you talking like a prince for once." She clenched a fist and pressed it into her other palm, her eyes darting from place to place. "Forget about that little horse and come with me. I have something to show you."

CHAPTER FORTY

Ayelet

Shihala did not take Ayelet to where she wanted to go most, but to where she needed to be.

In a puff of white she hoped had evaded Köle's senses, her feet once more stood in the brambles of the woods by the ruins. She could make out dappled cream columns through the thin veil of maples and smell the earthy bay leaves and sweetness of lime. The chasm between worlds reflected the moon like a pool, but nothing moved in or out. It was only open from this side.

She took a step closer to get a better look and pulled back, shifting her bare feet to avoid the prick of small sticks and thorns. Why did she keep throwing her shoes?

Ayelet stifled a sigh and looked at the now barren pistil of the alyasimin. There would be no way back to Jahmil if he forgot her once more. She pushed the black thought away and focused on the warmth she felt when he kissed her. The clearness in his eyes. The opals on her neck. The hopeful, nervous twitch of his lips when he asked if she trusted him. She *should* trust him. Allah, she wanted to. But the wound of being forgotten was still too fresh. She needed more time to heal. More time to believe he would not just disappear, by his choice or not, to more magic she didn't understand.

A twig snapped in the bushes ahead, dropping her low. She crept forward, careful to lift her legs high and set them down gently so as not to make a sound. A man with shoulder-length hair and the shadow of a molasses beard leaned against an acacia tree. She grinned.

"*Yu—*"

"Don't even think about it," Balian said, turning around with his arms crossed. His gaze was hard, and his lips twisted in the way they always did when he was looking for a fight.

Ayelet pouted. "How did you know I was there?"

"You're ripe with the stink of Shihala."

She glared.

"Where is Serap?" he asked, turning a cold eye to her antics.

"With—Still in Shihala, I think. I thought you were with her."

"Clearly I am not."

"Clearly," she said.

Frogs croaked between them, and an eagle screeched in the dark sky overhead.

"Why not?" she finally ventured to ask, just a little nervous Jahmil had kicked him out of Shihala from Thueban's back.

He flicked his eyes away from her.

"Balian?" She stepped across the prickly forest floor, wincing twice until she stood in front of him. She knit her brows together and then relaxed. "Ah, you came to rescue me, didn't you?"

His jaw twitched.

"Yes, you did." Her grin returned, and she poked a finger at him.

He grabbed her wrist and held it away from him. "Stop."

Her smile faded.

He snuck a glance at her, and his face softened. "Please, stop. No more teasing." He dropped his gaze to his feet. "I can't take it."

As much as Balian had hurt her, he had been a constant in her life, and she wanted his friendship back, even if everything else had changed. "Well, you are going to have to take it," she said, trying to make things light between them. Light and friendly, like they used to be.

"Ayelet," he growled. He looked as if he would say more, then he swept her towards him into a kiss.

She pushed away, tripping on a vine and tumbling onto her back. "Balian!"

He wouldn't even look at her, his teeth clenched and his cheeks wine-red. "You cannot have it both ways. Either be with me or leave me be." He ran his hands over his face and through his wild hair. "Please?"

She pushed herself up, brushing leaves from her purple robes. Mud now smeared her soft, white dress. She looked at Balian. At her feet. At the trees. And then back to him. "I am sorry."

"Right. Because you've chosen to be with *him*," he seethed. "Don't apologize to me."

She sighed and stood, knocking off the last bits of errant brush. "I have chosen him. But that is not why I am sorry."

He scoffed.

"Balian." She stepped up to him once more and bent around so he could see her. He snapped his head in the other direction. She bit her cheek and turned again, this time holding his face in place with her hands. "Balian!"

He stared daggers.

"I am sorry," she said. He jerked his head, and she held it firm. "I forgive you, Balian. And I am sorry I did not do so sooner."

His pinched brow tightened, then released. "I have regretted not going with you every single day of my life. When I wake up, when I sleep, when I swallow bread too good for my wretched stomach, I think of it."

"I am sorry I made you feel that you should. I know I did. But you were a child. We both were. And you have proven to me every single day that you would never let it happen again. So, thank you." She offered him a sweet smile, hoping he would believe her.

"But you still won't choose me?"

She bit her lip and shook her head.

He exhaled something between a sigh and groan. "I pity him."

"What?"

"That djinn, Jahmika, or whatever. I pity him the havoc you're going to wreak on his life." Balian smirked.

She scowled and punched him in the arm. She would have punched him again, but a thick mist of wisps rushed past her through the woods.

Köle.

She pushed Balian toward the edge of the trees. Not Köle. Nadir. She scrunched her brow and leaned closer. He was collecting all the bottles and jars he had tucked away before the battle into a knapsack on his back. He had indeed captured swaths of magic, little white breaths shimmering under midnight's moon. But there were far more than he could carry, and already jars were spilling out, sometimes breaking with a wisp's sigh of relief.

Balian slid beside her without a sound, and a tiny chill ran up her spine. She elbowed him and whispered, "Could you be a little louder next time?"

He smirked.

"What could Nadir possibly plan to do with all those jars?" she mused. "He can barely even carry them."

Balian leaned back against a tree, crossing his arms in the black shadows with an ease that made her envy him. "Probably trade them with Kadri." He shrugged.

"And how would he do that when she is not here?"

Balian raised a brow. "She's right down the hill."

"What?"

"I came upon this place just as Kadri was dumping a bunch of kids off on a passing group of janissaries who looked none too happy about it. She kicked them onto the soldiers and ran before they could protest too much. Then she set up camp in a thicket about a fersah to the south. She was yelling about how the djinn would regret ruining her life. Moaning about how she wished she had more wagons to take the magic to market. I think they're all bottled up in the same kind of jars we saw in Edirne, though they look nothing more than a bit of glittering air to me."

A small dollop of relief soothed her aching heart. At least that group of children was safe. Though there were still so many more to go. She snuck a side glance at Balian, then pulled away from the treeline and tapped the opals around her neck. "How much magic is already down there?"

"Enough that she has to keep the bulk of the jars covered so the magic doesn't catch the moonlight and announce her presence from Edirne to Istanbul."

Ayelet nodded, then flashed a smile and held out her hand. "Come with me?"

His eyes moved between her open palm and her eyes. "Yes."

She and Balian flew down the mountain, he, like a hawk, and she, like a baby grouse. After the third stick stabbed between her toes, Ayelet called a pair of wisps to whip the ground before her to clear the brush and slick it flat. While she still stubbed her toes on buried rocks and caught the sharp stray branches of wind-blown trees, she was able to quicken her pace and keep up with Balian.

When they arrived near Kadri's camp, her legs were more scrape than skin. She sat down to nurse a particularly stabbing wound while Balian scoped out Kadri's whereabouts. The henna-like lines around her scar still churned indecisively, and she traced the curls with her finger. Then she remembered Jahmil's tattoo... It had looked the same. She swiped a finger over the rough skin, but the swirling continued unbothered.

Why had Köle been so angry when he saw her scar? And why did Jahmil have a matching mark?

Her eyes widened, and she held her hands out in front of her. She bent each finger, imagining the lyre beneath. She had always been told she was marked by fate. When she was five and accidentally bumped into a magus at the market who had backed away in horror and signed against the Evil Eye. By Köle when he bought her from another slaver at the age of nine. And then, by the creepy peddler who whispered *ayelet* under his breath, and by everyone who heard her play her lyre afterward.

She had always assumed the instrument that gave her the ability to play faultless music and see the wisps was the mark she bore. But what if it was an *actual* mark?

The itch of anxiety crawled across her shoulders. The mark, her fate, had not yet been decided. What if the bone-reaching scar wasn't enough? What if Köle could mark her soul as his forever with magic this time? Magic she couldn't escape. She eyed the swirls again, tempted to rake them off. She and Jahmil loved each other, right? He said he would never leave her again. That he wanted her to be his queen. And yet, his tattoo still twined across his skin with uncertainty. Hers did, too.

She clenched her teeth and growled, "Why do you still move?"

"I'm going to assume you aren't talking to me," Balian drawled casually, returning with a light skip over the pitch-black terrain.

"I am not." Ayelet threw the hem of her dress down. "Did you find her?"

He nodded, and she followed, weaving through prickly bushes and budless saplings until the glow of the moon revealed Kadri moving thick jars with cork lids between the tarps covering two wagons. She must have restocked her supplies because her camp was full to the brim with empty containers, charms against the Evil Eye, and wagons that numbered the men one to one.

Balian took out a dagger and raised a brow, but Ayelet shook her head. She would handle Kadri herself. Balian bowed out of the way, and she stepped into the scattered light of the torches.

"Kadri, Kadri, my old friend," she announced herself to the camp.

Kadri froze with her back to her, and the large jar she had been holding *thunked* into the soft dirt. Then she snapped her fingers, and her men hustled around. Balian slid out of the trees to Ayelet's side.

"Now, this time I'm certain I have seen this same scene play out before." Ayelet smiled widely. "How many times must you surround me with your muscle to learn it does not work out well for you?"

Kadri spun around. "I no longer work with Köle, so if this is his business—"

"I do not come for Köle."

Kadri's face hardened. She pulled a jeweled dagger from her dress. "Then leave."

"I thought we were partners?"

Kadri scoffed and flicked her hand to the side. Two ugly men with legs the size of tree trunks lunged toward her. Balian made to jump in front, but Ayelet thrust her arm out and pushed him back. With her other hand, she called a pair of wisps from the woods and plunged them into the men's lungs. With the clench of her fist, she yanked them back out, any air coming with them. The two brutes stumbled and fell to their knees, gasping in tiny, painful breaths.

Balian's head darted between the struggling men and Ayelet. He took a wary step back. Kadri's eyes widened before collapsing into slits. She waved the rest of her men forward, and they converged like ants around their nest, swords drawn.

Ayelet pictured the lock in the prison and called wisp after wisp from the dark of the woods and into the hilts of their swords. Each one glowed as if soaked in the moon's blood, expanding until the metal could no longer hold itself together. The iron and wood burst out in needle-thin projectiles that grazed flesh, pierced eyes, and entered the backs of choking mouths and into screaming throats.

Some men fell. Others cried in agony, running into the dangers of the woods half-blind. The rest backed away, their fearful eyes trying to gauge whether she or Kadri was the bigger threat.

Kadri watched them abandon her one after another, horror morphing into visible rage.

"The rumors were true," she spat. "You sold your soul to a djinn!"

"No." Ayelet tugged a wisp that smacked Kadri's jaw shut with an audible snap. "*You* sold my soul to a djinn. And now you are going to pay me what I am owed."

Kadri managed to spit through her clenched teeth. "I have nothing left, remember? Köle took all my earthly possessions."

"And in return, you took his magic. Now, I think he would like it back," she said, a shadow of a plan forming in the back of her mind.

Kadri growled through her teeth, the wisp still pushing up against her jaw so her neck strained backward. "I thought you weren't working for Köle."

Ayelet smiled. "I am not."

CHAPTER FORTY-ONE

Jahmil

Jahmil's mother led him through the harem into her bed chamber where she had kept him trapped and naked. Where she had held him down and forced poison into his throat.

Being in the room again brought back a sharp twinge of resentment, but he was determined not to dwell on it. If he was ever going to be able to forgive himself for all the terrible things that he had done in following his father's misguided vision of total victory, then he first had to learn to forgive everyone else. He did forgive his mother, but he still did not trust her. Like Takisha, he was now uncomfortable being alone with her.

"What are we doing here? I don't have time—"

"Patience, *abnay*."

She opened her wardrobe, now stuffed with all her beautiful clothes. Pushing aside hangers, she reached to the back, and a loud click sounded. The false back of the wardrobe swung open into a dark tunnel of gray stone.

He didn't realize his mouth was hanging open until his mother touched his chin with one finger and closed it.

"Is this your conception of a joke?" he snarled.

She smirked, as close to a smile as her face was capable of. Then she raised her skirts and stepped inside, beckoning for him to follow with a slight tilt of her head.

They walked through the finely carved tunnels and down an endless twist of staircases. She held a glimmer of white fire on her hand to light the way.

"The harem used to be the Seat of Ahmar," she explained in a flat voice. "Before Qadira's grandmother had that garish pile of pearls constructed. These tunnels have been here for a thousand years, but she clearly isn't aware of them. Otherwise, she never would have tried to imprison me here."

They walked for what felt like a quarter turn of the First Moon, the anxiety spreading through his blood like the beginnings of a cold. Every step was slow and painful, the deep chew marks on his legs stealing the strength from his calf muscles. A dozen doors passed on either side of the hallway, some made of carved alabaster, others rotted wood. He wondered where each led, trying to visualize the palace complex above them, the city itself.

After a while, the doors disappeared, and the tunnel straightened. Stones gave way to clear glass. The waters of Buhayra Ruwarin shimmered above, sea creatures sailing by on shimmering fins like the wings of sky birds.

They crossed the lake and came to a circular hatch made of limestone with a handwheel lock at the center. His mother stepped back and lifted an eyebrow. He grabbed the bar and began to twist.

"Be warned," she said, backing away and lifting her skirt to her knees. "The chamber on the other side has been known to flood."

The lock popped. His wounds cried with strain as he pulled the door open. A wall of water rushed in. It knocked the air from his chest. Unsteady knees buckled, and he had to catch himself on the wall. His mother stepped demurely out of the way until it had settled. He was soaked and out of breath. She sneered at a tiny spot on her shoe, then breezed past him through the door, ordering him to close it behind them.

They went up a line of slippery stairs until they were standing under the free sky of Qaf once more. He cast an eye back at the lake; the City of Pearls was a small, shaking glimmer on the horizon. Mountains rose before them, sharp and craggy, dotted with tiny pink and green blossoms. She hitched up her skirt and began to ascend the steep rocks. When her foot slipped, Jahmil caught her arm and held her up. She laid her other hand on his and let him help her up the incline.

They came to an immense face of flat stone, a hundred feet high and twice as wide, smooth as a sheet of paper. In either direction, the ledge thinned so it would be impossible to go any further. He narrowed his eyes at her. "What now?"

She stepped back and took a long, slow breath. Then she lifted her arms, whispering a prayer he had never heard before. Her hands ignited with fire, and she sent streams of it at the rockface. It shimmered, then melted away in brown bubbles like sugar.

As Jahmil's eyes focused beyond the false wall, his lips quivered, and his teeth and fists clenched painfully. Five hundred drakontes coiled inside the massive chamber. Soldiers were lined against the wall like kindling, many of them still in blood-caked armor. For one horrible moment, he worried they were all dead, but then he noticed the gentle rise and fall of their chests. The drakontes and their riders were fast asleep.

His jaw twitched for words, a rant like none other brewing in his guts. But all that came out was a strangled, "You..."

"I wasn't going to let you execute a coup against Qadira," she said, putting back her shoulder and lifting her chin to gaze up at him. "The trothplight obligated her to take in the remainder of our refugees once the marriage had been completed. I could not have you and your pet snakes flying around and ruining everything."

"They are not pets." He clenched his jaw and looked down at his feet. "Do you know what I have been through looking for them?"

"I do." Her defiant gaze held his. Such a tiny woman with a presence even larger than that of the massive snakes hibernating peacefully in the dark cavern. "Are you prepared to forgive me for this as well?"

His blood boiled with such ferocity that fire licked at his fingertips without his summoning it. He glared at her, the word *traitor* thick on his tongue. He swallowed it.

"I suppose it makes no difference now," he said, then he lifted his hand and shot his fire at the head of the nearest drakonte.

Heatless white flames encircled the beast, slithering into its nose and eyes and waking it from the hibernation spell his mother had cast over it. The creature's mouth gaped open in a terrifying yawn, and its body shivered away the last flicker of sleep. Its glowing green eyes took in the surrounding scene, then when it saw its queen and amir, it bowed its head low to the ground.

Jahmil climbed on, careful to tuck his walking stick under him. His mother hurried to the body of one of the sleeping soldiers and drew the sword from his belt. She held it out to him.

He shook his head. "No."

Black smoke pooled in her eyes. "You mustn't go in unarmed."

"Wake the drakontes and have them ready to fly if needed."

With a last glance at her face, he guided the massive beast out towards the ledge, and they rocketed up into the sky. He forced the creature higher and higher until they were so far up they would have looked like little more than a strange bird from the ground. Then he turned the beast in a wide circle and spurred it at full speed to the east. Into Shihala and then beyond the crest of Orkeshi into Vespar.

His mind kept trying to regress into hideous imaginings of what might be happening to Ayelet. The pain in her eyes when he asked her what Köle had done to her, and she replied, *"Everything."*

He thought about the conversation he'd had with Serap about Ayelet and her past. That she had been a slave for a few years as a child before she managed to escape. Had Köle been her master then as well? There was a strange familiarity in her voice when she spoke about him, and that alone should have been enough of an answer, though he didn't want to believe it.

As horrible as it was to imagine her standing in a line in a slave market, thinking of her—as small and innocent as Serap—under the thumb of that monster was overwhelming. He knew from experience how cruel Köle could be, even to a small child. But he had suffered under his sword for but a single evening. A scant few minutes and the experience had scarred his soul as if it were a hundred hard years.

He was haunted by the doubt in her eyes when he asked her if she trusted him. But why would she? He had failed her in her moment of need. The exact second when she had been prepared to open her heart, he had left her in the cold, as every person had before him. She wore his necklace and kissed him with such sincerity, yet the words of love she had offered were in the past tense: *I loved you.* As if the feeling had only lasted one brief and fleeting moment that fell into nothing as soon as he left.

What hatred had she been nursing these last few days? Alone. Thinking he did not care. Suffering under the weight of her own nightmares as he stumbled through a blur of magic and politics.

And for all of that, he had let her go again. Or she had fled from him again. To fight her demons alone as she always had. Or if not alone, then with someone else. Someone who knew her in a way he never could because she would never allow him such closeness. Not after what he had done.

Let her not be alone. Whatever she chooses, let her not be alone.

The tattoo on his arm stung like fresh needles piercing the skin, like the dusting of iron from Köle's hideous bombard. The weight of his people, his position, still pressed down on him as ever before, coupled with the shame of the mistakes he had made trying to fight his father's war. But all of this paled in comparison to the weight of Ayelet's words. *You are worse than Balian. You are selfish. I mean to spare you... and myself.*

Whether any of that changed when the light of remembrance dawned in his eyes, it did not change what had to be done.

He would love her anyway.

Though they were flying too high to see details of the land, he still knew the moment they had passed over Shihala into the barrenness of Vespar.

Cracked, gray land. Tangles of dead black trees like coarse hairs. He followed the instructions Khayin had given him—nestled in the crook of the Shamaal Range, surrounded by the corpses of ash palms. And after a few wide loops in the air, he spotted it. A city of gray circles lay across the land like a massive target.

He angled the drakonte towards the center. As he drew closer, the coiled figure of Thueban was the first to come into view, and then Takisha's gleaming, bald head. They were waiting at the edge of what looked like a massive black mirror. It had a radius of a quarter of a *ghalwah*, filling the very center of the circular city. Just as Khayin said it would.

Takisha got to her feet as he brought the drakonte in to land. "Raqisa!" she cried, rushing towards the snake. "Jahmil, where did you find her?"

He was about to answer honestly, then stopped himself. Takisha would be furious if she found out what his mother had done: stealing the drakontes, enchanting them, hiding them away, and then lying to everyone about it. He didn't want to see the result should Takisha let loose her anger on her.

"Nevermind that. Just know that your remaining army is safe."

"Where are they?" she snarled.

"We don't need them for this." Jahmil stepped closer to the sealed-over caldera. When he gazed through the sharp, volcanic glass that now capped the hole, he saw only darkness below. But it wasn't ordinary darkness, not a simple lack of light. It was like staring down the throat of some hideous creature, an oversized ghoul stealing life and chewing the bones of death. Regurgitating it like cud, only to swallow again until not even the memory of life remained.

Looking at the sharp, crumbled ruins surrounding the glass, he could easily imagine his father and Khayin in this place, battling with the ifrit of wind until the great immortal creature was dead and they had access to the well of Vespar's magic. The very heart of the land, of the people. And then, like vampires, sucking away the life force.

But how had they done it? Had they needed the aid of someone like Ayelet? Was there anyone else like her?

Jahmil took a slow, deep breath and stepped out onto the sheet of glass. It shivered under his bare feet, more delicate than it looked. Surely it had not always been in this state, or someone would have broken the seal by now. It had to be Ayelet and her work with Köle. She had weakened it. He only had to finish the job.

The cold crept up through his skin, chilling his bones. He walked on.

"Jahmil!" Takisha hissed from the edge. "What are you doing?"

There was no answer. He didn't know what he was doing. All he knew for certain was this was the wound through which Vespar had lost all her lifeblood, and this was where Ayelet would have to direct the magic if it was ever going to live again. He had to open it, to peel back the scar tissue. Like a wound that had sealed over with infection left inside, only by reopening it could it ever truly heal.

"Jahmil!" Takisha called. "Come back here."

"I would remind you that you are sworn to stand by my irrational decisions," he said, glancing over his shoulder before resuming his cautious tread. "Do not try to save me. That is an order."

As he drew near the center of the dark circle, the glass cracked. A loud popping sound rolled in waves across the entire sheet. He crouched down and laid his fingertips on the surface. He felt something inside, a faint whisper calling to him. He half-expected to hear fury, to be admonished by the dying spirit of the land that had for so long been his enemy. But there was nothing like anger in the humanless voice. Instead, it was as gentle and pleading as a baby bird fallen from the nest. A broken wing tangled under its fragile body, it squeaked and struggled, and begged for something—anything—to come to its rescue.

More cracks formed under his feet, racing to the edges of the glass. Popping and crackling. He steeled himself against the fear lurching in his guts. There was no other way. He had to put this right. For his father. For Bakr. For Shihala.

For Ayelet.

He lifted his fist and punched the glass with all his strength. Takisha screamed from the edge, helplessly reaching for him. Cracks darted through the glass in every direction. He poured white fire into the fissures, and it quickened with the heat. It shattered into a million tiny shards. Jahmil fell into darkness.

CHAPTER FORTY-TWO

AYELET

AYELET STOOD BEFORE THE steps that led to darkness in the temple, and a chill ran down her spine.

Köle knew she was there. And she knew that he knew. But he would not come to her. He was the master, not her, or so he had made her believe all those years. And so it had been as far as mankind cared. But she was willing to accept his price this time. One lying, flighty soul for thousands—hundreds of thousands of children and the fate of Shihala and all of Qaf.

She touched a foot to the scar on her ankle, worried that fate would agree to the price as well and sell her for eternity. The "K" still swirled, and she couldn't decide whether to be thankful or not. It meant fate did not believe she had fully aligned herself with Köle despite all the awful things she had done. It also meant fate was not convinced she and Jahmil were meant to be together.

"Ada." A wisp blew sharply, stinging her cheek with Köle's call.

She descended and tried to keep her thoughts clear, her emotions steady. She had a plan. Balian waited at the chasm, the bottles of magic lined up around the edge of the silver pool. Kadri waited with him, helping under the threat of excruciating, wispy death. Ayelet had implanted a tail of magic into Kadri's lungs, so Kadri felt the pinch of her wrath every time she breathed, but even then, Ayelet did not trust her.

The doorway between the two worlds had not yet opened, but it would. She trusted Jahmil to do this; it was for the good of his kingdom, for Vespar, for all of Qaf. But with each step farther into the cool, musty ruins, she doubted more and more his promise to make her his queen, not because he lacked sincerity, but because it was impossible.

Takisha hadn't believed it. Balian had called her foolish. Jahmil's own mother had poisoned him to stop them from being together. Not even fate itself believed. And now she was certain she had figured out why. It was not Jahmil; he was far too noble. Far too kind and self-sacrificing, genuine and honest, shouldering the weight of the kingdom with no one to help him carry the burden even as it sucked the life from his blood.

No, it was not Jahmil that fate doubted. It was her.

She was the unreliable one. The *little human*. The marked one who was ruining Jahmil's life. He had been right. She was selfish, but not because she loved whoever she pleased for as long as she pleased. It was because she loved no one. Trusted no one. Though she wanted to with Jahmil.

"Ada!" Köle snapped. He waited for her in the entrance to the altar room, his red curtain soaking up light in the background. The faceless statues that lined the walls of the temple mocked her with their anonymity. "Do not tempt your master again!"

She sighed and stepped before him, wishing for the comforting weight of the lyre upon her waist. But even her companion of the last thirteen years had failed to be with her in the end.

Fitting.

"Show it to me," he hissed.

Stinging chills excoriated her lungs when she looked at him. The awful, sepulchral black of his eyes flickered with flashes of jade and a hunger she knew meant he would never let her go.

She couldn't help but smirk at the irony.

Köle's dry hand slapped her face so hard, the sound echoed in the empty ruins. Her cheek prickled, and a sliver of blood leaked like poison onto her tongue.

He snarled again, "Show it to me!"

Licking the iron from her split and shaking lip, she grabbed her skirts and lifted the hem.

He bent low and inhaled a screech that rivaled Thueban. Then he grabbed her leg with one leathery hand and sank the jagged nails of his other into her flesh, lacerating the skin of her ankle once more into the shape of a "K", as if he could force fate to decide.

She screamed and fell back, kicking and thrashing to get away. And just like every other time, she couldn't. His bruising grasp and slicing fingers etched himself into her lungs, her heart, her mind, until he'd finished marking her for the second time. The inky spirals seeped into the wound, mixing with her blood into the same wretched black that stared out from his eyes.

When at last he released her, he breathed out a chilling laugh. "I made you, Ada. I hunted you down from the moment you came squalling into Ard, the prophesied Marked One for this century, and forced magic into your blood to give you your power. You were marked by fate to be mine, to avenge Vespar and make Shihala and their pathetic amir pay for what they've done."

She pulled her ankle into herself, agony rippling through her bone, her flesh, and her muscle. She pulled and pulled on her mind, bringing herself into that place of nothing. The place she ran to when all hope had dimmed. A place where she did not have to feel.

A rumbling crack shattered the air, and a wave of wisps poured into the room, sloshing up the sides like thick cider in a cup. Her vision whited out completely, and the tender touch of wisps eased some of the pain in her leg. She strummed her fingers in the air, and a pathway cleared around her. Jahmil must be opening the chasm.

Köle shrieked in the mist, the bottomless black of his eyes visible through the veil.

"It is time, Ada. Time for you to fulfill your fate. And Ada," he whispered, his voice carrying like winter through cracks in a door. "If you fail me this time, I will carve a hundred lines into your eyes so you'll never see the amir again, a thousand holes into your throat so you will never whisper his name, and ten thousand scars with my name upon your pathetic heart so you will bleed and think only of me. And as for Jahmil Amir—" Köle chuckled cruelly. "—it will be far worse."

Köle scraped the air overhead with his bony fingers, and the ceiling of the temple ruins crumbled, dropping heavy blocks and worm-filled dirt into heaps around her. Then he called the wisps, and they obeyed, just as he expected them to, carrying him up to destroy, like revenge was the only thing in Qaf or Ard that mattered.

Ayelet sat numbly, staring at the white wisps of magic nipping at her feet and pulling her clothes up toward the cloudless sky. The space in her mind muffled the torrent of wisps and the calls of Köle.

"Ayelet!"

Her name. Her new name though it now felt old, sifting through the blanket of her mind.

"Ayelet," he called again. But it was the smattering of curses that made her look up at Balian. "Get up! The chasm is shattering, and that crazy djinn is hurling cannonballs and flinging knives at anything that moves. *You* dragged me into this mess, so your creepy ghost powers and crazy plan had better get me out."

She blinked once more before the images of strategically placed glass bottles and the dead lands of Vespar tumbled across her mind.

She did have a plan. A plan that would end Qaf's suffering... and her own for good. She jumped to her feet, wincing and limping whenever she used her scarred foot. Its inky blood leaked between her toes, leaving behind little human footprints as she leaped for Balian's outstretched hand. She fell short, but a trail of wisps caught her waist and lifted her with the gentleness of Jahmil when they had danced. She grabbed hold of Balian's rough hands and dragged herself to the surface just as the chasm burst open.

Magic flung in kaleidoscopic flakes of glass, hurling to their pinnacle, where they remained suspended until fading with a twinkle into the sky.

In the middle of the glittering breath of magic, dove Jahmil. Coming from the chasm, he already faced up, as if he had fallen head-first through the opening and now flew through the sky. Shimmering Thueban burst through behind him, his magnificent coils and mammoth wings catching moonlight before sliding under Jahmil with ease. Through the gateway between the two worlds twinkled the gray skies of Vespar, its blanched trees and grassless earth. A bald, hulking woman-warrior yelled curses behind him. Her own drakonte flew to catch her, and she caught its neck and swung around to its back.

Takisha.

Had she come once more to bring Jahmil to his senses? Or to help them fight?

Köle hissed out a chuckle, commanding wisps and flinging iron balls that burst in the sky to try to end them. Ayelet blinked twice more to take in the scene and then managed to pull her wits about her.

"Go, Balian," she said. "Wait for my signal."

He left her, eyes creased with concern that she had gone mad. She turned to Köle and took a shuddering breath. She would need time to gain an advantage. To get the wisps whirling in a funnel back to Vespar as Jahmil wished. *Inşallah*, if she could just get the magic going, the pull would sustain itself with her nearby as it had before. But Köle would never allow the magic to re-enter, which was why she needed Balian.

She climbed large marble blocks to stand next to Köle. He sneered at her, squeezing his nails into the back of her neck.

"No games this time, Ada. There will be no mercy if you test me!"

She nodded and cast her eyes to the ground, then lifted both her hands up slowly until they stretched as far as she could reach.

The signal.

She kept her face straight as she waited for Balian to reply. A single wisp. He was ready.

She took a step closer to Köle, fighting her natural revulsion. Then she brought her hands down in front of her and curled her fingers into fists, calling, calling the wisps to her. A wave rose up from the chasm, a white wall that shimmered lazily across the field and up the hill, not from Shihala, though it appeared to be so, but from the bottles lining the opening that Balian and the others now smashed.

"More," Köle hissed, glee filling his dead eyes as he fell for the deception.

He pushed a blade-filled whirlwind toward Thueban and Jahmil, and the creature hissed and pulled back. Takisha flew low between the trees, grabbing cannons and releasing them over the chasm. Twice, burning iron nearly seared her flesh. Then the shrill, desperate, and heart-rending cry of the bial'dabaye—of children—cracked through the thunder of billowing wisps. The sound of their suffering drove her forward and gave her strength.

There was purpose in staying. There was power in it.

Ayelet pulled her eyes from the battle in the sky, opened her palms, and curled her fingers once more. Another wave of white pulled towards them just as the first was arriving. She had not called the raw power of Shihala to the earth; she had called the bottled wisps to Köle, to trap him where he stood so he could not disappear through the thick veil of magic.

The gulf of wisps grew, spinning around them in thicker and thicker sheets. When she could see nothing beyond the wall of magic, she turned to Köle. His abysmally dark eyes flashed to hers with pure hate, staying her hands in fear. Instinct told her to run. Impulse, to fold upon herself and cower. She fought back the pain and the nothingness and closed her eyes. Then she lunged.

Grabbing Köle's cracked and weathered face, she pressed her hands against his cheeks and called the magic to her. His magic. He screamed and tried to disappear, but the blanket of wisps held him in. His cheeks sunk; his eyes fluttered with pure rage. Still, she pressed.

He reached out and dug his nails into her neck. Ayelet cried out as a slick, thick sickness lurched through her like her stomach was being pulled through the slats in her ribs.

"You think you can drain power from me?" he said in a whisper that consumed her. He dug his nails deeper. Pain stabbed at her wherever his skin touched, the warm drip of blood seeping down the sides of her throat. "You will die, Ada."

She screamed and tried to pull away, but the same magic that held Köle down trapped her in the bubble as well. She could not suck the magic from his blood without dying before she finished, and she could not escape.

Ayelet gazed at Köle's terrible eyes, at the obsession with ruling that had destroyed his very being. If she could not suck the power he craved from his blood, she would pull more in. Then maybe, like the lock in the prison, the magic would burst, shooting the wisps through the void and back into Vespar.

It was the last act of love she could do for Jahmil, choosing to stay to help him save his kingdom, the thing he loved most, the thing he would always be there for, even if it meant welcoming her fate at the side of the man who marked her. If fate decreed she and Köle be together, let it be so through death.

The wave of wisps spun around them in a circle, Ayelet gathering as much as she could before she would slam it into Köle, into herself, and into their blood. Again and again, she threw her fading plea into the wind.

First, a wall of wisps from the bottles that Balian broke below. And then, a torrent from above, made of any and every wisp on earth who felt her yearning. Wisps from the ruins, from the bial'dabaye, from any breeze that sighed with magic and could hear her song. And so she sang, the same melody she had shared with Jahmil in the smokeless firelight. And no matter Jahmil's promises of unspoken love or the fire of determination in his eyes as he sought to prove himself to her, she knew he could do nothing. She had always known. For what mortal could fight against the mark of fate? And what life was worth giving for hers?

When at last a great tornado of wisps cascaded around them in coruscating sparkles of tremendous power, she looked to Köle. His greedy, black eyes turned to hers, thinking he had won as he drained her life and flung swords at the heart of Jahmil. His cruel lips cracked in a horrid smile.

Then she yanked it all down.

Blow after blow of wisp entered Köle first. His eyes widened, and he howled. She grabbed his wrist, then slid around his back and pinned his arms to his chest, her face pressed against his bony, awful, persimmon-smelling back as she used magic to seal him off from fleeing.

He writhed, twisting his arms to lift hers higher, and bit her wrist, teeth scraping bone in an agony that blasted white spots against her vision. Angry droplets of blood flowed from her torn flesh, but she did not let go.

The wall of magic flowing from the edges of the chasm ceased, the bottles empty, but the freed magic of the earth still flooded down like a meteor shower coming together in a single lightning strike. And just as they flew into Köle, filling him up, they soaked into her as she held him to her breast. Köle's skin glowed white with burning heat. Still, she clung, until she, too, was glowing, shining brighter than the moon to rival the sun.

She looked up at the sky through the top of the swirling gusts of wisps. The whirlwind of blades had ceased. The cannonballs dropped midair and crashed into the earth. Takisha raged. And Jahmil...

She swore she saw his face through the torrent of wisps that encased her, staring at her with the stars as his backdrop, his diamond eyes fixed solely on hers, horrified. Broken. Desperate, furious, and oh-so-serious.

She smiled sadly and sang the final note of her song.

CHAPTER FORTY-THREE

JAHMIL

CRUDE WEAPONS AIMED THEMSELVES at the sky, powered by wisps of stolen magic. The great iron bombards fired on their own, trying to bring down him and Takisha. But Thueban was too quick and Takisha far too skilled a rider. She moved around the perimeter, snatching up cannons in her massive gloved hands, then rocketing high into the sky where she would send them plummeting to the earth. Craters of dust exploded as the machines shattered into pieces.

As Jahmil scanned for Ayelet, the sharp shriek of bial'dabaye scraped across his ears, and he turned to see a giant of a man with a whip trying to force a cackle of the creatures onto the field. Some lay twitching in the dirt already, the magic being drawn from their very eyes as they slowly and painfully transformed back into human children. Others were still firmly in their shapes, at least for the moment, nipping at Takisha's drakonte every time she swooped to the earth.

One bial'dabaye got its claws into the drakonte's neck and was lifted up as the snake soared back into the sky. Takisha lifted her sword to cut the beast's head off.

"No!" Jahmil cried and shot a ball of fire at her face, enough to disorient her and stay the killing blow. Her hold on the reins faltered, and the drakonte dipped to one side. The bial'dabaye lost its grip on the snake's scales and began to plummet.

Jahmil pressed Thueban into the path, catching the creature in his arms before it slammed into the ground. It clawed and twitched, catching his cheek, but its eyes were already changing as Ayelet pulled every free ounce of power toward her. By the time Thueban landed, Jahmil's arms no longer held a slobbering beast but a small boy, bruised and scratched, but alive.

He laid the boy under a tree to protect him and dashed toward the slave driver. As the bial'dabaye fell and began to transform, the bearlike man was gathering up the twitching, naked children and throwing them back in the pen, preserving them for future use.

When his dead brown eyes spotted Jahmil, the slave driver reeled back and snapped his whip. Jahmil caught it on his forearm, the strap of leather wrapping his shifting tattoo many times over. He yanked his arm back, pulling the whip away. The man stumbled, then drew a thick, short sword from his belt and barreled forward.

Jahmil dodged the first strike, his body arcing far back. The man brought his blade down to stab him, but Jahmil caught the man's arm and twisted it back. A sharp crack sounded as the elbow snapped. The sword fell.

A scream ripped through the air, human and in horrible pain. Ayelet.

Jahmil dropped the body in the dirt and turned, his eyes searching for Ayelet and Köle. The pair was no longer visible, entirely cocooned in a hissing cyclone of white magic. It funneled towards the center like water into a drain, raw magic so powerful as to rend a human body into liquid.

He prayed Ayelet's abilities somehow allowed her to withstand it, but the horrible truth was he still didn't know what she was capable of. Even more terrifying was that neither did she. She had always used her magic to draw things towards her, or so she had said. When they were together in the Moonless Night, she had pulled fountains of energy from all over Shihala with nothing more than a few plucks of her lyre. In his haze, he had broken the instrument, thinking that was what gave Ayelet her powers. But it had never been the lyre. The faint glow had been nothing more than the power Ayelet had imbued it with. Because she had loved it.

The tattoo of the Covenant swelled on his forearm. It connected him to Ayelet, made him a part of her and her a part of him. He could feel the intensity of the magic even now forcing its way into Ayelet. The flesh of his arm was inflamed like a massive white blister. It pulsed and shivered, about to pop.

Jahmil raced towards the wall of magic. His bare feet prickled with every step, iron ash and shards of wood. When he hit the curtain, the force of it threw him back. The wisps dashed through him, aching to reach Ayelet. To reach Köle. He was blinded by the garish light, the overwhelming cacophony.

He forced himself to his feet and tried again to enter, but every step was like battling a hurricane. As the magic pulsed through him, he grew strong. His wounds sealed, his bones hardened, even as his very skin felt like it was being torn away. But it wasn't enough. No amount of strength could help him push through.

A blister on his tattoo burst and began to bleed. He hissed in pain, his gaze turning to the mark. Shihala had forged a connection between them, something no amount of magic could break. Even if it was still shifting, still finding its place, it was there, written in ink that could never be scrubbed away. He turned back to the awesome cyclone. A part of him was already inside with her. He closed his eyes, searching for a way to her inside of himself.

The first sensation that came to him was pain—tattered fingernails tearing into his flesh, blood like mist on the wind. He felt a shriek of anger and desperation as Köle's eyes came into focus—sheets of white, unseeing and pulsing as the magic of Vespar rushed into him, filling him to the point of bursting. And Ayelet at his back, gripping him, holding him in place as the same overwhelming force rushed into her fragile, human body.

She did not have long.

Fear rushed at Jahmil from all sides, threatening to overwhelm his senses. He fought it back, that blackness that so easily made all things putrid. A song touched him, like vibrations crawling over his skin. As soft as a whisper, yet insistent. He breathed slowly, deeply, trying to focus through the rushing madness, reaching for the music.

Ayelet, of course. Humming to herself to focus, to control the direction of so much power. Her voice trembled, the tune breaking like waves against sharp rocks. Still, he knew the song. She had played it for him that first night, and he had heard it so many times before.

If only she could hear him and know he was there. That she didn't have to sing alone. Maybe she would reach out to him. Maybe she would be able to allow him through the barrier she had built up around herself so that he could stand at her side.

His hand went to his belt, the whisper-light feeling of the old wooden flute. He took up the ney and put the mouthpiece to his lips and breathed into it. The first warbling notes came out hardly recognizable, his concentration shot, his hands trembling, and his memory unsure. But he kept going. Ayelet's faltering hum was his guide. At last, he found the tune and played low and slow, calm and controlled. Three times he played the melody. He was beginning to feel it was hopeless when at last she reached for him.

Her humming stopped, and the cloud of magic mushroomed out, allowing a single fleeting glimpse of her and the swollen, pulsating figure of Köle. Jahmil darted through the break, reaching her moments before the swell of magic sealed back up. In the eye of the storm, trillions of tiny wisps whipped around them like droplets of water in the clouds. Sparkling into existence and then disappearing. They were funneling into Köle's mouth, his eyes, his ears. His white skin stretched, shivering blue veins pulsing. He had already swollen to twice his original size. And the ferocity of the cyclone was beginning to die down. He had swallowed everything, all the magic that had been lost to Vespar, and even more stolen from Shihala all crammed into his disgusting, bloated body, which now shone more brightly than the First Moon.

Jahmil looked at Ayelet. Her hair whipped around her violently. Her nose and lip were bleeding, her body shaking, her eyes clenched so tightly it looked painful. Her fingers held so tight to Köle that bones showed under her skin.

He touched one of her arms. She flinched and tightened her grip. He leaned in close to her ear and whispered, "Give me your hand."

She hesitated. Even with her eyes shut and the power of the universe flicking all around her, he saw the resistance on her face. With one hand she clenched Köle tighter, but the other loosened. He guided it towards himself, and as she had done that first day on Thueban's back, he used his two arms to form a triangle with hers.

The moment the symbol was completed, the magic inside of Ayelet followed the command. Their bodies did not have to pass through the triangle, as was the case with ordinary djinn apparation. The very mists of Qaf spirited them away. Ayelet's exhausted fingers lost their grip on Köle. Jahmil snatched him by the face, and the three of them fell together through the veil.

They landed in the hard dirt all in a pile with Köle at the bottom. Ayelet was convulsing, the power in her overwhelming her mind and her senses. Her skin was beginning to swell too, white lightning flickering through the surface. Jahmil's arm stung and burned. Another blister burst.

The gray sky of Vespar thundered above. Thick clouds roiled close to the ground, sweeping the barren landscape. What little will the broken bird of Vespar had left within Her was rallying to this place, aching for its own life force.

Jahmil lifted Ayelet into his arms as he stood and loped away from Köle. A lash of thunder louder than any he had ever heard sounded from the sky and the ground at once. Köle shook violently, and then a strangled scream tore from his throat. Ayelet winced, the lightning on her skin flickering with each convulsion.

A wisp of black wafted from her ankle. He turned his head to the side to look at the complex mark. Shifting black serifs twirled on her skin—the Covenant of Shihala.

He rested her weight against his shoulder and ran his fingers over the delicate swirls, the same as his, yet profaned. A deep scar in the shape of a K—old and yet fresh. Cut into the skin over and over in defiance of Allah and decency. Köle had tried to force his mark onto her, to make her his. And with his magic and hatred, he had succeeded in some small way. The scar had been there long before Shihala had kissed the same spot with Her magic.

Why had Shihala chosen that exact spot?

Another crack of thunder. He looked up and saw a pool of emptiness forming over Köle in the clouds, a blackness that ached towards the light in his body, growing steadily nearer. But that same desperation was reaching for Ayelet, for the power contained inside of her. Like a wounded animal, Vespar had lost Her senses. She would rip them both apart to get back what was Hers.

The strength in Jahmil's legs disappeared, and he lowered himself onto the scorched land, holding Ayelet close. He laid his hand over the wound, the impurity of Köle. Holding her body close in the crook of his other arm, he closed his eyes and summoned fire to his hand: gentle and unburning, as it had been the first time he kissed her.

"Please, Vespar," he said, turning his gaze to furious heavens. "She has done you no harm."

If Vespar took Ayelet in Her desperation, misled by the false covenant Köle had scratched into her bones, it would have to take him, too.

He had once given her a boot to protect her foot. Now, he wanted to enfold every bit of her. To take every cut, every nightmare, every moment into himself so that she could be free and unblemished. Let the fires scatter his psyche like shards of broken crystal. Let the beasts come and tear his body into ribbons. For no matter what happened to him, so long as she survived—so long as he could still hear her laughter—he knew he would be able to heal.

The pain on his forearm flared as if a knife tore through his muscles. He looked down and saw the cut bubbling up through his skin under the shivering lines of Shihala. He growled in pain, but his eyes stayed on her ankle, on his fire dancing up and down her skin. Her scar was fading.

A blast of thunder cracked the air so loudly that blood burst in his ears. A column of white fire struck the ground where Köle lay. The body exploded, and an infinite number of compact wisps burst forth, scattering in every direction in a rush of blinding light. Jahmil rolled on top of Ayelet, shielding her with his body. The intensity of the magic was overwhelming, falling from great heights even as the crushing weight of an ocean pressed down from above. His heart hammered. His body shriveled and expanded all at once.

He screamed, and then everything became silent.

CHAPTER FORTY-FOUR

AYELET

AYELET WOKE, SPYING A blurry silver mist and feathery clouds through cracked eyes, hints of pinks and salmons manifesting in the occasional shimmer of still air. She inhaled deeply, a heavy weight upon her chest and the smell of night-kissed breeze tempting her awake. Her ankle ached, but it was a far cry from the agony it had twisted with when Köle had marked her. She shivered at the memory, at the pain that followed when she clung to Köle to bring him to his death.

What happened?

One more inhale, and she opened her eyes wider. Pain spindled down her neck when she moved her head, and she remembered Köle's nails sinking into her flesh as he tried to kill her. Then white, agony, a song, and... a ney. She tried to sit, but something heavy lay across her, tucking her legs and arms up around her and cocooning her in a shell of safety. She raised a weak hand and ran her fingers over muslin and silk. Faintly warm skin and lush, soft hair. She took another shaky breath of moonlight, and her eyes widened as she fully woke to her senses.

"Jahmil?"

Silence.

"Jahmil!" She scrambled to free herself from his alarmingly lifeless arms. When she managed to squeeze out, she rolled Jahmil to his back and ran trembling hands over his chest and neck, stroking and patting his cheeks. "Jahmil. Jahmil, are you okay?"

His eyes remained shut, the eyelids peacefully smooth and his lips loose. Panic overtook her, sending her heart in a whirlwind far more violent than the one that had nearly killed her. What had happened? She had been so close. So close to ending Köle. So close to ending herself. What had Jahmil done?

She ran her fingers over his torn and stained kaftan and then laid her ear on his chest, listening, listening for the sound of his heart. A ney hung loosely from his hand, and she realized it was him she had heard in the torrent of pain. Jahmil, calling out to her. Coming for her when she had long lost hope of living, and fighting for her when even fate had written her off. She heard nothing but the rushing of her own anxious heart beating.

"Jahmil!" she cried and pulled herself up so she could lean forward and kiss him gently. His soft lips lay still. No urgency. No love... no life. She called wisps to her and found Vespar unwilling.

"No!" she yelled at the gray sky that already began to swirl with more stars than she had ever seen. Magic returning to Qaf.

She clenched her teeth, her fingers opening and closing, strumming the air as she yearned for her lyre. "Give me the magic! Please!" She raised Jahmil's hand to the sky in supplication, and his sleeve slipped down below his elbow.

Her breath caught. She dropped his hand and scooted away, the back of her palm pressed against her lips. A faint "K" lay in the center of a swirl of black vines, shifting slower and slower as if they neared fate's final decision.

"What have you done?" she whispered, pulling herself to her unsteady feet and turning fierce eyes on the shared skies of Qaf, of Vespar and Shihala. "That is *my* mark to bear," she cried. "*I* am the marked one. *I* am!"

She ripped her hem from her ankle and raised it up. Then fell back into the earth with a puff of dust. Where Köle had carved himself into her flesh now lay gentle, henna-like swirls moving peacefully, slower and slower as if they, too, had accepted Jahmil's sacrifice as fate.

She clawed at her ankle, raking her own short and chewed nails into her skin in hopes of forming the "K" once more, trying desperately, urgently to take it back. She looked to Jahmil's smooth face, to his arm that now carried Köle's horrid mark.

Frothing rage and a scorching sorrow ripped from her throat in a scream. Lightning thrashed the ground beside her.

She stood, feet apart, and thrust her hand into the air. "He is mine!" she cried.

Then, with all the love shattered within her, she grabbed the magic of unwilling Qaf and slammed it to the dirt, funneling it into Jahmil. The ground shook, the air cracked and rent with power, and the sky filled with a bright and bitter light.

When the surge of magic around her settled to the earth like stardust, and the silver of wisps glittered beneath Jahmil's skin, she inched forward. Exhausted, she lay her head once more on Jahmil's chest, hopelessly hoping to hear his heart beat once more.

A thrum.

The shiver of a beat deep down. She feared she imagined it and leaned in closer, breathing him in. Another beat quivered in his chest. Then three and four. Her heart picked up its pace, hearing life in the one it loved most. A gentle hand scooped hair from the back of her neck and ran warm fingers across her shoulders.

"Jahmil?" she could barely utter his name as she pulled herself up to look at him.

He smiled, his eyes fluttering in tones of gold and pale blue, an anxious dawn about to burst. "I really must get better servants."

She smiled and brushed the hair from his forehead. He pulled her closer before movement caught her periphery.

She flicked her gaze up to see a retreating man with pale blue skin and eyes filled with terror emerge from behind the worn-down building of a decaying city. Vespar's city. One that had been sucked dry like the rest of the war-torn country, but that could now be restored. A hint of recognition flittered its way through her mind. The man was the fidgety one from the marketplace.

Then, a stern-looking, light-purple-skinned woman with sharp cheekbones and garish robes stepped out from behind the crumbling walls and blocked him from sight. Ayelet gasped and scooted away from Jahmil, straight into the grip of waiting guards. How had she missed the sounds of their coming? Drawing the magic had drained her of everything, including her awareness or ability to think.

They lifted her to her feet but did not release her arms. Her muscles still shook with the toll of containing and releasing a world's worth of magic. She was certain if they did release her, she would tumble to the ground, helpless. She looked to Jahmil, who struggled to move. He called for her, but before she could answer, rough hands slapped over her mouth and, with the queen's glittering eyes watching, dragged her away.

With her remaining strength, Ayelet yanked one last wisp free from thirsty Vespar and slipped it into the mark on Jahmil's arm. Köle and fate's mark. Her mark. Then, light faded and restless darkness took her.

Dripping was all she heard for the longest time. An uneven *drip, plip, plop* of water on cold, rough stone nearby. But she was too tired to care. To move or fight or search or think. It was only when the dripping stopped, replaced by hungry chittering, that she found the motivation to open her eyes. In a burst of energy, she pulled herself upright and tucked her knees up close to her chest. Startled, a rat hissed and dodged for the shadows of the corner.

She shivered against the dank cold that always clung to dungeons and assessed her situation.

She had spent her life in many prisons; the one she now cowered in was not meant to torment, just unkindly detain. A bucket of dirty water sat in the corner, another empty one next to it for prisoners to relieve themselves. Patches of mold clung to moist wooden beams, and gold bars that could have bought a small kingdom on earth kept her in. With enough force, might she be able to break them? They were clearly effective at holding back djinn, but gold was soft and would only burn a hole in her pocket, not her skin.

Ayelet snuck a peek at her ankle once more. It no longer stung at all, and the swirls had nearly stopped. The "K" had disappeared entirely, and when she rubbed the bone beneath, it felt whole. She cocked her head to the side, certain she had seen the lingering pattern before, though she couldn't remember where.

Clunky footsteps followed by snippy, short ones neared her cage. She slipped the white dress over her ankle to hide it. Then she pulled herself to a stand, determined to minimize her dirty robes and hideously tangled hair with as much confidence as possible.

Orange torchlight lit the stone on the other side of the bars when tiny, heeled feet stepped into view. They belonged to the same sharp-boned woman she had seen in Vespar. In the shadows of the prison, her features looked far more severe. Hair pulled back tightly and encrusted with a net of gems, wide and puffed silk pants, each leg made of as much fabric as Ayelet's entire dress. Skin that hadn't seen a fleck of dirt in its entire life and instead was dusted with a ridiculous amount of sparkles. Her lipstick was far too warm a shade for her skin tone and her eyes far too cold. And on top of it all, a sharp crown caught flickers of light, casting reflections across Ayelet's face and clothes with seven large gems.

The queen pursed her lips. "So, *you're* the girl," she sneered. Not a compliment.

Ayelet tilted her head to the side. "And you are?"

"Qadira the Glistering, Queen of Ahmar."

"Never heard of you."

Qadira visibly bristled, every fleck of glitter on her skin burning like little fires. "No doubt because you were too busy trying to destroy all of Qaf."

Ayelet let out something between a sigh and a groan, making sure to heave her shoulders as obtusely as possible. "Can we skip the part where you accuse me of traitorous deeds and get on with sentencing me? That is what this is, is it not? A sentencing?"

Qadira's thin brows sliced together. Her mouth curled into a frown. "You speak boldly for someone imprisoned in a land that is not your own, which means you're either stupid or naïve. And seeing as how you attempted to work with the traitor Köle to drain the magic from Vespar and the rest of Qaf *and* tried to seduce the Prince of Shihala in his weakest moments, I know you're not naïve."

Ayelet wanted to fry Qadira on the spot. But her bones still quivered from nearly being blown apart, and Qaf still begrudged her use of wisps. Instead, she smirked. "Ah. I *have* heard of you."

Qadira made a tiny "hmph" noise and smiled cruelly, waiting for Ayelet to continue.

Ayelet was more than happy to oblige. "Yes, you're the *former* fiancée of Jahmil Amir, the woman a particularly trustworthy source described as something akin to a rat chewing on a prisoner's neck."

Lightning flashed in Qadira's eyes. She grabbed Ayelet's robes through the bars and pulled her hard against them, though the gold must have burned her skin where it touched. "Jahmil and I marry as soon as the Third Moon rises in the sky."

"You will not," Ayelet said simply, touching a hand to the opals around her neck.

Qadira spat a laugh in her face. "And what do you know of Jahmil? Of being a king and the price it costs to rule a kingdom? He is mine. And saving the pathetic people of Shihala was the price I paid for him."

Ayelet narrowed her eyes. "I trust Jahmil with everything I am."

Qadira snarled, her eyes glittering dangerously.

"Besides," Ayelet continued, not caring how big a fit Qadira threw. "No slave has ever loved its master. Or is that the only way anyone will marry you?"

Qadira's eyes widened, then her face crumpled into something angled and ugly. She released Ayelet, then grabbed her opals and yanked them off her neck.

"No!" Ayelet cried, reaching for the necklace.

"So this is Jahmil's nightmare catcher." She turned the necklace over in her hands, her expression filling with contempt. "Hardly fit for a queen, but far too lovely for the likes of you."

Ayelet grasped for it once more, desperate to keep her connection to Jahmil. Qadira yanked the opals back and threw them on the ground with a laugh far worse than the snarl of a bial'dabaye. Then, she stomped on it, shattering one of the delicate stones and Ayelet's heart with it.

"You will waste away in prison the rest of your days. And as you rot, wishing every day that you were dead, I want you to think of me wrapped in Jahmil's arms. Guards," she quipped, and two men appeared at attention. "Take her to Ashkult."

One of the soldiers whose face was a deep royal purple hesitated, eyeing her with the same wary look she had seen her whole life.

Qadira snarled and slapped his face, raking her nails deep into his skin so thick drops of red pooled in sharp stripes on his cheek. "Now!"

The man winced, nodding hastily as he took up his place by the cell door. Qadira spat on the ground in front of Ayelet, then disappeared down the hallway, her clicking footsteps as grating as grinding chalk between teeth.

Ayelet dropped to the floor and scooped up the opal necklace, marred by some of the blood still dripping from the soldier's face. The middle bead lay crushed, the chain broken beneath it so it no longer looped in an eternal circle, but hung limply as a string in her grasp. She waited for the hopeless emptiness to consume her as it always had in the past, but it had been replaced by the blinding heat of rage and unquenchable determination.

She had been wrong about the necklace. The opals were Jahmil's promise to marry her, to give her a future, but they were not their connection. That lay in their hearts and on the settling tattoos that whispered of more. Shihala's Covenant between them.

Ayelet twined her fingers around the cool beads and turned the fire of her wrath into the dark where Qadira had left a chill. Jahmil would never marry her. She was done waiting for fate to decide. She would be with him, whatever it took.

CHAPTER FORTY-FIVE

JAHMIL

HE WAS STILL IN a dreamy haze when the winds encircled him and he was lifted from the cold of Vespar and transported somewhere soft and perfumed. He still felt her beside him, Ayelet, holding him and keeping him safe. He had seen her smile, and that was all that mattered. She was alive and well enough to turn the corners of her lips. Whatever the fate of Shihala, or Vespar, or anything else, that was success. The pain in his bones was nothing, nor was the endless swirling of his mind.

"*Abnay,*" a voice said, a cold palm pressing his cheek. His eyes rolled painfully, aching to open. He twitched his limbs, a herculean effort.

He knew who it was speaking without needing to look up.

"*Marhabān*, Mother."

"I didn't tell her. *Wallahi*, I did not tell her."

He shook his head and opened his eyes. Her face looked dark and pale all at once, creased with unspoken worries, but in her eyes were golden sparkles of happiness. She leaned down and kissed his cheek. Was it the first time?

"Where am I?" he asked, trying to sit up. "Where is Ayelet?"

"I tried to stop her."

"Stop who?" The room came into focus, his own bed chamber at Ahmar. It shifted as if he were watching through lines of rain on cheap glass. He had never felt so tired.

A hand clasped his, hot and small. "Are you okay?"

He turned and saw Serap sitting at his bedside, a princess in her fine silks, yet with far too many cares written in her dewy eyes.

"I'm fine, *anisa*." He smiled at her. "But where is Ayelet?"

"Qadira took her to the dungeon," said his mother.

"What?" He shook his head. The words she said made sense on their own, but not in that order. "How could she? We were in Vespar..."

"You succeeded, *abnay*. Vespar's sky glimmers with the fire of Qaf and bathes the land in light. The Nine Kingdoms are whole again."

"I don't care." He rolled out of bed, forcing his feet to hold weight with the sheer power of will. Serap shrieked and covered her eyes. Jahmil looked down at his naked body, then flashed his eyes at his mother. "You have got to be joking!"

She snatched a robe from a nearby chair and rushed to give it to him. "Your clothes were filthy."

He wrapped the long-sleeved, ankle-length garment over his body and secured the belt tightly. Serap looked up between her fingers, her face redder than a poppy.

Grabbing his mother's shoulders, he squared her to him. "Where is Ayelet?"

"I told you. Qadira has sent her to Ashkult."

"But how did she find us?"

"It was Zamir," said Serap.

His eyes widened painfully. "Excuse me?"

"He's a snake." Serap shrugged. "I've been here a while now and I've been watching him watch you. Qadira bought him a long time ago. He followed you both when you left through the harem. I was going to tell you, but you're never around. And nobody listens to me anyway."

"Quite a little ally you have here," said his mother. She sounded incredulous, but her expression was decidedly pleased. She'd always wanted a daughter of her own.

"What grounds does Qadira have?" he asked, his head still spinning with a rush of blood. "Ayelet has done no wrong."

"She's human," said his mother. "No grounds are needed."

"I'll kill her."

"Jahmil, listen to me." She grabbed his chin, forcing him to look into her eyes. "I warned you that she had become obsessed. The news of the renaissance of Vespar and your part in it is spreading like wildfire. We don't need Qadira anymore and she knows it, but we still have a contract."

"Ala aljahim her contract!"

"If you do not marry her and sleep with her tonight, she will kill Ayelet."

He laughed at the absurdity. "Ayelet could destroy her with a glance."

"She is in Ashkult, a place without magic. A place where magic will not tread." She sighed and shook her head. "Within the frozen walls of that hell... *abnay*, your powerful love is nothing but a tiny human."

His breath puffed between his teeth, hissing and hot. "I'll go break her out."

She shook her head. "Your apartments are surrounded by a full regiment. You're not going anywhere. And neither am I."

He grabbed at his hair and sank onto the mattress, the weight of his mother's words landing like small stones piled on a slab to crush a victim to death. "Those are her options? A lifetime in Ashkult or death? They are the same."

"No." His mother bit her lip and shifted. "I have negotiated a plea with Qadira. First, you must wipe your own memory and marry Qadira at the rising of the Third Moon. Second, you must further agree to drink an elixir of romance at the commencement of your honeymoon. If conditions are met, Ayelet will be pardoned and returned to Ard. Her memory will be wiped clean and she will be given a stipend of forty pearls and allowed to live out the rest of her life undisturbed. If, however, you refuse the contract, she will remain at Ashkult and be executed slowly over the next four years by means of lashing, poisoning, and flaying."

He could not respond. It was everything he could do not to spit on the contract. "She's out of her mind."

"Yes," said his mother. "And you must not capitulate."

"Excuse me?"

"We have an opportunity to seize back Shihala for our people. If you lose your memory again and marry Qadira, it will severely hamper our efforts. The life of a single human is not worth the setbacks to the cause."

"That's your argument?" he raged, pushing her away. "Let her die?"

"You can't..." stammered Serap, her eyes darting between him and his mother. "You wouldn't."

He shook his head, glaring daggers at his mother. "After everything I have been through for her, how could you suggest—"

"What you did was for the good of Shihala."

"No. It wasn't." He cradled his face in his hands, his bones aching to collapse. "I know you don't understand it, but that doesn't matter. Shihala understands." He lifted his arm to show her the Covenant burned into his flesh. No longer did it shift and bend. It was set now and would never change.

His mother sighed quickly, then jutted out her chin. "Then marry the wench. I can make that work, too." She hurried to the window and gazed out at the shifting moons. "The people are gathering in the palace to witness the signing of the official contract. I'm certain she has the forgetting potion waiting for you there. You have thirty minutes to make up your mind."

With that, she left. Jahmil stood in the center of his room, clawing at the sides of his own head.

"There has to be something else we can do," said Serap, rising to come to his side. "You can't forget each other. Not again."

He ran his fingers over the tattoo on his arm. The K-shaped scar was visible under the lines, already faded, a part of the design. He smiled sadly and shook his head. "Shihala will remember."

"You're going to do it, aren't you?" Serap's eyes shimmered with tears, her face dotted with hard, red splotches.

He took a knee so he could look into her eyes. "Tell me your plan."

She pressed a hand over her mouth, and he watched as her body crumpled hopelessly into itself, the reality of the situation twisting her bones. The transformation was almost as painful to watch as a bial'dabaye turning back into a human, only this was not a monster returning to innocence. This was an innocent being awakened to the true monstrosity of the world. The fact that you can try your best, sacrifice everything, and still fail.

She began to cry and rushed from the room. Part of him wanted to follow her, but what could he possibly say?

His eyes scanned the room and found his wedding clothes laid out neatly over the changing screen. Loose white pants of silk so fine it felt frictionless, a structured brocade jacket that fell to the knee-line, inlaid with diamonds and aquamarine. A long strip of heavy, embroidered silk. Soft, white shoes made of doeskin. He changed into the clothes and tied the red and gold silk around his head in a wedding turban. But he took the shoes and threw them out of the window.

Jahmil sat down and waited. They would come for him when it was time.

He pressed a hand to his chest, hoping to feel the beat of his own heart. Nothing.

The sound of a ruckus down below stirred him, and he looked up lazily. He heard harsh voices and a crash. After some time the door burst open and the burned, tattered, and bloody figure of Takisha stepped inside. He smiled weakly.

"Jahmil," she breathed, rushing closer. She fell to her knees in front of him and gazed up at his face, even as several of Qadira's guards ran in behind her.

"It's all right," he said, glancing up at them. "She's only here to offer her well-wishes."

The guards shared a glance, then stepped outside the door, but they left it open. He would never again have a private conversation.

"I tried to stop them," she said, her words quick and heavy. "I could not get to you in time."

"It's all right."

"Why are you dressed like that? What is going on?"

"It's time, *Amiri*," said one guard, peeking his head into the room.

Jahmil nodded, then rose with a heavy sigh. He glanced at Takisha. "I'm getting married."

Her face fell even as her eyes clouded with white mist. "Why?"

"I have nothing left, Takisha." He shrugged and shook his head. "It's over. She wins."

"Where is Ayelet?"

"Ashkult."

Her features pinched with rage. "Qadira…"

"Of course. I should have seen it coming." He chuckled mirthlessly. "I'm not very good at my job."

"You can't."

He clapped his hand onto her massive, swollen shoulder and gave it a weak squeeze. "You should go back to Shihala. There's a lot of work to be done."

He stepped past her towards the door and into the hands of his jailers.

"Jahmil," she called, her deep voice sounding frayed and exhausted.

He let himself be led away. She may have called after him again, but he didn't understand it. He walked slowly and deliberately, the guards keeping perfect pace with him. The bailey had been decorated with lanterns and streamers. Peasants danced in the street, happy for their day off work and not particularly caring why it had been granted. Courtiers crammed the area around the palace, each jockeying for a better view of the royal wedding. They parted to let him through and cheered his name as he passed.

"*Alf mabrouk Ala alzifaf alsaʿeed!*" they called. *Heartiest congratulations on your happy nuptials.*

He stepped into the glittering palace and was led through to a room he had never entered before—a sprawling ballroom decorated with bursts of fire and flickering flowers. A wedding march played, a song so hideous it could hardly be called music. Qadira was already waiting on an upraised platform, draped in so much red silk and gems it was difficult to believe a person was wrapped inside. She wore a sheer veil over her mouth and nose, but he still saw her heavy lipstick beneath.

"*Taw'am al'ruwhi!*" she cried. *My soulmate.*

He stepped up to the podium and picked up the fluffy yellow quill on his side of the heavy scroll. Rows of delicate golden calligraphy and hideous words. Qadira's signature in shimmering purple ink. And there at the bottom of the page was the seal of the King of the Eastern Elm, the great arbitrator of Qaf. To break a deal sealed by him would bring instantaneous death to the offending party, burned from the inside out into a pile of cinder. When he went through with the wedding, Qadira would have to release Ayelet. There would be no option to double-cross him.

"Where are your shoes?" Qadira sneered.

He raised his brow. "Are you sure you want to ask me that?"

Her gaze flickered, features squishing to one side of her face. Then she laughed so loudly that it echoed through the massive chamber. "Oh, Jahmil. You're so delightfully eccentric."

"Let's get on with it," he said.

CHAPTER FORTY-SIX

AYELET

ASHKULT *WAS* A PRISON meant to torment.

Ayelet could tell even before she entered through the wall that imposed on the surrounding white void and strange lake of silver. Qadira had taken no chances transporting her there; the short, red-faced guards touched her with anxious eyes and whispered of her power to drain life. Ayelet supposed she had taken on the role of Köle now, his eternal servant left to do his will even after he vanished. She didn't have to have his mark upon her skin.

The ride there had been atop a drakonte, and the small goodness of knowing that Jahmil and Takisha had found their lost soldiers lifted her heavy feet. The second Qadira left her presence, biting manacles had been slapped on her arm, and she had been thrown in a box weighted with strange markings and material she had not yet seen on earth. It suffocated her. Not because she was a magical being, but because she breathed magic, even on earth. Part of her supposed that she had ever since she had been with Köle. Whatever the material, it repelled Shihala and Qaf and the wisps, same as the silver chains upon her hands.

She touched her ankle and looked up at the walls that disappeared into the sky, then entered darkness.

Inside the terrible prison, Ayelet sighed. Even though she was not a djinn, this place had no shortage of misery to inflict on humans. She closed her eyes and tried for the thousandth time to call magic from the air, but it hid from this terrible place. Even so, the guards trapped inside Ashkult seemed to have heard the rumors of her terrible treachery, for they only shoved her when necessary and feared looking into her eyes. One tried to take a blade to shave her hair—what must have happened to Takisha—but one glare and an ominous whisper had sent him retreating a step or two.

She was sure it wouldn't last; a couple of days here and they would fear her magic no more than her drab, human eyes. For now, it was a victory.

As grim-faced guards shuffled her over thin bridges of dripping stone and through the wailing of prisoners who had no hope—who hadn't had hope for a long, long time—Ayelet realized that she did. Even in this awful place, with Qadira's threats and no wisps of comfort, she still believed in Jahmil. Believed him.

A pair of glowing yellow eyes stared at her from one of the cells she passed. Ayelet smiled sadly at whoever they belonged to as the guards pulled her to a halt. A shrill creak echoed through the air as the guards dragged up a platform to take her down into the depths of Qaf's hell.

"I love you, Jahmil," she whispered under her breath.

A sneer sounded from the cell next to her, soft enough that only she could hear it. "I see you stopped Köle Amir, Ayelet."

She looked up from her manacles and bit the gasp on her tongue. Bottomless eyes stared out from creped skin and droopy brows. She would know the face and voice of the peddler anywhere.

"No thanks to you."

"Yet you are not happy."

She flicked eyes heavy with irony his way. "If you'd like your sacrifices to be happier about their lot, maybe you should ask them before marking them."

The peddler hissed a cackle, and the guards rammed the hilts of their swords into the door. He growled and disappeared. The platform reached their floor, and the guards pushed her to move. She ripped her shoulders away from their touch, and with a glare, set them back. Then she turned to the peddler's door.

"That's it? You made me a target of Köle, sent me to torture, rested the fate of a world I don't belong to on my shoulders, threaten even now to tear my only love from me, and yet you laugh?"

If the wisps had responded to the call she sent through the air, her fist would be as white as Jahmil's with magic. She kicked the door with her bare foot and welcomed the pain.

His awful eyes appeared once more in the tiny slits of his door's window. "You are mad at fate. Not me. And until your *love* asks his final two questions and fulfills his promise to end my life, I will gleefully take part in any suffering he may endure. But who says Shihala is done deciding anything?"

She lifted the hem of her skirt and shoved her ankle awkwardly against the door with a thud. "It looks set to me."

His glittering eyes took in the mark before he sneered and disappeared into the shadows.

"Peddler!" she yelled, not sure what more she wanted from him.

The guards had just found enough bravery to grab her arm when shouts echoed from the passageway behind them. Thuds shook the walls, and panicked soldiers streamed in from crevices in the maze of the prison. Ashkult was under siege. The extra guards surrounding her must have decided the immediate threat was more dangerous than she, for they left her, all but one, to make sure their walls weren't breached.

Ayelet flashed her eyes toward the strange mystic who had marked her Ayelet, but the cell shone empty and black.

The red guard holding her hand tightened his grasp, loosened it, then tightened again, glancing between her, the men rushing by, and the platform that would take him further into the fortress.

"Run now," Ayelet whispered in a tone she had learned from Jahmi, "and when I get free, I won't come back and suck the magic from every drop of your blood, shriveling your body, turning your bones into husks with nothing inside." She flicked her eyes down his body and then back up. "Along with your seed."

He scowled at her, the only act of defiance he had left, then released her and disappeared into the belly of Ashkult.

Ayelet glanced once more at the peddler's cell before running back across the stone bridge and toward the mouth of the prison. Thrice she had to pull herself into a shadow as guards ran by, but in this terrible place full of Qaf's monsters, a human could hide easily. The guards split in a fork before her, streaming up two distinct sets of stairs to gain higher ground. She creased her brow, then heard a familiar, spine-scraping screech.

"Thueban!"

No. Dozens of Thuebans—an army of drakontes. She ached to go outside, to see the army that had come, the army she hoped Jahmil had sent to free her. Aside from Jahmil, she did not know whom she could trust, but the atrium into the prison still held a dozen men. Half faced toward her, and half toward freedom.

One of the djinn caught sight of her. "There! Get her!" he cried, but he advanced no more than any of his companions.

She slid her feet apart and glared up through her lashes just as an iridescent djinn barrelled through the entrance. The metal door burst apart. Takisha, dressed from head to toe in gray, studded leather, pulled herself to full height and swung her sword at the nearest guard, who crumpled without fight.

Ayelet's eyes widened. The guards would come her way now. As Takisha thrashed the men at the front, the ones nearest Ayelet crept forward like she was a wild beast they planned to kill and eat.

Ayelet took step after step back, retreating while trying to look like she wasn't. Her hem brushed her ankle, and a deep sorrow ran up every nerve in her leg. Jahmil's sorrow. She clenched her fist and breathed in the stale, magicless air of Ashkult. Then she remembered where there was some magic. Just a wisp. She dropped to one knee and placed her hand on her scarless tattoo. Thinking of Jahmil, she pulled for magic, not from the air, but through Shihala's bond, through the mark fate placed upon them both.

Hesitant, resisting the oppression of Ashkult's walls and the silver lake outside, the wisp she had placed in his tattoo earlier slowly manifested. Ayelet did not yank this time but coaxed and pleaded. The wisp unfurled more readily, becoming a ball of soft, ethereal fabric in her hand. She smiled up at the guards and unleashed the magic. The wisp flew into eyes, through lungs, and out screaming teeth. What little magic hid in the skin of the guards, the wisp ripped out from under their fingernails, growing bit by bit into a glittering ball of power.

Takisha pummeled the guards at the front and Ayelet suffocated the ones in the back until they both twirled around to see each other. Before Ayelet could say anything, Takisha grabbed the front of her dress and hauled her out the doors. She threw Ayelet onto Thueban's back as he hovered nervously over the lake of silver, then jumped up herself.

As guards shot arrows and yelled in outrage, Thueban thrust into the sky, shielded by the army to their back. Ayelet grabbed Takisha's waist to stay on, her hands unable to fit fully around. Soon, they were out of reach, speeding through clouds toward a shining castle in the distance.

When their path smoothed and she grew used to the whip of wind against her ears, Ayelet leaned closer and asked the only question on her mind.

"Why?"

"Why what, little human?" Takisha asked, looking straight ahead.

"Why are you helping me? Jahmil said..." she trailed off, afraid Takisha might change her mind.

"Because..." Takisha tilted her head back just enough so Ayelet could see the sincerity in her eye. "Because I can't stand looking at his face... not like that. Not anymore."

Ayelet nodded, then creased her brow. "Why didn't Jahmil come himself?"

Takisha was silent for a moment. "He weds Qadira," she said solemnly.

Ayelet shot her eyes up to the sky above them. The Third Moon. "We've got to stop him!"

"I know that." Takisha sounded irritated. "Why do you think I braved the lake of silver? But even on Thueban, I don't think we can make it in time."

Ayelet bit her lip. "Then we show up, and he breaks his contract. He doesn't need that awful woman to keep Shihala anymore."

Takisha sighed.

"What?" Ayelet asked, concerned by the normally blunt warrior's silence.

"The deal he made with Qadira was to take a forgetting potion as soon as he signed the marriage contract. And then a love potion after that. It is also sealed by the King of Elm. A broken promise would mean death."

Ayelet growled and stood on Thueban's back, unable to stay seated. "How could he be so selfish! Again!"

Takisha reached back and yanked Ayelet down. "Don't be such a fool, risking your life like that after Jahmil gave up everything to save it."

Realization dawned on Ayelet. "Ashkult. He did it to get me out of that place, didn't he?"

"That place and worse."

Ayelet leaned around Takisha. The palace was still too far off. Anxiety ate away at her. Jahmil had lost enough for her. And she for him. She stood once more.

"Sit!" Takisha growled.

"No."

Takisha reached for her once more, but Ayelet stepped back, rallied her strength, and jumped. Thueban screeched and Takisha cursed. They plummeted after her as Ayelet forced Shihala to share Her magic. She used the wisps to rip three trees from the earth and make them into a triangle. Takisha swooped behind, reaching to grab her, before they burst through into earth's realm, Ayelet trailing extra wisps with her. She landed on Thueban's back as he slipped under her, Takisha cursing up a storm. Children screamed in terror and men cried out in alarm under earth's scorching sun. Ayelet used her wisps to do the same once more.

When the trees hovered in front, Ayelet called out to Takisha. "To Ahmar!"

But Takisha waved her off, already angling Thueban for a grand entrance. The drakonte screeched as they blasted once more between the two worlds and over the glittering city. Soldiers stumbled back as Thueban flew just past the ramparts, calling out in alarm and readying weapons. But they darted past all that and straight for the palace decked out in flowers, ribbons, and sparkling fountains.

A giant circular window cut into thousands of colored pieces in the pattern of Qaf's seven moons shone with the light of the ceremony inside. Takisha yanked Thueban forward, and they shattered through it. Glass burst onto the crowd below. People ran for cover. Guards regrouped.

Jahmil froze, yellow pen in hand and half his name written on a glittering scroll. Qadira screamed at her guardsmen, who closed ranks around her.

Ayelet jumped from Thueban's back and landed on the floor in a crouch, leaving the snake to ripple around the room, cracking wood and breaking windows. Takisha cackled with joy at the destruction.

Ayelet said nothing. Qadira spat hate at her feet. And Jahmil just stared, his jaw open and his brow knit tight. She walked over, ripped the pen from his hand, and snapped it in half. Then she grabbed the document and turned to the wretched queen.

"Give that back," Qadira seethed. "Guards!"

Ayelet tossed it into the air and called the wisps to grab it. Then she had them circle Qadira slowly, the parchment's edges tattering a little more with every rotation.

Jahmil said nothing, gazing at her with an open mouth, but the edges of his lips were turning up.

Qadira's eyes widened, and she took a step back, her men muscling even closer to seal off the path between Ayelet and their terrible queen.

"He signed it." Qadira's chin quivered. "It doesn't matter he didn't quite finish. His magic is in the paper. It is a promise sealed by Shihala and Ahmar. By Qaf itself! He must forget about you and love me. You are nothing!"

Ayelet ran a wisp through Qadira's ceremonial dress until it came up with the poison she had planned to use on Jahmil. With the curl of her finger, she uncorked the lid and dragged the shining liquid out, suspended by a wisp that snaked through the air toward her gaping mouth.

"Your contract means nothing," Ayelet said, taking step after step toward the queen.

Qadira's guards hesitated, black fear growing in their eyes as the Marked One neared. Ayelet heard the whispers at her back, even now. The Sorceress. The Destroyer of Worlds. The Savior of Vespar.

"It is signed!" Qadira insisted, her voice tinted with the faintest trill.

Ayelet whipped the parchment in front of Qadira, then cell by cell drew out the magic. The contract that tried to bind the magic of Qaf disintegrated into black dust that glinted with purple sparkles. The outline of the seal at the bottom flickered and disappeared.

"Shihala does not recognize your union."

Qadira's lavender face burned fuschia as anger blotched her cheeks. She pushed past her guard and tried to rake her sharp nails into Ayelet's flesh, but Ayelet twitched a finger, and a wisp caught the queen's hand. She wrapped the magic around the queen's bony wrist and yanked it so she scratched her own cheek.

"How dare you?" Qadira's lips quivered. "You're not even djinn! You're just some pathetic human. A disgusting monster of Köle Amir's making."

Ayelet clenched her fist so that a whirlwind consumed them and she could see only Qadira's severe face and the white of magic. She stepped forward in the eerie quiet at the center of the mini-storm, pulling the river of forgetting potion closer to Qadira's lips.

"You speak boldly for someone who is imprisoned in magic that is not your own, and we both know you're not naïve." She walked up to the queen, stopping just in front. "Jahmil will not be seduced by your sick manipulations. Shihala forbids it," Ayelet said and lifted the hem of her skirt.

Qadira scoffed before she caught sight of the tattooed mark. Her eyes widened. "How did you— Who has—" She screamed, but the magic whisked away the sound.

She lunged at Ayelet once more, but glistening tendrils lashed her arms and held her back. Then slowly, slowly, with every twitch of Ayelet's little finger, the wisps sucked the magic from Qadira's skin.

Ayelet spoke in a whisper. "Shihala has indeed sealed a union this day. But it is clearly not yours." Qadira opened her mouth to speak, and Ayelet snapped it shut.

"Your contract is null. Your kingdom is more loyal to the amir than you. And your very existence causes the magic of Qaf to shiver in disgust."

Qadira's face fell, trepidation filling her cruel eyes. The magic continued to drain from her face, her lavender skin now a faintly purple-tinted white. No luster. No glow.

Ayelet pulled the potion so it trailed the queen's hideous lips. "If you ever come near Jahmil again, I will see to it you forget your own name. There will be no place on Qaf or Ard you can hide that I will not find you. No flower will bloom when you are near, no gentle breeze will ever touch your face. You will be haunted with every step for abusing the magic of Qaf for your petty, personal whims, and I will see to it that no life grows in that barren wasteland you call a womb."

Qadira glared as if she would say more. Ayelet turned before she could answer, not caring for whatever she had to say. She walked the whirlwind over to Jahmil and swept him gently inside. She smiled and took his hand, bringing him close and pulling back his sleeve to reveal the tattoo on his arm. It was as set as hers, the hint of a "K" tangled up in the same pattern of Shihala's skies that wrapped her ankle. She kissed each moon, then followed the warmth of his skin up his arm and onto his neck.

"Now, what do you have to say for yourself?"

CHAPTER FORTY-SEVEN

Jahmil

For a moment he could not move, could not even breathe as the impossibility of Ayelet caressed his skin. And then, like magma rushing to burst from a volcano, he began to laugh. And laugh. A laughter so intense that he could not breathe, or see, or even think. His abs burned, tears stung his eyes, his legs quivered. He wiped his eyes and tried to focus on everything that was in front of him.

Thueban coiled through the crowd, scattering Qadira's hateful sycophants. Takisha stood at the edge of it all with her broad shoulders, screaming a resounding call of "Death!" and threatening to eviscerate anybody who came near. And Qadira with blood on her cheek. Qadira gazing with an open mouth. Qadira twitching, and seething, itching for revenge and yet unable to do anything.

The Queen of Ahmar, the viper, the constrictor. The creature that had haunted his dreams for nearly a year. She was speechless.

The laughter redoubled, and he grabbed his stomach, barely able to keep himself from falling to his knees. Ayelet said something, but he couldn't understand it. She could have been calling him the biggest fool to ever live and it would not have mattered. He could not stop laughing. And by Allah, it felt wonderful.

Panting, he struggled to gain control of himself. He reached for Ayelet and took her wrist in his hand. He looked down at her too-serious eyes, and it was almost too much. He tried to speak over and over, but laughter kept cutting him off until he couldn't remember what he was trying to say.

Ayelet scowled, though the corners of her lips turned. "You are a silly man, did you know that?"

He almost spat on her, he laughed so hard. He forced himself to breathe, to contain it, to shove it down. But when he looked at her, he couldn't help the ridiculous smile that grew on his face. He started her name several times before he managed to say, "Ayelet."

"I have a mind to throw a shoe at you," she pouted. "Except neither of us is wearing any."

"Who needs them?" he said, pulling her to his chest.

She grinned, then appeared to remember something. She slapped his arm. "No more leaving me in dungeons and making deals to forget me!"

He took a long slow breath, his fuzzy vision finally focusing on her, though he could not see anything else. It did not matter. "Who are you again?"

She growled out a laugh, then put her hands on his face and pulled him closer. "Just someone looking for your servant. I have something to give him."

"He's such a miserable, useless buffoon, I doubt he deserves it." He pressed his forehead against hers. "But go on. I'll be sure he gets it."

She narrowed her eyes, playfully suspicious. "I am not sure if I can trust you. I hear you are terrible at your job."

"What job?"

Ayelet bit her lip with a smile, then looked down. She pulled the opal necklace from her pocket, its center bead crushed and its chain broken. "Qadira…" she said, a small frown on her flushed face. "But I can fix it… I think. Perhaps I can beg another opal off you for a song?" Her doe eyes looked up at him hopefully.

"That will do well enough, my queen. And be all the more beautiful for its trials." He ran his fingertips gently over her cheek. "Until then, I know another thing you can sleep with that will bring you glad dreams."

She blushed with a giggle, slapping his shoulder before grabbing him and pulling him in for a kiss. "You are not being serious about this at all."

"Somebody told me that I ought to laugh more."

"Takisha?"

"Yes, it must have been. You know, I always do everything she tells me."

"Is that so? I cannot seem to get you to do anything I tell you."

He smirked. "You don't hit me hard enough."

A beam broke from the ceiling, landing with a harsh crack behind them. Jahmil raised his gaze and realized a battle was taking place in the surrounding palace. More drakontes had arrived, joining Takisha and Thueban in tearing through the forces of Ahmar. Wisps churned in the air and shot down in thick columns, keeping Qadira and her soldiers in place while she screamed like the petulant child she was. He turned back to Ayelet. "Maybe we should get out of here."

She took one look around the room, hushing the wisps that still spun around them. "Yes. Definitely."

"Where would you like to go? We can go anywhere."

"But what about Shihala?"

"Shihala understands," he said. "The day will come when She will ask us to repay Her for everything she has done for us. Until then, She already has a queen who loves Her more than anything."

Ayelet ran her fingers down his arms and circled them over his tattoo. "And what do you love more than anything?"

"That's tricky." He bit his bottom lip and cast his gaze away. "I'm quite fond of baklava."

She nodded. "Yes. I can see how baklava could ruin your life." She poked his stomach. "Good thing we will have Serap here to help you eat it."

He lifted her chin, drawing her nearer until their lips were a scant inch apart. "You," he said.

Her eyes glistened, and she laughed that impossible, beautiful laugh that filled up his soul. The laugh that had changed his entire life. There was nothing he could do but draw her in and kiss her.

And for the first time, he felt spoiled.

Scan below to read the epilogue!

https://dl.bookfunnel.com/nu2z5e1
932

Remember, reviews are an author's bread and butter! If you enjoyed The Covenant of Shihala, please leave a review on Amazon, Goodreads, or eightmoonspublishing.com.

And don't forget to check out our **new releases** and **extra content** on our website!

GLOSSARY OF TERMS

PLACES:

Ahmar: one of the Nine Kingdoms of Qaf, ruled by Queen Qadira.

Ard: the world of humans.

Ashkult: an internationally utilized, inescapable prison. Built in an area of Qaf where there is no magic.

Buhayra Ruwarin: the lake that surrounds The City of Pearls

Buhayrat Alzaybiq: the lake of quicksilver that surrounds Ashkult.

Edirne: a city in Thrace (Greece), ruled by the Ottoman Empire.

Ghaluma: one of the Nine Kingdoms of Qaf, located on the Lower Continent. The location of Ashkult.

Karzusan: capital of Shihala.

Orkeshi: mountainous borderlands between Shihala.

Qaf: the world of the djinn.

Rananbar: a city at the borders of Shihala, Ahmar, and Vespar.

Shihala: one of the Nine Kingdoms of Qaf, ruled by Dowager Queen Zalika and her son, Prince Jahmil. They are in exile in the court of Ahmar since the lands were overtaken by the Vaspars.

Tel Keveh: a city in Vespar

The City of Pearls: capital of Ahmar.

Vespar: one of the Nine Kingdoms of Qaf, which currently occupies the territory of Shihala and is on the brink of invading Ahmar. Ruled by Princess Vespasia since the death of her father, King Harduk, and her brother, Prince Köle.

Zabriya: one of the Nine Kingdoms of Qaf, located on the Lower Continent.a kingdom of Qaf

Arabic phrases:

Adhhab mae Allah - go with God

Alhamdulillah - thank God/praise God

Allah yahmini - God protect me

Astaghfirullah - God forgive me

Bihaqi alsama' - for heaven's sake

Bismillah - in the name of God

Inshallah (Turk. inşallah) - hopefully, God willing

Kun hadi - be calm/calm down

La 'atamanā - I hope not?

Lā 'ilāha 'illā-llāh - there is no God but Allah

La'anaha Allah - God damn it

Mashallah (Turk. maşallah) - what God has willed has happened

Sallah-llahu 'alayhi wa-salam - peace be upon him (used in reference to the Prophet Muhammad)

Takun 'alā al-salam - be at peace

Tarajae – retreat

Taw'am ruhwi - my soulmate

Wallahi - I swear to God

Ya Allah - oh my god

Yalak min 'ahmaq - you fool

Misc. Words/Terms

Abnay - my son (Ar.)

Al'ama - blindness [damnit] (Ar.)

Al'amir alsaghir - little prince (Ar.)

Ala aljahim - to hell (Ar.)

al-Baqarah - a chapter of the Quran (Ar.)

Allah'a şükür - thank God (Turk.)

Amiri - my prince (Ar.)

Anisa - companion, friend (Ar.)

Boş ver - never mind (Turk.)

Efendi - lord, master (Turk.)

Eimlaq - giant (Ar.)

Ekmek - bread (Turk.)

Fersah - an Ottoman unit of measurement, about 6-7 km

Fırıncılık - bakery (Turk.)

Ghalwah - an ancient Arabic unit of measurement, about 230 m

Habibi (m) / habibati (f) - my dear/darling (Ar.)

Ignis fatuus - lit. *giddy flame*, will-o'-the-wisp (Lat.) pl. fatui

Jahannam - hell (Ar.)

Jamilati (f) - beautiful one (Ar.)

Kafir - infidel, unbeliever (Ar.)

Kahrolası - goddamn (Turk.)

Kanatlı yılan - winged serpents (Turk.)

Majnun - crazy [one] (Ar.)

Malikati - my queen (Ar.)

Nazar boncuğu - an Evil Eye amulet (Turk.)

Nene - lit. *grandmother*, a form of address for elderly women (Turk.)

Parasang - a Persian unit of measurement, about 6 km

Pide - a type of cheese-bread (Turk.)

Poğaça - a stuffed roll (Turk.)

Qut mukhif - scaredy cat (Ar.)

Sadiq Allah - friend of God (Ar.)

Sayida(t) - lady, miss (Ar.)

Sharmouta - whore/prostitute (Ar.)

Wali - Islamic Saint [Sufism] (Ar.)

The Five Directions:

Bahamut, Janu'ub, Sharq, Gharb, and Shamaal

GUIDE TO DJINN EYE COLORS

Black: Fear. Mist swirling in the eyes

Blue: Hope, Anticipation

Green: Jealousy, Envy

Purple: Sadness, Grief, Despair

Gold: Happiness, Joy

Pink: Anxiety, Nervousness

Red: Lust. Glows in pupils

Silver: Compassion, Commiseration

White: Shock, Surprise. Lines like lightning

Yellow: Disgust, Disdain, Loathing

Orange: Embarrassment, Humiliation

Copper: Confidence, Bravery, Pride

Brown: Malice

Gray: Awe, Amazement

Eyes are Clear: Honesty, Forthrightness

Eyes flash with bright light: Anger

Colors do not match what is being said: Deceit

THE EIGHT MOONS OF QAF

Time:

Time is measured in degrees based on the orbit of the First Moon. One degree is equal to roughly four minutes. And 15 degrees is equally to roughly one hour.

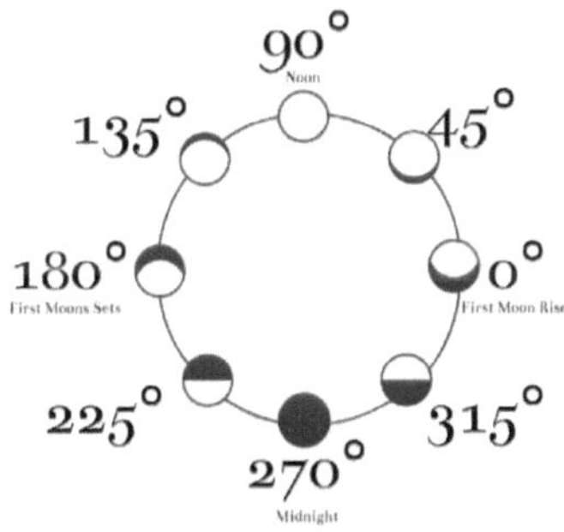

The Eight Moons of Qaf

- **The First Moon:**

A rough, rusty sphere of copper. The First Moon is the largest and brightest of the eight, taking up a full eighth of the sky when it is full. The path of the First Moon is the Qafian equivalent of 'daylight' and it is their main means of telling time. It comes up in the sharq and sets over the Bahamut Sea.

- **The Second Moon:**

Quick-moving silver moon that passes through the sky about ten and half times every 360 degrees. This moon follows the first moon, rising sharq and setting bahamut.

- **The Third Moon:**

Pale pink, this moon crosses the sky perpendicular to the first moon, bouncing back and forth as it chases the swish of the Bahamut's tail. It rises janu'ub/gharb to shamaal. It is common lore that the Bahamut's former lover lives on this celestial body, pulling and yearning for its true love and creating the Qafian tides. The position of the third moon is preferred for telling time because it is always visible except for when it dips behind each horizon.

- **The Fourth Moon (Lover's Moon):**

A dim yellow, this moon is nearly impossible to see when the First Moon is out. It only shines brightly during Qaf's *night.* It is often referred to when saying people are up to no good because only criminals, ne'er do wells, and lovers stay up late enough to see the Fourth Moon.

This moon passes twice for every single pass of the First Moon, once during Qaf's day unseen, then once through Qaf's night when visible. This moon rises sharq/shamaal to bahamut/shamaal.

- **The Fifth Moon (Witch's Moon):**

The witch's moon of soft green that passes through the sky five times, following the Five Winds and crossing the sky 45 degrees (or 3 hours in Ard equivalence) at a time (with another 45 degrees to pass over to the other side beneath Qaf).

It starts sharq and crosses to bahamut, then rises in janu'ub and sets shamaal, then rises gharb and sets sharq, then inverts and rises bahamut and sets janu'ub, then rises shamaal and sets gharb, then rises sharq and sets bahamut like it started. This follows a 405 degree (or 27 hour)/27 day pentagon cycle and is difficult to track. It is the fortune teller's moon as they track its erratic behavior through the heavens and is often associated with Saqueia and the 5 Winds.

- **The Sixth Moon:**

A soft-white moon that crosses the sky three times, 30 degrees after the rise of the First Moon, 60 degrees after midday, and at midnight. It travels from janu'ub to shamaal on each pass. It is the easiest moon to tell time by, has a medium heat, and most resembles Ard's moon.

- **The Seventh Moon (Shadow Moon):**

This moon appears in odd years as a black circle in the sky that blots out the stars but does not give off any of its own light or heat. It takes an entire year to pass over the sky, and then is gone for an entire year. The measurement of Qaf's year and the seasons are determined by the movements of this moon.

It rises sharq/shamaal and sets gharb, dividing the upper and lower continents. It separates them but also forces them to look toward each other whenever they look at it and reminds them they share Qaf. Wars take place more often in the year this moon is hidden. It is also believed by some that it gives off no heat or light because it is the servant of a celestial that is dead or away or because the celestial they serve is.

- **The Eighth Moon:**

A rare bright blue moon that only rises once every thirteen years—The Festival of the Eighth Moon. It rises janu'ub and sets bahamut/shamaal, rising directly behind

Fyre. Every 130 years the appearance of the eighth moon will coincide with every other moon being visible in the sky. This is the "Festival of the Eight Moons," Qaf's most important holiday as it only comes once in most djinn's lifetimes.

It is the warmest moon, and Fyrans believe it serves the Origin, gaining its power from beneath Qaf like lava and only appearing rarely as a reminder to Qaf that the Origin is equal in power to the Bahamut, Celestials, and other minor deities.

- **The Moonless Night:**

Every fourteen cycles of the First Moon in a shadow year of the Seventh Moon comes The Moonless Night, when all of the Eight Moons of Qaf are hidden beyond the horizon. During this time, all heat is sucked from the land and the stars shine their brightest. It does not last the whole night.

About the Authors

Kyro Dean has written over 20 novels, including The Baron's Ghost, which can be found on Kindle Vella. The only thing she loves more than her plants is spending time with her family and making friends and connections. In addition to her works for Eight Moons Publishing, she owns and edits for the blog, Vanilla Grass Writing Resources. She loves to speak and present and has shared her knowledge at many conferences. Check out her website for the most recent updates.

Laya V Smith's debut novel "The Lumbermill", published by Black Rose Writing, won the 2021 Maxy Award for Best Thriller and was a finalist for 2021 IAN Award for Best Debut Novel. To date she has written over thirty novels. When she isn't writing or reading, you can usually find her daydreaming, cooking, laughing at stand-up comedy, or playing with her children.

For more information about Kyro and Laya or to connect on social media, please visit www.eightmoonspublishing.com.

THANK YOU

GRATITUDE FROM KYRO, LAYA, AND JANELLE

Kyro Dean and Laya V Smith would like to extend our sincerest thanks to all the professionals who worked with us on this project. Wes Dean for writing Jahmil and Ayelet's theme song. George Patsouras for illustrating our beautiful cover, and James Owen for helping us to perfect it. Our editor, Keri Karandrakis, for crossing all those t's and dotting all those i's. Ibrahim Salman for helping us with the Arabic. George Ellington for consulting on the Turkish and acting as our alpha reader. And Rakisha, our insightful sensitivity reader. Finally, we want to recognize our wonderful and devoted publicist, Janelle Youngstrom, for her hard work and unflappable enthusiasm.

The authors also want to thank all the people who supported us on Kickstarter and helped make this book a reality, especially Josh Wilcox, the enigmatic Ooky Spooky, Wes Dean, Holly Dean, Rosanna Root-Garey, Daniel Murrieta, Rachel Erickson, Carrie Sykes, Jacob Sparks, Mary Denslow, Douglas Smith, and George Ellington. You helped us make Qaf great.

www.ingramcontent.com/pod-product-compliance
Lightning Source LLC
Chambersburg PA
CBHW051002210726
48287CB00004B/1340